THE GREATEST

AMERICAN SHORT STORIES

The Greatest

American Short Stories

TWENTY CLASSICS OF OUR HERITAGE

EDITED BY *A. Grove Day*

WEBSTER DIVISION, McGRAW-HILL BOOK COMPANY

ST. LOUIS   NEW YORK   SAN FRANCISCO   DALLAS   TORONTO   LONDON

THE GREATEST AMERICAN SHORT STORIES

Library of Congress Catalog Card Number: 52-11507

07-016170-4

Twenty-first Printing

ACKNOWLEDGMENTS

"The Celebrated Jumping Frog of Calaveras County" by Mark Twain reprinted by permission of Harper & Brothers.

"The Wonderful Tar-Baby Story" by Joel Chandler Harris reprinted by permission of Lucien Harris.

"The Lady or the Tiger?" by Frank R. Stockton reprinted by permission of Charles Scribner's Sons.

"The Open Boat" by Stephen Crane reprinted from *Twenty Stories* by Stephen Crane, by permission of Alfred A. Knopf, Inc. Copyright 1925 by William H. Crane.

"The Gift of the Magi" by O. Henry, from *The Four Million* by O. Henry, copyright 1906 by Doubleday & Company, Inc. and reprinted by permission.

"Paul's Case" by Willa Cather reprinted from *Youth and the Bright Medusa* by Willa Cather, by permission of Alfred A. Knopf, Inc. Copyright 1905, 1932 by Willa Cather.

"The Lost Phoebe" by Theodore Dreiser, from *Free and Other Stories* by Theodore Dreiser, by permission of a special arrangement with Mrs. Theodore Dreiser. Copyright 1918 by Boni and Liveright, Inc.

"The Fourth Man" by John Russell, copyright 1917 by P. F. Collier & Son, reprinted by permission of Brandt & Brandt.

"I'm a Fool" by Sherwood Anderson reprinted from *Horses and Men*, copyright 1924 by Eleanor Anderson, reprinted by permission of Harold Ober Associates.

"Haircut" by Ring Lardner reprinted from *The Love Nest and Other Stories* by Ring Lardner; copyright 1926 by Charles Scribner's Sons; used by permission of the publishers.

"The Devil and Daniel Webster" by Stephen Vincent Benét, from *Selected Works of Stephen Vincent Benét*, published by Rinehart & Company, Inc. Copyright, 1936, by Stephen Vincent Benét.

"The Leader of the People" by John Steinbeck, from *The Portable Steinbeck*, copyright 1938, 1943 by John Steinbeck. Reprinted by permission of The Viking Press, Inc., New York.

"The Secret Life of Walter Mitty" by James Thurber, copyright 1939 by James Thurber and reprinted by permission of the author from *The New Yorker*.

"The Bear" by William Faulkner, copyright 1942 by The Curtis Publishing Co., reprinted by permission of Harold Ober Associates.

Contents

[v]

The Flowering of the
American Short Story

THE MOST POPULAR type of American literature over the past century has been the short story. Its brevity, the variety of its forms, and its sharp impact have made it especially fitted to the American temperament. Short stories have been enjoyed by high-brow and lowbrow alike. Most of the writers of short fiction have maintained a high level of competence, and many of them have revealed a genius for creating great stories. No other nation can show such a high record, on both quantity and quality, in this very modern type of literature.

The origins of the short story are found in the widespread romantic movement that began in the early nineteenth century and awakened in literature a new interest in the wondrous, the emotional, and the colorful aspects of life in both high and low places. By study, experiment, and luck, a few earlier American writers worked out a new theory of what this kind of short prose fiction might be. The history of the short story in America shows many variations and many modifications and passing fads, but a general advance in both theory and practice has been made, so that today there is broad agreement among writers on the possibilities of this form of fiction, and there is as well a high order of craftsmanship shown in the average story.

Progress has indeed been made in short-story art. Ordinary nineteenth-century fiction strikes today's reader as clumsy and old-

[1]

fashioned. A few early writers, however, through their genius produced stories that have become classics—stories that every educated American is presumed to have read. It is to the inventive powers of these and later writers that we can attribute the transition from the loose, episodic tale to the unified, compressed short story.

Can one find, previous to 1820, any examples of the "modern" kind of short story? Many types of short fiction can be discovered in the world's literature. These include the early myths and legends of various races, the widespread folk tales and fairy tales, the fables such as those of Aesop, and the animal tales of Reynard the Fox or Old Man Coyote. One finds the parable, a story invented to demonstrate a moral or religious truth; the edifying little stories of Hannah More; and other uses of invented actions to preach a moral. One finds also the sketch, which exhibits characters or settings but which lacks a plot. Certain older prose pieces might be considered to resemble closely the modern short story: the Biblical episodes of Ruth or the prodigal son; Petronius' "Matron of Ephesus" or the "Cupid and Psyche" of Apuleius; some of the tales of the Arabian Nights adventures; pieces by the Elizabethan "novella" writers, Nashe, Greene, and Lodge; a few of the tales from Boccaccio's *Decameron*; and stories inserted in essays or novels, such as Addison's "Vision of Mirza" (1711) or Scott's "Wandering Willie's Tale" (1824). But one might say that all these types, which accidentally resemble the short story in many ways, lack one or more of the main qualities of the modern form.

The romantic "tale" popular in Europe in the early nineteenth century is closest to the short story, which developed from it. A number of these tales, such as those by the German writers E. T. W. Hoffman and Ludwig Tieck, were widely enjoyed, but they were episodic in structure, rambling in style, feeble in motivation, and lacking in the strong unity and singleness of effect that the modern stories aim at. Characters in the tales were often fantastic, and the events whimsical and inexplicable. Many such tales were written by Irving, Hawthorne, and Poe, but these three American authors slowly developed a new form, which for want of a better name is called the modern short story.

Washington Irving can be credited with the earliest examples. Influenced by his reading of European tales and the *Spectator* sketches—particularly the Sir Roger de Coverley series—Irving added deeper characterization, some humor, restraint, and realistic touches.

Irving's *Sketch Book*, the first part of which was published in 1819, set a fashion of writing that was widely imitated. However, except for a few justly celebrated stories—"Rip Van Winkle," "The Legend of Sleepy Hollow," and "The Devil and Tom Walker"—Irving remained a sketch writer with no strong theory of fiction. "For my part," he wrote in the introduction to his *Tales of a Traveller*, "I consider a story merely as a frame upon which to stretch my materials. It is the play of thought, and sentiment, and language; the weaving in of characters, lightly, yet expressively delineated; the familiar and faithful exhibition of scenes in common life; and the half-concealed vein of humor that is often playing through the whole—these are among what I aim at, and upon which I felicitate myself in proportion as I think I succeed." This pioneer writer of the short story in English scarcely concerned himself with plot.

Nathaniel Hawthorne began publishing short fiction in 1830, and for more than twenty years his work appeared—often unsigned or under pseudonyms—in various publications. He began writing before the day of the popular magazine, and his chief outlet was the "annual," a kind of fancy gift book containing engravings and a miscellany of Irvingesque sketches and Byronic verse. In many of his best stories he came close to the later ideal of a unified narrative.

Hawthorne's earliest interest lay in the novel, but when his first novel failed he turned to writing tales, as he called them, in the romantic mode of the annuals. He often used the situations found in the work of the German taletellers—fanciful adventures, horror, supernatural events, odd legends, and contemplation of death—but his deep moral sense and artistic taste usually kept him from extravagance. He likewise avoided weak sentimentality. Many of his tales are properly short stories in the modern sense. His style is clear and harmonious and yet filled with suggestive overtones and hints of mystery. On the other hand, his characters are seldom individuals, and are often walking personifications of virtues or vices. He is concerned with atmosphere, and the strong impression of a setting is frequently the main effect recalled after reading a Hawthorne piece—the atmosphere along with the "moral."

Hawthorne's stories are mirrors of his moods but are seldom morbid. He turned the romantic tale from a toy of fantasy and frivolity to an instrument for spiritual teaching. He demonstrated that the story could be a unified study of one intense situation. And he made fiction respectable, even in staid New England. After more than a century, he still ranks as one of the greatest story writers of the world.

The short fiction of Hawthorne includes three types. One is the New England legend or historical incident, such as "The Gray Champion." Another is the story of ordinary life, like "The White Old Maid." Most typical, however, is his use of imagined events to point a moral; his best pieces—"The Ambitious Guest," "The Minister's Black Veil," "The Great Stone Face," "Ethan Brand," "Rappaccini's Daughter," "Young Goodman Brown," "The Birthmark," and "Dr. Heidigger's Experiment"—are never free of allegory, the symbolic drama of ideas.

Hawthorne never stated any theory of the short story, but Poe evolved his own theory from a study of his fellow taleteller. "If wise," observed Poe of the story writer in a review of Hawthorne's *Twice-Told Tales* in *Graham's Magazine*, May, 1842, "he has not fashioned his thoughts to accommodate his incidents; but having conceived, with deliberate care, a certain unique or single *effect* to be wrought out, he then invents such incidents—he then combines such events as may best aid him in establishing the preconceived effect. If his very initial sentence tend not to the outbringing of this effect, then he has failed in his first step. In the whole composition there should be no word written, of which the tendency, direct or indirect, is not to the one preëstablished design."

Edgar Allan Poe, who preached this gospel of the "single effect," was a contemporary of Hawthorne. Alike in their imaginative power and indrawn personalities, they differed in many ways. Poe's mind dwelt upon fantastic incidents, grim and horrid details, startling emotions, and suspense. Lacking the balance that a sense of humor might give, Poe was saved from bathos or farce chiefly by a careful study of his audience and his craft. He was a pioneer "magazinist" and editor, and used his born cleverness to discover the kinds of fiction that readers would buy. He was a master of the story of situation and the story of atmosphere. His style was compact and vivid, but too often feverish. In many ways, his work was as grotesque as that of the German tale writers, but he insisted upon an internal story unity that they lacked. As a result, Poe is read as eagerly today as any other fiction writer of the days before the Civil War. His work, although it had little immediate effect upon other writers, slowly became popular in other countries—particularly in France, where the short story was coming into vogue—and today he towers as one of the giants in the world-wide history of the short story.

Poe never sought realism, for romantic novelty and variety were demanded by the magazine readers of his day. His fiction may be listed under four headings: descriptive pieces, which are little more than pictorial sketches; tales of the grotesque, which deal with ludicrous ideas often heightened into witty burlesques; tales of the arabesque, a group that includes most of his best short stories, touching on death, the supernatural, terror, and scientific romance; and tales of ratiocination, which are the prototypes of our modern detective story. Famous examples of the arabesque are "William Wilson," "The Black Cat," "The Tell-Tale Heart," "The Pit and the Pendulum," "The Fall of the House of Usher," and "Ligeia." Poe wrote four tales of ratiocination—"The Murders in the Rue Morgue," "The Mystery of Marie Rogêt," "The Purloined Letter," and "The Gold Bug"—in which a problem in deduction is offered the reader and solved by the brilliant intellect of Poe's detective. Poe was thus the father of the modern story of detection.

Poe's contribution to the evolution of the short story lay in his recognition that the brevity of this form demands a single striking effect; that the short story differs from longer fiction not only in length but in purpose; that the writing of magazine stories could be a calculated technique; and that the public of his day desired to have their minds shocked by vivid representation of grotesque, terrible, supernatural, witty, scientific, or otherwise startling events.

The triumvirate—Irving, Hawthorne, and Poe—had worked out a rationale of the short story, but it did not exert a great influence on popular American writers before the Civil War. Among these purveyors to the mass tastes, only a few are remembered today. The prolific and journalistic Nat P. Willis, prophetic of O. Henry, was the most important mid-century fiction writer, but his brittle pieces have not lasted. Better remembered is Edward Everett Hale, but chiefly for one story, "The Man Without a Country," which in length approaches the novelette. The brilliant amateur Fitz-James O'Brien, whose fiction appeared in the magazines during the decade before the end of the Civil War, is recollected for two stories—"The Diamond Lens" and "What Was It?"—which, although reminiscent of Poe, lend to their impossible main events a strong foundation of realistic detail.

One great writer of shorter fiction before the Civil War was Herman Melville. He is best known as a novelist, but in 1855 he put out the lengthy "Benito Cereno," which has been called the greatest short story ever written. This ironic masterpiece of ominous foreboding was based on an actual event, but Melville's atmospheric retelling bears the mark of a great creation.

The end of the Civil War brought a strong conviction that America was a big country with many interesting regions inside its borders. The most popular school of fiction that grew up was labeled "local color," and reflected this new interest in exploiting regional story materials just as the industrial expansion of the era was exploiting its physical resources. Readers realized that America held many strange corners filled with odd types of people who spoke often in curious dialects. From 1865 to 1900, the most popular stories were those that satisfied this demand for local color—that is, stories putting emphasis upon regional setting, the effects of geography upon action, unusual characters, and dialect or other regional variations in speech habits.

The earlier writings of Mark Twain reflect this regional interest, and his brief story, "The Celebrated Jumping Frog of Calaveras County," set in California in the early days, is a tall tale of the kind which had been popular in frontier journalism for many years. Mark Twain's power of evoking the life of a locality is best found in his novels, however, and except for the sardonic "The Man That Corrupted Hadleyburg" (1899), few of his short stories have become classics.

Bret Harte, more than any other writer, set the fashion for local-color fiction. His instant success in 1868 with "The Luck of Roaring Camp" lay in his combining well-known appeals—a mixture of sentiment, pathos, humor, ironic contrasts, and whimsical characters—with a new setting, the California gold camp.

Harte's defects—mawkishness, subordination of plausibility to striking event, and theatrical excesses—are obvious. But he was a master of the brief form, and his great contribution lay in the adaptation of old methods to new scenery. Using a striking situation played within a highly colored setting, and painting in broad and strong strokes, he could create a powerful impression on the reader—the impression of a flashing interaction between the character and his environment. Harte is at his best when the setting seems to emerge almost with the force of a personality, to play a dominant role in the story.

Harte had shown the way, and in the next decades a variety of talented writers, urged on by the magazine editors, ransacked the corners of the continent for fresh settings and striking local characters and customs.

Harper's Magazine was founded in 1850; the *Atlantic Monthly* began in 1857, with James Russell Lowell as its first editor; and *Scribner's Monthly* started in 1870. These new and lively family periodicals offered their pages to fiction writers who could mirror America to itself, and the encouragement they gave brought forth many new writers from many parts of the nation.

This search for the picturesque resulted in the reign of regionalism that continued up to the 1890's. The earliest form was romantic. It is found in the presentation of New England by Rose Terry Cooke and Harriet Beecher Stowe; in the stories of the Great

Lakes and other sections by Constance Fenimore Woolson, a grandniece of James Fenimore Cooper; in the Tennessee Mountain sketches of Mary N. Murfree, who wrote under the name of Charles Egbert Craddock; and in the tales of the Arkansas cane-brakes by Alice French, whose pseudonym was Octave Thanet. The South had a busy local-color movement that included such names as George Washington Cable with his *Old Creole Days*, Joel Chandler Harris, Thomas Nelson Page, and Kate Chopin with *Bayou Folks*. Even the remote Pacific was represented by Charles Warren Stoddard in *South-Sea Idyls*. The tendency to use heavier dialect—the attempt to convey local speech through complicated spellings to give phonetic representation—ran riot in the later localized romances, and the dialect story exhausted itself by 1890.

Regional realism took an almost concurrent course with the romantic aspect. The movement found its roots in Henry James and William Dean Howells. These two important writers were better known as novelists, but their influence on all fiction was great. They stood for integrity of workmanship, for literature as a conscious and self-critical art.

Henry James began publishing short stories in 1865. In the next decade, twenty-four of them appeared. His method required the larger scope of novelette or novel, however, and most of his short stories are lengthy. His masterpiece, "The Turn of the Screw," takes as much space in its development as does the usual novelette. On one level—this story has several—it is a ghost story; on another it is a profound psychological study of evil. James sometimes used American settings, but his best works offer the international scene as viewed through the eyes of traveling Americans. James, as a keen critic of artistic technique, often wrote about the relation of an artist to his art; this idea is found in such stories as "The Madonna of the Future" and "The Lesson of the Master." The realism of Henry James was a cool avoidance of romantic treatment rather than a positive doctrine, and he seldom set out to describe ordinary people in a true-to-life situation. This literary master wrote for a select audience about a select class of cultured people, and his interest lay less in stirring action than in complex human relationships, analyzed in a subtle and careful style. His concentration on immediate aspects and significant details made him a forerunner of writers of the impressionist school.

The realism of William Dean Howells was the deliberate program of a practical editor and fiction writer. He created few short stories, but the title of one of them—"A Romance of Real Life," which is close to an essay-like sketch—suggests his idea of finding interesting material in the revelation of ordinary characters drawn from the contemporary scene. His questions furnish a definition of realism in fiction: "Is it clear, simple, unaffected? Is it true to human experience generally?" Howells fostered many younger writers who later felt that his realism was not real enough, and who went on to write fiction of the naturalistic sort.

Followers of the Howells kind of realism produced much creditable work up through the end of the century. Sarah Orne Jewett's stories of the Maine coast appeared in the best monthly magazines from 1873 to 1899. Mary E. Wilkins Freeman, another New England realist, brought an intensely original mind to the matter-of-fact portrayal of character. A third New Englander was Alice Brown, whose *Meadow Grass* appeared in 1895. Other well-balanced regional stories that flourished in the 1890's came from the pens of James Lane Allen of Kentucky; Hamlin Garland, whose stories of the "Middle Border" exemplified his theory of "veritism," a more intense and harsher realism; Margaret Deland of Pennsylvania; and William Allen White of Kansas.

A disciple of Henry James was Edith Wharton. Her short stories as well as her novels reflect his serious craftsmanship, his interest in moral dilemmas, and his aloof concern for culture. In her novelette *Ethan Frome*, however, Mrs. Wharton gives a sterner picture of New Englanders than that found in most of the Howells school of realists.

A few important writers around the turn of the century applied the theory of naturalism, originating in France, to the American scene. This theory had several tenets, but in general it considered the fiction writer as a social scientist whose first task was to present objectively all aspects of society. Actually, the writers of naturalism felt that the seamier side of life had been neglected by previous writers and, impelled by modern ideas of determinism and the lack of free will in the complex modern period, concentrated on the plight of the individual trapped by heredity and environment. They felt that the realism of Howells was too timid, and that it avoided grappling with the animal side of man's nature. The naturalists have been condemned for their frankness in dealing with human instincts, for exaggerating sordid and pessimistic details, and for concentrating upon characters who are unintelligent, neurotic, underprivileged, or broken by circumstances. These writers were serious in their intentions, however, and the daring experiments of such naturalists as Stephen Crane (his best known story is "The Open Boat"), Frank Norris (whose "A Deal in Wheat" appeared in 1903), Harold Frederic, and Theodore Dreiser had a marked effect upon many later American writers of our century.

Jack London, who wrote many stories about simple, vigorous characters, often used grim details such as those used also by the naturalists. He is often classed with them, although, dominated by a crude idea of the "survival of the fittest," he had as a main quality a primitivism which showed elemental men in violent conflict against nature or against other men.

A popular taleteller of the 1890's was Ambrose Bierce. His stories deal with war, death, and horror, but are less in the tradition of Poe than in that of Fitz-James O'Brien. Bierce frequently used the surprise ending, but often it was a mere *tour de force*, and the revelation of withheld facts did not cause the reader to revise his ideas about the deeper meaning of the story. This kind of ending became almost a mannerism with Bierce, as can be seen by reading "An Occurrence at Owl Creek Bridge," "The Damned Thing," "A Horseman in the Sky," "One of the Missing," or "The Coup de Grâce." Yet often Bierce's ironic method and grim detail can give the reader the true shiver of terror.

Another who wrote horror stories—an old form that has persisted through the history of fiction to the present—was F. Marion

Crawford, whose "The Upper Berth" is deservedly famed. A classic of terror is Charlotte P. Gilman's "The Yellow Wall-Paper."

Light fiction is found in the later nineteenth century with Thomas Bailey Aldrich, Frank R. Stockton, Henry Cuyler Bunner, and Richard Harding Davis, all of whom combined comedy and adventure with clever and vigorous action. Aldrich is mainly remembered for his "Margery Daw," the ending of which plays an amusing hoax on the reader. Stockton is even more widely known for his trick story, "The Lady or the Tiger?" He frequently took a fantastic situation and treated it seriously; but more often his stories are imaginative yarns told with whimsical humor. Bunner, whose collection *Short Sixes* appeared in 1890, wrote charming pieces dealing lightly with commonplace city dwellers. Davis, with a gay air, turned out over a period of fifteen years many successful stories of colorful action, such as "Gallegher," the Van Bibber series, "The Bar Sinister," and "The Boy Scout." The story of plot, which plays a joke on the reader and is narrated in an amusing and even slangy manner, is found in these four writers; it was thus not invented by O. Henry, although he became the best known practitioner in this popular type.

The stories of William Sydney Porter, who used the pseudonym O. Henry, appeared from 1899 to the year of his death, 1910. He wrote at first of unusual people adventuring in strange places; later, his stories of life in a metropolis brought the pleasure of recognition to the man, and woman, in the street. Much of his popularity grew from his sympathy for the underdog. O. Henry had himself often been that underdog. The reading public loved him, but they loved most his open heart and broad humor.

O. Henry, often acclaimed as an innovator, in reality was giving the wider audience what it wanted. He was original only in his brisk style. Most of the ingredients that he mixed into his brief but frequent excursions into journalistic entertainment were not new with him. His humor is a strong quality, but it is usually that of the exaggerated tall tale. His characters are mere puppets or grotesques, speaking a language never heard outside his pages.

He never sought truth, but merely a broad chuckle. The art of compression he could have learned from such earlier masters as Harte, Rudyard Kipling, and Guy de Maupassant. His plots are commonly mere anecdotes or contrived, and sometimes creaking, vehicles for his style. Even the surprise ending that became his trade-mark might have been derived, as has been said, from Aldrich, Stockton, Bunner, or Bierce. The typical O. Henry story whose ending is an ironic whirligig is at first attractive to a reader, but after he has found many stories that end in the same way, the unusual stunt itself becomes usual and trite.

The unfortunate effect of the O. Henry boom was to create a crop of imitators who, encouraged by the market to be found in the tremendous expansion of the mass magazines, embarked on the business of earning a living by supplying this demand for middle-class fiction. The short story took the direction of commercialism. Writing fiction became a matter of feeding the public what it wanted. Overemphasis upon "plot"—the contrivance of new and increasingly incredible situations and complications—became the rule, and all the other qualities of a good story were neglected in the scramble for new plots. Some of these later writers of magazine fiction were masters of their craft. Such storytellers as Wilbur Daniel Steele, John Russell, and Richard Connell took the plot story as far as it could logically go. But serious writers of the short story still remained interested in the attempt to portray real people in fiction, and both the impressionistic school of Henry James and the naturalistic school of Crane and Norris are prominent when one looks at the outstanding short stories of America in the twentieth century.

The existence in the past half century of several hundred magazines in America whose columns have demanded increasing floods of fiction to satisfy a mass audience has resulted in a rather misleading division of the modern story between the "commercial" and the "artistic." It is true that a majority of printed stories have been written to fit a narrow formula that avoids controversy, and that most writers of our era have looked upon their work less as a high art than as a craft practiced to earn a living. Yet the level of their work has been higher, in moral and educational values, than that found in such competing forms of popular entertainment as the vaudeville stage, the movies, the radio, television, and the comic books. Well-edited magazines are available for almost every level of literary taste, from the plot-heavy "pulps" to the "quality" monthlies such as *Harper's Magazine* and the *Atlantic*. The demand for fiction has been so great that thousands of mediocre stories have been printed. But the past fifty years have shown the true flowering of the American short story. Never before have so many talented writers been offered so broad an audience and such wide popular encouragement. Never have the standards of technical excellence been so high. And never has the chance been so slight that a writer of genius will struggle and perish without recognition and reward. Nor is it true that fiction of the highest artistic merit has inevitably been found in the smaller and more esoteric periodicals. Some of the finest stories of our time have been first published in the million-circulation magazines.

The tastes of readers have been heightened by the offering of school and college courses in reading and writing the short story; by the publication of such annual collections as *The O. Henry Memorial Award Prize Stories* (1918 on, currently edited by Herschel Brickell) and *The Best Short Stories* (edited by Edward J. O'Brien from 1915 to 1941, and since then by Martha Foley); and by the publication of innumerable anthologies of selected stories of many kinds.

Several "little magazines" have taken the lead in developing new kinds of stories. One of the best was *Story*, founded in 1931 in Vienna in mimeographed form by Whit Burnett and his wife, Martha Foley; until it ceased publication in 1948, it encouraged writers of several nations to send in experimental work.

The *New Yorker* has been an influence of a sophisticated sort; it developed a brief sketch form that fitted the smart and sometimes disillusioned tone of the magazine, which has published such celebrities as Dorothy Parker, "Leonard Q. Ross," and James Thurber.

The *Saturday Evening Post, Collier's,* and the *American Maga-*

zine, sometimes attacked for conventionalism, have nevertheless opened their pages to such masters of the solid, popular story as Edna Ferber, Ellis Parker Butler, Fannie Hurst, Richard Connell, Roark Bradford, Irvin S. Cobb, and Thomas Beer. The *Post* sought stories of the American heritage by Stephen Vincent Benét, Walter D. Edmonds, and MacKinlay Kantor; it has often given wide readership to fine work by first-rate authors such as Sinclair Lewis, William Faulkner, Ring Lardner, and Joseph Hergesheimer.

The outstanding types of lasting short stories in the twentieth century have been satirical, realistic, naturalistic, psychological, and impressionistic.

Foremost satirists of American complacency have been Sinclair Lewis (first American to be awarded the Nobel prize in literature), Ring Lardner, and James Thurber. The powers of Lewis lent themselves more easily to the novel, but Lardner, who never succeeded in the longer form, in his short stories held up a sardonic mirror to Americans. James Thurber's wry prose expresses with bitter pathos the frustrations of modern city life and the eternal battle between the sexes.

Regional realism of the Garland variety has been welcomed in our century. Notable are Willa Cather, who wrote about the people of the prairies as well as those of Eastern cities; Dorothy Canfield Fisher of New England, with *Hillsboro People*; and Ruth Suckow, whose *Iowa Interiors* contains sympathetic studies of plain folk.

Realism in portraying the "jazz age" after World War I is found in the stories of F. Scott Fitzgerald and Katharine Brush. The hectic tales of Fitzgerald did much to focus the disillusion of the days of flapper and lounge lizard, those smart young people who sought relief from boredom by means of bathtub gin and casual loves.

Naturalism in the twentieth century has been a dominant force, both in selection of previously untouched fiction subjects and in experiments in style. Its practitioners have, it seems, overthrown all the old taboos and have reveled in unhappy endings, shocking physical details, psychopathic minds, amoral attitudes, and unpleasantness in general.

Sherwood Anderson turned his back on the conventional short story and in *Winesburg, Ohio* (1919) produced psychological sketches of frustrated people in a small Middle Western town. His style, influenced by the experiments of Gertrude Stein *(Three Lives,* 1909), attempted to restore the rhythm of spoken narrative. With kindly insight he presented the inner struggles of troubled souls who are broken by forces they can never understand, who imprison their lives in a cage of false values. Often his tales were plotless, but when he controlled his sprawling materials he produced such revealing stories as "I'm a Fool" and "I Want to Know Why."

Ernest Hemingway, whose attitude and style have been dominating forces on our time, learned much from both Stein and Anderson. Ever since the "lost generation" of the 1920's accepted him as their spokesman he has been the pontiff of naturalism in the short story. His attitude—one cannot call it a philosophy—is a negation of all human values except a hard-boiled stoicism. His hatred of sham, his frank admiration for physical endurance and bodily pleasures, and his denial of human choice—all these qualities put him in the naturalist camp. Most of his characters are primitive and unreflective; they are superanimals living by a simple code—the code of the sportsman, the gambler, the bullfighter, the criminal, the soldier—and too often he glorifies the merely virile. But his style is so perfectly matched to his materials that his best work is as likely to last as anything else written in his era. This terse style, unapproached by his many imitators, is misleadingly simple in both diction and syntax. One must read between the lines, for suggestion replaces description; one must magnify, for understatement and apparently casual talk are highly significant. His sentences are short and colloquial and seldom complex. But his style is elemental rather than elementary, and gets a controlled result because Hemingway is a shrewd and painstaking craftsman, a master of the single effect.

The method of naturalism found wider use during the depression years of the 1930's by writers with strong social consciousness. John Steinbeck handled it skillfully in such novels as *The Grapes of*

Wrath, but in some of his short stories, like "The Red Pony" and "The Leader of the People," he is content to tell an earthy narrative of ranch life in the Salinas Valley of California.

William Faulkner's naturalism is tinged with a nightmare quality that partakes at times of deliberate melodrama. His people are tortured or terrified, victims of sinister emotions and unnamed sins. His plots often deal with the decay of Southern aristocracy and the rise of vulgar pretenders, and the pathological horror is sometimes lightened by a touch of macabre humor. With Erskine Caldwell, another Southern naturalist, both the humor and the horror are intensified to the point where credibility is almost lost. In both Caldwell and Faulkner, in fact, the extremes of naturalism are pushed far beyond the original goals and rebound toward fantasy and a return to the Gothic tale.

The naturalist group often handled sensational and terrifying subjects. More conventional twentieth-century writers of the story of horror, haunting, and the supernatural include Irvin S. Cobb, Charles Caldwell Dobie, Helen R. Hull, Edith Wharton, and August Derleth.

Psychological studies of character are written more often as the century goes on. In a sense, good writers of all epochs have been expert practical psychologists, but the use of types taken over from clinical histories has seldom resulted in first-rate fiction. Most successful, perhaps, has been Conrad Aiken, whose work has a marked Freudian flavor. In "Silent Snow, Secret Snow" he gives a touching picture of a boy whose mind is shutting itself off more and more from the world around him.

Impressionism, which today has gone far beyond the experiments of Henry James, has been influenced strongly by the Russian writer Anton Chekhov and the British writer Katherine Mansfield. The impressionist story, which seems to have a haphazard structure and delineates character in a casual tone that gives a vivid effect of living reality, is actually far from plotless. Suspense in this type of story, however, comes less from a contrived plot than from a skillfully aroused curiosity about the deepest complexities of human emotions. Most active in presenting this newer sort of story are

Katherine Anne Porter, Eudora Welty, and Caroline Gordon. If plot is "motivated action," Miss Porter's celebrated story "Flowering Judas" does not lack a plot; the author skillfully shows a character in a dilemma, the tone delicately suggests the theme of betrayal, and the solution which reveals the decision of the leading figure is couched in the symbols of a dream. This most modern type of character story—whose possibilities are endless, since variations in human nature are infinite—is a new experience in the world of fiction. The American short story has indeed covered a long road since the days of Irving and Hawthorne.

Today the dictum of William Dean Howells in *Criticism and Fiction* (1891) is as true as ever: "I am not sure that the Americans have not brought the short story nearer perfection in the all-round sense than almost any other people, and for reasons very simple and near at hand. It might be argued from the national hurry and impatience that it was a literary form peculiarly adapted to the American temperament, but I suspect that its extraordinary development among us is owing to more tangible facts. The success of American magazines, which is nothing less than prodigious, is only commensurate with their excellence. Their sort of success is not only from the courage to decide what ought to please, but from the knowledge of what does please; and it is probable that, aside from the pictures, it is the short stories which please the readers of our best magazines." Short stories are congenial to the American mood, and the demand for them has produced a supply of great stories by great American authors.

What of the future of the American short story? In spite of the growing competition of other forms of diversion, it is likely that, so long as people read at all, they will still demand well-written short fiction. This peculiarly American form should continue to attract readers and challenge writers. The chief types of story may be expected to maintain themselves, and experiment will still go on. If one may venture predictions, it might seem that the merely drab and defeatist naturalistic story has about run its course. The impressionistic James-Chekhov-Mansfield story of character will, on the other hand, further come into its own. And a rather new type—science fiction, as written by Ray Bradbury and many other excellent dreamers about the future as glorified or cursed by scientific creation—has now become popular, perhaps because it offers a freer scope for depicting the world not as it is but as it might be. If the pendulum swing of extreme realism is soon reversed, it can only return in the direction of romanticism. Is it too much to expect that the same stimuli—wonder, emotion, and fancy—which gave birth to the short story in the nineteenth century will carry readers in a new romanticism toward atom-propelled adventures in far galaxies of the imagination?

The ghost of Hendrick Hudson sent
Rip on an amazing adventure. . . .

Rip Van Winkle

WASHINGTON IRVING (1783–1859)

When Washington Irving, first American short-story writer, was born in New York during the Revolution, the city was still in the hands of the British, and he died on the eve of the American Civil War. His life thus spanned our first great national era, and as America's first professional man of letters he produced a wide shelf of essays, histories, biographies, and tales; but his work in the creation of the short story was finished early.

His father, a merchant and patriot soldier, gave to his eleventh child the name of his former commander-in-chief. When Washington came to New York in 1789 to be inaugurated as President, he gave the boy his blessing. The lad's education was casual, and he spent much time in the colorful streets of the city whose history he was later to write in humorous vein, or shooting squirrels along the banks of the Hudson. He studied law, but was more interested in writing light pieces for his brother Peter's Morning Chronicle.

He went abroad in 1804 for his health and traveled in Europe for two years. On his return he was admitted to the bar, and began contributing sketches to Salmagundi (1807–1808), and produced his comic Knickerbocker History of New York (1809).

After further literary and editorial labors, Irving went to Liverpool to manage a branch of the family business, and did not return for seventeen years. He began to write to support himself, and at this time produced The Sketch Book, which made him famous and gave him entree into the best circles abroad. Residence in Germany, France, and Spain (where he collected material for his life of Columbus, his history of the conquest of Granada, and especially his charming Tales of the Alhambra) produced grist for his literary mill, and when he returned home in 1832 he was recognized as America's foremost man of letters.

A trip to the Indian country resulted in several volumes about Western America. He lived at his estate, "Sunnyside," near Tarrytown, New York, until 1842, when after declining various other political honors he accepted the post of minister to Spain and served in Madrid for four years. The major effort of his later period was a life of his great namesake, Washington; he saw the fifth and final volume in print before he died of a heart attack in 1859. He had broken fresh ground in several important branches of writing—particularly the early short story—and well earned the title, "father of American literature."

Both "Rip Van Winkle" and "The Legend of Sleepy Hollow," Irving's two best stories, were ascribed to Diedrich Knickerbocker in The Sketch Book, by "Geoffrey Crayon, Bart.," the first part of which appeared in May, 1819; Knickerbocker had been the pseudonym of Irving for his burlesque History of New York. In addition to the items in both parts of The Sketch Book, Irving's principal short pieces appear in Bracebridge Hall (1822), Tales of a Traveler (1824), and Wolfert's Roost (1855).

> By Woden, God of Saxons,
> From whence comes Wensday, that is Wodensday.
> Truth is a thing that ever I will keep
> Unto thylke day in which I creep into
> My sepulchre—
>
> CARTWRIGHT

WHOEVER HAS MADE a voyage up the Hudson must remember the Kaatskill mountains. They are a dismembered branch of the great Appalachian family, and are seen away to the west of the river, swelling up to a noble height, and lording it over the surrounding country. Every change of season, every change of weather, indeed, every hour of the day, produces some change in the magical hues and shapes of these mountains, and they are regarded by all the good wives, far and near, as perfect barometers. When the weather is fair and settled, they are clothed in blue and purple, and print their bold outlines on the clear evening sky; but sometimes, when the rest of the landscape is cloudless, they will gather a hood of gray vapors about their summits, which, in the last rays of the setting sun, will glow and light up like a crown of glory.

At the foot of these fairy mountains, the voyager may have descried the light smoke curling up from a village, whose shingle-roofs gleam among the trees, just where the blue tints of the upland melt away into the fresh green of the nearer landscape. It is a little village, of great antiquity, having been founded by some of the Dutch colonists, in the early times of the province, just about the beginning of the government of the good Peter Stuyvesant (may he rest in peace!) and there were some of the houses of the original settlers standing within a few years, built of small yellow bricks brought from Holland, having latticed windows and gable fronts, surmounted with weathercocks.

In that same village and in one of these very houses (which, to tell the precise truth, was sadly time-worn and weather-beaten), there lived many years since, while the country was yet a province of Great Britain, a simple good-natured fellow, of the name of Rip Van Winkle. He was a descendant of the Van Winkles who figured so gallantly in the chivalrous days of Peter Stuyvesant, and accompanied him to the siege of Fort Christina. He inherited, however, but little of the martial character of his ancestors. I have observed that he was a simple good-natured man; he was, moreover, a kind neighbor, and an obedient henpecked husband. Indeed, to the latter circumstance might be owing that meekness of spirit which gained him such universal popularity; for those men are most apt to be obsequious and conciliating abroad, who are under the discipline of shrews at home. Their tempers, doubtless, are rendered pliant and malleable in the fiery furnace of domestic tribulation, and a curtain lecture is worth all the sermons in the world for teaching the virtues of patience and long-suffering. A termagant wife may, therefore, in some respects, be considered a tolerable blessing; and if so, Rip Van Winkle was thrice blessed.

Certain it is that he was a great favorite among all the good wives of the village, who, as usual with the amiable sex, took his part in all family squabbles; and never failed, whenever they talked those matters over in their evening gossipings, to lay all the blame on Dame Van Winkle. The children of the village, too, would shout with joy whenever he approached. He assisted at their sports, made their playthings, taught them to fly kites and shoot marbles, and told them long stories of ghosts, witches, and Indians. Whenever he went dodging about the village, he was surrounded by a troop of them hanging on his skirts, clambering on his back, and playing a thousand tricks on him with impunity; and not a dog would bark at him throughout the neighborhood.

The great error in Rip's composition was an insuperable aversion to all kinds of profitable labor. It could not be from the want of assiduity or perseverance; for he would sit on a wet rock, with a rod as long and heavy as a Tartar's lance, and fish all day without a murmur, even though he should not be encouraged by a single nibble. He would carry a fowling-piece on his shoulder for hours together, trudging through woods and swamps, and up hill and down dale, to shoot a few squirrels or wild pigeons. He would never refuse to assist a neighbor even in the roughest toil, and was a foremost man at all country frolics for husking Indian corn, or building stone fences; the women of the village, too, used to employ him to run their errands, and to do such little odd jobs as their less obliging husbands would not do for them. In a word, Rip was ready to attend to anybody's business but his own; but as to doing family duty, and keeping his farm in order, he found it impossible.

In fact, he declared it was of no use to work on his farm; it was the most pestilent little piece of ground in the whole country; everything about it went wrong, and would go wrong, in spite of him. His fences were continually falling to pieces; his cow would either go astray, or get among the cabbages; weeds were sure to grow quicker in his fields than anywhere else; the rain always made a point of setting in just as he had some outdoor work to do; so that though his patrimonial estate had dwindled away under his management, acre by acre, until there was little more left than a mere patch of Indian corn and potatoes, yet it was the worst con-ditioned farm in the neighborhood.

His children, too, were as ragged and wild as if they belonged to nobody. His son Rip, an urchin begotten in his own likeness, promised to inherit the habits, with the old clothes, of his father. He was generally seen trooping like a colt at his mother's heels, equipped in a pair of his father's cast-off galligaskins which he had much ado to hold up with one hand, as a fine lady does her train in bad weather.

Rip Van Winkle, however, was one of those happy mortals, of foolish, well-oiled dispositions, who take the world easy, eat white bread or brown, whichever can be got with least thought or trouble, and would rather starve on a penny than work for a pound. If left to himself, he would have whistled life away in perfect contentment; but his wife kept continually dinning in his ears about his idleness, his carelessness, and the ruin he was bringing on his family. Morning, noon, and night, her tongue was incessantly going, and everything he said or did was sure to produce a torrent of household eloquence. Rip had but one way of replying to all lectures of the kind, and that, by frequent use, had grown into a habit. He shrugged his shoulders, shook his head, cast up his eyes, but said nothing. This, however, always provoked a fresh volley from his wife; so that he was fain to draw off his forces, and take to the outside of the house—the only side which, in truth, belongs to a henpecked husband.

Rip's sole domestic adherent was his dog Wolf, who was as much henpecked as his master; for Dame Van Winkle regarded them as companions in idleness, and even looked upon Wolf with an evil eye, as the cause of his master's going so often astray. True it is, in all points of spirit, befitting an honorable dog, he was as courageous an animal as ever scoured the woods—but what courage can withstand the ever-during and all-besetting terrors of a woman's tongue? The moment Wolf entered the house, his crest fell, his tail drooped to the ground, or curled between his legs, he sneaked about with a gallows air, casting many a sidelong glance at Dame Van Winkle, and at the least flourish of a broomstick or ladle, he would fly to the door with yelping precipitation.

Times grew worse and worse with Rip Van Winkle as years of matrimony rolled on; a tart temper never mellows with age, and a sharp tongue is the only edged tool that grows keener with constant use. For a long while he used to console himself, when driven from home, by frequenting a kind of perpetual club of the sages, philosophers, and other idle personages of the village; which held its sessions on a bench before a small inn, designated by a rubicund portrait of His Majesty George the Third. Here they used to sit in the shade through a long lazy summer's day, talking listlessly over village gossip, or telling endless sleepy stories about nothing. But it would have been worth any statesman's money to have heard the profound discussions that sometimes took place, when by chance an old newspaper fell into their hands from some passing traveler. How solemnly they would listen to the contents, as drawled out by Derrick Van Bummel, the schoolmaster, a dapper learned little man, who was not to be daunted by the most gigantic word in the dictionary; and how sagely they would deliberate upon public events some months after they had taken place.

The opinions of this junto were completely controlled by Nicholas Vedder, a patriarch of the village, and landlord of the inn, at the door of which he took his seat from morning till night, just moving sufficiently to avoid the sun and keep in the shade of a large tree; so that the neighbors could tell the hour by his movements as accurately as by a sundial. It is true he was rarely heard to speak, but smoked his pipe incessantly. His adherents, however (for every great man has his adherents), perfectly understood him, and knew how to gather his opinions. When anything that was read or related displeased him, he was observed to smoke his pipe vehemently, and to send forth short, frequent, and angry puffs, but when pleased he would inhale the smoke slowly and tranquilly, and emit it in light and placid clouds; and sometimes, taking the pipe from his mouth, and letting the fragrant vapor curl about his nose, would gravely nod his head in token of perfect approbation.

From even this stronghold the unlucky Rip was at length routed by his termagant wife, who would suddenly break in upon the tranquillity of the assemblage and call the members all to naught; nor was that august personage, Nicholas Vedder himself, sacred from the daring tongue of this terrible virago, who charged him outright with encouraging her husband in habits of idleness.

Poor Rip was at last reduced almost to despair; and his only alternative, to escape from the labor of the farm and the clamor of his wife, was to take gun in hand and stroll away into the woods. Here he would sometimes seat himself at the foot of a tree, and share the contents of his wallet with Wolf, with whom he sympathized as a fellow-sufferer in persecution. "Poor Wolf," he would say, "thy mistress leads thee a dog's life of it; but never mind, my lad, whilst I live thou shalt never want a friend to stand by thee!" Wolf would wag his tail, look wistfully in his master's face, and if dogs can feel pity, I verily believe he reciprocated the sentiment with all his heart.

In a long ramble of the kind on a fine autumnal day, Rip had unconsciously scrambled to one of the highest parts of the Kaatskill mountains. He was after his favorite sport of squirrel-shooting, and the still solitudes had echoed and reëchoed with the reports of his gun. Panting and fatigued, he threw himself, late in the afternoon, on a green knoll, covered with mountain herbage, that crowned the brow of a precipice. From an opening between the trees he could overlook all the lower country for many a mile of rich woodland. He saw at a distance the lordly Hudson, far, far below him, moving on its silent but majestic course, with the reflection of a purple cloud, or the sail of a lagging bark, here and there sleeping on its glassy bosom, and at last losing itself in the blue highlands.

On the other side he looked down into a deep mountain glen, wild, lonely, and shagged, the bottom filled with fragments from the impending cliffs, and scarcely lighted by the reflected rays of the setting sun. For some time Rip lay musing on this scene; evening was gradually advancing; the mountains began to throw their long blue shadows over the valleys; he saw that it would be dark long before he could reach the village, and he heaved a heavy sigh when he thought of encountering the terrors of Dame Van Winkle.

As he was about to descend, he heard a voice from a distance, hallooing, "Rip Van Winkle! Rip Van Winkle!" He looked round, but could see nothing but a crow winging its solitary flight across the mountain. He thought his fancy must have deceived him, and turned again to descend, when he heard the same cry ring through the still evening air: "Rip Van Winkle! Rip Van Winkle!"—at the same time Wolf bristled up his back, and, giving a loud growl, skulked to his master's side, looking fearfully down into the glen. Rip now felt a vague apprehension stealing over him; he looked anxiously in the same direction, and perceived a strange figure slowly toiling up the rocks, and bending under the weight of something he carried on his back. He was surprised to see any human being in this lonely and unfrequented place; but supposing it to be some one of the neighborhood in need of his assistance, he hastened down to yield it.

On nearer approach he was still more surprised at the singularity of the stranger's appearance. He was a short, square-built old fellow, with thick bushy hair and a grizzled beard. His dress was of the antique Dutch fashion—a cloth jerkin, strapped round the waist— several pair of breeches, the outer one of ample volume, decorated with rows of buttons down the sides, and bunches at the knees. He bore on his shoulder a stout keg, that seemed full of liquor, and made signs for Rip to approach and assist him with the load. Though rather shy and distrustful of this new acquaintance, Rip complied with his usual alacrity; and mutually relieving each other, they clambered up a narrow gully, apparently the dry bed of a mountain torrent. As they ascended, Rip every now and then heard long rolling peals, like distant thunder, that seemed to issue out of a deep ravine, or rather cleft, between lofty rocks, towards which their rugged path conducted. He paused for an instant, but supposing it to be the muttering of one of those transient thunder-showers which often take place in mountain heights, he proceeded. Passing through the ravine, they came to a hollow, like a small amphitheater, surrounded by perpendicular precipices, over the brinks of which impending trees shot their branches, so that you only caught glimpses of the azure sky and the bright evening cloud. During the whole time Rip and his companion had labored on in silence, for though the former marveled greatly what could be the object of carrying a keg of liquor up this wild mountain; yet there was something strange and incomprehensible about the unknown, that inspired awe and checked familiarity.

On entering the amphitheater, new objects of wonder presented themselves. On a level spot in the center was a company of odd-

looking personages playing at ninepins. They were dressed in a
quaint outlandish fashion; some wore short doublets, others jerkins,
with long knives in their belts, and most of them had enormous
breeches, of similar style with that of the guide's. Their visages, too,
were peculiar; one had a large head, broad face, and small piggish
eyes; the face of another seemed to consist entirely of nose, and
was surmounted by a white sugar-loaf hat, set off with a little red
cock's tail. They all had beards, of various shapes and colors. There
was one who seemed to be the commander. He was a stout old
gentleman, with a weather-beaten countenance; he wore a laced
doublet, broad belt and hanger, high-crowned hat and feather, red
stockings, and high-heeled shoes, with roses in them. The whole
group reminded Rip of the figures in an old Flemish painting, in
the parlor of Dominie Van Shaick, the village parson, and which
had been brought over from Holland at the time of the settlement.

What seemed particularly odd to Rip was, that though these
folks were evidently amusing themselves, yet they maintained the
gravest faces, the most mysterious silence, and were, withal, the
most melancholy party of pleasure he had ever witnessed. Nothing
interrupted the stillness of the scene but the noise of the balls,
which, whenever they were rolled, echoed along the mountains like
rumbling peals of thunder.

As Rip and his companion approached them, they suddenly
desisted from their play, and stared at him with such fixed, statue-
like gaze, and such strange, uncouth, lackluster countenances, that
his heart turned within him, and his knees smote together. His
companion now emptied the contents of the keg into large flagons,
and made signs to him to wait upon the company. He obeyed with
fear and trembling; they quaffed the liquor in profound silence,
and then returned to their game.

By degrees Rip's awe and apprehension subsided. He even ventured, when no eye was fixed upon him, to taste the beverage, which
he found had much of the flavor of excellent Hollands. He was
naturally a thirsty soul, and was soon tempted to repeat the draught.
One taste provoked another; and he reiterated his visits to the
flagon so often. that at length his senses were overpowered, his

eyes swam in his head, his head gradually declined, and he fell into a deep sleep.

On waking, he found himself on the green knoll whence he had first seen the old man of the glen. He rubbed his eyes—it was a bright sunny morning. The birds were hopping and twittering among the bushes, and the eagle was wheeling aloft, and breasting the pure mountain breeze. "Surely," thought Rip, "I have not slept here all night." He recalled the occurrences before he fell asleep. The strange man with a keg of liquor—the mountain ravine —the wild retreat among the rocks—the woebegone party at nine-pins—the flagon—"Oh! that flagon! that wicked flagon!" thought Rip; "what excuse shall I make to Dame Van Winkle?"

He looked round for his gun, but in place of the clean well-oiled fowling-piece, he found an old flintlock lying by him, the barrel incrusted with rust, the lock falling off, and the stock worm-eaten. He now suspected that the grave roysters of the mountain had put a trick upon him, and, having dosed him with liquor, had robbed him of his gun. Wolf, too, had disappeared, but he might have strayed away after a squirrel or partridge. He whistled after him, and shouted his name, but all in vain; the echoes repeated his whistle and shout, but no dog was to be seen.

He determined to revisit the scene of the last evening's gambol, and, if he met with any of the party, to demand his dog and gun. As he rose to walk he found himself stiff in the joints, and wanting in his usual activity. "These mountain beds do not agree with me," thought Rip; "and if this frolic should lay me up with a fit of rheumatism, I shall have a blessed time with Dame Van Winkle." With some difficulty he got down into the glen: he found the gully up which he and his companion had ascended the preceding evening; but, to his astonishment, a mountain stream was now foaming down it—leaping from rock to rock, and filling the glen with babbling murmurs. He, however, made shift to scramble up its sides, working his toilsome way through thickets of birch, sassafras, and witch-hazel, and sometimes tripped up or entangled by the wild grapevines that twisted their coils or tendrils from tree to tree, and spread a kind of network in his path.

At length he reached to where the ravine had opened through the cliffs to the amphitheater; but no traces of such opening remained. The rocks presented a high impenetrable wall, over which the torrent came tumbling in a sheet of feathery foam, and fell into a broad, deep basin, black from the shadows of the surrounding forest. Here, then, poor Rip was brought to a stand. He again called and whistled after his dog; he was only answered by the cawing of a flock of idle crows, sporting high in air about a dry tree that overhung a sunny precipice; and who, secure in their elevation, seemed to look down and scoff at the poor man's perplexities. What was to be done?—the morning was passing away, and Rip felt famished for want of his breakfast. He grieved to give up his dog and his gun; he dreaded to meet his wife; but it would not do to starve among the mountains. He shook his head, shouldered the rusty firelock, and, with a heart full of trouble and anxiety, turned his steps homeward.

As he approached the village he met a number of people, but none whom he knew, which somewhat surprised him, for he had thought himself acquainted with everyone in the country round. Their dress, too, was of a different fashion from that to which he was accustomed. They all stared at him with equal marks of surprise, and, whenever they cast their eyes upon him, invariably stroked their chins. The constant recurrence of this gesture induced Rip, involuntarily, to do the same—when, to his astonishment, he found his beard had grown a foot long!

He had now entered the skirts of the village. A troop of strange children ran at his heels, hooting after him, and pointing at his gray beard. The dogs, too, not one of which he recognized for an old acquaintance, barked at him as he passed. The very village was altered; it was larger and more populous. There were rows of houses which he had never seen before, and those which had been his familiar haunts had disappeared. Strange names were over the doors—strange faces at the windows—everything was strange. His mind now misgave him; he began to doubt whether both he and the world around him were not bewitched. Surely this was his native village, which he had left but the day before. There stood the Kaatskill mountains—there ran the silver Hudson at a distance —there was every hill and dale precisely as it had always been. Rip was sorely perplexed. "That flagon last night," thought he, "has addled my poor head sadly!"

It was with some difficulty that he found the way to his own house, which he approached with silent awe, expecting every moment to hear the shrill voice of Dame Van Winkle. He found the house gone to decay—the roof fallen in, the windows shattered, and the doors off the hinges. A half-starved dog that looked like Wolf was skulking about it. Rip called him by name, but the cur snarled, showed his teeth, and passed on. This was an unkind cut indeed—"My very dog," sighed poor Rip, "has forgotten me!"

He entered the house, which, to tell the truth, Dame Van Winkle had always kept in neat order. It was empty, forlorn, and apparently abandoned. The desolateness overcame all his connubial fears—he called loudly for his wife and children—the lonely chambers rang for a moment with his voice, and then all again was silence.

He now hurried forth, and hastened to his old resort, the village inn—but it too was gone. A large, rickety, wooden building stood in its place, with great gaping windows, some of them broken and mended with old hats and petticoats, and over the door was painted, "The Union Hotel, by Jonathan Doolittle." Instead of the great tree that used to shelter the quiet little Dutch inn of yore, there was now reared a tall naked pole, with something on the top that looked like a red nightcap, and from it was fluttering a flag, on which was a singular assemblage of stars and stripes—all this was strange and incomprehensible. He recognized on the sign, however, the ruby face of King George, under which he had smoked so many a peaceful pipe; but even this was singularly metamorphosed. The red coat was changed for one of blue and buff, a sword was held in the hand instead of a scepter, the head was decorated with a cocked hat, and underneath was painted in large characters, GENERAL WASHINGTON.

There was, as usual, a crowd of folks about the door, but none that Rip recollected. The very character of the people seemed changed. There was a busy, bustling, disputatious tone about it, instead of the accustomed phlegm and drowsy tranquillity. He looked in vain for the sage Nicholas Vedder, with his broad face, double chin, and fair long pipe, uttering clouds of tobacco-smoke instead of idle speeches; or Van Bummel, the schoolmaster, doling forth the contents of an ancient newspaper. In place of these, a lean, bilious-looking fellow, with his pockets full of handbills, was haranguing vehemently about rights of citizens—elections— members of Congress—liberty—Bunker's Hill—heroes of seventy- six—and other words, which were a perfect Babylonish jargon to the bewildered Van Winkle.

The appearance of Rip, with his long grizzled beard, his rusty fowling-piece, his uncouth dress, and an army of women and children at his heels, soon attracted the attention of the tavern politicians. They crowded round him, eyeing him from head to foot with great curiosity. The orator bustled up to him, and, draw- ing him partly aside, inquired "on which side he voted?" Rip stared in vacant stupidity. Another short but busy little fellow pulled him by the arm, and, rising on tiptoe, inquired in his ear, "Whether he was Federal or Democrat?" Rip was equally at a loss to comprehend the question; when a knowing, self-important old gentleman, in a sharp cocked hat, made his way through the crowd, putting them to the right and left with his elbows as he passed, and planting himself before Van Winkle, with one arm akimbo, the other resting on his cane, his keen eyes and sharp hat penetrating, as it were, into his very soul, demanded in an austere tone, "What brought him to the election with a gun on his shoulder, and a mob at his heels, and whether he meant to breed a riot in the village?"—"Alas! gentlemen," cried Rip, somewhat dismayed, "I am a poor quiet man, a native of the place, and a loyal subject of the king, God bless him!"

Here a general shout burst from the bystanders—"A tory! a tory! a spy! a refugee! hustle him! away with him!" It was with great difficulty that the self-important man in the cocked hat restored order; and, having assumed a tenfold austerity of brow, demanded again of the unknown culprit, what he came there for, and whom he was seeking? The poor man humbly assured him that he meant no harm, but merely came there in search of some of his neighbors, who used to keep about the tavern.

"Well—who are they?—name them."

Rip bethought himself a moment, and inquired, "Where's Nicholas Vedder?"

There was a silence for a little while, when an old man replied in a thin piping voice, "Nicholas Vedder? Why, he is dead and gone these eighteen years! There was a wooden tombstone in the church-yard that used to tell all about him, but that's rotten and gone too."

"Where's Brom Dutcher?"

"Oh, he went off to the army in the beginning of the war; some say he was killed at the storming of Stony Point—others say he was drowned in a squall at the foot of Antony's Nose. I don't know—he never came back again."

"Where's Van Bummel, the schoolmaster?"

"He went off to the wars too, was a great militia general, and is now in Congress."

Rip's heart died away at hearing of these sad changes in his home and friends, and finding himself thus alone in the world. Every answer puzzled him too, by treating of such enormous lapses of time, and of matters which he could not understand; war—Congress—Stony Point;—he had no courage to ask after any more friends, but cried out in despair, "Does nobody here know Rip Van Winkle?"

"Oh, Rip Van Winkle!" exclaimed two or three. "Oh, to be sure! That's Rip Van Winkle yonder, leaning against the tree."

Rip looked, and beheld a precise counterpart of himself, as he went up the mountain: apparently as lazy, and certainly as ragged. The poor fellow was now completely confounded. He doubted his own identity, and whether he was himself or another man. In the midst of his bewilderment, the man in the cocked hat demanded who he was, and what was his name?

"God knows," exclaimed he, at his wits' end; "I'm not myself—I'm somebody else—that's me yonder—no—that's somebody else got into my shoes—I was myself last night, but I fell asleep on the mountain, and they've changed my gun, and everything's changed, and I'm changed, and I can't tell what's my name, or who I am!"

The bystanders began now to look at each other, nod, wink significantly, and tap their fingers against their foreheads. There was a whisper, also, about securing the gun, and keeping the old fellow from doing mischief, at the very suggestion of which the self-important man in the cocked hat retired with some precipitation. At this critical moment a fresh comely woman pressed through the throng to get a peep at the gray-bearded man. She had a chubby child in her arms, which, frightened at his looks, began to cry. "Hush, Rip," cried she, "hush, you little fool; the old man won't hurt you." The name of the child, the air of the mother, the tone of her voice, all awakened a train of recollections in his mind.

"What is your name, my good woman?" asked he.

"Judith Gardenier."

"And your father's name?"

"Ah, poor man, Rip Van Winkle was his name, but it's twenty years since he went away from home with his gun, and never has been heard of since—his dog came home without him; but whether he shot himself, or was carried away by the Indians, nobody can tell. I was then but a little girl."

Rip had but one question more to ask; but he put it with a faltering voice,—

"Where's your mother?"

"Oh, she too had died but a short time since; she broke a blood-vessel in a fit of passion at a New England pedlar."

There was a drop of comfort, at least, in this intelligence. The honest man could contain himself no longer. He caught his daughter and her child in his arms. "I am your father!" cried he—"Young Rip Van Winkle once—old Rip Van Winkle now!—Does nobody know poor Rip Van Winkle?"

All stood amazed, until an old woman, tottering out from among the crowd, put her hand to her brow, and peering under it in his

face for a moment, exclaimed, "Sure enough! It is Rip Van Winkle
—it is himself! Welcome home again, old neighbor— Why, where
have you been these twenty long years?"

Rip's story was soon told, for the whole twenty years had been
to him but as one night. The neighbors stared when they heard
it; some were seen to wink at each other, and put their tongues
in their cheeks: and the self-important man in the cocked hat,
who, when the alarm was over, had returned to the field, screwed
down the corners of his mouth, and shook his head—upon which
there was a general shaking of the head throughout the assemblage.

It was determined, however, to take the opinion of old Peter
Vanderdonk, who was seen slowly advancing up the road. He was
a descendant of the historian of that name, who wrote one of the
earliest accounts of the province. Peter was the most ancient in-
habitant of the village, and well versed in all the wonderful events
and traditions of the neighborhood. He recollected Rip at once,
and corroborated his story in the most satisfactory manner. He
assured the company that it was a fact, handed down from his
ancestor the historian, that the Kaatskill mountains had always
been haunted by strange beings. That it was affirmed that the great
Hendrick Hudson, the first discoverer of the river and country,
kept a kind of vigil there every twenty years, with his crew of the
Half-moon; being permitted in this way to revisit the scenes of his
enterprise, and keep a guardian eye upon the river, and the great
city called by his name. That his father had once seen them in
their old Dutch dresses playing at ninepins in a hollow of the
mountain; and that he himself had heard, one summer afternoon,
the sound of their balls, like distant peals of thunder.

To make a long story short, the company broke up, and returned
to the more important concerns of the election. Rip's daughter
took him home to live with her; she had a snug, well-furnished
house, and a stout cheery farmer for her husband, whom Rip recollected for one of the urchins that used to climb upon his back.
As to Rip's son and heir, who was the ditto of himself, seen leaning against the tree, he was employed to work on the farm; but

evinced an hereditary disposition to attend to anything else but his business.

Rip now resumed his old walks and habits; he soon found many of his former cronies, though all rather the worse for the wear and tear of time; and preferred making friends among the rising generation, with whom he soon grew into great favor.

Having nothing to do at home, and being arrived at that happy age when a man can be idle with impunity, he took his place once more on the bench at the inn door, and was reverenced as one of the patriarchs of the village, and a chronicle of the old times "before the war." It was some time before he could get into the regular track of gossip, or could be made to comprehend the strange events that had taken place during his torpor. How that there had been a revolutionary war—that the country had thrown off the yoke of Old England—and that, instead of being a subject of His Majesty George the Third, he was now a free citizen of the United States. Rip, in fact, was no politician; the changes of states and empires made but little impression on him; but there was one species of despotism under which he had long groaned, and that was—petticoat government. Happily that was at an end; he had got his neck out of the yoke of matrimony, and could go in and out whenever he pleased without dreading the tyranny of Dame Van Winkle. Whenever her name was mentioned, however, he shook his head, shrugged his shoulders, and cast up his eyes; which might pass either for an expression of resignation to his fate, or joy at his deliverance.

He used to tell his story to every stranger that arrived at Mr. Doolittle's hotel. He was observed at first to vary on some points every time he told it, which was, doubtless, owing to his having so recently awaked. It at last settled down precisely to the tale I have related, and not a man, woman, or child in the neighborhood but knew it by heart. Some always pretended to doubt the reality of it, and insisted that Rip had been out of his head, and that this was one point on which he always remained flighty. The old Dutch inhabitants, however, almost universally gave it full credit. Even to this day they never hear a thunderstorm of a summer afternoon about the Kaatskill, but they say Hendrick Hudson and his crew are at their game of ninepins; and it is a common wish of all hen-pecked husbands in the neighborhood, when life hangs heavy on their hands, that they might have a quieting draught out of Rip Van Winkle's flagon.

The Ambitious Guest

NATHANIEL HAWTHORNE (1804–1864)

Still ranked after more than a century as one of the
foremost short-story writers in any language, Hawthorne was born in Salem, Massachusetts, son of a
Puritan family that went back to 1630 in America.

His father died when the boy was four. A slight
lameness, the result of an injury at baseball, increased the lad's natural solitariness, and he read
widely, especially the writers of romances. He was
able as a youth to spend a year in the wilderness of
Maine.

After taking a degree at Bowdoin College in
Maine, he passed a dozen years in Salem, a recluse
learning his literary art. Vacations he spent vaga-
bonding about New England and New York,
where he found settings for many of his best stories.
He won a growing reputation as a contributor to
the New England Magazine and to The Token, an
annual gift book. In 1837, the publication of the
first series of Twice-Told Tales brought him a
wider audience.

Thereafter he worked as editor, historian, and writer of tales for children—A Wonder-Book (1852) and Tanglewood Tales (1853)—that are still read. From 1839 to 1841, he held a job in the Salem Custom House. He lived much of the time during the next year at Brook Farm, a socialistic community which was to give him material for a novel. He married Sophia Peabody in 1842, and for the next three years they lived in the Old Manse at historic Concord, Massachusetts, as neighbors to the celebrated Transcendentalist group that included Bronson Alcott, William Ellery Channing, Ralph Waldo Emerson, and Henry David Thoreau.

Hawthorne returned to the Salem Custom House in 1845 and there came upon the inspiration for The Scarlet Letter (1850), which at once became a best seller. His The House of Seven Gables (1851) was written at Pittsfield, Massachusetts, where his friend Herman Melville was at work on Moby Dick.

Returning to Concord, Hawthorne wrote a campaign biography of his Bowdoin classmate Franklin Pierce, and was rewarded with the consulship at Liverpool. For the next seven years he lived in England, except for a year in Italy. He returned to Concord in 1860. The Civil War affected him greatly and disturbed his flow of thought. Four unfinished novels were published after his death.

One of Hawthorne's favorite themes was that one's hopes in life are seldom realized; this theme is ironically expressed in "The Ambitious Guest," first published in the New England Magazine, June, 1835. His shorter pieces were published in Twice-Told Tales (first series, 1837; second series,

1842) *and* The Snow-Image and Other Twice-Told Tales (1852). *These had previously appeared in early American magazines.*

ONE SEPTEMBER NIGHT a family had gathered round their hearth, and piled it high with the driftwood of mountain streams, the dry cones of the pine, and the splintered ruins of great trees that had come crashing down the precipice. Up the chimney roared the fire, and brightened the room with its broad blaze. The faces of the father and mother had a sober gladness; the children laughed; the eldest daughter was the image of Happiness at seventeen; and the aged grandmother, who sat knitting in the warmest place, was the image of Happiness grown old. They had found the "herb, heart's-ease," in the bleakest spot of all New England. This family were situated in the Notch of the White Hills, where the wind was sharp throughout the year, and pitilessly cold in the winter—giving their cottage all its fresh inclemency before it descended on the valley of the Saco. They dwelt in a cold spot and a dangerous one; for a mountain towered above their heads, so steep, that the stones would often rumble down its sides and startle them at midnight.

The daughter had just uttered some simple jest that filled them all with mirth, when the wind came through the Notch and seemed to pause before their cottage—rattling the door, with a sound of wailing and lamentation, before it passed into the valley. For a moment it saddened them, though there was nothing unusual in the tones. But the family were glad again when they perceived that the latch was lifted by some traveler, whose footsteps had been unheard amid the dreary blast which heralded his approach, and wailed as he was entering, and went moaning away from the door.

Though they dwelt in such a solitude, these people held daily converse with the world. The romantic pass of the Notch is a great artery, through which the lifeblood of internal commerce is continually throbbing between Maine, on one side, and the Green Mountains and the shores of the St. Lawrence, on the other. The stagecoach always drew up before the door of the cottage. The wayfayer, with no companion but his staff, paused here to exchange a word, that the sense of loneliness might not utterly overcome him ere he could pass through the cleft of the mountain, or reach the first house in the valley. And here the teamster, on his way to Portland market, would put up for the night; and, if a bachelor, might sit an hour beyond the usual bed-time, and steal a kiss from the mountain maid at parting. It was one of those primitive taverns where the traveler pays only for food and lodging, but meets with a homely kindness beyond all price. When the footsteps were heard, therefore, between the outer door and the inner one, the whole family rose up, grandmother, children, and all, as if about to welcome some one who belonged to them, and whose fate was linked with theirs.

The door was opened by a young man. His face at first wore the melancholy expression, almost despondency, of one who travels a wild and bleak road, at nightfall and alone, but soon brightened up when he saw the kindly warmth of his reception. He felt his heart spring forward to meet them all, from the old woman, who wiped a chair with her apron, to the little child that held out its arms to him. One glance and smile placed the stranger on a foot-ing of innocent familiarity with the eldest daughter.

"Ah, this fire is the right thing!" cried he; "especially when there is such a pleasant circle round it. I am quite benumbed; for the Notch is just like the pipe of a great pair of bellows; it has blown a terrible blast in my face all the way from Bartlett."

"Then you are going towards Vermont?" said the master of the house, as he helped to take a light knapsack off the young man's shoulders.

"Yes; to Burlington, and far enough beyond," replied he. "I meant to have been at Ethan Crawford's tonight; but a pedestrian lingers along such a road as this. It is no matter; for, when I saw this good fire, and all your cheerful faces, I felt as if you had kindled it on purpose for me, and were waiting my arrival. So I shall sit down among you, and make myself at home."

The frank-hearted stranger had just drawn his chair to the fire when something like a heavy footstep was heard without, rushing down the steep side of the mountain, as with long and rapid strides, and taking such a leap in passing the cottage as to strike the opposite precipice. The family held their breath, because they knew the sound, and their guest held his by instinct.

"The old mountain has thrown a stone at us, for fear we should forget him," said the landlord, recovering himself. "He sometimes nods his head and threatens to come down; but we are old neighbors, and agree together pretty well upon the whole. Besides we have a sure place of refuge hard by if he should be coming in good earnest."

Let us now suppose the stranger to have finished his supper of bear's meat; and, by his natural felicity of manner, to have placed himself on a footing of kindness with the whole family, so that they talked as freely together as if he belonged to their mountain brood. He was of a proud, yet gentle spirit—haughty and reserved among the rich and great; but ever ready to stoop his head to the lowly cottage door, and be like a brother or a son at the poor man's fireside. In the household of the Notch he found warmth and simplicity of feeling, the pervading intelligence of New England, and a poetry of native growth, which they had gathered when they little thought of it from the mountain peaks and chasms, and at the very threshold of their romantic and dangerous abode. He had traveled far and alone; his whole life, indeed, had been a solitary path; for, with the lofty caution of his nature, he had kept himself apart from those who might otherwise have been his companions. The family, too, though so kind and hospitable, had that consciousness of unity among themselves, and separation from the world at large, which, in every domestic circle, should still keep a holy place where no stranger may intrude. But this evening a prophetic sympathy impelled the refined and educated youth to pour out his heart before the simple mountaineers, and constrained them to answer him with the same free confidence. And thus it should have been. Is not the kindred of a common fate a closer tie than that of birth?

The secret of the young man's character was a high and abstracted ambition. He could have borne to live an undistinguished life, but not to be forgotten in the grave. Yearning desire had been transformed to hope; and hope, long cherished, had become like certainty that, obscurely as he journeyed now, a glory was to beam on all his pathway—though not, perhaps, while he was treading it. But when posterity should gaze back into the gloom of what was now the present, they would trace the brightness of his footsteps, brightening as meaner glories faded, and confess that a gifted one had passed from his cradle to his tomb with none to recognize him.

"As yet," cried the stranger—his cheek glowing and his eye flashing with enthusiasm—"as yet, I have done nothing. Were I to vanish from the earth tomorrow, none would know so much of me as you: that a nameless youth came up at nightfall from the valley of the Saco, and opened his heart to you in the evening, and passed through the Notch by sunrise, and was seen no more. Not a soul would ask, 'Who was he? Whither did the wanderer go?' But I cannot die till I have achieved my destiny. Then, let Death come! I shall have built my monument!"

There was a continual flow of natural emotion, gushing forth amid abstracted reverie, which enabled the family to understand this young man's sentiments, though so foreign from their own. With quick sensibility of the ludicrous, he blushed at the ardor into which he had been betrayed.

"You laugh at me," said he, taking the eldest daughter's hand, and laughing himself. "You think my ambition as nonsensical as if I were to freeze myself to death on the top of Mount Washington, only that people might spy at me from the country round about. And, truly, that would be a noble pedestal for a man's statue!"

"It is better to sit here by this fire!" answered the girl, blushing, "and be comfortable and contented, though nobody thinks about us."

"I suppose," said her father, after a fit of musing, "there is something natural in what the young man says; and if my mind had been turned that way, I might have felt just the same. It is strange, wife, how his talk has set my head running on things that are pretty certain never to come to pass."

"Perhaps they may," observed the wife. "Is the man thinking what he will do when he is a widower?"

"No, no!" cried he, repelling the idea with reproachful kindness. "When I think of your death, Esther, I think of mine, too. But I was wishing we had a good farm in Bartlett, or Bethlehem, or Littleton, or some other township round the White Mountains; but not where they could tumble on our heads. I should want to stand well with my neighbors and be called Squire, and sent to General Court for a term or two; for a plain, honest man may do as much good there as a lawyer. And when I should be grown quite an old man, and you an old woman, so as not to be long apart, I might die happy enough in my bed, and leave you all crying around me. A slate gravestone would suit me as well as a marble one—with just my name and age, and a verse of a hymn, and something to let people know that I lived an honest man and died a Christian."

"There now!" exclaimed the stranger; "it is our nature to desire a monument, be it slate or marble, or a pillar of granite, or a glorious memory in the universal heart of man."

"We're in a strange way, tonight," said the wife, with tears in her eyes. "They say it's a sign of something, when folks' minds go a wandering so. Hark to the children!"

They listened accordingly. The younger children had been put to bed in another room, but with an open door between, so that they could be heard talking busily among themselves. One and all seemed to have caught the infection from the fireside circle, and were outvying each other in wild wishes, and childish projects of what they would do when they came to be men and women. At length a little boy, instead of addressing his brothers and sisters, called out to his mother.

"I'll tell you what I wish, mother," cried he. "I want you and father and grandma'm, and all of us, and the stranger too, to start right away, and go and take a drink out of the basin of the Flume!"

Nobody could help laughing at the child's notion of leaving a warm bed, and dragging them from a cheerful fire, to visit the basin of the Flume—a brook which tumbles over the precipice, deep within the Notch. The boy had hardly spoken when a wagon rattled along the road, and stopped a moment before the door. It appeared to contain two or three men, who were cheering their hearts with the rough chorus of a song, which resounded, in broken notes, between the cliffs, while the singers hesitated whether to continue their journey or put up here for the night.

"Father," said the girl, "they are calling you by name."

But the good man doubted whether they had really called him, and was unwilling to show himself too solicitous of gain by inviting people to patronize his house. He therefore did not hurry to the door; and the lash being soon applied, the travelers plunged into the Notch, still singing and laughing, though their music and mirth came back drearily from the heart of the mountain.

"There, mother!" cried the boy, again. "They'd have given us a ride to the Flume."

Again they laughed at the child's pertinacious fancy for a night ramble. But it happened that a light cloud passed over the daughter's spirit; she looked gravely into the fire, and drew a breath that was almost a sigh. It forced its way, in spite of a little struggle to repress it. Then starting and blushing, she looked quickly round the circle, as if they had caught a glimpse into her bosom. The stranger asked what she had been thinking of.

"Nothing," answered she, with a downcast smile. "Only I felt lonesome just then."

"Oh, I have always had a gift of feeling what is in other people's hearts," said he, half seriously. "Shall I tell the secrets of yours? For I know what to think when a young girl shivers by a warm hearth, and complains of lonesomeness at her mother's side. Shall I put these feelings into words?"

"They would not be a girl's feelings any longer if they could be put into words," replied the mountain nymph, laughing, but avoiding his eye.

All this was said apart. Perhaps a germ of love was springing in their hearts, so pure that it might blossom in Paradise, since it could not be matured on earth; for women worship such gentle dignity as his; and the proud, contemplative, yet kindly soul is oftenest captivated by simplicity like hers. But while they spoke softly, and he was watching the happy sadness, the lightsome shadows, the shy yearnings of a maiden's nature, the wind through the Notch took a deeper and drearier sound. It seemed, as the fanciful stranger said, like the choral strain of the spirits of the blast, who in old Indian times had their dwellings among these mountains, and made their heights and recesses a sacred region. There was a wail along the road, as if a funeral were passing. To chase away the gloom, the family threw pine branches on their fire, till the dry leaves crackled and the flame arose, discovering once again a scene of peace and humble happiness. The light hovered about them fondly, and caressed them all. There were the little faces of the children, peeping from their bed apart, and here the father's frame of strength, the mother's subdued and careful mien, the high-browed youth, the budding girl, and the good old grandam, still knitting in the warmest place. The aged woman looked up from her task, and, with fingers ever busy, was the next to speak.

"Old folks have their notions," said she, "as well as young ones. You've been wishing and planning, and letting your heads run on one thing and another, till you've set my mind a wandering too. Now what should an old woman wish for, when she can go but a step or two before she comes to her grave? Children, it will haunt me night and day till I tell you."

"What is it, mother?" cried the husband and wife at once.

Then the old woman, with an air of mystery which drew the circle closer round the fire, informed them that she had provided

her grave-clothes some years before—a nice linen shroud, a cap
with a muslin ruff, and everything of a finer sort than she had worn
since her wedding day. But this evening an old superstition had
strangely recurred to her. It used to be said, in her younger days, that
if anything were amiss with a corpse, if only the ruff were not
smooth, or the cap did not set right, the corpse in the coffin and
beneath the clods would strive to put up its cold hands and arrange
it. The bare thought made her nervous.

"Don't talk so, grandmother!" said the girl, shuddering.

"Now"—continued the old woman, with singular earnestness,
yet smiling strangely at her own folly—"I want one of you, my
children—when your mother is dressed and in the coffin—I want
one of you to hold a looking-glass over my face. Who knows but
I may take a glimpse at myself, and see whether all's right?"

"Old and young, we dream of graves and monuments," murmured the stranger youth. "I wonder how mariners feel when the
ship is sinking, and they, unknown and undistinguished, are to
be buried together in the ocean—that wide and nameless sepul-
chre?"

For a moment, the old woman's ghastly conception so engrossed
the minds of her hearers that a sound abroad in the night, rising like
the roar of a blast, had grown broad, deep, and terrible, before the
fated group were conscious of it. The house and all within it
trembled; the foundations of the earth seemed to be shaken, as if
this awful sound were the peal of the last trump. Young and
old exchanged one wild glance, and remained an instant, pale,
affrighted, without utterance, or power to move. Then the same
shriek burst simultaneously from all the lips.

"The Slide! The Slide!"

The simplest words must intimate, but not portray, the unutter-
able horror of the catastrophe. The victims rushed from their
cottage, and sought refuge in what they deemed a safer spot—
where, in contemplation of such an emergency, a sort of barrier
had been reared. Alas! they had quitted their security, and fled right
into the pathway of destruction. Down came the whole side of
the mountain, in a cataract of ruin. Just before it reached the house,

the stream broke into two branches—shivered not a window there, but overwhelmed the whole vicinity, blocked up the road, and annihilated everything in its dreadful course. Long ere the thunder of the great Slide had ceased to roar among the mountains, the mortal agony had been endured, and the victims were at peace. Their bodies were never found.

The next morning, the light smoke was seen stealing from the cottage chimney up the mountain side. Within, the fire was yet smouldering on the hearth, and the chairs in a circle round it, as if the inhabitants had but gone forth to view the devastation of the Slide, and would shortly return, to thank Heaven for their miraculous escape. All had left separate tokens, by which those who had known the family were made to shed a tear for each. Who has not heard their name? The story has been told far and wide, and will forever be a legend of these mountains. Poets have sung their fate.

There were circumstances which led some to suppose that a stranger had been received into the cottage on this awful night, and had shared the catastrophe of all its inmates. Others denied that there were sufficient grounds for such a conjecture. Woe for the high-souled youth, with his dream of Earthly Immortality! His name and person utterly unknown; his history, his way of life, his plans, a mystery never to be solved, his death and his existence equally a doubt! Whose was the agony of that death moment?

Carnival time in Rome—and Montresor
schemed an act of vengeance. . . .

The Cask of Amontillado

EDGAR ALLAN POE (1809–1849)

The two stories here taken from Poe's best work
represent two types of writing in which he excelled
—the Gothic tale of horror and the tale of ratiocination that is the direct ancestor of our modern detective story.

The life of the unhappy genius who wrote them
was in many ways as macabre and unfortunate as
one of his own stories. The future poet, critic, and
short-story writer was born in Boston, Massachusetts, son of a pair of traveling actors, both of whom
died when he was an infant. The child became the
foster son of John Allan, Scottish merchant of
Richmond, Virginia, and was thereafter known as
Edgar Allan Poe.

The boy went abroad with Allan and spent the
years 1815 to 1820 in Scottish and English schools.
Returning to Richmond, Poe began writing verses;
he was already a brilliant, Byronic young man,
spoiled by "great expectations." He went to the
University of Virginia in 1826, but left after one

term, when his foster father refused to pay his gentlemanly gambling debts.

The following year, after a quarrel with Allan, Poe left for Boston and had his first book printed, Tamerlane (1827). The same year, penniless, he enlisted in the United States Army under the name of Edgar A. Perry. He was sent to garrison duty at Fort Moultrie, near Charleston, South Carolina, the scene of his story "The Gold Bug." He became regimental sergeant-major in 1829, and was given an honorable discharge in order to enter West Point, where Allan had obtained an appointment for him. When Allan later disowned him, Poe deliberately neglected his duties and was dismissed in 1831.

He returned to Baltimore and began getting his sketches in print in 1832; his "MS. Found in a Bottle" won a fifty-dollar prize, and he obtained a place on the staff of the Southern Literary Messenger. His work was brilliant, but worry and poverty had caused him to take to drinking to stave off his growing melancholy.

His foster father had died in 1834, leaving Poe not a penny. He romantically married his fourteen-year-old cousin, Virginia Clemm, in 1836, and took her and her mother to live in New York. The year was one of financial panic in America, and Poe was glad to move to Philadelphia, where he served as coeditor of Burton's Gentleman's Magazine for a year and literary editor of Graham's Magazine for a year and a half. These were his most productive times, but his labors were sadly underpaid, and his future was clouded by failure to finance a proposed magazine of his own and by the knowledge that his young wife was suffering from tuberculosis.

The pair returned to New York in 1844, where

Poe became a free-lance writer and editor of the Broadway Journal. His wife died in January, 1847, and thereafter Poe's search for another wife—rich widows were his ideal now—had an element of odd comedy. On the eve of marrying an early sweetheart, Poe went to Baltimore, where he disappeared for five days. It is thought that an election gang of the time plied him with drink and dragged him about the city, making him vote for their candidate. He died in the hospital on October 7, 1849, a self-consuming genius who first defined and demonstrated the theory of the modern short story.

"The Cask of Amontillado" first appeared in the November, 1846, issue of Godey's Lady's Book. "The Purloined Letter" was first published in The Gift (annual) for 1845. Poe's first collection of short prose writings was Tales of the Grotesque and Arabesque (1840). His collected stories have frequently been reprinted in various editions.

THE THOUSAND INJURIES of Fortunato I had borne as I best could, but when he ventured upon insult I vowed revenge. You, who so well know the nature of my soul, will not suppose, however, that I gave utterance to a threat. *At length* I would be avenged; this was a point definitely settled—but the very definitiveness with which it was resolved precluded the idea of risk. I must not only punish but punish with impunity. A wrong is unredressed when retribution overtakes its redresser. It is equally unredressed when the avenger fails to make himself felt as such to him who has done the wrong.

It must be understood that neither by word nor deed had I

given Fortunato cause to doubt my good will. I continued, as was
my wont, to smile in his face, and he did not perceive that my smile
now was at the thought of his immolation.

He had a weak point—this Fortunato—although in other regards
he was a man to be respected and even feared. He prided himself
on his connoisseurship in wine. Few Italians have the true virtuoso
spirit. For the most part their enthusiasm is adopted to suit the
time and opportunity, to practise imposture upon the British and
Austrian *millionaires*. In painting and gemmary, Fortunato, like
his countrymen, was a quack, but in the matter of old wines he
was sincere. In this respect I did not differ from him materially;
I was skilful in the Italian vintages myself, and bought largely whenever I could.

It was about dusk, one evening during the supreme madness of
the carnival season, that I encountered my friend. He accosted
me with excessive warmth, for he had been drinking much. The
man wore motley. He had on a tight-fitting parti-striped dress,
and his head was surmounted by the conical cap and bells. I was
so pleased to see him that I thought I should never have done wring-
ing his hand.

I said to him—"My dear Fortunato, you are luckily met. How
remarkably well you are looking today. But I have received a pipe
of what passes for Amontillado, and I have my doubts."

"How?" said he. "Amontillado? A pipe? Impossible! And in the
middle of the carnival!"

"I have my doubts," I replied; "and I was silly enough to pay
the full Amontillado price without consulting you in the matter.
You were not to be found, and I was fearful of losing a bargain."

"Amontillado!"

"I have my doubts."

"Amontillado!"

"And I must satisfy them."

"Amontillado!"

"As you are engaged, I am on my way to Luchresi. If any one
has a critical turn it is he. He will tell me—"

"Luchresi cannot tell Amontillado from sherry."

"And yet some fools will have it that his taste is a match for your own."

"Come, let us go."

"Whither?"

"To your vaults."

"My friend, no; I will not impose upon your good nature. I perceive you have an engagement. Luchresi—"

"I have no engagement;—come."

"My friend, no. It is not the engagement, but the severe cold with which I perceive you are afflicted. The vaults are insufferably damp. They are encrusted with nitre."

"Let us go, nevertheless. The cold is merely nothing. Amontillado! You have been imposed upon. And as for Luchresi, he cannot distinguish sherry from Amontillado."

Thus speaking, Fortunato possessed himself of my arm; and putting on a mask of black silk and drawing a *roquelaure* closely about my person, I suffered him to hurry me to my palazzo.

There were no attendants at home; they had absconded to make merry in honor of the time. I had told them that I should not return until the morning, and had given them explicit orders not to stir from the house. These orders were sufficient, I well knew, to insure their immediate disappearance, one and all, as soon as my back was turned.

I took from their sconces two flambeaux, and giving one to Fortunato, bowed him through several suites of rooms to the archway that led into the vaults. I passed down a long and winding staircase, requesting him to be cautious as he followed. We came at length to the foot of the descent, and stood together upon the damp ground of the catacombs of the Montresors.

The gait of my friend was unsteady, and the bells upon his cap jingled as he strode.

"The pipe," he said.

"It is farther on," said I; "but observe the white web-work which gleams from these cavern walls."

He turned towards me, and looked into my eyes with two filmy orbs that distilled the rheum of intoxication.

"Nitre?" he asked, at length.

"Nitre," I replied. "How long have you had that cough?"

"Ugh! ugh! ugh!—ugh! ugh! ugh!—ugh! ugh! ugh!—ugh! ugh! ugh!—ugh! ugh! ugh!"

My poor friend found it impossible to reply for many minutes.

"It is nothing," he said, at last.

"Come," I said, with decision, "we will go back; your health is precious. You are rich, respected, admired, beloved; you are happy, as once I was. You are a man to be missed. For me it is no matter. We will go back; you will be ill, and I cannot be responsible. Besides, there is Luchresi—"

"Enough," he said; "the cough is a mere nothing; it will not kill me. I shall not die of a cough."

"True—true," I replied; "and, indeed, I had no intention of alarming you unnecessarily—but you should use all proper caution. A draught of this Medoc will defend us from the damps."

Here I knocked off the neck of a bottle which I drew from a long row of its fellows that lay upon the mould.

"Drink," I said, presenting him the wine.

He raised it to his lips with a leer. He paused and nodded to me familiarly, while his bells jingled.

"I drink," he said, "to the buried that repose around us."

"And I to your long life."

He again took my arm, and we proceeded.

"These vaults," he said, "are extensive."

"The Montresors," I replied, "were a great and numerous family."

"I forget your arms."

"A huge human foot d'or, in a field azure; the foot crushes a serpent rampant whose fangs are imbedded in the heel."

"And the motto?"

"*Nemo me impune lacessit.*" *

"Good!" he said.

The wine sparkled in his eyes and the bells jingled. My own fancy grew warm with the Medoc. We had passed through long walls of piled skeletons, with casks and puncheons intermingling,

* No one attacks me with impunity.

into the inmost recesses of catacombs. I paused again, and this time I made bold to seize Fortunato by an arm above the elbow.

"The nitre!" I said; "see, it increases. It hangs like moss upon the vaults. We are below the river's bed. The drops of moisture trickle among the bones. Come, we will go back ere it is too late. Your cough—"

"It is nothing," he said; "let us go on. But first, another draught of the Medoc."

I broke and reached him a flagon of De Grâve. He emptied it at a breath. His eyes flashed with a fierce light. He laughed and threw the bottle upwards with a gesticulation I did not understand.

I looked at him in surprise. He repeated the movement—a grotesque one.

"You do not comprehend?" he said.

"Not I," I replied.

"Then you are not of the brotherhood."

"How?"

"You are not of the masons."

"Yes, yes," I said; "yes, yes."

"You? Impossible! A mason?"

"A mason," I replied.

"A sign," he said, "a sign."

"It is this," I answered, producing from beneath the folds of my *roquelaure* a trowel.

"You jest," he exclaimed, recoiling a few paces. "But let us proceed to the Amontillado."

"Be it so," I said, replacing the tool beneath the cloak and again offering my arm. He leaned upon it heavily. We continued our route in search of the Amontillado. We passed through a range of low arches, descended, passed on, and descending again, arrived at a deep crypt, in which the foulness of the air caused our flambeaux rather to glow than flame.

At the most remote end of the crypt there appeared another less spacious. Its walls had been lined with human remains, piled to the vault overhead, in the fashion of the great catacombs of Paris. Three sides of this interior crypt were still ornamented in this manner. From the fourth side the bones had been thrown down, and lay promiscuously upon the earth, forming at one point a mound of some size. Within the wall thus exposed by the displacing of the bones, we perceived a still interior crypt or recess, in depth about four feet, in width three, in height six or seven. It seemed to have been constructed for no especial use within itself, but formed merely the interval between two of the colossal supports of the roof of the catacombs, and was backed by one of their circumscribing walls of solid granite.

It was in vain that Fortunato, uplifting his dull torch, endeavored to pry into the depth of the recess. Its termination the feeble light did not enable us to see.

"Proceed," I said; "herein is the Amontillado. As for Luchresi—"

"He is an ignoramus," interrupted my friend, as he stepped unsteadily forward, while I followed immediately at his heels. In an instant he had reached the extremity of the niche, and finding his progress arrested by the rock, stood stupidly bewildered. A moment more and I had fettered him to the granite. In its surface were two iron staples, distant from each other about two feet, horizontally. From one of these depended a short chain, from the other a padlock. Throwing the links about his waist, it was but the work of a few seconds to secure it. He was too much astounded to resist. Withdrawing the key I stepped back from the recess.

"Pass your hand," I said, "over the wall; you cannot help feeling the nitre. Indeed, it is *very* damp. Once more let me *implore* you to return. No? Then I must positively leave you. But I must first render you all the little attentions in my power."

"The Amontillado!" ejaculated my friend, not yet recovered from his astonishment.

"True," I replied; "the Amontillado."

As I said these words I busied myself among the pile of bones of which I have before spoken. Throwing them aside, I soon uncovered a quantity of building stone and mortar. With these materials and with the aid of my trowel, I began vigorously to wall up the entrance of the niche.

I had scarcely laid the first tier of masonry when I discovered that the intoxication of Fortunato had in a great measure worn off. The earliest indication I had of this was a low moaning cry from the depth of the recess. It was *not* the cry of a drunken man. There was then a long and obstinate silence. I laid the second tier, and the third, and the fourth; and then I heard the furious vibrations of the chain. The noise lasted for several minutes, during which, that I might hearken to it with the more satisfaction, I ceased my labors and sat down upon the bones. When at last the clanking subsided, I resumed the trowel, and finished without interruption the fifth, the sixth, and the seventh tier. The wall was now nearly upon a level with my breast. I again paused, and holding the flambeaux over the mason-work, threw a few feeble rays upon the figure within.

A succession of loud and shrill screams, bursting suddenly from the throat of the chained form, seemed to thrust me violently back. For a brief moment I hesitated, I trembled. Unsheathing my rapier, I began to grope with it about the recess; but the thought of an instant reassured me. I placed my hand upon the solid fabric of the catacombs, and felt satisfied. I reapproached the wall; I replied to the yells of him who clamored. I re-echoed, I aided, I surpassed them in volume and in strength. I did this, and the clamorer grew still.

It was now midnight, and my task was drawing to a close. I had completed the eighth, the ninth and the tenth tier. I had finished a portion of the last and the eleventh; there remained but a single stone to be fitted and plastered in. I struggled with its weight; I placed it partially in its destined position. But now there came from out the niche a low laugh that erected the hairs upon my head. It was succeeded by a sad voice, which I had difficulty in recognizing as that of the noble Fortunato. The voice said—

"Ha! ha! ha!—he! he! he!—a very good joke, indeed—an excellent jest. We shall have many a rich laugh about it at the palazzo—he! he! he!—over our wine—he! he! he!"

"The Amontillado!" I said.

"He! he! he!—he! he! he!—yes, the Amontillado. But is it not getting late? Will not they be awaiting us at the palazzo, the Lady Fortunato and the rest? Let us be gone."

"Yes," I said, "let us be gone."

"*For the love of God, Montresor!*"

"Yes," I said, "for the love of God!"

But to these words I hearkened in vain for a reply. I grew impatient. I called aloud—

"Fortunato!"

No answer. I called again—

"Fortunato!"

No answer still. I thrust a torch through the remaining aperture and let it fall within. There came forth in return only a jingling of the bells. My heart grew sick; it was the dampness of the catacombs that made it so. I hastened to make an end of my labor. I forced the last stone into its position; I plastered it up. Against the new masonry I reërected the old rampart of bones. For the half of a century no mortal has disturbed them. *In pace requiescat!*

> *"Perhaps the mystery is a little too plain," said Dupin.* . . .

The Purloined Letter

*Nil sapientiæ odiosius acumine nimio.** SENECA

AT PARIS JUST AFTER DARK one gusty evening in the autumn of 18——, I was enjoying the twofold luxury of meditation and a meerschaum, in company with my friend C. Auguste Dupin, in his little back library, or book-closet, *au troisième, No. 33, Rue Dunôt, Faubourg St. Germain.* For one hour at least we had maintained a profound silence; while each, to any casual observer, might have seemed intently and exclusively occupied with the curling eddies of smoke that oppressed the atmosphere of the chamber. For myself, however, I was mentally discussing certain topics which had formed matter for conversation between us at an earlier period of the evening; I mean the affair of the Rue Morgue, and the mystery attending the murder of Marie Rogêt. I looked upon it, therefore, as something of a coincidence, when the door of our apartment was thrown open and admitted our old acquaintance, Monsieur G——, the Prefect of the Parisian police.

We gave him a hearty welcome; for there was nearly half as much of the entertaining as of the contemptible about the man, and we had not seen him for several years. We had been sitting in the dark, and Dupin now arose for the purpose of lighting a lamp, but sat down again, without doing so, upon G——'s saying that he had called to consult us, or rather to ask the opinion of

* Nothing is more hateful to good sense than too much penetration.

my friend, about some official business which had occasioned a great deal of trouble.

"If it is any point requiring reflection," observed Dupin, as he forbore to enkindle the wick, "we shall examine it to better purpose in the dark."

"That is another of your odd notions," said the Prefect, who had a fashion of calling every thing "odd" that was beyond his comprehension, and thus lived amid an absolute legion of "oddities."

"Very true," said Dupin, as he supplied his visitor with a pipe, and rolled towards him a comfortable chair.

"And what is the difficulty now?" I asked. "Nothing more in the assassination way, I hope?"

"Oh, no; nothing of that nature. The fact is, the business is *very* simple indeed, and I make no doubt that we can manage it sufficiently well ourselves; but then I thought Dupin would like to hear the details of it, because it is so excessively *odd*."

"Simple and odd," said Dupin.

"Why, yes; and not exactly that, either. The fact is, we have all been a good deal puzzled because the affair *is* so simple, and yet baffles us altogether."

"Perhaps it is the very simplicity of the thing which puts you at fault," said my friend.

"What nonsense you *do* talk!" replied the Prefect, laughing heartily.

"Perhaps the mystery is a little *too* plain," said Dupin.

"Oh, good heavens! Who ever heard of such an idea?"

"A little *too* self-evident."

"Ha! ha! ha!—ha! ha! ha!—ho! ho! ho!"—roared our visitor, profoundly amused, "oh, Dupin, you will be the death of me yet!"

"And what, after all, *is* the matter on hand?" I asked.

"Why, I will tell you," replied the Prefect, as he gave a long, steady, and contemplative puff, and settled himself in his chair. "I will tell you in a few words; but, before I begin, let me caution you that this is an affair demanding the greatest secrecy, and that

I should most probably lose the position I now hold, were it known that I confided it to any one."

"Proceed," said I.

"Or not," said Dupin.

"Well, then; I have received personal information, from a very high quarter, that a certain document of the last importance has been purloined from the royal apartments. The individual who purloined it is known; this beyond a doubt; he was seen to take it. It is known, also, that it still remains in his possession."

"How is this known?" asked Dupin.

"It is clearly inferred," replied the Prefect, "from the nature of the document, and from the non-appearance of certain results which would at once arise from its passing *out* of the robber's possession;—that is to say, from his employing it as he must design in the end to employ it."

"Be a little more explicit," I said.

"Well, I may venture so far as to say that the paper gives its holder a certain power in a certain quarter where such power is immensely valuable." The Prefect was fond of the cant of diplomacy.

"Still I do not quite understand," said Dupin.

"No? Well; the disclosure of the document to a third person, who shall be nameless, would bring in question the honor of a personage of most exalted station; and this fact gives the holder of the document an ascendancy over the illustrious personage whose honor and peace are so jeopardized."

"But this ascendancy," I interposed, "would depend upon the robber's knowledge of the loser's knowledge of the robber. Who would dare—"

"The thief," said G——, "is the Minister D——, who dares all things, those unbecoming as well as those becoming a man. The method of the theft was not less ingenious than bold. The document in question—a letter, to be frank—had been received by the personage robbed while alone in the royal *boudoir*. During its perusal she was suddenly interrupted by the entrance of the other exalted personage from whom especially it was her wish to conceal it.

After a hurried and vain endeavor to thrust it in a drawer, she was forced to place it, open as it was, upon a table. The address, however, was uppermost, and, the contents thus unexposed, the letter escaped notice. At this juncture enters the Minister D——. His lynx eye immediately perceives the paper, recognizes the hand-writing of the address, observes the confusion of the personage addressed, and fathoms her secret. After some business transactions, hurried through in his ordinary manner, he produces a letter some-what similar to the one in question, opens it, pretends to read it, and then places it in close juxtaposition to the other. Again he converses, for some fifteen minutes, upon the public affairs. At length, in taking leave, he takes also from the table the letter to which he had no claim. Its rightful owner saw, but, of course, dared not call attention to the act, in the presence of the third personage who stood at her elbow. The minister decamped; leaving his own letter—one of no importance—upon the table."

"Here, then," said Dupin to me, "you have precisely what you demand to make the ascendancy complete—the robber's knowledge of the loser's knowledge of the robber."

"Yes," replied the Prefect; "and the power thus attained has, for some months past, been wielded, for political purposes, to a very dangerous extent. The personage robbed is more thoroughly convinced, every day, of the necessity of reclaiming her letter. But this, of course, cannot be done openly. In fine, driven to despair, she has committed the matter to me."

"Than whom," said Dupin, amid a perfect whirlwind of smoke, "no more sagacious agent could, I suppose, be desired, or even imagined."

"You flatter me," replied the Prefect; "but it is possible that some such opinion may have been entertained."

"It is clear," said I, "as you observe, that the letter is still in pos-session of the minister; since it is this possession, and not any employment of the letter, which bestows the power. With the employment the power departs."

"True," said G——; "and upon this conviction I proceeded. My first care was to make thorough search of the minister's hotel; and here my chief embarrassment lay in the necessity of searching without his knowledge. Beyond all things, I have been warned of the danger which would result from giving him reason to suspect our design."

"But," said I, "you are quite *au fait* in these investigations. The Parisian police have done this thing often before."

"Oh yes; and for this reason I did not despair. The habits of the minister gave me, too, a great advantage. He is frequently absent from home all night. His servants are by no means numerous. They sleep at a distance from their master's apartment, and, being chiefly Neapolitans, are readily made drunk. I have keys, as you know, with which I can open any chamber or cabinet in Paris. For three months a night has not passed, during the greater part of which I have not been engaged, personally, in ransacking the D—— hotel. My honor is interested, and, to mention a great secret, the reward is enormous. So I did not abandon the search until I had become fully satisfied that the thief is a more astute man than myself. I fancy that I have investigated every nook and corner of the premises in which it is possible that the paper can be concealed."

"But is it not possible," I suggested, "that although the letter may be in possession of the minister, as it unquestionably is, he may have concealed it elsewhere than upon his own premises?"

"This is barely possible," said Dupin. "The present peculiar condition of affairs at court, and especially of those intrigues in which D—— is known to be involved, would render the instant availability of the document—its susceptibility of being produced at a moment's notice—a point of nearly equal importance with its possession."

"Its susceptibility of being produced?" said I.

"That is to say, of being *destroyed*," said Dupin.

"True," I observed; "the paper is clearly then upon the premises. As for its being upon the person of the minister, we may consider that as out of the question."

"Entirely," said the Prefect. "He has been twice waylaid, as if by footpads, and his person rigorously searched under my own inspection."

"You might have spared yourself this trouble," said Dupin. "D——, I presume, is not altogether a fool, and, if not, must have anticipated these waylayings, as a matter of course."

"Not *altogether* a fool," said G——, "but then he's a poet, which I take to be only one remove from a fool."

"True," said Dupin, after a long and thoughtful whiff from his meerschaum, "although I have been guilty of certain doggerel myself."

"Suppose you detail," said I, "the particulars of your search."

"Why, the fact is, we took our time, and we searched *everywhere*. I have had long experience in these affairs. I took the entire building, room by room; devoting the nights of a whole week to each. We examined, first, the furniture of each apartment. We opened every possible drawer; and I presume you know that, to a properly trained police agent, such a thing as a *secret* drawer is impossible. Any man is a dolt who permits a 'secret' drawer to escape him in a search of this kind. The thing is *so* plain. There is a certain amount of bulk—of space—to be accounted for in every cabinet. Then we have accurate rules. The fiftieth part of a line could not escape us. After the cabinets we took the chairs. The cushions we probed with the fine long needles you have seen me employ. From the tables we removed the tops."

"Why so?"

"Sometimes the top of a table, or other similarly arranged piece of furniture, is removed by the person wishing to conceal an article; then the leg is excavated, the article deposited within the cavity, and the top replaced. The bottoms and tops of bedposts are employed in the same way."

"But could not the cavity be detected by sounding?" I asked.

"By no means, if, when the article is deposited, a sufficient wadding of cotton be placed around it. Besides, in our case, we were obliged to proceed without noise."

"But you could not have removed—you could not have taken to pieces *all* articles of furniture in which it would have been possible to make a deposit in the manner you mention. A letter may be compressed into a thin spiral roll, not differing much in shape or bulk from a large knitting-needle, and in this form it might be inserted into the rung of a chair, for example. You did not take to pieces all the chairs?"

"Certainly not; but we did better—we examined the rungs of every chair in the hotel, and, indeed, the jointings of every description of furniture, by the aid of a most powerful microscope. Had there been any traces of recent disturbance we should not have failed to detect it instantly. A single grain of gimlet-dust, for example, would have been as obvious as an apple. Any disorder in the gluing—any unusual gaping in the joints—would have sufficed to insure detection."

"I presume you looked to the mirrors, between the boards and the plates, and you probed the beds and the bedclothes, as well as the curtains and carpets."

"That of course; and when we had absolutely completed every particle of the furniture in this way, then we examined the house itself. We divided its entire surface into compartments, which we numbered, so that none might be missed; then we scrutinized each individual square inch throughout the premises, including the two houses immediately adjoining, with the microscope, as before."

"The two houses adjoining!" I exclaimed; "you must have had a great deal of trouble."

"We had; but the reward offered is prodigious."

"You include the *grounds* about the houses?"

"All the grounds are paved with brick. They gave us comparatively little trouble. We examined the moss between the bricks, and found it undisturbed."

"You looked among D——'s papers, of course, and into the books of the library?"

"Certainly; we opened every package and parcel; we not only opened every book, but we turned over every leaf in each volume, not contenting ourselves with a mere shake, according to the fashion of some of our police officers. We also measured the thickness of every book-*cover*, with the most accurate admeasurement, and applied to each the most jealous scrutiny of the microscope. Had any of the bindings been recently meddled with, it would have been utterly impossible that the fact should have escaped observation. Some five or six volumes, just from the hands of the binder, we carefully probed, longitudinally, with the needles."

"You explored the floors beneath the carpets?"

"Beyond doubt. We removed every carpet, and examined the boards with the microscope."

"And the paper on the walls?"

"Yes."

"You looked into the cellars?"

"We did."

"Then," I said, "you have been making a miscalculation, and the letter is *not* upon the premises, as you suppose."

"I fear you are right there," said the Prefect. "And now, Dupin, what would you advise me to do?"

"To make a thorough re-search of the premises."

"That is absolutely needless," replied G——. "I am not more sure that I breathe than I am that the letter is not at the hotel."

"I have no better advice to give you," said Dupin. "You have, of course, an accurate description of the letter?"

"Oh yes!"—And the Prefect, producing a memorandum book, proceeded to read aloud a minute account of the internal, and especially of the external appearance of the missing document. Soon after finishing the perusal of this description, he took his departure, more entirely depressed in spirits than I had ever known the good gentleman before.

In about a month afterwards he paid us another visit, and found us occupied very nearly as before. He took a pipe and a chair and entered into some ordinary conversation. At length I said:

"Well, but G——, what of the purloined letter? I presume you have at last made up your mind that there is no such thing as over-reaching the minister?"

"Confound him, say I—yes; I made the reëxamination, however, as Dupin suggested—but it was all labor lost, as I knew it would be."

"How much was the reward offered, did you say?" asked Dupin.

"Why, a very great deal—a *very* liberal reward—I don't like to say how much, precisely; but one thing I *will* say, that I wouldn't mind giving my individual check for fifty thousand francs to any one who could obtain me that letter. The fact is, it is becoming of more and more importance every day; and the reward has been lately doubled. If it were trebled, however, I could do no more than I have done."

"Why, yes," said Dupin, drawlingly, between the whiffs of his meerschaum, "I really—think, G——, you have not exerted your-self—to the utmost in this matter. You might—do a little more, I think, eh?"

"How?—in what way?"

"Why—puff, puff—you might—puff, puff,—employ counsel in the matter, eh?—puff, puff, puff. Do you remember the story they tell of Abernethy?"

"No; hang Abernethy!"

"To be sure! Hang him and welcome. But, once upon a time, a certain rich miser conceived the design of sponging upon this Abernethy for a medical opinion. Getting up, for this purpose, an ordinary conversation in a private company, he insinuated his case to the physician, as that of an imaginary individual.

" 'We will suppose,' said the miser, 'that his symptoms are such and such; now, doctor, what would *you* have directed him to take?'

" 'Take!' said Abernethy, 'why, take *advice*, to be sure.' "

"But," said the Prefect, a little discomposed, "I am *perfectly* willing to take advice, and to pay for it. I would *really* give fifty thousand francs to any one who would aid me in the matter."

"In that case," replied Dupin, opening a drawer, and producing a checkbook, "you may as well fill me up a check for the amount mentioned. When you have signed it, I will hand you the letter."

I was astounded. The Prefect appeared absolutely thunder-stricken. For some minutes he remained speechless and motion-less, looking incredulously at my friend with open mouth, and eyes that seemed starting from their sockets; then, apparently recover-ing himself in some measure, he seized a pen, and after several pauses and vacant stares, finally filled up and signed a check for fifty thousand francs, and handed it across the table to Dupin. The latter examined it carefully and deposited it in his pocketbook; then, unlocking an *escritoire*, took thence a letter and gave it to the Prefect. This functionary grasped it in a perfect agony of joy, opened it with a trembling hand, cast a rapid glance at its contents, and then, scrambling and struggling to the door, rushed at length unceremoniously from the room and from the house, without having uttered a syllable since Dupin had requested him to fill up the check.

When he had gone, my friend entered into some explanations.

"The Parisian police," he said, "are exceedingly able in their way. They are persevering, ingenious, cunning, and thoroughly versed in the knowledge which their duties seem chiefly to demand. Thus, when G—— detailed to us his mode of searching the premises at the Hotel D——, I felt entire confidence in his having made a satisfactory investigation—so far as his labors extended."

"So far as his labors extended?" said I.

"Yes," said Dupin. "The measures adopted were not only the best of their kind, but carried out to absolute perfection. Had the letter been deposited within the range of their search, these fellows would, beyond a question, have found it."

I merely laughed—but he seemed quite serious in all that he said.

"The measures, then," he continued, "were good in their kind, and well executed; their defect lay in their being inapplicable to the case, and to the man. A certain set of highly ingenious resources are, with the Prefect, a sort of Procrustean bed, to which he forcibly adapts his designs. But he perpetually errs by being too deep or too shallow for the matter in hand; and many a schoolboy is a better reasoner than he. I knew one about eight years of age whose success at guessing in the game of 'even and odd' attracted universal admiration. This game is simple, and is played with marbles. One player holds in his hand a number of these toys, and demands of another whether that number is even or odd. If the guess is right, the guesser wins one; if wrong, he loses one. The boy to whom I allude won all the marbles of the school. Of course he had some principle of guess ing; and this lay in mere observation and admeasurement of the astuteness of his opponents. For example, an arrant simpleton is his opponent, and, holding up his closed hand, asks, 'Are they even or odd?' Our schoolboy replies, 'odd,' and loses; but upon the second trial he wins, for he then says to himself, 'The simpleton had them even upon the first trial, and his amount of cunning is just sufficient to make him have them odd upon the second; I will therefore guess odd';—he guesses odd, and wins. Now, with a simpleton a degree above the first, he would have reasoned thus: 'This fellow finds that in the first instance I guessed odd, and, in the second, he will propose to himself upon the first impulse, a simple variation from even to odd, as did the first simpleton; but then a second thought will suggest that this is too simple a variation, and finally he will decide upon putting it even as before. I will therefore guess even';—he guesses even, and wins. Now this mode of reasoning in the schoolboy, whom his fellows termed 'lucky,'—what, in its last analysis, is it?"

"It is merely," I said, "an identification of the reasoner's intellect with that of his opponent."

"It is," said Dupin; "and, upon inquiring of the boy by what means he effected the *thorough* identification in which his success consisted, I received answer as follows: 'When I wish to find out how wise, or how stupid, or how good, or how wicked is any one, or what are his thoughts at the moment, I fashion the expression of my face, as accurately as possible, in accordance with the expression of his, and then wait to see what thoughts or sentiments arise in my mind or heart, as if to match or correspond with the expression.' This response of the schoolboy lies at the bottom of all the spurious profundity which has been attributed to Rochefoucauld, to La Bougive, to Machiavelli, and to Campanella."

"And the identification," I said, "of the reasoner's intellect with that of his opponent, depends, if I understand you aright, upon the accuracy with which the opponent's intellect is admeasured."

"For its practical value it depends upon this," replied Dupin; "and the Prefect and his cohort fail so frequently, first, by default of this identification, and, secondly, by ill-admeasurement, or

rather through non-admeasurement, of the intellect with which
they are engaged. They consider only their *own* ideas of ingenuity;
and, in searching for any thing hidden, advert only to the modes in
which *they* would have hidden it. They are right in this much—that
their own ingenuity is a faithful representative of that of *the mass*;
but when the cunning of the individual felon is diverse in character
from their own, the felon foils them, of course. This always happens
when it is above their own, and very usually when it is below. They
have no variation of principle in their investigations; at best, when
urged by some unusual emergency—by some extraordinary reward
—they extend or exaggerate their old modes of *practice*, without
touching their principles. What, for example, in this case of D——,
has been done to vary the principle of action? What is all this
boring, and probing, and sounding, and scrutinizing with the microscope, and dividing the surface of the building into registered square
inches—what is it all but an exaggeration *of the application* of the
one principle or set of principles of search, which are based upon
the one set of notions regarding human ingenuity, to which the
Prefect, in the long routine of his duty, has been accustomed? Do
you not see he has taken it for granted that *all* men proceed to conceal a letter,—not exactly in a gimlet-hole bored in a chair-leg—
but, at least, in *some* out-of-the-way hole or corner suggested by the
same tenor of thought which would urge a man to secrete a letter
in a gimlet-hole bored in a chair-leg? And do you not see, also, that
such *recherchés* nooks for concealment are adapted only for ordinary
occasions, and would be adopted only by ordinary intellects; for, in
all cases of concealment, a disposal of the article concealed—a disposal of it in this *recherché* manner,—is, in the very first instance,
presumable and presumed; and thus its discovery depends, not at
all upon the acumen, but altogether upon the mere care, patience,
and determination of the seekers; and where the case is of importance—or, what amounts to the same thing in the policial eyes,
when the reward is of magnitude,—the qualities in question have
never been known to fail. You will now understand what I mean in
suggesting that, had the purloined letter been hidden anywhere
within the limits of the Prefect's examination—in other words, had

the principle of its concealment been comprehended within the principles of the Prefect—its discovery would have been a matter altogether beyond question. This functionary, however, has been thoroughly mystified; and the remote source of his defeat lies in the supposition that the minister is a fool, because he has acquired renown as a poet. All fools are poets; this the Prefect *feels*; and he is merely guilty of a *non distributio medii* in thence inferring that all poets are fools."

"But is this really the poet?" I asked. "There are two brothers, I know; and both have attained reputation in letters. The minister I believe has written learnedly on the Differential Calculus. He is a mathematician, and no poet."

"You are mistaken; I know him well; he is both. As poet *and* mathematician, he would reason well; as mere mathematician, he could not have reasoned at all, and thus would have been at the mercy of the Prefect."

"You surprise me," I said, "by these opinions, which have been contradicted by the voice of the world. You do not mean to set at naught the well-digested idea of centuries. The mathematical reason has long been regarded as *the* reason *par excellence*."

" '*Il y a à parier*,' " replied Dupin, quoting from Chamfort, " '*que toute idée publique, toute convention reçue, est une sottise, car elle a convenu au plus grand nombre.*' * The mathematicians, I grant you, have done their best to promulgate the popular error to which you allude, and which is none the less an error for its promulgation as truth. With an art worthy a better cause, for example, they have insinuated the term 'analysis' into application to algebra. The French are the originators of this particular deception; but if a term is of any importance—if words derive any value from applicability—then 'analysis' conveys 'algebra' about as much as, in Latin, '*ambitus*' implies 'ambition,' '*religio*' 'religion,' or '*homines honesti*,' a set of *honorable* men."

"You have a quarrel on hand, I see," said I, "with some of the algebraists of Paris; but proceed."

* It is to be wagered that every popular idea, every accepted convention, is a fallacy, because it has been agreed to by the majority.

"I dispute the availability, and thus the value, of that reason which is cultivated in any special form other than the abstractly logical. I dispute, in particular, the reason educed by mathematical study. The mathematics are the science of form and quantity; mathematical reasoning is merely logic applied to observation upon form and quantity. The great error lies in supposing that even the truths of what is called *pure* algebra are abstract or general truths. And this error is so egregious that I am confounded at the universality with which it has been received. Mathematical axioms are *not* axioms of general truth. What is true of *relation*—of form and quantity—is often grossly false in regard to morals, for example. In this latter science it is very usually *un*true that the aggregated parts are equal to the whole. In chemistry also the axiom fails. In the consideration of motive it fails; for two motives, each of a given value, have not, necessarily, a value, when united, equal to the sum of their values apart. There are numerous other mathematical truths which are only truths within the limits of *relation*. But the mathematician argues, from his *finite truths*, through habit, as if they were of an absolutely general applicability—as the world indeed imagines them to be. Bryant, in his very learned 'Mythology,' mentions an analogous source of error, when he says that 'although the Pagan fables are not believed, yet we forget ourselves continually, and make inferences from them as existing realities.' With the algebraists, however, who are Pagans themselves, the 'Pagan fables' *are* believed, and the inferences are made, not so much through lapse of memory, as through an unaccountable addling of the brains. In short, I never yet encountered the mere mathematician who could be trusted out of equal roots, or one who did not clandestinely hold it as a point of his faith that $x^2 + px$ was absolutely and unconditionally equal to q. Say to one of these gentlemen, by way of experiment, if you please, that you believe occasions may occur where $x^2 + px$ is *not* altogether equal to q, and, having made him understand what you mean, get out of his reach as speedily as convenient, for, beyond doubt, he will endeavor to knock you down.

"I mean to say," continued Dupin, while I merely laughed at his last observations, "that if the minister had been no more than a mathematician, the Prefect would have been under no necessity of giving me this check. I knew him, however, as both mathematician and poet, and my measures were adapted to his capacity, with reference to the circumstances by which he was surrounded. I knew him as a courtier, too, and as a bold *intrigant*. Such a man, I considered, could not fail to be aware of the ordinary policial modes of action. He could not have failed to anticipate—and events have proved that he did not fail to anticipate—the waylayings to which he was subjected. He must have foreseen, I reflected, the secret investigations of his premises. His frequent absences from home at night, which were hailed by the Prefect as certain aids to his success, I regarded only as *ruses*, to afford opportunity for thorough search to the police, and thus the sooner to impress them with the conviction to which G——, in fact, did finally arrive—the conviction that the letter was not upon the premises. I felt, also, that the whole train of thought which I was at some pains in detailing to you just now, concerning the invariable principle of policial action in searches for articles concealed—I felt that this whole train of thought would necessarily pass through the mind of the minister. It would imperatively lead him to despise all the ordinary *nooks* of concealment. *He* could not, I reflected, be so weak as not to see that the most intricate and remote recess of his hotel would be as open as his commonest closets to the eyes, to the probes, to the gimlets, and to the microscopes of the Prefect. I saw, in fine, that he would be driven, as a matter of course, to *simplicity*, if not deliberately induced to it as a matter of choice. You will remember, perhaps, how desperately the Prefect laughed when I suggested, upon our first interview, that it was just possible this mystery troubled him so much on account of its being so *very* self-evident."

"Yes," said I, "I remember his merriment well. I really thought he would have fallen into convulsions."

"The material world," continued Dupin, "abounds with very strict analogies to the immaterial; and thus some color of truth has been given to the rhetorical dogma that metaphor, or simile, may be made to strengthen an argument, as well as to embellish a description. The principle of the *vis inertiæ*, for example, seems to be identical in physics and metaphysics. It is not more true in the former, that a large body is with more difficulty set in motion than a smaller one, and that its subsequent *momentum* is commensurate with this difficulty, than it is, in the latter, that intellects of the vaster capacity, while more forcible, more constant, and more eventful in their movements than those of inferior grade, are yet the less readily moved, and more embarrassed and full of hesitation in the first few steps of their progress. Again: have you ever noticed which of the street signs, over the shop doors, are the most attractive of attention?"

"I have never given the matter a thought," I said.

"There is a game of puzzles," he resumed, "which is played upon a map. One party playing requires another to find a given word—the name of town, river, state or empire—any word, in short, upon the motley and perplexed surface of the chart. A novice in the game generally seeks to embarrass his opponents by giving them the most minutely-lettered names; but the adept selects such words as stretch, in large characters, from one end of the chart to the other. These, like the over-largely lettered signs and placards of the street, escape observation by dint of being excessively obvious; and here the physical oversight is precisely analogous with the moral inapprehension by which the intellect suffers to pass unnoticed those considerations which are too obtrusively and too palpably self-evident. But this is a point, it appears, somewhat above or beneath the understanding of the Prefect. He never once thought it probable, or possible, that the minister had deposited the letter immediately beneath the nose of the whole world, by way of best preventing any portion of that world from perceiving it.

"But the more I reflected upon the daring, dashing, and discriminating ingenuity of D——; upon the fact that the document must always have been *at hand*, if he intended to use it to good purpose; and upon the decisive evidence, obtained by the Prefect, that it was not hidden within the limits of that dignitary's ordinary search—the more satisfied I became that, to conceal this letter, the minister had resorted to the comprehensive and sagacious expedient of not attempting to conceal it at all.

"Full of these ideas, I prepared myself with a pair of green spectacles, and called one fine morning, quite by accident, at the ministerial hotel. I found D—— at home, yawning, lounging, and dawdling, as usual, and pretending to be in the last extremity of *ennui*. He is, perhaps, the most really energetic human being now alive—but that is only when nobody sees him.

"To be even with him, I complained of my weak eyes, and lamented the necessity of the spectacles, under cover of which I cautiously and thoroughly surveyed the apartment, while seemingly intent only upon the conversation of my host.

"I paid special attention to a large writing-table near which he sat, and upon which lay confusedly some miscellaneous letters and other papers, with one or two musical instruments and a few books. Here, however, after a long and very deliberate scrutiny, I saw nothing to excite particular suspicion.

"At length my eyes, in going the circuit of the room, fell upon a trumpery filigree card-rack of pasteboard, that hung dangling by a dirty blue ribbon, from a little brass knob just beneath the middle of the mantelpiece. In this rack, which had three or four compart-ments, were five or six visiting cards and a solitary letter. This last was much soiled and crumpled. It was torn nearly in two, across the middle—as if a design, in the first instance, to tear it entirely up as worthless, had been altered, or stayed, in the second. It had a large black seal, bearing the D—— cipher *very* conspicuously, and was addressed, in a diminutive female hand, to D——, the minister, himself. It was thrust carelessly, and even, as it seemed, con-temptuously, into one of the upper divisions of the rack.

"No sooner had I glanced at this letter, than I concluded it to be that of which I was in search. To be sure, it was, to all appearance, radically different from the one of which the Prefect had read us so minute a description. Here the seal was large and black, with the D—— cipher; there it was small and red, with the ducal arms of the S—— family. Here, the address, to the minister, was diminutive and feminine; there the superscription, to a certain royal personage, was markedly bold and decided; the size alone formed a point of correspondence. But, then, the *radicalness* of these differences, which was excessive; the dirt; the soiled and torn condition of the paper, so inconsistent with the *true* methodical habits of D——, and so suggestive of a design to delude the beholder into an idea of the worthlessness of the document; these things, together with the hyperobtrusive situation of this document, full in the view of every visitor, and thus exactly in accordance with the conclusions to which I had previously arrived; these things, I say, were strongly corroborative of suspicion, in one who came with the intention to suspect.

"I protracted my visit as long as possible, and, while I maintained a most animated discussion with the minister, on a topic which I knew well had never failed to interest and excite him, I kept my attention really riveted upon the letter. In this examination, I committed to memory its external appearance and arrangement in the rack; and also fell, at length, upon a discovery which set at rest whatever trivial doubt I might have entertained. In scrutinizing the edges of the paper, I observed them to be more *chafed* than seemed necessary. They presented the *broken* appearance which is manifested when a stiff paper, having been once folded and pressed with a folder, is refolded in a reversed direction, in the same creases or edges which had formed the original fold. This discovery was sufficient. It was clear to me that the letter had been turned, as a glove, inside out, redirected, and resealed. I bade the minister good morning, and took my departure at once, leaving a gold snuffbox upon the table.

"The next morning I called for the snuffbox, when we resumed, quite eagerly, the conversation of the preceding day. While thus engaged, however, a loud report, as if of a pistol, was heard immediately beneath the windows of the hotel, and was succeeded by a series of fearful screams, and the shoutings of a mob. D—— rushed to a casement, threw it open, and looked out. In the meantime, I stepped to the card-rack, took the letter, put it in my pocket, and replaced it by a *fac-simile* (so far as regards externals), which I had carefully prepared at my lodgings; imitating the D—— cipher, very readily, by means of a seal formed of bread.

"The disturbance in the street had been occasioned by the frantic behavior of a man with a musket. He had fired it among a crowd of women and children. It proved, however, to have been without ball, and the fellow was suffered to go his way as a lunatic or a drunkard. When he had gone, D—— came from the window, whither I had followed him immediately upon securing the object in view. Soon afterwards I bade him farewell. The pretended lunatic was a man in my own pay."

"But what purpose had you," I asked, "in replacing the letter by a *fac-simile*? Would it not have been better, at the first visit, to have seized it openly, and departed?"

"D——," replied Dupin, "is a desperate man, and a man of nerve. His hotel, too, is not without attendants devoted to his interests. Had I made the wild attempt you suggest, I might never have left the ministerial presence alive. The good people of Paris might have heard of me no more. But I had an object apart from these considerations. You know my political prepossessions. In this matter, I act as a partisan of the lady concerned. For eighteen months the minister has had her in his power. She has now him in hers; since, being unaware that the letter is not in his possession, he will proceed with his exactions as if it was. Thus will he inevitably commit himself, at once, to his political destruction. His downfall, too, will not be more precipitate than awkward. It is all very well to talk about the *facilis descensus Averni*; but in all kinds of climbing, as Catalani said of singing, it is far more easy to get up than to come down. In the present instance I have no sympathy—at least no pity—for him who descends. He is that *monstrum horrendum*, an unprincipled man of genius. I confess, however, that I should like very well to know the precise character of his thoughts, when, being defied by her whom the Prefect terms 'a certain personage,' he is reduced to opening the letter which I left for him in the card-rack."

"How? Did you put anything particular in it?"

"Why—it did not seem altogether right to leave the interior blank—that would have been insulting. D——, at Vienna once, did me an evil turn, which I told him, quite good-humouredly, that I should remember. So, as I knew he would feel some curiosity in regard to the identity of the person who had outwitted him, I thought it a pity not to give him a clue. He is well acquainted with my MS., and I just copied into the middle of the blank sheet the words—

> '——Un dessein si funeste,
> S'il n'est digne d'Atrée, est digne de Thyeste.' *

They are to be found in Crébillon's 'Atrée.' "

* A scheme so fatal, if not worthy of Atreus, is worthy of Thyestes.

Smiley would bet on anything—but in
a stranger he met his match. . . .

The Celebrated Jumping Frog of Calaveras County

MARK TWAIN (1835–1910)

Every American knows something of the life of
America's great storyteller, born Samuel Lang-
horne Clemens in Florida, Missouri, and better
known throughout the world as Mark Twain.

The lad's boyhood, much like that of his own
Tom Sawyer and Huckleberry Finn, was spent in
Hannibal, Missouri, a town on the Mississippi
River. Sam, when his father died, was apprenticed
to his brother Orion, who ran a country newspaper,
and at the type case the boy learned not only a useful trade but the elements of journalistic writing.

After wandering about the Eastern states as a
journeyman printer, the young man mastered the
glamorous vocation of Mississippi steamboat pilot,
as he was to relate in Life on the Mississippi (1883).

During the Civil War, after an interlude of aim-
less soldiering, he joined his brother, who was secre-

tary to the governor of the Territory of Nevada, in a trip across the West to the rich silver mines of the Comstock Lode. Tiring of an unremunerative fling at prospecting, Sam became a reporter for the Virginia City Enterprise, and there first used the pseudonym Mark Twain.

A meeting with "Artemus Ward," noted humorist, aroused Mark's interest in writing for a wider audience, and in San Francisco, where he went to escape the echoes of a ridiculous duel, he met and compared notes with Bret Harte. In California he wrote his "Jumping Frog" story, which made him a national figure. After a roving assignment in the Hawaiian Islands, he went to New York and joined the steamship cruise to the Holy Land that resulted in his first important book, The Innocents Abroad (1869).

The last forty years of his life were marked by the writing of other great travel books, novels, stories, and humorous sketches, along with financial ups and downs, journeys about the world, and family joys and misfortunes. At the time of his death at Stormfield, Redding, Connecticut, he was America's most popular and beloved man of letters. His reputation as a humorist still overshadows the brooding pessimist who wrote "The Man That Corrupted Hadleyburg" and The Mysterious Stranger.

"The Jumping Frog" first appeared in the New York Saturday Press on November 18, 1865, and was immediately reprinted around the world. It was first collected in The Celebrated Jumping Frog of Calaveras County, and Other Sketches (1867), Mark Twain's first book.

IN COMPLIANCE WITH the request of a friend of mine, who wrote me from the East, I called on good-natured, garrulous old Simon Wheeler, and inquired after my friend's friend, *Leonidas W.* Smiley, as requested to do, and I hereunto append the result. I have a lurking suspicion that *Leonidas W.* Smiley is a myth; that my friend never knew such a personage; and that he only conjectured that, if I asked old Wheeler about him, it would remind him of his infamous *Jim* Smiley, and he would go to work and bore me nearly to death with some infernal reminiscence of him as long and tedious as it should be useless to me. If that was the design, it certainly succeeded.

I found Simon Wheeler dozing comfortably by the barroom stove of the old, dilapidated tavern in the ancient mining camp of Angel's, and I noticed that he was fat and baldheaded, and had an expression of winning gentleness and simplicity upon his tranquil countenance. He roused up and gave me good-day. I told him a friend of mine had commissioned me to make some inquiries about a cherished companion of his boyhood named *Leonidas W.* Smiley—*Rev. Leonidas W.* Smiley—a young minister of the Gospel, who he had heard was at one time a resident of Angel's Camp. I added that, if Mr. Wheeler could tell me anything about this Rev. Leonidas W. Smiley, I would feel under many obligations to him.

Simon Wheeler backed me into a corner and blockaded me there with his chair, and then sat me down and reeled off the monotonous narrative which follows this paragraph. He never smiled, he never frowned, he never changed his voice from the gentle-flowing key to which he tuned the initial sentence, he never betrayed the slightest suspicion of enthusiasm; but all through the interminable narrative there ran a vein of impressive earnestness and sincerity, which showed me plainly that, so far from his imagining that there was anything ridiculous or funny about his story, he regarded it as a really important matter, and admitted its two heroes as men of transcendent genius in *finesse*. To me, the spectacle of a man drifting serenely along through such a queer yarn without ever smiling was exquisitely absurd. As I said before, I asked him to tell me what he knew of Rev. Leonidas W. Smiley, and he replied as follows. I let him go on in his own way, and never interrupted him once.

There was a feller here once by the name of *Jim* Smiley, in the winter of '49—or maybe it was the spring of '50—I don't recollect exactly, somehow, though what makes me think it was one or the other is because I remember the big flume wasn't finished when he first came to the camp; but anyway, he was the curiousest man about always betting on anything that turned up you ever see, if he could get anybody to bet on the other side; and if he couldn't, he'd change sides. Any way what suited the other man would suit him—any way just so's he got a bet, *he* was satisfied. But still he was lucky, uncommon lucky—he most always come out winner. He was always ready and laying for a chance; there couldn't be no solit'ry thing mentioned but that feller'd offer to bet on it, and take any side you please, as I was just telling you. If there was a horse-race, you'd find him flush, or you'd find him busted at the end of it; if there was a dog-fight, he'd bet on it; if there was a cat-fight, he'd bet on it; if there was a chicken-fight, he'd bet on it; why, if there was two birds setting on a fence, he would bet you which one would fly first; or if there was a camp meeting, he would be there reg'lar, to bet on Parson Walker, which he judged to be the best exhorter about here, and so he was, too, and a good man. If he even seen a straddle-bug start to go anywheres, he would bet you how long it would take him to get wherever he was going to, and if you took him up, he would foller that straddle-bug to Mexico but what he would find out where he was bound for and how long he was on the road. Lots of the boys here has seen that Smiley, and can tell you about him. Why, it never made no difference to *him*—he would bet on *anything*—the dangdest feller. Parson Walker's wife laid very sick once, for a good while, and it seemed as if they warn't going to save her; but one morning he came in, and Smiley asked how she was, and he said she was considerable better—thank the Lord for his inf'nit mercy—and coming on so smart that, with the blessing of Prov'dence, she'd get well yet; and Smiley, before he thought, says, "Well, I'll risk two-and-a-half that she don't, anyway."

Thish-yer Smiley had a mare—the boys called her the fifteen-minute nag, but that was only in fun, you know, because, of course, she was faster than that—and he used to win money on that horse, for all she was so slow and always had the asthma, or the distemper, or the consumption, or something of that kind. They used to give her two or three hundred yards start, and then pass her under way; but always at the fag-end of the race she'd get excited and desperate-like, and come cavorting and straddling up, and scattering her legs around limber, sometimes in the air, and sometimes out to one side amongst the fences, and kicking up m-o-r-e dust, and raising m-o-r-e racket with her coughing and sneezing and blowing her nose—and always fetch up at the stand just about a neck ahead, as near as you could cipher it down.

And he had a little small bull pup, that to look at him you'd think he wan't worth a cent but to set around and look ornery and lay for a chance to steal something. But as soon as money was up on him, he was a different dog; his under-jaw'd begin to stick out like the fo'castle of a steamboat, and his teeth would uncover, and shine savage like the furnaces. And a dog might tackle him, and bullyrag him, and bite him, and throw him over his shoulder two or three times, and Andrew Jackson—which was the name of the pup—Andrew Jackson would never let on but what *he* was satisfied, and hadn't expected nothing else—and the bets being doubled and doubled on the other side all the time, till the money was all up; and then all of a sudden he would grab that other dog jest by the j'int of his hind leg and freeze to it—not claw, you understand, but only jest grip and hang on till they throwed up the sponge, if it was a year. Smiley always come out winner on that pup, till he harnessed a dog once that didn't have no hind legs, because they'd been sawed off by a circular saw, and when the thing had gone along far enough, and the money was all up, and he come to make a snatch for his pet holt, he saw in a minute how he'd been imposed on, and how the other dog had him in the door, so to speak, and he 'peared surprised, and then he looked sorter discouraged-like, and didn't try no more to win the fight, and so he got shucked out bad. He give Smiley a look, as much to say his heart was broke and it was *his* fault for putting up a dog that hadn't no hind legs for him to take holt of, which was his main dependence in a fight, and then he limped off a piece and laid down and died. It was a good pup, was that Andrew Jackson, and would have made a name for hisself if he'd lived, for the stuff was in him, and he had genius—I know it, because he hadn't no opportunities to speak of, and it don't stand to reason that a dog could make such a fight as he could under them circumstances, if he hadn't no talent. It always makes me feel sorry when I think of that last fight of his'n, and the way it turned out.

Well, thish-yer Smiley had rat-tarriers, and chicken-cocks, and tomcats, and all them kind of things, till you couldn't rest, and you couldn't fetch nothing for him to bet on but he'd match you. He ketched a frog one day, and took him home, and said he cal'klated to edercate him; and so he never done nothing for these three months but set in his back yard and learn that frog to jump. And you bet you he *did* learn him, too. He'd give him a little punch behind, and the next minute you'd see that frog whirling in the air like a doughnut—see him turn one summerset, or maybe a couple, if he got a good start, and come down flat-footed and all right, like a cat. He got him up so in the matter of catching flies, and kept him in practice so constant, that he'd nail a fly every time as far as he could see him. Smiley said all a frog wanted was education, and he could do most anything—and I believe him. Why, I've seen him set Dan'l Webster down here on this floor—Dan'l Webster was the name of the frog—and sing out, "Flies, Dan'l, flies!" and quicker'n you could wink, he'd spring straight up, and snake a fly off'n the counter there, and flop down on the floor again as solid as a gob of mud, and fall to scratching the side of his head with his hind foot as indifferent as if he hadn't no idea he'd been doin' any more'n any frog might do. You never see a frog so modest and straight-for'ard as he was, for all he was so gifted. And when it come to fair and square jumping on the dead level, he could get over more ground at one straddle than any animal of his breed you ever see. Jumping on a dead level was his strong suit, you understand; and when it come to that, Smiley would ante up money on him as long as he had a red. Smiley was monstrous proud of his frog, and well he might be, for fellers that had traveled and been everywhere all said he laid over any frog that ever *they* see.

Well, Smiley kept the beast in a little lattice box, and he used to fetch him downtown sometimes and lay for a bet. One day a feller—a stranger in the camp, he was—come across him with his box, and says:

"What might it be that you've got in the box?"

And Smiley says, sorter indifferent like, "It might be a parrot, or it might be a canary, maybe, but it ain't—it's only just a frog."

An' the feller took it, and looked at it careful, and turned it round this way and that, and says, "H'm—so 'tis. Well, what's *he* good for?"

"Well," Smiley says, easy and careless, "he's good enough for *one* thing, I should judge—he can outjump ary frog in Calaveras county."

The feller took the box again, and took another long, particular look, and give it back to Smiley, and says, very deliberate, "Well, I don't see no p'ints about that frog that's any better'n any other frog."

"Maybe you don't," Smiley says. "Maybe you understand frogs, and maybe you don't understand 'em; maybe you've had experience, and maybe you ain't only a amature, as it were. Anyways, I've got *my* opinion, and I'll risk forty dollars that he can outjump any frog in Calaveras county."

And the feller studied a minute, and then says, kinder sad like, "Well, I'm only a stranger here, and I ain't got no frog; but if I had a frog, I'd bet you."

And then Smiley says, "That's all right—that's all right—if you'll hold my box a minute, I'll go and get you a frog." And so the feller took the box, and put up his forty dollars along with Smiley's, and set down to wait.

So he set there a good while thinking and thinking to hisself, and then he got the frog out and pried his mouth open and took a teaspoon and filled him full of quail shot—filled him pretty near up to his chin—and set him on the floor. Smiley he went to the swamp and slopped around in the mud for a long time, and finally he ketched a frog, and fetched him in, and give him to this feller, and says:

"Now, if you're ready, set him alongside of Dan'l, with his fore-paws just even with Dan'l, and I'll give the word." Then he says, "One—two—three—jump!" and him and the feller touched up the frogs from behind, and the new frog hopped off, but Dan'l give a heave, and hysted up his shoulders—so—like a Frenchman, but it wasn't no use—he couldn't budge; he was planted as solid as an an-vil, and he couldn't no more stir than if he was anchored out. Smiley was a good deal surprised, and he was disgusted too, but he didn't have no idea what the matter was, of course.

The feller took the money and started away; and when he was going out at the door, he sorter jerked his thumb over his shoulder—this way—at Dan'l, and says again, very deliberate, "Well, I don't see no p'ints about that frog that's any better'n any other frog."

Smiley he stood scratching his head and looking down at Dan'l a long time, and at last he says, "I do wonder what in the nation that frog throw'd off for—I wonder if there ain't something the matter with him—he 'pears to look mighty baggy, somehow." And he ketched Dan'l by the nap of the neck, and lifted him up and says, "Why, blame my cats, if he don't weigh five pounds!" and turned him upside down, and he belched out a double handful of shot. And then he see how it was, and he was the maddest man—he set the frog down and took out after that feller, but he never ketched him. And—

Here Simon Wheeler heard his name called from the front yard, and got up to see what was wanted. And turning to me as he moved away, he said: "Just set where you are, stranger, and rest easy—I ain't going to be gone a second."

But, by your leave, I did not think that a continuation of the history of the enterprising vagabond *Jim* Smiley would be likely to afford me much information concerning the Rev. *Leonidas* W. Smiley, and so I started away.

At the door I met the sociable Wheeler returning, and he buttonholed me and recommenced:

"Well, thish-yer Smiley had a yeller one-eyed cow that didn't have no tail, only jest a short stump like a bannanner, and—"

"Oh, hang Smiley and his afflicted cow!" I muttered, good-naturedly, and bidding the old gentleman good-day, I departed.

The gambler knew a losing game
when he saw one. . . .

The Outcasts of Poker Flat

BRET HARTE (1836–1902)

Bret Harte's long literary career never lived up to
its early promise. He was born Francis Brett Harte
in Albany, New York, of English, Dutch, and
Jewish descent. His father was an impoverished
schoolteacher, and the family wandered from city
to city in the Eastern states.

The boy left school at thirteen to earn his living,
but he had early ransacked his father's collection
of English literature (his favorite authors were to
be Irving, Dickens, and Hawthorne), and at the
age of eleven had published a poem in a New York
newspaper.

His mother, widowed in 1845, went to California
in 1853 and remarried there. Young Frank followed
by way of Nicaragua, and thus entered the state
that was to be the background of his most famous
writings. He drifted about, working at odd jobs,
tutoring, serving as express messenger, and visiting
the mining camps, although, frail and delicate, he
probably never wielded a pick for a living. At Ar-

[91]

cata he learned to set type on the town newspaper and practiced the writing trade, but his condemnation in that paper of the brutal massacre of some sixty peaceful Indians caused him to leave Arcata for San Francisco in 1860.

During the next three years, more than a hundred of his poems and sketches appeared in the Golden Era. He was given a sinecure in the branch mint and became a literary leader in the city by the Golden Gate.

His great chance came when, as first editor of the Overland Monthly, he decided to make the magazine a reflection of the booming life of the Pacific slope. In the second number he printed "The Luck of Roaring Camp," the first story in his new local-color style. It was an immediate hit—especially in the East and in Europe, where the California gold mines were a romantic milieu—but it was attacked as "immoral," and Harte prudently held back for six months the publication of "The Outcasts of Poker Flat."

His world-wide reputation as a humorist came in 1870 with the appearance of the poem "Plain Language from Truthful James" ("The Heathen Chinee"). In the same year, his first important book was published in Boston. He made a triumphal progress to the East and was given a ten-thousand-dollar contract for twelve contributions to the Atlantic Monthly. He had always been a cosmopolite at heart, and his seventeen years in California had not made him a frontiersman. He was slender in build and foppish in dress, and in ill health for most of his life.

As the literary lion of America and Europe, he wrote steadily and slaved as a lecturer to support the expensive tastes of his wife and children. He left America in 1878 never to return, to serve as consul in Russia and then at Glasgow, Scotland. From 1885 until his death he lived in London, where his fame still lasted long after America had almost forgotten him. He turned out stories, sketches, and plays on the old formula, but the magic was gone; his best work had been done before he was thirty-five, in the invention of the dramatic wild-West story, by adapting the Dickens method to the colorful and fresh locale of the California gold camps.

"The Outcasts of Poker Flat" first appeared in the Overland Monthly in January, 1869, and was collected in The Luck of Roaring Camp and Other Stories, the first and best of Harte's long list of volumes of stories, novels, poems, plays, and parodies.

As MR. JOHN OAKHURST, gambler, stepped into the main street of Poker Flat on the morning of the twenty-third of November, 1850, he was conscious of a change in its moral atmosphere since the preceding night. Two or three men, conversing earnestly together, ceased as he approached, and exchanged significant glances. There was a Sabbath lull in the air, which, in a settlement unused to Sabbath influences, looked ominous.

Mr. Oakhurst's calm, handsome face betrayed small concern of these indications. Whether he was conscious of any predisposing cause was another question. "I reckon they're after somebody," he reflected; "likely it's me." He returned to his pocket the handker-

chief with which he had been whipping away the red dust of Poker
Flat from his neat boots, and quietly discharged his mind of any
further conjecture.

In point of fact, Poker Flat was "after somebody." It had lately
suffered the loss of several thousand dollars, two valuable horses,
and a prominent citizen. It was experiencing a spasm of virtuous
reaction, quite as lawless and ungovernable as any of the acts that
had provoked it. A secret committee had determined to rid the
town of all improper persons. This was done permanently in regard
to two men who were then hanging from the boughs of a sycamore
in the gulch, and temporarily in the banishment of certain other
objectionable characters. I regret to say that some of these were
ladies. It is but due to the sex, however, to state that their impro-
priety was professional, and it was only in such easily established
standards of evil that Poker Flat ventured to sit in judgment.

Mr. Oakhurst was right in supposing that he was included in
this category. A few of the committee had urged hanging him as
a possible example, and a sure method of reimbursing themselves
from his pockets of the sums he had won from them. "It's agin
justice," said Jim Wheeler, "to let this yer young man from Roaring Camp—an entire stranger—carry away our money." But a
crude sentiment of equality residing in the breasts of those who
had been fortunate enough to win from Mr. Oakhurst overruled
this narrower local prejudice.

Mr. Oakhurst received his sentence with philosophic calmness,
none the less coolly that he was aware of the hesitation of his judges.
He was too much of a gambler not to accept Fate. With him life
was at best an uncertain game, and he recognized the usual percentage in favor of the dealer.

A body of armed men accompanied the deported wickedness of
Poker Flat to the outskirts of the settlement. Besides Mr. Oakhurst,
who was known to be a coolly desperate man, and for whose intimi-
dation the armed escort was intended, the expatriated party consisted of a young woman familiarly known as "The Duchess"; another, who had gained the infelicitous title of "Mother Shipton";
and "Uncle Billy," a suspected sluice-robber and confirmed drunk-

ard. The cavalcade provoked no comments from the spectators, nor was any word uttered by the escort. Only, when the gulch which marked the uttermost limit of Poker Flat was reached, the leader spoke briefly and to the point. The exiles were forbidden to return at the peril of their lives.

As the escort disappeared, their pent-up feelings found vent in a few hysterical tears from the Duchess, some bad language from Mother Shipton, and a Parthian volley of expletives from Uncle Billy. The philosophic Oakhurst alone remained still. He listened calmly to Mother Shipton's desire to cut somebody's heart out, to the repeated statements of the Duchess that she would die on the road, and to the alarming oaths that seemed to be bumped out of Uncle Billy as he rode forward. With the easy good humor characteristic of his class, he insisted upon exchanging his own riding-horse, Five Spot, for the sorry mule which the Duchess rode. But even this act did not draw the party into any closer sympathy. The young woman readjusted her somewhat draggled plumes with a feeble, faded coquetry; Mother Shipton eyed the possessor of Five Spot with malevolence, and Uncle Billy included the whole party in one sweeping anathema.

The road to Sandy Bar—a camp that, not having as yet experienced the regenerating influences of Poker Flat, consequently seemed to offer some invitation to the emigrants—lay over a steep mountain range. It was distant a day's severe journey. In that advanced season, the party soon passed out of the moist, temperate regions of the foothills into the dry, cold bracing air of the Sierras. The trail was narrow and difficult. At noon the Duchess, rolling out of her saddle upon the ground, declared her intention of going no farther, and the party halted.

The spot was singularly wild and impressive. A wooded amphitheater, surrounded on three sides by precipitous cliffs of naked granite, sloped gently toward the crest of another precipice that overlooked the valley. It was undoubtedly the most suitable spot for a camp, had camping been advisable. But Mr. Oakhurst knew that scarcely half the journey to Sandy Bar was accomplished, and the party were not equipped or provisioned for delay. This fact he pointed out to his companions curtly, with a philosophic commentary on the folly of "throwing up their hands before the game was played out." But they were furnished with liquor, which in this emergency stood them in place of food, fuel, rest, and prescience. In spite of his remonstrances, it was not long before they were more or less under its influence. Uncle Billy passed rapidly from a bellicose state into one of stupor, the Duchess became maudlin, and Mother Shipton snored. Mr. Oakhurst alone remained erect, leaning against a rock, calmly surveying them.

Mr. Oakhurst did not drink. It interfered with a profession which required coolness, impassiveness, and presence of mind, and, in his own language, he "couldn't afford it." As he gazed at his recumbent fellow-exiles, the loneliness begotten of his pariah-trade, his habits of life, his very vices, for the first time seriously oppressed him. He bestirred himself in dusting his black clothes, washing his hands and face, and other acts characteristic of his studiously neat habits, and for a moment forgot his annoyance. The thought of deserting his weaker and more pitiable companions never perhaps occurred to him. Yet he could not help feeling the want of that excitement which, singularly enough, was most conducive to that calm equanimity for which he was notorious. He looked at the gloomy walls that rose a thousand feet sheer above the circling pines around him; at the sky, ominously clouded; at the valley below, already deepening into shadow. And, doing so, suddenly he heard his own name called.

A horseman slowly ascended the trail. In the fresh, open face of the newcomer Mr. Oakhurst recognized Tom Simson, otherwise known as "The Innocent" of Sandy Bar. He had met him some months before over a "little game," and had, with perfect equanimity, won the entire fortune—amounting to some forty dollars—of that guileless youth. After the game was finished, Mr. Oakhurst drew the youthful speculator behind the door and thus addressed him: "Tommy, you're a good little man, but you can't gamble worth a cent. Don't try it over again." He then handed him his money back, pushed him gently from the room, and so made a devoted slave of Tom Simson.

There was a remembrance of this in his boyish and enthusiastic greeting of Mr. Oakhurst. He had started, he said, to go to Poker Flat to seek his fortune. "Alone?" No, not exactly alone; in fact— a giggle—he had run away with Piney Woods. Didn't Mr. Oakhurst remember Piney? She that used to wait on the table at the Temperance House? They had been engaged a long time, but old Jake Woods had objected, and so they had run away, and were going to Poker Flat to be married, and here they were. And they were tired out, and how lucky it was they had found a place to camp and company. All this the Innocent delivered rapidly, while Piney—a stout, comely damsel of fifteen—emerged from behind the pine tree, where she had been blushing unseen, and rode to the side of her lover.

Mr. Oakhurst seldom troubled himself with sentiment, still less with propriety; but he had a vague idea that the situation was not felicitous. He retained, however, his presence of mind sufficiently to kick Uncle Billy, who was about to say something, and Uncle Billy was sober enough to recognize in Mr. Oakhurst's kick a superior power that would not bear trifling. He then endeavored to dissuade Tom Simson from delaying further, but in vain. He even pointed out the fact that there was no provision, nor means of making a camp. But, unluckily, the Innocent met this objection by assuring the party that he was provided with an extra mule loaded with provisions, and by the discovery of a rude attempt at a log-house near the trail. "Piney can stay with Mrs. Oakhurst," said the Innocent, pointing to the Duchess, "and I can shift for myself."

Nothing but Mr. Oakhurst's admonishing foot saved Uncle Billy from bursting into a roar of laughter. As it was, he felt compelled to retire up the canyon until he could recover his gravity. There he confided the joke to the tall pine trees, with many slaps of his leg, contortions of his face, and the usual profanity. But when he returned to the party, he found them seated by a fire—for the air had grown strangely chill and the sky overcast—in apparently amicable conversation. Piney was actually talking in an impulsive, girlish fashion to the Duchess, who was listening with an interest and animation she had not shown for many days. The Innocent was holding forth, apparently with equal effect, to Mr. Oakhurst and Mother Shipton, who was actually relaxing into amiability. "Is this yer a d—d picnic?" said Uncle Billy, with inward scorn, as he surveyed the sylvan group, the glancing firelight, and the tethered animals in the foreground. Suddenly an idea mingled with the alcoholic fumes that disturbed his brain. It was apparently of a jocular nature, for he felt impelled to slap his leg again and cram his fist into his mouth.

As the shadows crept slowly up the mountain, a slight breeze rocked the tops of the pine trees, and moaned through their long and gloomy aisles. The ruined cabin, patched and covered with pine boughs, was set apart for the ladies. As the lovers parted, they unaffectedly exchanged a kiss, so honest and sincere that it might have been heard above the swaying pines. The frail Duchess and the malevolent Mother Shipton were probably too stunned to remark upon this last evidence of simplicity, and so turned without a word to the hut. The fire was replenished, the men lay down before the door, and in a few minutes were asleep.

Mr. Oakhurst was a light sleeper. Toward morning he awoke benumbed and cold. As he stirred the dying fire, the wind, which was now blowing strongly, brought to his cheek that which caused the blood to leave it—snow!

He started to his feet with the intention of awakening the sleepers, for there was no time to lose. But turning to where Uncle Billy had been lying, he found him gone. A suspicion leaped to his brain and a curse to his lips. He ran to the spot where the mules had been tethered; they were no longer there. The tracks were already rapidly disappearing in the snow.

The momentary excitement brought Mr. Oakhurst back to the fire with his usual calm. He did not waken the sleepers. The Innocent slumbered peacefully, with a smile on his good-humored, freckled face; the virgin Piney slept beside her frailer sisters as sweetly as though attended by celestial guardians, and Mr. Oakhurst, drawing his blanket over his shoulders, stroked his mustachios and waited for the dawn. It came slowly in the whirling mist of

snowflakes, that dazzled and confused the eye. What could be
seen of the landscape appeared magically changed. He looked over
the valley, and summed up the present and future in two words—
"Snowed in!"

A careful inventory of the provisions, which, fortunately for the
party, had been stored within the hut, and so escaped the felonious
fingers of Uncle Billy, disclosed the fact that with care and prudence
they might last ten days longer. "That is," said Mr. Oakhurst, *sotto
voce* to the Innocent, "if you're willing to board us. If you ain't—
and perhaps you'd better not—you can wait till Uncle Billy gets
back with provisions." For some occult reason, Mr. Oakhurst could
not bring himself to disclose Uncle Billy's rascality, and so offered
the hypothesis that he had wandered from the camp and had accidentally stampeded the animals. He dropped a warning to the
Duchess and Mother Shipton, who of course knew the facts of their
associate's defection. "They'll find out the truth about us *all*,
when they find out anything," he added, significantly, "and there's
no good frightening them now."

Tom Simson not only put all his worldly store at the disposal of
Mr. Oakhurst, but seemed to enjoy the prospect of their enforced
seclusion. "We'll have a good camp for a week, and then the snow'll
melt, and we'll all go back together." The cheerful gayety of the
young man and Mr. Oakhurst's calm infected the others. The
Innocent, with the aid of pine boughs, extemporized a thatch for
the roofless cabin, and the Duchess directed Piney in the rearrange-
ment of the interior with a taste and tact that opened the blue eyes
of that provincial maiden to their fullest extent.

"I reckon now you're used to fine things at Poker Flat," said
Piney. The Duchess turned away sharply to conceal something that
reddened her cheek through its professional tint, and Mother Shipton requested Piney not to "chatter." But when Mr. Oakhurst returned from a weary search for the trail, he heard the sound of
happy laughter echoed from the rocks. He stopped in some alarm,
and his thoughts first naturally reverted to the whisky, which he
had prudently *cached*. "And yet it don't somehow sound like

whisky," said the gambler. It was not until he caught sight of the blazing fire through the still blinding storm, and the group around it, that he settled to the conviction that it was "square fun."

Whether Mr. Oakhurst had *cached* his cards with the whisky as something debarred the free access of the community, I cannot say. It was certain that, in Mother Shipton's words, he "didn't say cards once" during the evening. Haply the time was beguiled by an accordion produced somewhat ostentatiously by Tom Simson, from his pack. Notwithstanding some difficulties attending the manipulation of this instrument, Piney Woods managed to pluck several reluctant melodies from its keys, to an accompaniment by the Innocent on a pair of bone castinets. But the crowning festivity of the evening was reached in a rude camp-meeting hymn, which the lovers, joining hands, sang with great earnestness and vociferation. I fear that a certain defiant tone and Covenanter's swing to its chorus, rather than any devotional quality, caused it speedily to infect the others, who at last joined in the refrain:

> I'm proud to live in the service of the Lord,
> And I'm bound to die in His army.

The pines rocked, the storm eddied and whirled above the miserable group, and the flames of their altar leaped heavenward, as if in token of the vow.

At midnight the storm abated, the rolling clouds parted, and the stars glittered keenly above the sleeping camp. Mr. Oakhurst, whose professional habits had enabled him to live on the smallest possible amount of sleep, in dividing the watch with Tom Simson, somehow managed to take upon himself the greater part of that duty. He excused himself to the Innocent, by saying that he had "often been a week without sleep." "Doing what?" asked Tom. "Poker!" replied Oakhurst, sententiously. "When a man gets a streak of luck —real luck—he don't get tired. The luck gives in first. Luck," continued the gambler, reflectively, "is a mighty queer thing. All you know about it for certain is that it's bound to change. And it's finding out when it's going to change that makes you. We've had a streak of bad luck since we left Poker Flat—you come along, and slap you get into it, too. If you can hold your cards right along you're all right. For," added the gambler, with cheerful irrelevance,

> "I'm proud to live in the service of the Lord,
> And I'm bound to die in His army."

The third day came, and the sun, looking through the white-curtained valley, saw the outcasts divide their slowly decreasing store of provisions for the morning meal. It was one of the peculiarities of that mountain climate that its rays diffused a kindly warmth over the wintry landscape, as if in regretful commiseration of the past. But it revealed drift on drift of snow piled high around the hut; a hopeless, uncharted, trackless sea of white lying below the rocky shores to which the castaways still clung. Through the marvelously clear air, the smoke of the pastoral village of Poker Flat rose miles away. Mother Shipton saw it, and from a remote pinnacle of her rocky fastness, hurled in that direction a final malediction. It was her last vituperative attempt, and perhaps for that reason was invested with a certain degree of sublimity. It did her good, she privately informed the Duchess, "Just to go out there and cuss, and see." She then set herself to the task of amusing "the child," as she and the Duchess were pleased to call Piney. Piney was no chicken, but it was a soothing and ingenious theory of the pair thus to account for the fact that she didn't swear and wasn't improper.

When night crept up again through the gorges, the reedy notes of the accordion rose and fell in fitful spasms and long-drawn gasps by the flickering campfire. But music failed to fill entirely the aching void left by insufficient food, and a new diversion was proposed by Piney—storytelling. Neither Mr. Oakhurst nor his female companions caring to relate their personal experiences, this plan would have failed, too, but for the Innocent. Some months before he had chanced upon a stray copy of Mr. Pope's ingenious translation of the Iliad. He now proposed to narrate the principal incidents of that poem—having thoroughly mastered the argument and fairly forgotten the words—in the current vernacular of Sandy Bar. And so for the rest of that night the Homeric demigods again walked the earth. Trojan bully and wily Greek wrestled in the winds, and the great pines in the canyon seemed to bow to the wrath of the son of Peleus. Mr. Oakhurst listened with quiet satisfaction. Most especially was he interested in the fate of "Ash-heels," as the Innocent persisted in denominating the "swift-footed Achilles."

So with small food and much of Homer and the accordion, a week passed over the heads of the outcasts. The sun again forsook them, and again from leaden skies the snowflakes were sifted over the land. Day by day closer around them drew the snowy circle, until at last they looked from their prison over drifted walls of dazzling white, that towered twenty feet above their heads. It became more and more difficult to replenish their fires, even from the fallen trees beside them, now half-hidden in the drifts. And yet no one complained. The lovers turned from the dreary prospect and looked into each other's eyes, and were happy. Mr. Oakhurst settled himself coolly to the losing game before him. The Duchess, more cheerful than she had been, assumed the care of Piney. Only Mother Shipton—once the strongest of the party—seemed to sicken and fade. At midnight on the tenth day she called Oakhurst to her side. "I'm going," she said, in a voice of querulous weakness, "but don't say anything about it. Don't waken the kids. Take the bundle from under my head and open it." Mr. Oakhurst did so. It contained Mother Shipton's rations for the last week, untouched. "Give 'em to the child," she said, pointing to the sleeping Piney. "You've starved yourself," said the gambler. "That's what they call it," said the woman, querulously, as she lay down again, and, turning her face to the wall, passed quietly away.

The accordion and the bones were put aside that day, and Homer was forgotten. When the body of Mother Shipton had been committed to the snow, Mr. Oakhurst took the Innocent aside, and showed him a pair of snowshoes, which he had fashioned from the old packsaddle. "There's one chance in a hundred to save her yet," he said, pointing to Piney; "but it's there," he added, pointing toward Poker Flat. "If you can reach there in two days she's safe." "And you?" asked Tom Simson. "I'll stay here," was the curt reply.

The lovers parted with a long embrace. "You are not going, too?" said the Duchess, as she saw Mr. Oakhurst apparently waiting to accompany him. "As far as the canyon," he replied. He turned suddenly, and kissed the Duchess, leaving her pallid face aflame, and her trembling limbs rigid with amazement.

Night came, but not Mr. Oakhurst. It brought the storm again and the whirling snow. Then the Duchess, feeding the fire, found that some one had quietly piled beside the hut enough fuel to last a few days longer. The tears rose to her eyes, but she hid them from Piney.

The women slept but little. In the morning, looking into each other's faces, they read their fate. Neither spoke; but Piney, accepting the position of the stronger, drew near and placed her arm around the Duchess's waist. They kept this attitude for the rest of the day. That night the storm reached its greatest fury, and, rending asunder the protecting pines, invaded the very hut.

Toward morning they found themselves unable to feed the fire, which gradually died away. As the embers slowly blackened, the Duchess crept closer to Piney, and broke the silence of many hours: "Piney, can you pray?" "No, dear," said Piney, simply. The Duchess, without knowing exactly why, felt relieved, and putting her head upon Piney's shoulder, spoke no more. And so reclining, the younger and purer pillowing the head of her soiled sister upon her virgin breast, they fell asleep.

The wind lulled as if it feared to waken them. Feathery drifts of snow, shaken from the long pine boughs, flew like white-winged birds, and settled about them as they slept. The moon through the rifted clouds looked down upon what had been the camp. But all human stain, all trace of earthly travail, was hidden beneath the spotless mantle mercifully flung from above.

They slept all that day and the next, nor did they waken when voices and footsteps broke the silence of the camp. And when pitying fingers brushed the snow from their wan faces, you could scarcely have told, from the equal peace that dwelt upon them, which was she that had sinned. Even the Law of Poker Flat recognized this, and turned away, leaving them still locked in each other's arms.

But at the head of the gulch, on one of the largest pine trees, they found the deuce of clubs pinned to the bark with a bowie knife. It bore the following, written in pencil, in a firm hand:

†

BENEATH THIS TREE
LIES THE BODY
OF
JOHN OAKHURST,
WHO STRUCK A STREAK OF BAD LUCK
ON THE 23D OF NOVEMBER, 1850,
AND
HANDED IN HIS CHECKS
ON THE 7TH OF DECEMBER, 1850.

†

And pulseless and cold, with a derringer by his side and a bullet in his heart, though still calm as in life, beneath the snow lay he who was at once the strongest and yet the weakest of the outcasts of Poker Flat.

"Bred en bawn in a brier-patch,
Brer Fox!" . . .

The Wonderful Tar-Baby Story

JOEL CHANDLER HARRIS (1848-1908)

The great Southern humorist, editor, and taleteller
was born near Eatonton, Georgia, and spent only
about a year of his life away from his native state.

His father, an Irish laborer, deserted his wife
shortly before Joel was born. To help support his
mother, the boy became a typesetter on The
Countryman, a popular newspaper printed on the
plantation of Turnwold. Here the lore of the South
entered his brain along with the African animal
tales of the slave quarters.

After the surrender of Lee in 1865, the young
journalist worked for a while in Macon and in New
Orleans, but in 1867 he returned to Eatonton and
began a long career as paragraph writer, columnist,
and editor.

The first Uncle Remus sketches appeared in his
column of the Atlanta Constitution and were at
once widely enjoyed and translated into many
languages. In 1907, Harris established Uncle Remus's Magazine with his son Julian.

The energy, good nature, and deep humor of Joel Chandler Harris made him widely loved beyond the bounds of sectionalism. He was intensely shy and retiring, and a slight speech defect kept him from joining a lecture tour with George Washington Cable and Mark Twain. Only after much persuasion did he spend a night at the White House as the guest of his admirer, President Theodore Roosevelt.

Harris published eight volumes of Uncle Remus tales, seven volumes of Georgia sketches, several books for children, and two novels. "The Wonderful Tar-Baby Story," which was the most beloved of his Negro dialect pieces, comprises three sections from Harris's first book, Uncle Remus: His Songs and His Sayings (1881). This story is found, in variant versions, in folklore from many different parts of the world; it probably originated not in Africa but in India.

ONE EVENING RECENTLY, the lady whom Uncle Remus calls "Miss Sally" missed her little seven-year-old boy. Making search for him through the house and through the yard, she heard the sound of voices in the old man's cabin, and, looking through the window, saw the child sitting by Uncle Remus. His head rested against the old man's arm, and he was gazing with an expression of the most intense interest into the rough, weather-beaten face that beamed so kindly upon him. This is what "Miss Sally" heard:

"Bimeby, one day, arter Brer Fox bin doin' all dat he could fer

ter ketch Brer Rabbit, en Brer Rabbit bin doin' all he could fer
to keep 'im fum it, Brer Fox say to hisse'f dat he'd put up a game
on Brer Rabbit, en he ain't mo'n got de wuds out'n his mouf twel
Brer Rabbit come a lopin' up de big road, lookin' des ez plump,
en ez fat, en ez sassy ez a Moggin hoss in a barley-patch.

" 'Hol' on dar, Brer Rabbit,' sez Brer Fox, sezee.

" 'I ain't got time, Brer Fox,' sez Brer Rabbit, sezee, sorter
mendin' his licks.

" 'I wanter have some confab wid you, Brer Rabbit,' sez Brer Fox,
sezee.

" 'All right, Brer Fox, but you better holler fum whar you stan'.
I'm monstus full er fleas dis mawnin',' sez Brer Rabbit, sezee.

" 'I seed Brer B'ar yistiddy,' sez Brer Fox, sezee, 'en he sorter
rake me over de coals kaze you en me ain't make frens en live
naberly, en I told 'im dat I'd see you.'

"Den Brer Rabbit scratch one year wid his off hinefoot sorter
jub'usly, en den he ups en sez, sezee:

" 'All a settin', Brer Fox. Spose'n you drap roun' ter-morrer en
take dinner wid me. We ain't got no great doin's at our house, but
I speck de old 'oman en de chilluns kin sorter scramble roun' en git
up sump'n fer ter stay yo' stummuck.'

" 'I'm 'gree'ble, Brer Rabbit,' sez Brer Fox, sezee.

" 'Den I'll 'pen' on you,' sez Brer Rabbit, sezee.

"Nex' day, Mr. Rabbit an' Miss Rabbit got up soon, 'fo' day,
en raided on a gyarden like Miss Sally's out dar, en got some
cabbiges, en some roas'n years, en some sparrer-grass, en dey fix up
a smashin' dinner. Bimeby one er de little Rabbits, playin' out
in de backyard, come runnin' in hollerin', 'Oh, ma! oh, ma! I seed
Mr. Fox a comin'!' En den Brer Rabbit he tuck de chilluns by der
years en make um set down, en den him and Miss Rabbit sorter
dally roun' waitin' for Brer Fox. En dey keep on waitin', but no
Brer Fox ain't come. Atter 'while Brer Rabbit goes to de do', easy
like, en peep out, en dar, stickin' fum behime de cornder, wuz de
tip-een' er Brer Fox tail. Den Brer Rabbit shot de do' en sot down,
en put his paws behime his years en begin fer ter sing:

" 'De place wharbouts you spill de grease,
    Right dar youer boun' ter slide,
    An' whar you fine a bunch er ha'r,
    You'll sholy find de hide.'

"Nex' day, Brer Fox sont word by Mr. Mink, en skuze hisse'f kaze he wuz too sick fer ter come, en he ax Brer Rabbit fer to come en take dinner wid him, en Brer Rabbit say he wuz 'gree'ble.

"Bimeby, w'en de shadders wuz at der shortes', Brer Rabbit he sorter brush up en santer down ter Brer Fox's house, en w'en he got dar, he hear somebody groanin', en he look in de do' en dar he see Brer Fox settin' up in a rockin' cheer all wrop up wid flannil, en he look mighty weak. Brer Rabbit look all 'roun', he did, but he ain't see no dinner. De dishpan wuz settin' on de table, en close by wuz a kyarvin' knife.

" 'Look like you gwineter have chicken fer dinner, Brer Fox,' sez Brer Rabbit, sezee.

" 'Yes, Brer Rabbit, deyer nice, en fresh, en tender,' sez Brer Fox, sezee.

"Den Brer Rabbit sorter pull his mustarsh, en say: 'You ain't got no calamus root, is you, Brer Fox? I done got so now dat I can't eat no chicken 'ceppin she's seasoned up wid calamus root.' En wid dat Brer Rabbit lipt out er de do' and dodge 'mong de bushes, en sot dar watchin' fer Brer Fox; en he ain't watch long, nudder, kaze Brer Fox flung off de flannil en crope out er de house en got whar he could cloze in on Brer Rabbit, en bimeby Brer Rabbit holler out: 'Oh, Brer Fox! I'll des put yo' calamus root out yer on dish yer stump. Better come git it while hit's fresh,' and wid dat Brer Rabbit gallop off home. En Brer Fox ain't never kotch 'im yet, en w'at's mo', honey, he ain't gwineter."

"Didn't the fox *never* catch the rabbit, Uncle Remus?" asked the little boy next evening.

"He come mighty nigh it, honey, sho's you born—Brer Fox did. One day atter Brer Rabbit fool 'im wid dat calamus root, Brer Fox went ter wuk en got 'im some tar, en mix it wid some turkentime, en fix up a contrapshun w'at he call a Tar-Baby, en he tuck dish yer Tar-Baby en he sot 'er in de big road, en den he lay off in de bushes fer to see w'at de news wuz gwineter be. En he didn't hatter wait long, nudder, kaze bimeby here come Brer Rabbit pacin' down de road—lippity-clippity, clippity-lippity—dez ez sassy ez a jay-bird. Brer Fox, he lay low. Brer Rabbit come prancin' 'long twel he spy de Tar-Baby, en den he fotch up on his behime legs like he wuz 'stonished. De Tar-Baby, she sot dar, she did, en Brer Fox, he lay low.

" 'Mawnin'!' sez Brer Rabbit, sezee—'nice wedder dis mawnin',' sezee.

"Tar-Baby ain't sayin' nothin', en Brer Fox, he lay low.

" 'How duz yo' sym'tums seem ter segashuate?' sez Brer Rabbit, sezee.

"Brer Fox, he wink his eye slow, en lay low, en de Tar-Baby, she ain't sayin' nothin'.

" 'How you come on, den? Is you deaf?' sez Brer Rabbit, sezee. 'Kaze if you is, I kin holler louder,' sezee.

"Tar-Baby lay still, en Brer Fox, he lay low.

" 'Youer stuck up, dat's w'at you is,' sez Brer Rabbit, sezee, 'en I'm gwineter kyore you, dat's w'at I'm a gwineter do,' sezee.

"Brer Fox, he sorter chuckle in his stummuck, he did, but Tar-Baby ain't sayin' nothin'.

" 'I'm gwineter larn you howter talk ter 'specttubble fokes ef hit's de las' ack,' sez Brer Rabbit, sezee. 'Ef you don't take off dat hat en tell me howdy, I'm gwineter bus' you wide open,' sezee.

"Tar-Baby stay still, en Brer Fox, he lay low.

"Brer Rabbit keep on axin' 'im, en de Tar-Baby, she keep on sayin' nothin', twel present'y Brer Rabbit draw back wid his fis', he did, en blip he tuck 'er side er de head. Right dar's whar he broke his merlasses jug. His fis' stuck, en he can't pull loose. De tar hilt 'im. But Tar-Baby, she stay still, en Brer Fox, he lay low.

" 'Ef you don't lemme loose, I'll knock you agin,' sez Brer Rabbit, sezee, en wid dat he fotch 'er a wipe wid de udder han', en dat stuck. Tar-Baby, she ain't sayin' nothin', en Brer Fox, he lay low.

" 'Tu'n me loose, fo' I kick de natal stuffin' outen you,' sez Brer

Rabbit, sezee, but de Tar-Baby, she ain't sayin' nothin'. She des hilt on, en den Brer Rabbit lose de use er his feet in de same way. Brer Fox, he lay low. Den Brer Rabbit squall out dat ef de Tar-Baby don't tu'n 'im loose he butt 'er cranksided. En den he butted, en his head got stuck. Den Brer Fox, he sa'ntered fort', lookin' des ez innercent ez one er yo' mammy's mockin'birds.

" 'Howdy, Brer Rabbit,' sez Brer Fox, sezee. 'You look sorter stuck up dis mawnin',' sezee, en den he rolled on de groun', en laughed en laughed twel he couldn't laugh no mo'. 'I speck you'll take dinner wid me dis time, Brer Rabbit. I done laid in some cal-amus root, en I ain't gwineter take no skuse,' sez Brer Fox, sezee."

Here Uncle Remus paused, and drew a two-pound yam out of the ashes.

"Did the fox eat the rabbit?" asked the little boy to whom the story had been told.

"Dat's all de fur de tale goes," replied the old man. "He mout, en den agin he moutent. Some say Jedge B'ar come 'long en loosed 'im—some say he didn't. I hear Miss Sally callin'. You better run 'long."

"Uncle Remus," said the little boy one evening, when he found the old man with little or nothing to do, "did the fox kill and eat the rabbit when he caught him with the Tar-Baby?"

"Law, honey, ain't I tell you 'bout dat?" replied the old darkey, chuckling slyly. "I 'clar ter grashus I ought er tole you dat, but old man Nod wuz ridin' on my eyeleds 'twel a leetle mo'n I'd a dis'member'd my own name, en den on to dat here come yo' mammy hollerin' atter you.

"W'at I tell you w'en I fus' begin? I tole you Brer Rabbit wuz a monstus soon creetur; leas' ways dat's w'at I laid out fer ter tell you. Well, den, honey, don't you go en make no udder calkalashuns, kaze in dem days Brer Rabbit en his fambly wuz at de head er de gang w'en enny racket wuz on han', en dar dey stayed. 'Fo' you begins ter wipe yo' eyes 'bout Brer Rabbit, you wait en see whar'-bouts Brer Rabbit gwineter fetch up at. But dat's needer yer ner dar.

"W'en Brer Fox fine Brer Rabbit mixt up wid de Tar-Baby, he feel mighty good, en he roll on de groun' en laff. Bimeby he up'n say, sezee:

" 'Well, I speck I got you dis time, Brer Rabbit,' sezee; 'maybe I ain't, but I speck I is. You been runnin' roun' here sassin' atter me a mighty long time, but I speck you done come ter de een' er de row. You bin cuttin' up yo' capers en bouncin' 'roun' in dis neighberhood ontwel you come ter b'leeve yo'se'f de boss er de whole gang. En den youer allers some'rs whar you got no bizness,' sez Brer Fox, sezee. 'Who ax you fer ter come en strike up a 'quaintance wid dish yer Tar-Baby? En who stuck you up dar whar you iz? Nobody in de roun' worril. You des tuck en jam yo'se'f on dat Tar-Baby widout waitin' fer enny invite,' sez Brer Fox, sezee, 'en dar you is, en dar you'll stay twel I fixes up a bresh-pile and fires her up, kaze I'm gwineter bobbycue you dis day, sho,' sez Brer Fox, sezee.

"Den Brer Rabbit talk mighty 'umble.

" 'I don't keer w'at you do wid me, Brer Fox,' sezee, 'so you don't fling me in dat brier-patch. Roas' me, Brer Fox,' sezee, 'but don't fling me in dat brier-patch,' sezee.

" 'Het's so much trouble fer ter kindle a fier,' sez Brer Fox, sezee, 'dat I speck I'll hatter hang you,' sezee.

" 'Hang me des ez high ez you please, Brer Fox,' sez Brer Rabbit, sezee, 'but do fer de Lord's sake don't fling me in dat brier-patch,' sezee.

" 'I ain't got no string,' sez Brer Fox, sezee, 'en now I speck I'll hatter drown you,' sezee.

" 'Drown me des ez deep ez you please, Brer Fox,' sez Brer Rabbit, sezee, 'but do don't fling me in dat brier-patch,' sezee.

" 'Dey ain't no water nigh,' sez Brer Fox, sezee, 'en now I speck I'll hatter skin you,' sezee.

" 'Skin me, Brer Fox,' sez Brer Rabbit, sezee, 'snatch out my eyeballs, t'ar out my years by de roots, en cut off my legs,' sezee, 'but do please, Brer Fox, don't fling me in dat brier-patch,' sezee.

"Co'se Brer Fox wanter hurt Brer Rabbit bad ez he kin, so he cotch 'im by de behime legs en slung 'im right in de middle er de brier-patch. Dar wuz a considerbul flutter whar Brer Rabbit struck de bushes, en Brer Fox sorter hang 'roun' fer to see w'at wuz gwineter happen. Bimeby he hear somebody call 'im, en way up de hill he see Brer Rabbit settin' cross-legged on a chinkapin log koamin' de pitch outen his har wid a chip. Den Brer Fox know dat he bin swop off mighty bad. Brer Rabbit wuz bleedzed fer ter fling back some er his sass, en he holler out:

"'Bred en bawn in a brier-patch, Brer Fox—bred en bawn in a brier-patch!' en wid dat he skip out des ez lively ez a cricket in de embers."

*Which did the princess doom her lover
to embrace—*

The Lady or the Tiger?

FRANK R. STOCKTON (1834–1902)

The favorite humorous writer of the 1880's was
born in Philadelphia, Pennsylvania, of an old and
influential New Jersey family. Young Frank, after
graduating from high school, unwilling to study
medicine as his father wished, became a wood en-
graver and practiced this craft for some years.

He began contributing to children's magazines in
1867, and was made assistant editor of St. Nicholas
when this famous monthly was founded in 1873.
Here he remained until 1881, when he was able to
support himself by writing imaginative novels and
short stories for grownups. The wide success of
Rudder Grange (1879), an episodic and farcical
novel, established him as a popular author of cheerful and sometimes fantastic fiction.

He continued to write in this vein until almost
the end of his lengthy life. His later years were
spent at Nutley and Convent Station, New Jersey,
and in West Virginia near Harpers Ferry.

"The Lady or the Tiger?" first appeared in Century Magazine in November, 1882, and was collected in a volume of the same title in 1884. It created a sensation at once. Its charm lies in the delightful practical joke it plays on the reader. This is probably the cleverest trick story ever written. Pestered by readers who wanted him to give them the right answer to his riddle, Stockton wrote a similar story, "The Discourager of Hesitancy," and said that to anyone who could logically solve this second dilemma, he would divulge the answer to the first! Stockton's best later stories are found in A Chosen Few (1895). His fiction has been collected in twenty-three volumes.

IN THE VERY olden time, there lived a semibarbaric king, whose ideas, though somewhat polished and sharpened by the progressiveness of distant Latin neighbors, were still large, florid, and untrammelled, as became the half of him which was barbaric. He was a man of exuberant fancy, and, withal, of an authority so irresistible that, at his will, he turned his varied fancies into facts. He was greatly given to self-communing; and when he and himself agreed upon anything, the thing was done. When every member of his domestic and political systems moved smoothly in its appointed course, his nature was bland and genial; but whenever there was a little hitch, and some of his orbs got out of their orbits, he was blander and more genial still, for nothing pleased him so much as to make the crooked straight, and crush down uneven places.

Among the borrowed notions by which his barbarism had become semified was that of the public arena, in which, by exhibitions of manly and beastly valor, the minds of his subjects were refined and cultured.

But even here the exuberant and barbaric fancy asserted itself. The arena of the king was built, not to give the people an opportunity of hearing the rhapsodies of dying gladiators, nor to enable them to view the inevitable conclusion of a conflict between religious opinions and hungry jaws, but for purposes far better adapted to widen and develop the mental energies of the people. This vast amphitheater, with its encircling galleries, its mysterious vaults, and its unseen passages, was an agent of poetic justice, in which crime was punished, or virtue rewarded, by the decrees of an impartial and incorruptible chance.

When a subject was accused of a crime of sufficient importance to interest the king, public notice was given that on an appointed day the fate of the accused person would be decided in the king's arena,—a structure which well deserved its name; for, although its form and plan were borrowed from afar, its purpose emanated solely from the brain of this man, who, every barleycorn a king, knew no tradition to which he owed more allegiance than pleased his fancy, and who ingrafted on every adopted form of human thought and action the rich growth of his barbaric idealism.

When all the people had assembled in the galleries, and the king, surrounded by his court, sat high up on his throne of royal state on one side of the arena, he gave a signal, a door beneath him opened, and the accused subject stepped out into the amphitheater. Directly opposite him, on the other side of the enclosed space, were two doors, exactly alike and side by side. It was the duty and the privilege of the person on trial to walk directly to these doors and open one of them. He could open either door he pleased: he was subject to no guidance or influence but that of the aforementioned impartial and incorruptible chance. If he opened the one, there came out of it a hungry tiger, the fiercest and most cruel that could be procured, which immediately sprang upon him, and tore him to pieces, as a punishment for his guilt. The moment that the case of the criminal was thus decided, doleful iron bells were clanged, great wails went up from the hired mourners posted on the outer rim of the arena, and the vast audience, with bowed heads and downcast hearts, wended slowly their homeward way, mourning gently that one so young and fair, or so old and respected, should have merited so dire a fate.

But, if the accused person opened the other door, there came forth from it a lady, the most suitable to his years and station that his majesty could select among his fair subjects; and to this lady he was immediately married, as a reward of his innocence. It mattered not that he might already possess a wife and family, or that his affections might be engaged upon an object of his own selection: the king allowed no such subordinate arrangements to interfere with his great scheme of retribution and reward. The exercises, as in the other instance, took place immediately, and in the arena. Another door opened beneath the king, and a priest, followed by a band of choristers, and dancing maidens blowing joyous airs on golden horns and treading an epithalamic measure, advanced to where the pair stood, side by side; and the wedding was promptly and cheerily solemnized. Then the gay brass bells rang forth their merry peals, the people shouted glad hurrahs, and the innocent man, preceded by children strewing flowers on his path, led his bride to his home.

This was the king's semibarbaric method of administering justice. Its perfect fairness is obvious. The criminal could not know out of which door would come the lady: he opened either he pleased, without having the slightest idea whether, in the next instant, he was to be devoured or married. On some occasions the tiger came out of one door, and on some out of the other. The decisions of this tribunal were not only fair, they were positively determinate: the accused person was instantly punished if he found himself guilty; and, if innocent, he was rewarded on the spot, whether he liked it or not. There was no escape from the judgments of the king's arena.

The institution was a very popular one. When the people gathered together on one of the great trial days, they never knew whether they were to witness a bloody slaughter or a hilarious wedding. This element of uncertainty lent an interest to the occasion which it could not otherwise have attained. Thus, the masses were entertained and pleased, and the thinking part of the community could bring no charge of unfairness against this plan; for did not the accused person have the whole matter in his own hands?

This semibarbaric king had a daughter as blooming as his most florid fancies, and with a soul as fervent and imperious as his own. As is usual in such cases, she was the apple of his eye, and was loved by him above all humanity. Among his courtiers was a young man of that fineness of blood and lowness of station common to the conventional heroes of romance who love royal maidens. This royal maiden was well satisfied with her lover, for he was handsome and brave to a degree unsurpassed in all this kingdom; and she loved him with an ardor that had enough of barbarism in it to make it exceedingly warm and strong. This love affair moved on happily for many months, until one day the king happened to discover its existence. He did not hesitate nor waver in regard to his duty in the premises. The youth was immediately cast into prison, and a day was appointed for his trial in the king's arena. This, of course, was an especially important occasion; and his majesty, as well as all the people, was greatly interested in the workings and development of this trial. Never before had such a case occurred; never before had a subject dared to love the daughter of a king. In afteryears such things became commonplace enough; but then they were, in no slight degree, novel and startling.

The tiger-cages of the kingdom were searched for the most savage and relentless beasts, from which the fiercest monster might be selected for the arena; and the ranks of maiden youth and beauty throughout the land were carefully surveyed by competent judges, in order that the young man might have a fitting bride in case fate did not determine for him a different destiny. Of course, everybody knew that the deed with which the accused was charged had been done. He had loved the princess, and neither he, she, nor any one else thought of denying the fact; but the king would not think of allowing any fact of this kind to interfere with the workings of the tribunal, in which he took such great delight and satisfaction. No matter how the affair turned out, the youth would be disposed of;

and the king would take an æsthetic pleasure in watching the course of events, which would determine whether or not the young man had done wrong in allowing himself to love the princess.

The appointed day arrived. From far and near the people gathered, and thronged the great galleries of the arena; and the crowds, unable to gain admittance, massed themselves against its outside walls. The king and his court were in their places, opposite the twin doors,—those fateful portals, so terrible in their similarity.

All was ready. The signal was given. A door beneath the royal party opened, and the lover of the princess walked into the arena. Tall, beautiful, fair, his appearance was greeted with a low hum of admiration and anxiety. Half the audience had not known so grand a youth had lived among them. No wonder the princess loved him! What a terrible thing for him to be there!

As the youth advanced into the arena, he turned, as the custom was, to bow to the king: but he did not think at all of that royal personage; his eyes were fixed upon the princess, who sat to the right of her father. Had it not been for the moiety of barbarism in her nature, it is probable that lady would not have been there; but her intense and fervid soul would not allow her to be absent on an occasion in which she was so terribly interested. From the moment that the decree had gone forth, that her lover should decide his fate in the king's arena, she had thought of nothing, night or day, but this great event and the various subjects connected with it. Possessed of more power, influence, and force of character than any one who had ever before been interested in such a case, she had done what no other person had done,—she had possessed herself of the secret of the doors. She knew in which of the two rooms, that lay behind those doors, stood the cage of the tiger, with its open front, and in which waited the lady. Through these thick doors, heavily curtained with skins on the inside, it was impossible that any noise or suggestion should come from within to the person who should approach to raise the latch of one of them; but gold, and the power of a woman's will, had brought the secret to the princess.

And not only did she know in which room stood the lady ready to emerge, all blushing and radiant, should her door be opened, but she knew who the lady was. It was one of the fairest and loveliest of the damsels of the court who had been selected as the reward of the accused youth, should he be proved innocent of the crime of aspiring to one so far above him; and the princess hated her. Often had she seen, or imagined that she had seen, this fair creature throwing glances of admiration upon the person of her lover, and sometimes she thought these glances were perceived and even returned. Now and then she had seen them talking together; it was but for a moment or two, but much can be said in a brief space; it may have been on most unimportant topics, but how could she know that? The girl was lovely, but she had dared to raise her eyes to the loved one of the princess; and, with all the intensity of the savage blood transmitted to her through long lines of wholly barbaric ancestors, she hated the woman who blushed and trembled behind that silent door.

When her lover turned and looked at her, and his eye met hers as she sat there paler and whiter than any one in the vast ocean of anxious faces about her, he saw, by that power of quick perception which is given to those whose souls are one, that she knew behind which door crouched the tiger, and behind which stood the lady. He had expected her to know it. He understood her nature, and his soul was assured that she would never rest until she had made plain to herself this thing, hidden to all other lookers-on, even to the king. The only hope for the youth in which there was any element of certainty was based upon the success of the princess in discovering this mystery; and the moment he looked upon her, he saw she had succeeded, as in his soul he knew she would succeed.

Then it was that his quick and anxious glance asked the question: "Which?" It was as plain to her as if he shouted it from where he stood. There was not an instant to be lost. The question was asked in a flash; it must be answered in another.

Her right arm lay on the cushioned parapet before her. She raised her hand, and made a slight, quick movement toward the right. No one but her lover saw her. Every eye but his was fixed on the man in the arena.

He turned, and with a firm and rapid step he walked across the empty space. Every heart stopped beating, every breath was held, every eye was fixed immovably upon that man. Without the slightest hesitation, he went to the door on the right, and opened it.

Now, the point of the story is this: Did the tiger come out of that door, or did the lady?

The more we reflect upon this question, the harder it is to answer. It involves a study of the human heart which leads us through devious mazes of passion, out of which it is difficult to find our way. Think of it, fair reader, not as if the decision of the question depended upon yourself, but upon that hot-blooded, semibarbaric princess, her soul at a white heat beneath the combined fires of despair and jealousy. She had lost him, but who should have him?

How often, in her waking hours and in her dreams, had she started in wild horror, and covered her face with her hands as she thought of her lover opening the door on the other side of which waited the cruel fangs of the tiger!

But how much oftener had she seen him at the other door! How in her grievous reveries had she gnashed her teeth, and torn her hair, when she saw his start of rapturous delight as he opened the door of the lady! How her soul had burned in agony when she had seen him rush to meet that woman, with her flushing cheek and sparkling eye of triumph; when she had seen him lead her forth, his whole frame kindled with the joy of recovered life; when she had heard the glad shouts from the multitude, and the wild ringing of the happy bells; when she had seen the priest, with his joyous followers, advance to the couple, and make them man and wife before her very eyes; and when she had seen them walk away together upon their path of flowers, followed by the tremendous shouts of the hilarious multitude, in which her one despairing shriek was lost and drowned!

Would it not be better for him to die at once, and go to wait for her in the blessed regions of semibarbaric futurity?

And yet, that awful tiger, those shrieks, that blood!

Her decision had been indicated in an instant, but it had been made after days and nights of anguished deliberation. She had known she would be asked, she had decided what she would answer, and, without the slightest hesitation, she had moved her hand to the right.

The question of her decision is one not to be lightly considered, and it is not for me to presume to set myself up as the one person able to answer it. And so I leave it with all of you: Which came out of the opened door—the lady, or the tiger?

The man in the noose dropped and was
as one already dead. . . .

An Occurrence
at Owl Creek Bridge

AMBROSE BIERCE (1842–1914?)

Master of the witty, cynical, and horrible, Bierce
hated most of his family and most of humanity.
He was born into a Puritanical household in a log
cabin on Horse Cave Creek in Ohio. His uncle
Lucius paid for the only schooling young Ambrose
had—a year at Kentucky Military Institute before
that school burned down.

The outbreak of the Civil War gave Bierce a release from home and an army career that shaped
the rest of his life. He enlisted as a drummer boy,
fought bravely throughout four years, was severely
wounded at Kenesaw Mountain, and emerged as
a brevet major.

After the war, he obtained his discharge from
service in San Francisco, entered journalism as a
cartoonist and writer of political squibs, and by
1868 was editor of the News Letter. His first story

was published in 1871 in Bret Harte's Overland
Monthly. In the same year, he married and went
to join the literary life of London. He did not return to California until 1876.

For more than a decade thereafter, he was the
literary dictator of the Pacific Coast, as editor of
the Wasp and biting critic of the "Prattler" column. He befriended many a young writer, but his
work became more bitter as his disillusion with life
mounted. From 1897 to 1909, he was a Washington
correspondent for the Hearst newspapers.

He returned to California for the last time in
1913, on his way to Mexico looking for another
war. There he disappeared in 1914, probably murdered in the revolution then raging between Car-
ranza and Pancho Villa.

The short stories of Bierce appear mainly in his
Tales of Soldiers and Civilians (1891) and Can
Such Things Be? (1893), collected from the San
Francisco Examiner. "An Occurrence at Owl
Creek Bridge" first appeared in book form in the
1891 volume.

A MAN STOOD UPON a railroad bridge in northern Alabama, looking down into the swift water twenty feet below. The
man's hands were behind his back, the wrists bound with a cord. A
rope closely encircled his neck. It was attached to a stout cross-timber
above his head and the slack fell to the level of his knees. Some
loose boards laid upon the sleepers supporting the metals of the
railway supplied a footing for him and his executioners—two
private soldiers of the Federal army, directed by a sergeant who in

civil life may have been a deputy sheriff. At a short remove upon the same temporary platform was an officer in the uniform of his rank, armed. He was a captain. A sentinel at each end of the bridge stood with his rifle in the position known as "support," that is to say, vertical in front of the left shoulder, the hammer resting on the forearm thrown straight across the chest—a formal and unnatural position, enforcing an erect carriage of the body. It did not appear to be the duty of these two men to know what was occurring at the center of the bridge; they merely blockaded the two ends of the foot planking that traversed it.

Beyond one of the sentinels nobody was in sight; the railroad ran straight away into a forest for a hundred yards, then, curving, was lost to view. Doubtless there was an outpost farther along. The other bank of the stream was open ground—a gentle acclivity topped with a stockade of vertical tree trunks, loopholed for rifles, with a single embrasure through which protruded the muzzle of a brass cannon commanding the bridge. Midway of the slope between the bridge and fort were the spectators—a single company of infantry in line, at "parade rest," the butts of the rifles on the ground, the barrels inclining slightly backward against the right shoulder, the hands crossed upon the stock. A lieutenant stood at the right of the line, the point of his sword upon the ground, his left hand resting upon his right. Excepting the group of four at the center of the bridge, not a man moved. The company faced the bridge, staring stonily, motionless. The sentinels, facing the banks of the stream, might have been statues to adorn the bridge. The captain stood with folded arms, silent, observing the work of his subordinates, but making no sign. Death is a dignitary who when he comes announced is to be received with formal manifestations of respect, even by those most familiar with him. In the code of military etiquette silence and fixity are forms of deference.

The man who was engaged in being hanged was apparently about thirty-five years of age. He was a civilian, if one might judge from his habit, which was that of a planter. His features were good—a straight nose, firm mouth, broad forehead, from which his long, dark hair was combed straight back, falling behind his ears to the collar of his well-fitting frock coat. He wore a mustache and pointed beard, but no whiskers; his eyes were large and dark gray, and had a kindly expression which one would hardly have expected in one whose neck was in the hemp. Evidently this was no vulgar assassin. The liberal military code makes provision for hanging many kinds of persons, and gentlemen are not excluded.

The preparations being complete, the two private soldiers stepped aside and each drew away the plank upon which he had been standing. The sergeant turned to the captain, saluted and placed himself immediately behind that officer, who in turn moved apart one pace. These movements left the condemned man and the sergeant standing on the two ends of the same plank, which spanned three of the cross-ties of the bridge. The end upon which the civilian stood almost, but not quite, reached a fourth. This plank had been held in place by the weight of the captain; it was now held by that of the sergeant. At a signal from the former the latter would step aside, the plank would tilt and the condemned man go down between two ties. The arrangement commended itself to his judgment as simple and effective. His face had not been covered nor his eyes bandaged. He looked a moment at his "unsteadfast footing," then let his gaze wander to the swirling water of the stream racing madly beneath his feet. A piece of dancing driftwood caught his attention and his eyes followed it down the current. How slowly it appeared to move! What a sluggish stream!

He closed his eyes in order to fix his last thoughts upon his wife and children. The water, touched to gold by the early sun, the brooding mists under the banks at some distance down the stream, the fort, the soldiers, the piece of drift—all had distracted him. And now he became conscious of a new disturbance. Striking through the thought of his dear ones was a sound which he could neither ignore nor understand, a sharp, distinct, metallic percussion like the stroke of a blacksmith's hammer upon the anvil; it had the same ringing quality. He wondered what it was, and whether immeasurably distant or near by—it seemed both. Its recurrence was regular, but as slow as the tolling of a death knell. He waited each stroke with impatience and—he knew not why—

apprehension. The intervals of silence grew progressively longer; the delays became maddening. With their greater infrequency the sounds increased in strength and sharpness. They hurt his ear like the thrust of a knife; he feared he would shriek. What he heard was the ticking of his watch.

He unclosed his eyes and saw again the water below him. "If I could free my hands," he thought, "I might throw off the noose and spring into the stream. By diving I could evade the bullets and, swimming vigorously, reach the bank, take to the woods and get away home. My home, thank God, is as yet outside their lines; my wife and little ones are still beyond the invader's farthest advance."

As these thoughts, which have here to be set down in words, were flashed into the doomed man's brain rather than evolved from it, the captain nodded to the sergeant. The sergeant stepped aside.

Peyton Farquhar was a well-to-do planter, of an old and highly respected Alabama family. Being a slave owner and like other slave owners a politician, he was naturally an original secessionist and ardently devoted to the Southern cause. Circumstances of an imperious nature, which it is unnecessary to relate here, had prevented him from taking service with the gallant army that had fought the disastrous campaigns ending with the fall of Corinth, and he chafed under the inglorious restraint, longing for the release of his energies, the larger life of the soldier, the opportunity for distinction. That opportunity, he felt, would come, as it comes to all in war time. Meanwhile he did what he could. No service was too humble for him to perform in aid of the South, no adventure too perilous for him to undertake if consistent with the character of a civilian who was at heart a soldier, and who in good faith and without too much qualification assented to at least a part of the frankly villainous dictum that all is fair in love and war.

One evening while Farquhar and his wife were sitting on a rustic bench near the entrance to his grounds, a gray-clad soldier rode up to the gate and asked for a drink of water. Mrs. Farquhar was only too happy to serve him with her own white hands. While she was fetching the water her husband approached the dusty horseman and inquired eagerly for news from the front.

"The Yanks are repairing the railroads," said the man, "and are getting ready for another advance. They have reached the Owl Creek bridge, put it in order and built a stockade on the north bank. The commandant has issued an order, which is posted everywhere, declaring that any civilian caught interfering with the railroad, its bridges, tunnels or trains will be summarily hanged. I saw the order."

"How far is it to the Owl Creek bridge?" Farquhar asked.

"About thirty miles."

"Is there no force on this side the creek?"

"Only a picket post half a mile out, on the railroad, and a single sentinel at this end of the bridge."

"Suppose a man—a civilian and student of hanging—should elude the picket post and perhaps get the better of the sentinel," said Farquhar, smiling, "what could he accomplish?"

The soldier reflected. "I was there a month ago," he replied. "I observed that the flood of last winter had lodged a great quantity of driftwood against the wooden pier at this end of the bridge. It is now dry and would burn like tow."

The lady had now brought the water, which the soldier drank. He thanked her ceremoniously, bowed to her husband and rode away. An hour later, after nightfall, he repassed the plantation, going northward in the direction from which he had come. He was a Federal scout.

As Peyton Farquhar fell straight downward through the bridge he lost consciousness and was as one already dead. From this state he was awakened—ages later, it seemed to him—by the pain of a sharp pressure upon his throat, followed by a sense of suffocation. Keen, poignant agonies seemed to shoot from his neck downward through every fiber of his body and limbs. These pains appeared to flash along well-defined lines of ramification and to beat with an inconceivably rapid periodicity. They seemed like streams of pulsating fire heating him to an intolerable temperature. As to his head, he was conscious of nothing but a feeling of fullness—of congestion. These sensations were unaccompanied by thought. The intellectual part of his nature was already effaced; he had power only to feel, and feeling was torment. He was conscious of motion. Encompassed in a luminous cloud, of which he was now merely the fiery heart, without material substance, he swung through unthinkable arcs of oscillation, like a vast pendulum. Then all at once, with terrible suddenness, the light about him shot upward with the noise of a loud plash; a frightful roaring was in his ears, and all was cold and dark. The power of thought was restored; he knew that the rope had broken and he had fallen into the stream. There was no additional strangulation; the noose about his neck was already suffocating him and kept the water from his lungs. To die of hanging at the bottom of a river!—the idea seemed to him ludicrous. He opened his eyes in the darkness and saw above him a gleam of light, but how distant, how inaccessible! He was still sinking, for the light became fainter and fainter until it was a mere glimmer. Then it began to grow and brighten, and he knew that he was rising toward the surface—knew it with reluctance, for he was now very comfortable. "To be hanged and drowned," he thought, "that is not so bad; but I do not wish to be shot. No; I will not be shot; that is not fair."

He was not conscious of an effort, but a sharp pain in his wrist apprised him that he was trying to free his hands. He gave the struggle his attention, as an idler might observe the feat of a juggler, without interest in the outcome. What splendid effort!—what magnificent, what superhuman strength! Ah, that was a fine endeavor! Bravo! The cord fell away; his arms parted and floated upward, the hands dimly seen on each side in the growing light. He watched them with a new interest as first one and then the other pounced upon the noose at his neck. They tore it away and thrust it fiercely aside, its undulations resembling those of a water snake. "Put it back, put it back!" He thought he shouted these words to his hands, for the undoing of the noose had been succeeded by the direst pang that he had yet experienced. His neck ached horribly; his brain was on fire; his heart, which had been fluttering faintly, gave a great leap, trying to force itself out at his mouth. His whole body was racked and wrenched with an insupportable anguish! But his disobedient hands gave no heed to the command. They beat the water vigorously with quick, downward strokes, forcing him to the surface. He felt his head emerge; his eyes were blinded by the sunlight; his chest expanded convulsively, and with a supreme and crowning agony his lungs engulfed a great draught of air, which instantly he expelled in a shriek!

He was now in full possession of his physical senses. They were, indeed, preternaturally keen and alert. Something in the awful disturbance of his organic system had so exalted and refined them that they made record of things never before perceived. He felt the ripples upon his face and heard their separate sounds as they struck. He looked at the forest on the bank of the stream, saw the individual trees, the leaves and the veining of each leaf—saw the very insects upon them: the locusts, the brilliant-bodied flies, the gray spiders stretching their webs from twig to twig. He noted the prismatic colors in all the dewdrops upon a million blades of grass. The humming of the gnats that danced above the eddies of the stream, the beating of the dragonflies' wings, the strokes of the water-spiders' legs, like oars which had lifted their boat—all these made audible music. A fish slid along beneath his eyes and he heard the rush of its body parting the water.

He had come to the surface facing down the stream; in a moment the visible world seemed to wheel slowly round, himself the pivotal point, and he saw the bridge, the fort, the soldiers upon the bridge, the captain, the sergeant, the two privates, his executioners. They were in silhouette against the blue sky. They shouted and gesticulated, pointing at him. The captain had drawn his pistol, but did not fire; the others were unarmed. Their movements were grotesque and horrible, their forms gigantic.

Suddenly he heard a sharp report and something struck the water smartly within a few inches of his head, spattering his face with spray. He heard a second report, and saw one of the sentinels with his rifle at his shoulder, a light cloud of blue smoke rising from the muzzle. The man in the water saw the eye of the man on the bridge gazing into his own through the sights of the rifle. He observed that it was a gray eye and remembered having read that gray eyes were keenest, and that all famous marksmen had them. Nevertheless, this one had missed.

A counter-swirl had caught Farquhar and turned him half round; he was again looking into the forest on the bank opposite the fort. The sound of a clear, high voice in a monotonous singsong now rang out behind him and came across the water with a distinctness that pierced and subdued all other sounds, even the beating of the ripples in his ears. Although no soldier, he had frequented camps enough to know the dread significance of that deliberate, drawling, aspirated chant; the lieutenant on shore was taking a part in the morning's work. How coldly and pitilessly—with what an even, calm intonation, presaging and enforcing tranquillity in the men—with what accurately measured intervals fell those cruel words:

"Attention, company! . . . Shoulder arms! . . . Ready! . . . Aim! . . . Fire!"

Farquhar dived—dived as deeply as he could. The water roared in his ears like the voice of Niagara, yet he heard the dulled thunder of the volley and, rising again toward the surface, met shining bits of metal, singularly flattened, oscillating slowly downward. Some of them touched him on the face and hands, then fell away, continuing their descent. One lodged between his collar and neck; it was uncomfortably warm and he snatched it out.

As he rose to the surface, gasping for breath, he saw that he had been a long time under water; he was perceptibly farther down stream—nearer to safety. The soldiers had almost finished reloading; the metal ramrods flashed all at once in the sunshine as they were drawn from the barrels, turned in the air, and thrust into their sockets. The two sentinels fired again, independently and ineffectually.

The hunted man saw all this over his shoulder; he was now swimming vigorously with the current. His brain was as energetic as his arms and legs; he thought with the rapidity of lightning.

"The officer," he reasoned, "will not make that martinet's error a second time. It is as easy to dodge a volley as a single shot. He has probably already given the command to fire at will. God help me, I cannot dodge them all!"

An appalling splash within two yards of him was followed by a loud, rushing sound, *diminuendo*, which seemed to travel back through the air to the fort and died in an explosion which stirred the very river to its deeps! A rising sheet of water curved over him, fell down upon him, blinded him, strangled him! The cannon had taken a hand in the game. As he shook his head free from the commotion of the smitten water he heard the deflected shot humming through the air ahead, and in an instant it was cracking and smashing the branches in the forest beyond.

"They will not do that again," he thought; "the next time they will use a charge of grape. I must keep my eye upon the gun; the smoke will apprise me—the report arrives too late; it lags behind the missile. That is a good gun."

Suddenly he felt himself whirled round and round—spinning like a top. The water, the banks, the forests, the now distant bridge, fort and men—all were commingled and blurred. Objects were represented by their colors only; circular horizontal streaks of color—that was all he saw. He had been caught in a vortex and was being whirled on with a velocity of advance and gyration that made him giddy and sick. In a few moments he was flung upon the gravel at the foot of the left bank of the stream—the southern bank—and behind a projecting point which concealed him from his enemies. The sudden arrest of his motion, the abrasion of one of his hands on the gravel, restored him, and he wept with delight. He dug his fingers into the sand, threw it over himself in handfuls and audibly blessed it. It looked like diamonds, rubies, emeralds; he could think of nothing beautiful which it did not resemble. The trees upon the bank were giant garden plants; he noted a definite order in their arrangement, inhaled the fragrance of their blooms. A strange, roseate light shone through the spaces among their trunks and the wind made in their branches the music of Æolian harps. He had no wish to perfect his escape—was content to remain in that enchanting spot until retaken.

A whiz and rattle of grapeshot among the branches high above his head roused him from his dream. The baffled cannoneer had fired him a random farewell. He sprang to his feet, rushed up the sloping bank, and plunged into the forest.

All that day he traveled, laying his course by the rounding sun. The forest seemed interminable; nowhere did he discover a break in it, not even a woodman's road. He had not known that he lived in so wild a region. There was something uncanny in the revelation.

By nightfall he was fatigued, footsore, famishing. The thought of his wife and children urged him on. At last he found a road which led him in what he knew to be the right direction. It was as wide and straight as a city street, yet it seemed untraveled. No fields bordered it, no dwelling anywhere. Not so much as the barking of a dog suggested human habitation. The black bodies of the trees formed a straight wall on both sides, terminating on the horizon in a point, like a diagram in a lesson in perspective. Overhead, as he looked up through this rift in the wood, shone great golden stars looking unfamiliar and grouped in strange constellations. He was sure they were arranged in some order which had a secret and malign significance. The wood on either side was full of singular noises, among which—once, twice, and again—he distinctly heard whispers in an unknown tongue.

His neck was in pain and lifting his hand to it he found it horribly swollen. He knew that it had a circle of black where the rope had bruised it. His eyes felt congested; he could no longer close them. His tongue was swollen with thirst; he relieved its fever by thrusting it forward from between his teeth into the cold air. How softly the turf had carpeted the untraveled avenue—he could no longer feel the roadway beneath his feet!

Doubtless, despite his suffering, he had fallen asleep while walking, for now he sees another scene—perhaps he has merely recovered from a delirium. He stands at the gate of his own home. All is as he left it, and all bright and beautiful in the morning sunshine. He must have traveled the entire night. As he pushes open the gate and passes up the wide white walk, he sees a flutter of female garments; his wife, looking fresh and cool and sweet, steps down from the veranda to meet him. At the bottom of the steps she stands waiting, with a smile of ineffable joy, an attitude of matchless grace and dignity. Ah, how beautiful she is! He springs forward with extended arms. As he is about to clasp her he feels a stunning blow upon the back of the neck; a blinding white light blazes all about him with a sound like the shock of a cannon—then all is darkness and silence!

Peyton Farquhar was dead; his body, with a broken neck, swung gently from side to side beneath the timbers of the Owl Creek bridge.

> To the four men in the boat, the shore
> was so near and yet so far. . . .

The Open Boat

STEPHEN CRANE (1871–1900)

Named for an ancestor who had signed the Dec-
laration of Independence, Crane was born in a
Methodist parsonage in Newark, New Jersey,
where his father was a minister. His life as a boy
in Port Jervis and Asbury Park, New Jersey, gave
him material for his lively and realistic Whilom-
ville Stories (1900), which anticipated Booth Tar-
kington's Penrod.

After two years in a military academy at Clave-
rack, he entered Lafayette College and later went
to Syracuse University. College ended with his
mother's death in 1890. After a term as professional
baseball player (he had been team captain at Syracuse), he became a reporter for several New York
newspapers and explored the world around him,
particularly the slum area of the Bowery. His first
story, dealing with this seamy side of life, was too
grim for the magazines of his day; when he published it with borrowed money, the book lay unsold
on the shelves.

Sudden fame came to Crane at the age of twenty-four when his story of a recruit's adventures in the Civil War, The Red Badge of Courage, was published in 1895. The realism of this most celebrated American novel of battle was gained through Crane's power of imagination, for all he knew of the Civil War was what he had read and heard from veterans. In the same year he put out a volume of poems, The Black Riders, experiments with an early form of "free verse."

The Little Regiment, short stories of the Civil War, appeared in 1896, and in that winter Crane was sent by a newspaper syndicate on a trip to the West and Mexico, where he had various exciting encounters among cowboys and bandits, and gathered material for some of his best stories. His novel had labeled him as a "war writer," however, and the remainder of his short life was to be spent following the wars.

Cuba was rebelling against its Spanish masters, and at the end of 1896 Crane was sent to report on the activities of gunrunners. He sailed from Jacksonville, Florida, on a small steamer loaded with guns and cartridges for the insurrectos. The vessel sank off the coast and Crane was one of the four men in the last boat to leave. As related in "The Open Boat," they rowed for fifty hours to Mosquito Inlet, where a wave broke the oiler's back as they swam ashore. This story is as close to factual reporting as Crane's active imagination ever permitted him to come, but it is also creative literature.

The next year he went to Greece to cover the war with Turkey, but he fell ill and accomplished little. In the autumn he went to England with his bride, Cora Taylor, who had come from America to nurse him. He took a cottage in Surrey and continued to write, even though his house was overrun by curious visitors. Here he first met such important literary friends as Henry James, Joseph Conrad, and H. G. Wells.

The Spanish-American War broke out in April, 1898, and Crane, after being rejected for naval service, left for Cuba as a special correspondent. He was officially mentioned for bravery at Guantánamo, and his experiences resulted in Wounds in the Rain (1900).

Again he was broken in health, and although by now he had many ardent friends in America, he went back to England after Christmas, 1899. His last year was spent at rambling Brede Place in Sussex, where in spite of the growing inroads of tuberculosis he finished several more books. He died at Badenweiler in the Black Forest of Germany, in 1900, not yet thirty years old, leaving behind at least one great novel and a number of masterly short stories.

"The Open Boat" was first published in Scribner's Magazine in June, 1897, and in book form in The Open Boat and Other Tales of Adventure (1898). Crane's collected works in twelve volumes were edited by Wilson Follett. His best short stories appear in Men, Women, and Boats (1921), edited by Vincent Starrett, and in Twenty Stories (1940), edited by Carl Van Doren.

NONE OF THEM KNEW the color of the sky. Their eyes glanced level, and were fastened upon the waves that swept toward them. These waves were of the hue of slate, save for the tops, which were of foaming white, and all of the men knew the colors of the sea. The horizon narrowed and widened, and dipped and rose, and at all times its edge was jagged with waves that seemed thrust up in points like rocks.

Many a man ought to have a bathtub larger than the boat which here rode upon the sea. These waves were most wrongfully and barbarously abrupt and tall, and each froth-top was a problem in small-boat navigation.

The cook squatted in the bottom, and looked with both eyes at the six inches of gunwale which separated him from the ocean. His sleeves were rolled over his fat forearms, and the two flaps of his unbuttoned vest dangled as he bent to bail out the boat. Often he said, "Gawd! That was a narrow clip." As he remarked it he invariably gazed eastward over the broken sea.

The oiler, steering with one of the two oars in the boat, sometimes raised himself suddenly to keep clear of water that swirled in over the stern. It was a thin little oar, and it seemed often ready to snap.

The correspondent, pulling at the other oar, watched the waves and wondered why he was there.

The injured captain, lying in the bow, was at this time buried in that profound dejection and indifference which comes, temporarily at least, to even the bravest and most enduring when, willy-nilly, the firm fails, the army loses, the ship goes down. The mind of the master of a vessel is rooted deep in the timbers of her, though he command for a day or a decade; and this captain had on him the stern impression of a scene in the grays of dawn of seven turned faces, and later a stump of a topmast with a white ball on it, that slashed to and fro at the waves, went low and lower, and down. Thereafter there was something strange in his voice. Although steady, it was deep with mourning, and of a quality beyond oration or tears.

"Keep 'er a little more south, Billie," said he.

"A little more south, sir," said the oiler in the stern.

A seat in his boat was not unlike a seat upon a bucking broncho, and by the same token a broncho is not much smaller. The craft pranced and reared and plunged like an animal. As each wave came, and she rose for it, she seemed like a horse making at a fence outrageously high. The manner of her scramble over these walls of water was a mystic thing, and, moreover, at the top of them were ordinarily these problems in white water, the foam racing down from the summit of each wave requiring a new leap, and a leap from the air. Then, after scornfully bumping a crest, she would slide and race and splash down a long incline, and arrive bobbing and nodding in front of the next menace.

A singular disadvantage of the sea lies in the fact that after successfully surmounting one wave you discover that there is another behind it just as important and just as nervously anxious to do something effective in the way of swamping boats. In a ten-foot dinghy one can get an idea of the resources of the sea in the line of waves that is not probable to the average experience which is never at sea in a dinghy. As each slaty wall of water approached, it shut all else from the view of the men in the boat, and it was not difficult to imagine that this particular wave was the final outburst of the ocean, the last effort of the grim water. There was a terrible grace in the move of the waves, and they came in silence, save for the snarling of the crests.

In the wan light the faces of the men must have been gray. Their eyes must have glinted in strange ways as they gazed steadily astern. Viewed from a balcony, the whole thing would doubtless have been weirdly picturesque. But the men in the boat had no time to see it, and if they had had leisure, there were other things to occupy their minds. The sun swung steadily up the sky, and they knew it was broad day because the color of the sea changed from slate to emerald green streaked with amber lights, and the foam was like tumbling snow. The process of the breaking day was unknown to them. They were aware only of this effect upon the color of the waves that rolled toward them.

In disjointed sentences the cook and the correspondent argued as to the difference between a lifesaving station and a house of refuge. The cook had said: "There's a house of refuge just north of the Mosquito Inlet Light, and as soon as they see us they'll come off in their boat and pick us up."

"As soon as who see us?" said the correspondent.

"The crew," said the cook.

"Houses of refuge don't have crews," said the correspondent. "As I understand them, they are only places where clothes and grub are stored for the benefit of shipwrecked people. They don't carry crews."

"Oh, yes, they do," said the cook.

"No, they don't," said the correspondent.

"Well, we're not there yet, anyhow," said the oiler, in the stern.

"Well," said the cook, "perhaps it's not a house of refuge that I'm thinking of as being near Mosquito Inlet Light; perhaps it's a lifesaving station."

"We're not there yet," said the oiler in the stern.

As the boat bounced from the top of each wave the wind tore through the hair of the hatless men, and as the craft plopped her stern down again the spray slashed past them. The crest of each of these waves was a hill, from the top of which the men surveyed for a moment a broad tumultuous expanse, shining and wind-riven. It was probably splendid, it was probably glorious, this play of the free sea, wild with lights of emerald and white and amber.

"Bully good thing it's an on-shore wind," said the cook. "If not, where would we be? Wouldn't have a show."

"That's right," said the correspondent.

The busy oiler nodded his assent.

Then the captain, in the bow, chuckled in a way that expressed humor, contempt, tragedy, all in one. "Do you think we've got much of a show now, boys?" said he.

Whereupon the three were silent, save for a trifle of hemming and hawing. To express any particular optimism at this time they felt to be childish and stupid, but they all doubtless possessed this sense of the situation in their minds. A young man thinks doggedly at such times. On the other hand, the ethics of their condition was decidedly against any open suggestion of hopelessness. So they were silent.

"Oh, well," said the captain, soothing his children, "we'll get ashore all right."

But there was that in his tone which made them think; so the oiler quoth, "Yes! If this wind holds."

The cook was bailing. "Yes! If we don't catch hell in the surf."

Canton-flannel gulls flew near and far. Sometimes they sat down on the sea, near patches of brown seaweed that rolled over the waves with a movement like carpets on a line in a gale. The birds sat comfortably in groups, and they were envied by some in the dinghy, for the wrath of the sea was no more to them than it was to a covey of prairie chickens a thousand miles inland. Often they came very close and stared at the men with black bead-like eyes. At these times they were uncanny and sinister in their unblinking scrutiny, and the men hooted angrily at them, telling them to be gone. One came, and evidently decided to alight on the top of the captain's head. The bird flew parallel to the boat and did not circle, but made short sidelong jumps in the air in chicken-fashion. His black eyes were wistfully fixed upon the captain's head. "Ugly brute," said the oiler to the bird. "You look as if you were made with a jackknife." The cook and the correspondent swore darkly at the creature. The captain naturally wished to knock it away with the end of the heavy painter, but he did not dare to do it, because anything resembling an emphatic gesture would have capsized this freighted boat; and so, with his open hand, the captain gently and carefully waved the gull away. After it had been discouraged from the pursuit the captain breathed easier on account of his hair, and others breathed easier because the bird struck their minds at this time as being somehow gruesome and ominous.

In the meantime the oiler and the correspondent rowed. And

also they rowed. They sat together in the same seat, and each rowed an oar. Then the oiler took both oars; then the correspondent took both oars; then the oiler; then the correspondent. They rowed and they rowed. The very ticklish part of the business was when the time came for the reclining one in the stern to take his turn at the oars. By the very last star of truth, it is easier to steal eggs from under a hen than it was to change seats in the dinghy. First the man in the stern slid his hand along the thwart and moved with care, as if he were of Sèvres. Then the man in the rowing-seat slid his hand along the other thwart. It was all done with the most extraordinary care. As the two sidled past each other, the whole party kept watchful eyes on the coming wave, and the captain cried: "Look out, now! Steady, there!"

The brown mats of seaweed that appeared from time to time were like islands, bits of earth. They were travelling, apparently, neither one way nor the other. They were, to all intents, stationary. They informed the men in the boat that it was making progress slowly toward the land.

The captain, rearing cautiously in the bow after the dinghy soared on a great swell, said that he had seen the lighthouse at Mosquito Inlet. Presently the cook remarked that he had seen it. The correspondent was at the oars then, and for some reason he too wished to look at the lighthouse; but his back was toward the far shore, and the waves were important, and for some time he could not seize an opportunity to turn his head. But at last there came a wave more gentle than the others, and when at the crest of it he swiftly scoured the western horizon.

"See it?" said the captain.

"No," said the correspondent, slowly; "I didn't see anything."

"Look again," said the captain. He pointed. "It's exactly in that direction."

At the top of another wave the correspondent did as he was bid, and this time his eyes chanced on a small, still thing on the edge of the swaying horizon. It was precisely like a point of a pin. It took an anxious eye to find a lighthouse so tiny.

"Think we'll make it, Captain?"

"If this wind holds and the boat don't swamp, we can't do much else," said the captain.

The little boat, lifted by each towering sea and splashed viciously by the crests, made progress that in the absence of seaweed was not apparent to those in her. She seemed just a wee thing wallowing, miraculously top up, at the mercy of five oceans. Occasionally a great spread of water, like white flames, swarmed into her.

"Bail her, cook," said the captain, serenely.

"All right, Captain," said the cheerful cook.

It would be difficult to describe the subtle brotherhood of men that was here established on the seas. No one said that it was so. No one mentioned it. But it dwelt in the boat, and each man felt it warm him. They were a captain, an oiler, a cook, and a correspondent, and they were friends—friends in a more curiously ironbound degree than may be common. The hurt captain, lying against the water-jar in the bow, spoke always in a low voice and calmly; but he could never command a more ready and swiftly obedient crew than the motley three of the dinghy. It was more than a mere recognition of what was best for the common safety. There was surely in it a quality that was personal and heartfelt. And after this devotion to the commander of the boat, there was this comradeship, that the correspondent, for instance, who had been taught to be cynical of men, knew even at the time was the best experience of his life. But no one said that it was so. No one mentioned it.

"I wish we had a sail," remarked the captain. "We might try my overcoat on the end of an oar, and give you two boys a chance to rest." So the cook and the correspondent held the mast and spread wide the overcoat; the oiler steered; and the little boat made good way with her new rig. Sometimes the oiler had to scull sharply to keep a sea from breaking into the boat, but otherwise sailing was a success.

Meanwhile the lighthouse had been growing slowly larger. It had now almost assumed color, and appeared like a little gray shadow on the sky. The man at the oars could not be prevented from turning his head rather often to try for a glimpse of this little gray shadow.

At last, from the top of each wave, the men in the tossing boat could see land. Even as the lighthouse was an upright shadow on the sky, this land seemed but a long black shadow on the sea. It certainly was thinner than paper. "We must be about opposite New Smyrna," said the cook, who had coasted this shore often in schooners. "Captain, by the way, I believe they abandoned that lifesaving station there about a year ago."

"Did they?" said the captain.

The wind slowly died away. The cook and the correspondent were not now obliged to slave in order to hold high the oar. But the waves continued their old impetuous swooping at the dinghy, and the little craft, no longer under way, struggled woundily over them. The oiler or the correspondent took the oars again.

Shipwrecks are apropos of nothing. If men could only train for them and have them occur when the men had reached pink condition, there would be less drowning at sea. Of the four in the dinghy none had slept any time worth mentioning for two days and two nights previous to embarking in the dinghy, and in the excitement of clambering about the deck of a foundering ship they had also forgotten to eat heartily.

For these reasons, and for others, neither the oiler nor the correspondent was fond of rowing at this time. The correspondent wondered ingenuously how in the name of all that was sane could there be people who thought it amusing to row a boat. It was not an amusement; it was a diabolical punishment, and even a genius of mental aberrations could never conclude that it was anything but a horror to the muscles and a crime against the back. He mentioned to the boat in general how the amusement of rowing struck him, and the weary-faced oiler smiled in full sympathy. Previously to the foundering, by the way, the oiler had worked a double watch in the engine-room of the ship.

"Take her easy now, boys," said the captain. "Don't spend yourselves. If we have to run a surf you'll need all your strength, because we'll sure have to swim for it. Take your time."

Slowly the land arose from the sea. From a black line it became a line of black and a line of white—trees and sand. Finally the captain said that he could make out a house on the shore. "That's the house of refuge, sure," said the cook. "They'll see us before long, and come out after us."

The distant lighthouse reared high. "The keeper ought to be able to make us out now, if he's looking through a glass," said the captain. "He'll notify the lifesaving people."

"None of those other boats could have got ashore to give word of this wreck," said the oiler, in a low voice, "else the lifeboat would be out hunting us."

Slowly and beautifully the land loomed out of the sea. The wind came again. It had veered from the northeast to the southeast. Finally a new sound struck the ears of the men in the boat. It was the low thunder of the surf on the shore. "We'll never be able to make the lighthouse now," said the captain. "Swing her head a little more north, Billie."

"A little more north, sir," said the oiler.

Whereupon the little boat turned her nose once more down the wind, and all but the oarsman watched the shore grow. Under the influence of this expansion, doubt and direful apprehension were leaving the minds of the men. The management of the boat was still most absorbing, but it could not prevent a quiet cheerfulness. In an hour, perhaps, they would be ashore.

Their backbones had become thoroughly used to balancing in the boat, and they now rode this wild colt of a dinghy like circus men. The correspondent thought that he had been drenched to the skin, but happening to feel in the top pocket of his coat, he found therein eight cigars. Four of them were soaked with sea-water; four were perfectly scatheless. After a search, somebody produced three dry matches; and thereupon the four waifs rode impudently in their little boat and, with an assurance of an impending rescue shining in their eyes, puffed at the big cigars, and judged well and ill of all men. Everybody took a drink of water.

· · ·

"Cook," remarked the captain, "there don't seem to be any signs of life about your house of refuge."

"No," replied the cook. "Funny they don't see us!"

A broad stretch of lowly coast lay before the eyes of the men. It was of low dunes topped with dark vegetation. The roar of the surf was plain, and sometimes they could see the white tip of a wave as it spun up the beach. A tiny house was blocked out black upon the sky. Southward, the slim lighthouse lifted its little gray length.

Tide, wind, and waves were swinging the dinghy northward. "Funny they don't see us," said the men.

The surf's roar was here dulled, but its tone was nevertheless thunderous and mighty. As the boat swam over the great rollers the men sat listening to this roar. "We'll swamp sure," said everybody.

It is fair to say here that there was not a lifesaving station within twenty miles in either direction; but the men did not know this fact, and in consequence they made dark and opprobrious remarks concerning the eyesight of the nation's lifesavers. Four scowling men sat in the dinghy and surpassed records in the invention of epithets.

"Funny they don't see us."

The light-heartedness of a former time had completely faded. To their sharpened minds it was easy to conjure pictures of all kinds of incompetency and blindness and, indeed, cowardice. There was the shore of the populous land, and it was bitter and bitter to them that from it came no sign.

"Well," said the captain, ultimately, "I suppose we'll have to make a try for ourselves. If we stay out here too long, we'll none of us have strength left to swim after the boat swamps."

And so the oiler, who was at the oars, turned the boat straight for the shore. There was a sudden tightening of muscles. There was some thinking.

"If we don't all get ashore," said the captain—"if we don't all get ashore, I suppose you fellows know where to send news of my finish?"

They then briefly exchanged some addresses and admonitions. As for the reflections of the men, there was a great deal of rage in them. Perchance they might be formulated thus: "If I am going to be drowned—if I am going to be drowned—if I am going to be drowned, why, in the name of the seven mad gods who rule the sea, was I allowed to come thus far and contemplate sand and trees? Was I brought here merely to have my nose dragged away as I was about to nibble the sacred cheese of life? It is preposterous. If this old ninny-woman, Fate, cannot do better than this, she should be deprived of the management of men's fortunes. She is an old hen who knows not her intention. If she has decided to drown me, why did she not do it in the beginning and save me all this trouble? The whole affair is absurd.—But no; she cannot mean to drown me. She dare not drown me. She cannot drown me. Not after all this work." Afterward the man might have had an impulse to shake his fist at the clouds. "Just you drown me, now, and then hear what I call you!"

The billows that came at this time were more formidable. They seemed always just about to break and roll over the little boat in a turmoil of foam. There was a preparatory and long growl in the speech of them. No mind unused to the sea would have concluded that the dinghy could ascend these sheer heights in time. The shore was still afar. The oiler was a wily surfman. "Boys," he said swiftly, "she won't live three minutes more, and we're too far out to swim. Shall I take her to sea again, Captain?"

"Yes; go ahead!" said the captain.

This oiler, by a series of quick miracles and fast and steady oarsmanship, turned the boat in the middle of the surf and took her safely to sea again.

There was a considerable silence as the boat bumped over the furrowed sea to deeper water. Then somebody in gloom spoke: "Well, anyhow, they must have seen us from the shore by now."

The gulls went in slanting flight up the wind toward the gray, desolate east. A squall, marked by dingy clouds and clouds brick-red like smoke from a burning building, appeared from the southeast.

"What do you think of those lifesaving people? Ain't they peaches?"

"Funny they haven't seen us."

"Maybe they think we're out here for sport! Maybe they think we're fishin'. Maybe they think we're damned fools."

It was a long afternoon. A changed tide tried to force them southward, but wind and wave said northward. Far ahead, where coastline, sea, and sky formed their mighty angle, there were little dots which seemed to indicate a city on the shore.

"St. Augustine?"

The captain shook his head. "Too near Mosquito Inlet."

And the oiler rowed, and then the correspondent rowed; then the oiler rowed. It was a weary business. The human back can become the seat of more aches and pains than are registered in books for the composite anatomy of a regiment. It is a limited area, but it can become the theater of innumerable muscular conflicts, tangles, wrenches, knots, and other comforts.

"Did you ever like to row, Billie?" asked the correspondent.

"No," said the oiler; "hang it!"

When one exchanged the rowing-seat for a place in the bottom of the boat, he suffered a bodily depression that caused him to be careless of everything save an obligation to wiggle one finger. There was cold sea-water swashing to and fro in the boat, and he lay in it. His head, pillowed on a thwart, was within an inch of the swirl of a wave-crest, and sometimes a particularly obstreperous sea came inboard and drenched him once more. But these matters did not annoy him. It is almost certain that if the boat had capsized he would have tumbled comfortably out upon the ocean as if he felt sure that it was a great soft mattress.

"Look! There's a man on the shore!"

"Where?"

"There! See 'im? See 'im?"

"Yes, sure! He's walking along."

"Now he's stopped. Look! He's facing us!"

"He's waving at us!"

"So he is! By thunder!"

"Ah, now we're all right! Now we're all right! There'll be a boat out here for us in half an hour."

"He's going on. He's running. He's going up to that house there."

The remote beach seemed lower than the sea, and it required a searching glance to discern the little black figure. The captain saw a floating stick, and they rowed to it. A bath towel was by some weird chance in the boat, and, tying this on the stick, the captain waved it. The oarsman did not dare turn his head, so he was obliged to ask questions.

"What's he doing now?"

"He's standing still again. He's looking, I think.—There he goes again—toward the house.—Now he's stopped again."

"Is he waving at us?"

"No, not now; he was, though."

"Look! There comes another man!"

"He's running."

"Look at him go, would you!"

"Why, he's on a bicycle. Now he's met the other man. They're both waving at us. Look!"

"There comes something up the beach."

"What the devil is that thing?"

"Why, it looks like a boat."

"Why, certainly, it's a boat."

"No; it's on wheels."

"Yes, so it is. Well, that must be the lifeboat. They drag them along shore on a wagon."

"That's the lifeboat, sure."

"No, by God, it's—it's an omnibus."

"I tell you it's a lifeboat."

"It is not! It's an omnibus. I can see it plain. See? One of these big hotel omnibuses."

"By thunder, you're right. It's an omnibus, sure as fate. What do you suppose they are doing with an omnibus? Maybe they are going around collecting the life-crew, hey?"

"That's it, likely. Look! There's a fellow waving a little black flag. He's standing on the steps of the omnibus. There come those other two fellows. Now they're all talking together. Look at the fellow with the flag. Maybe he ain't waving it!"

"That ain't a flag, is it? That's his coat. Why, certainly, that's his coat."

"So it is; it's his coat. He's taken it off and is waving it around his head. But would you look at him swing it!"

"Oh, say, there isn't any lifesaving station there. That's just a winter-resort hotel omnibus that has brought over some of the boarders to see us drown."

"What's that idiot with the coat mean? What's he signalling, anyhow?"

"It looks as if he were trying to tell us to go north. There must be a lifesaving station up there."

"No; he thinks we're fishing. Just giving us a merry hand. See? Ah, there, Willie!"

"Well, I wish I could make something out of those signals. What do you suppose he means?"

"He don't mean anything; he's just playing."

"Well, if he'd just signal to us to try the surf again, or to go to sea and wait, or go north, or go south, or go to hell, there would be some reason in it. But look at him! He just stands there and keeps his coat revolving like a wheel. The ass!"

"There come more people."

"Now there's quite a mob. Look! Isn't that a boat?"

"Where? Oh, I see where you mean. No, that's no boat."

"That fellow is still waving his coat."

"He must think we like to see him do that. Why don't he quit it? It don't mean anything."

"I don't know. I think he is trying to make us go north. It must be that there's a lifesaving station there somewhere."

"Say, he ain't tired yet. Look at 'im wave!"

"Wonder how long he can keep that up. He's been revolving his coat ever since he caught sight of us. He's an idiot. Why aren't they getting men to bring a boat out? A fishing-boat—one of those big yawls—could come out here all right. Why don't he do something?"

"Oh, it's all right now."

"They'll have a boat out here for us in less than no time, now that they've seen us."

A faint yellow tone came into the sky over the low land. The shadows on the sea slowly deepened. The wind bore coldness with it, and the men began to shiver.

"Holy smoke!" said one, allowing his voice to express his impious mood. "If we keep on monkeying out here! If we've got to flounder out here all night!"

"Oh, we'll never have to stay here all night. Don't you worry. They've seen us now, and it won't be long before they'll come chasing out after us."

The shore grew dusky. The man waving a coat blended gradually into this gloom, and it swallowed in the same manner the omnibus and the group of people. The spray, when it dashed uproariously over the side, made the voyagers shrink and swear like men who were being branded.

"I'd like to catch the chump who waved the coat. I feel like socking him one, just for luck."

"Why? What did he do?"

"Oh, nothing, but then he seemed so damned cheerful."

In the meantime the oiler rowed, and then the correspondent rowed, and then the oiler rowed. Gray-faced and bowed forward, they mechanically, turn by turn, plied the leaden oars. The form of the lighthouse had vanished from the southern horizon, but finally a pale star appeared, just lifting from the sea. The streaked saffron in the west passed before the all-merging darkness, and the sea to the east was black. The land had vanished, and was expressed only by the low and drear thunder of the surf.

"If I am going to be drowned—if I am going to be drowned— if I am going to be drowned, why, in the name of the seven mad gods who rule the sea was I allowed to come thus far and contemplate sand and trees? Was I brought here merely to have my nose dragged away as I was about to nibble the sacred cheese of life?"

The patient captain, drooped over the water-jar, was sometimes obliged to speak to the oarsman.

"Keep her head up! Keep her head up!"

"Keep her head up, sir." The voices were weary and low.

This was surely a quiet evening. All save the oarsman lay heavily and listlessly in the boat's bottom. As for him, his eyes were just capable of noting the tall black waves that swept forward in a most sinister silence, save for an occasional subdued growl of a crest.

The cook's head was on a thwart, and he looked without interest at the water under his nose. He was deep in other scenes. Finally he spoke. "Billie," he murmured, dreamfully, "what kind of pie do you like best?"

"Pie!" said the oiler and the correspondent, agitatedly. "Don't talk about those things, blast you!"

"Well," said the cook, "I was just thinking about ham sandwiches, and—"

A night on the sea in an open boat is a long night. As darkness settled finally, the shine of the light, lifting from the sea in the south, changed to full gold. On the northern horizon a new light appeared, a small bluish gleam on the edge of the waters. These two lights were the furniture of the world. Otherwise there was nothing but waves.

Two men huddled in the stern, and distances were so magnificent in the dinghy that the rower was enabled to keep his feet partly warm by thrusting them under his companions. Their legs indeed extended far under the rowing-seat until they touched the feet of the captain forward. Sometimes, despite the efforts of the tired oarsman, a wave came piling into the boat, an icy wave of the night, and the chilling water soaked them anew. They would twist their bodies for a moment and groan, and sleep the dead sleep once more, while the water in the boat gurgled about them as the craft rocked.

The plan of the oiler and the correspondent was for one to row until he lost the ability, and then arouse the other from his sea-water couch in the bottom of the boat.

The oiler plied the oars until his head drooped forward and the overpowering sleep blinded him; and he rowed yet afterward. Then he touched a man in the bottom of the boat, and called his name. "Will you spell me for a little while?" he said meekly.

"Sure, Billie," said the correspondent, awakening and dragging himself to a sitting position. They exchanged places carefully, and the oiler, cuddling down in the sea-water at the cook's side, seemed to go to sleep instantly.

The particular violence of the sea had ceased. The waves came without snarling. The obligation of the man at the oars was to keep the boat headed so that the tilt of the rollers would not capsize her, and to preserve her from filling when the crests rushed past. The black waves were silent and hard to be seen in the darkness. Often one was almost upon the boat before the oarsman was aware.

In a low voice the correspondent addressed the captain. He was not sure that the captain was awake, although this iron man seemed to be always awake. "Captain, shall I keep her making for that light north, sir?"

The same steady voice answered him. "Yes. Keep it about two points off the port bow."

The cook had tied a life belt around himself in order to get even the warmth which this clumsy cork contrivance could donate, and he seemed almost stove-like when a rower, whose teeth invariably chattered wildly as soon as he ceased his labor, dropped down to sleep.

The correspondent, as he rowed, looked down at the two men sleeping underfoot. The cook's arm was around the oiler's shoulders, and, with the fragmentary clothing and haggard faces, they were the babes of the sea—a grotesque rendering of the old babes in the wood.

Later he must have grown stupid at his work, for suddenly there was a growling of water, and a crest came with a roar and a swash into the boat, and it was a wonder that it did not set the cook afloat in his life belt. The cook continued to sleep, but the oiler sat up, blinking his eyes and shaking with the new cold.

"Oh, I'm awful sorry, Billie," said the correspondent, contritely.

"That's all right, old boy," said the oiler, and lay down again and was asleep.

Presently it seemed that even the captain dozed, and the correspondent thought that he was the one man afloat on all the ocean. The wind had a voice as it came over the waves, and it was sadder than the end.

There was a long, loud swishing astern of the boat, and a gleaming trail of phosphorescence, like blue flame, was furrowed on the black waters. It might have been made by a monstrous knife.

Then there came a stillness, while the correspondent breathed with open mouth and looked at the sea.

Suddenly there was another swish and another long flash of bluish light, and this time it was alongside the boat, and might almost have been reached with an oar. The correspondent saw an enormous fin speed like a shadow through the water, hurling the crystalline spray and leaving the long glowing trail.

The correspondent looked over his shoulder at the captain. His face was hidden, and he seemed to be asleep. He looked at the babes of the sea. They certainly were asleep. So, being bereft of sympathy, he leaned a little way to one side and swore softly into the sea.

But the thing did not then leave the vicinity of the boat. Ahead or astern, on one side or the other, at intervals long or short, fled the long sparkling streak, and there was to be heard the *whirroo* of the dark fin. The speed and power of the thing was greatly to be admired. It cut the water like a gigantic and keen projectile.

The presence of this biding thing did not affect the man with the same horror that it would if he had been a picnicker. He simply looked at the sea dully and swore in an undertone.

Nevertheless, it is true that he did not wish to be alone with the thing. He wished one of his companions to awake by chance and keep him company with it. But the captain hung motionless over the water-jar, and the oiler and the cook in the bottom of the boat were plunged in slumber.

• • •

"If I am going to be drowned—if I am going to be drowned—if I am going to be drowned, why, in the name of the seven mad gods who rule the sea, was I allowed to come thus far and contemplate sand and trees?"

During this dismal night, it may be remarked that a man would conclude that it was really the intention of the seven mad gods to drown him, despite the abominable injustice of it. For it was certainly an abominable injustice to drown a man who had worked so hard, so hard. The man felt it would be a crime most unnatural. Other people had drowned at sea since galleys swarmed with painted sails, but still—

When it occurs to a man that nature does not regard him as important, and that she feels she would not maim the universe by disposing of him, he at first wishes to throw bricks at the temple, and he hates deeply the fact that there are no bricks and no temples. Any visible expression of nature would surely be pelleted with his jeers.

Then, if there be no tangible thing to hoot, he feels, perhaps, the desire to confront a personification and indulge in pleas, bowed to one knee, and with hands supplicant, saying, "Yes, but I love myself."

A high cold star on a winter's night is the word he feels that she says to him. Thereafter he knows the pathos of his situation.

The men in the dinghy had not discussed these matters, but each had, no doubt, reflected upon them in silence and according to his mind. There was seldom any expression upon their faces save the general one of complete weariness. Speech was devoted to the business of the boat.

To chime the notes of his emotion, a verse mysteriously entered the correspondent's head. He had even forgotten that he had forgotten this verse, but it suddenly was in his mind.

A soldier of the Legion lay dying in Algiers;
There was lack of woman's nursing, there was dearth of woman's
tears;

But a comrade stood beside him, and he took that comrade's
  hand,
And he said, "I never more shall see my own, my native land."

In his childhood the correspondent had been made acquainted
with the fact that a soldier of the Legion lay dying in Algiers, but
he had never regarded the fact as important. Myriads of his school-
fellows had informed him of the soldier's plight, but the dinning
had naturally ended by making him perfectly indifferent. He had
never considered it his affair that a soldier of the Legion lay dying
in Algiers, nor had it appeared to him as a matter for sorrow. It
was less to him than the breaking of a pencil's point.

Now, however, it quaintly came to him as a human, living thing.
It was no longer merely a picture of a few throes in the breast of
a poet, meanwhile drinking tea and warming his feet at the grate;
it was an actuality—stern, mournful, and fine.

The correspondent plainly saw the soldier. He lay on the sand
with his feet out straight and still. While his pale left hand was
upon his chest in an attempt to thwart the going of his life, the
blood came between his fingers. In the far Algerian distance, a city
of low square forms was set against a sky that was faint with the
last sunset hues. The correspondent, plying the oars and dreaming
of the slow and slower movements of the lips of the soldier, was
moved by a profound and perfectly impersonal comprehension.
He was sorry for the soldier of the Legion who lay dying in Algiers.

The thing which had followed the boat and waited had evidently
grown bored at the delay. There was no longer to be heard the
slash of the cutwater, and there was no longer the flame of the long
trail. The light in the north still glimmered, but it was apparently
no nearer to the boat. Sometimes the boom of the surf rang in the
correspondent's ears, and he turned the craft seaward then and
rowed harder. Southward, some one had evidently built a watch-
fire on the beach. It was too low and too far to be seen, but it made
a shimmering, roseate reflection upon the bluff in back of it, and
this could be discerned from the boat. The wind came stronger,

and sometimes a wave suddenly raged out like a mountain cat, and there was to be seen the sheen and sparkle of a broken crest.

The captain, in the bow, moved on his water-jar and sat erect. "Pretty long night," he observed to the correspondent. He looked at the shore. "Those lifesaving people take their time."

"Did you see that shark playing around?"

"Yes, I saw him. He was a big fellow, all right."

"Wish I had known you were awake."

Later the correspondent spoke into the bottom of the boat. "Billie!" There was a slow and gradual disentanglement. "Billie, will you spell me?"

"Sure," said the oiler.

As soon as the correspondent touched the cold, comfortable sea-water in the bottom of the boat and had huddled close to the cook's life belt he was deep in sleep, despite the fact that his teeth played all the popular airs. This sleep was so good to him that it was but a moment before he heard a voice call his name in a tone that demonstrated the last stages of exhaustion. "Will you spell me?"

"Sure, Billie."

The light in the north had mysteriously vanished, but the correspondent took his course from the wide-awake captain.

Later in the night they took the boat farther out to sea, and the captain directed the cook to take one oar at the stern and keep the boat facing the seas. He was to call out if he should hear the thunder of the surf. This plan enabled the oiler and the correspondent to get respite together. "We'll give those boys a chance to get into shape again," said the captain. They curled down and, after a few preliminary chatterings and trembles, slept once more the dead sleep. Neither knew they had bequeathed to the cook the company of another shark, or perhaps the same shark.

As the boat caroused on the waves, spray occasionally bumped over the side and gave them a fresh soaking, but this had no power to break their repose. The ominous slash of the wind and the water affected them as it would have affected mummies.

"Boys," said the cook, with the notes of every reluctance in his voice, "she's drifted in pretty close. I guess one of you had better take her to sea again." The correspondent, aroused, heard the crash of the toppled crests.

As he was rowing, the captain gave him some whisky-and-water, and this steadied the chills out of him. "If I ever get ashore and anybody shows me even a photograph of an oar—"

At last there was a short conversation.

"Billie!—Billie, will you spell me?"

"Sure," said the oiler.

When the correspondent again opened his eyes, the sea and the sky were each of the gray hue of the dawning. Later, carmine and gold was painted upon the waters. The morning appeared finally, in its splendor, with a sky of pure blue, and the sunlight flamed on the tips of the waves.

On the distant dunes were set many little black cottages, and a tall white windmill reared above them. No man, nor dog, nor bicycle appeared on the beach. The cottages might have formed a deserted village.

The voyagers scanned the shore. A conference was held in the boat. "Well," said the captain, "if no help is coming, we might better try a run through the surf right away. If we stay out here much longer we will be too weak to do anything for ourselves at all." The others silently acquiesced in this reasoning. The boat was headed for the beach. The correspondent wondered if none ever ascended the tall wind-tower, and if then they never looked seaward. This tower was a giant, standing with its back to the plight of the ants. It represented in a degree, to the correspondent, the serenity of nature amid the struggles of the individual—nature in the wind, and nature in the vision of men. She did not seem cruel to him then, nor beneficent, nor treacherous, nor wise. But she was indifferent, flatly indifferent. It is, perhaps, plausible that a man in this situation, impressed with the unconcern of the universe, should see the innumerable flaws of his life, and have them taste wickedly in his mind, and wish for another chance. A distinction between right and wrong seems absurdly clear to him, then, in this new ignorance of the grave-edge, and he understands that if he were given another opportunity he would mend his conduct and his words, and be better and brighter during an introduction or at a tea.

"Now, boys," said the captain, "she is going to swamp sure. All we can do is to work her in as far as possible, and then when she swamps, pile out and scramble for the beach. Keep cool now, and don't jump until she swamps sure."

The oiler took the oars. Over his shoulders he scanned the surf. "Captain," he said, "I think I'd better bring her about and keep her head-on to the seas and back her in."

"All right, Billie," said the captain. "Back her in." The oiler swung the boat then, and, seated in the stern, the cook and the correspondent were obliged to look over their shoulders to contemplate the lonely and indifferent shore.

The monstrous inshore rollers heaved the boat high until the men were again enabled to see the white sheets of water scudding up the slanted beach. "We won't get in very close," said the captain. Each time a man could wrest his attention from the rollers, he turned his glance toward the shore, and in the expression of the eyes during this contemplation there was a singular quality. The correspondent, observing the others, knew that they were not afraid, but the full meaning of their glances was shrouded.

As for himself, he was too tired to grapple fundamentally with the fact. He tried to coerce his mind into thinking of it, but the mind was dominated at this time by the muscles, and the muscles said they did not care. It merely occurred to him that if he should drown it would be a shame.

There were no hurried words, no pallor, no plain agitation. The men simply looked at the shore. "Now, remember to get well clear of the boat when you jump," said the captain.

Seaward the crest of a roller suddenly fell with a thunderous crash, and the long white comber came roaring down upon the boat.

"Steady now," said the captain. The men were silent. They turned their eyes from the shore to the comber and waited. The boat slid up the incline, leaped at the furious top, bounced over it, and swung down the long back of the wave. Some water had been shipped, and the cook bailed it out.

But the next crest crashed also. The tumbling, boiling flood of white water caught the boat and whirled it almost perpendicular. Water swarmed in from all sides. The correspondent had his hands on the gunwale at this time, and when the water entered at that place he swiftly withdrew his fingers, as if he objected to wetting them.

The little boat, drunken with this weight of water, reeled and snuggled deeper into the sea.

"Bail her out, cook! Bail her out!" said the captain.

"All right, Captain," said the cook.

"Now, boys, the next one will do for us sure," said the oiler. "Mind to jump clear of the boat."

The third wave moved forward, huge, furious, implacable. It fairly swallowed the dinghy, and almost simultaneously the men tumbled into the sea. A piece of life belt had lain in the bottom of the boat, and as the correspondent went overboard he held this to his chest with his left hand.

The January water was icy, and he reflected immediately that it was colder than he had expected to find it off the coast of Florida. This appeared to his dazed mind as a fact important enough to be noted at the time. The coldness of the water was sad; it was tragic. This fact was somehow mixed and confused with his opinion of his own situation, so that it seemed almost a proper reason for tears. The water was cold.

When he came to the surface he was conscious of little but the noisy water. Afterward he saw his companions in the sea. The oiler was ahead in the race. He was swimming strongly and rapidly. Off to the correspondent's left, the cook's great white and corked back bulged out of the water; and in the rear the captain was hanging with his one good hand to the keel of the overturned dinghy.

There is a certain immovable quality to a shore, and the correspondent wondered at it amid the confusion of the sea.

It seemed also very attractive; but the correspondent knew that it was a long journey, and he paddled leisurely. The piece of life preserver lay under him, and sometimes he whirled down the incline of a wave as if he were on a hand-sled.

But finally he arrived at a place in the sea where travel was beset with difficulty. He did not pause swimming to inquire what manner of current had caught him, but there his progress ceased. The shore was set before him like a bit of scenery on a stage, and he looked at it and understood with his eyes each detail of it.

As the cook passed, much farther to the left, the captain was calling to him, "Turn over on your back, cook! Turn over on your back and use the oar."

"All right, sir." The cook turned on his back, and, paddling with an oar, went ahead as if he were a canoe.

Presently the boat also passed to the left of the correspondent, with the captain clinging with one hand to the keel. He would have appeared like a man raising himself to look over a board fence if it were not for the extraordinary gymnastics of the boat. The correspondent marvelled that the captain could still hold to it.

They passed on nearer to shore—the oiler, the cook, the captain—and following them went the water-jar, bouncing gaily over the seas.

The correspondent remained in the grip of this strange new enemy—a current. The shore, with its white slope of sand and its green bluff topped with little silent cottages, was spread like a picture before him. It was very near to him then, but he was impressed as one who, in a gallery, looks at a scene from Brittany or Algiers.

He thought: "I'm going to drown? Can it be possible? Can it be possible? Can it be possible?" Perhaps an individual must consider his own death to be the final phenomenon of nature.

But later a wave perhaps whirled him out of this small deadly current, for he found suddenly that he could again make progress toward the shore. Later still he was aware that the captain, clinging with one hand to the keel of the dinghy, had his face turned away from the shore and toward him, and was calling his name. "Come to the boat! Come to the boat!"

In his struggle to reach the captain and the boat, he reflected that when one gets properly wearied, drowning must really be a comfortable arrangement—a cessation of hostilities accompanied by a large degree of relief; and he was glad of it, for the main thing in his mind for some moments had been horror of the temporary agony. He did not wish to be hurt.

Presently he saw a man running along the shore. He was undressing with most remarkable speed. Coat, trousers, shirt, everything flew magically off him.

"Come to the boat!" called the captain.

"All right, Captain." As the correspondent paddled, he saw the captain let himself down to bottom and leave the boat. Then the correspondent performed his one little marvel of the voyage. A large wave caught him and flung him with ease and supreme speed completely over the boat and far beyond it. It struck him even then as an event in gymnastics and a true miracle of the sea. An overturned boat in the surf is not a plaything to a swimming man.

The correspondent arrived in water that reached only to his waist, but his condition did not enable him to stand for more than a moment. Each wave knocked him into a heap, and the undertow pulled at him.

Then he saw the man who had been running and undressing, and undressing and running, come bounding into the water. He dragged ashore the cook, and then waded toward the captain; but the captain waved him away and sent him to the correspondent. He was naked—naked as a tree in winter; but a halo was about his head, and he shone like a saint. He gave a strong pull, and a long drag, and a bully heave at the correspondent's hand. The correspondent, schooled in the minor formulæ, said, "Thanks, old man." But suddenly the man cried, "What's that?" He pointed a swift finger. The correspondent said, "Go."

In the shallows, face downward, lay the oiler. His forehead touched sand that was periodically, between each wave, clear of the sea.

The correspondent did not know all that transpired afterward. When he achieved safe ground he fell, striking the sand with each particular part of his body. It was as if he had dropped from a roof, but the thud was grateful to him.

It seems that instantly the beach was populated with men with blankets, clothes, and flasks, and women with coffee-pots and all the remedies sacred to their minds. The welcome of the land to the men from the sea was warm and generous; but a still and dripping shape was carried slowly up the beach, and the land's welcome for it could only be the different and sinister hospitality of the grave.

When it came night, the white waves paced to and fro in the moonlight, and the wind brought the sound of the great sea's voice to the men on the shore, and they felt that they could then be interpreters.

What is the finest Christmas present
you could give your lover?

The Gift of the Magi

O. HENRY (1862–1910)

Best know by his pen name, William Sydney Porter drew upon an adventurous career for his whirligig stories of "life's little ironies."

He was born in Greensboro, North Carolina. His father was a doctor who spent most of his time trying to invent a perpetual-motion water wheel; his mother died when the boy was only three. Young Bill left school at fifteen and worked for five years in an uncle's drug store. He went to Texas in 1882 and for two years lived on a ranch, a setting that is later found in his stories.

Thereafter he lived in Austin, Texas, a small but lively town, and worked as clerk, draftsman, and bank teller. He had married and had begun to contribute sketches and stories to various newspapers, and in 1894 he resigned from the bank and spent all his time on a humorous weekly, The Rolling Stone, which failed after a year.

He was summoned back to Austin in 1896 to stand trial for alleged embezzlement of funds dur-

ing his former tellership in the bank. Had he returned, it is likely that he would have been ac-
quitted, for there were only slight irregularities in
his accounts. But in a moment of panic he fled to
New Orleans and thence to Honduras. His life as
a fugitive in Central America was drawn upon for
his first published book, Cabbages and Kings
(1904). He traveled with Al Jennings, famous out-
law, to South America and Mexico.

News that his wife was fatally ill brought Porter
back to Austin, where his trial resulted in a five-year
sentence to the Federal Ward of the Ohio State
Penitentiary. This term was later reduced for
exemplary behavior. He worked in the prison
pharmacy, slept in comfort in the hospital, and occasionally roamed the streets at night. He was allowed to write and sell stories written in the penitentiary (his famous pseudonym may have been
taken from the name of a prison guard), and he
collected many stories from his fellow prisoners,
among whom was Al Jennings. One of these stories
was later adapted as the play Alias Jimmy Valen-
tine.

O. Henry was released in 1901, and a year later
arrived in New York, whose slangy laureate he was
to become. He fell in love with "Bagdad-on-the-
Subway," as he called it, and thereafter, like a
caliph in disguise, haunted the streets and parks of
the city and drew a thousand types of humanity
into his net. His output of stories was great—his
collected short pieces run to twelve volumes—but
most of them were written under threats of editors
who had paid for these popular stories in advance.

In the last decade of his life, he turned out his
shelf of short stories, most of them on the ingenious formula which he made his own. The uncon-

ventional twist of his endings long ago became a tiresome convention, however, and today it is hard to see how a generation of readers could devour with delight each O. Henry volume as it appeared. His heavy use of current slang also dated his writing. The warmth of his heart and his love for Everyman—anybody in any street might be the hero or heroine of an O. Henry tale—have preserved many of his stories for those who enjoy his comic irony. The Society of Arts and Sciences founded in 1918 an annual O. Henry Memorial Award for the best American short story.

"The Gift of the Magi" first appeared in the New York Sunday World, December 10, 1905, and was first collected in The Four Million (1906).

ONE DOLLAR and eighty-seven cents. That was all. And sixty cents of it was in pennies. Pennies saved one and two at a time by bulldozing the grocer and the vegetable man and the butcher until one's cheeks burned with the silent imputation of parsimony that such close dealing implied. Three times Della counted it. One dollar and eighty-seven cents. And the next day would be Christmas.

There was clearly nothing to do but flop down on the shabby little couch and howl. So Della did it. Which instigates the moral reflection that life is made up of sobs, sniffles, and smiles, with sniffles predominating.

While the mistress of the home is gradually subsiding from the first stage to the second, take a look at the home. A furnished flat at $8 per week. It did not exactly beggar description, but it certainly had that word on the lookout for the mendicancy squad.

In the vestibule below was a letterbox into which no letter would go, and an electric button from which no mortal finger could coax a ring. Also appertaining thereunto was a card bearing the name "Mr. James Dillingham Young."

The "Dillingham" had been flung to the breeze during a former period of prosperity when its possessor was being paid $30 per week. Now, when the income was shrunk to $20, the letters of "Dillingham" looked blurred, as though they were thinking seriously of contracting to a modest and unassuming D. But whenever Mr. James Dillingham Young came home and reached his flat above, he was called "Jim" and greatly hugged by Mrs. James Dillingham Young, already introduced to you as Della. Which is all very good.

Della finished her cry and attended to her cheeks with the powder rag. She stood by the window and looked out dully at a gray cat walking a gray fence in a gray backyard. Tomorrow would be Christmas Day and she had only $1.87 with which to buy Jim a present. She had been saving every penny she could for months, with this result. Twenty dollars a week doesn't go far. Expenses had been greater than she had calculated. They always are. Only $1.87 to buy a present for Jim. Her Jim. Many a happy hour she had spent planning for something nice for him. Something fine and rare and sterling—something just a little bit near to being worthy of the honor of being owned by Jim.

There was a pier glass between the windows of the room. Perhaps you have seen a pier glass in an $8 flat. A very thin and very agile person may, by observing his reflection in a rapid sequence of longitudinal strips, obtain a fairly accurate conception of his looks. Della, being slender, had mastered the art.

Suddenly she whirled from the window and stood before the glass. Her eyes were shining brilliantly, but her face had lost its color within twenty seconds. Rapidly she pulled down her hair and let it fall to its full length.

Now, there were two possessions of the James Dillingham Youngs in which they both took a mighty pride. One was Jim's gold watch that had been his father's and his grandfather's. The other was

Della's hair. Had the Queen of Sheba lived in the flat across the airshaft, Della would have let her hair hang out the window some day to dry just to depreciate Her Majesty's jewels and gifts. Had King Solomon been the janitor, with all his treasures piled up in the basement, Jim would have pulled out his watch every time he passed, just to see him pluck at his beard from envy.

So now Della's beautiful hair fell about her rippling and shining like a cascade of brown waters. It reached below her knee and made itself almost a garment for her. And then she did it up again nervously and quickly. Once she faltered for a minute and stood still while a tear or two splashed on the worn red carpet.

On went her old brown jacket; on went her old brown hat. With a whirl of skirts and with the brilliant sparkle still in her eyes, she fluttered out the door and down the stairs to the street.

Where she stopped the sign read: "Mme. Sofronie. Hair Goods of All Kinds." One flight up Della ran, and collected herself, panting. Madame, large, too white, chilly, hardly looked the "Sofronie."

"Will you buy my hair?" asked Della.

"I buy hair," said Madame. "Take yer hat off and let's have a sight at the looks of it."

Down rippled the brown cascade.

"Twenty dollars," said Madame, lifting the mass with a practiced hand.

"Give it to me quick," said Della.

Oh, and the next two hours tripped by on rosy wings. Forget the hashed metaphor. She was ransacking the stores for Jim's present.

She found it at last. It surely had been made for Jim and no one else. There was no other like it in any of the stores, and she had turned all of them inside out. It was a platinum fob chain simple and chaste in design, properly proclaiming its value by substance alone and not by meretricious ornamentation—as all good things should do. It was even worthy of The Watch. As soon as she saw it she knew that it must be Jim's. It was like him. Quietness and value—the description applied to both. Twenty-one dollars they took from her for it, and she hurried home with the 87 cents. With that chain on his watch Jim might be properly anxious about the time in any company. Grand as the watch was, he sometimes looked at it on the sly on account of the old leather strap that he used in place of a chain.

When Della reached home her intoxication gave way a little to prudence and reason. She got out her curling irons and lighted the gas and went to work repairing the ravages made by generosity added to love. Which is always a tremendous task, dear friends— a mammoth task.

Within forty minutes her head was covered with tiny, close-lying curls that made her look wonderfully like a truant schoolboy. She looked at her reflection in the mirror long, carefully, and critically.

"If Jim doesn't kill me," she said to herself, "before he takes a second look at me, he'll say I look like a Coney Island chorus girl. But what could I do—oh! what could I do with a dollar and eighty-seven cents?"

At 7 o'clock the coffee was made and the frying pan was on the back of the stove hot and ready to cook the chops.

Jim was never late. Della doubled the fob chain in her hand and sat on the corner of the table near the door that he always entered. Then she heard his step on the stair away down on the first flight, and she turned white for just a moment. She had a habit of saying little silent prayers about the simplest everyday things, and now she whispered: "Please God, make him think I am still pretty."

The door opened and Jim stepped in and closed it. He looked thin and very serious. Poor fellow, he was only twenty-two—and to be burdened with a family! He needed a new overcoat and he was without gloves.

Jim stepped inside the door, as immovable as a setter at the scent of quail. His eyes were fixed upon Della, and there was an expression in them that she could not read, and it terrified her. It was not anger, nor surprise, nor disapproval, nor horror, nor any of the sentiments that she had been prepared for. He simply stared at her fixedly with that peculiar expression on his face.

Della wriggled off the table and went for him.

"Jim, darling," she cried, "don't look at me that way. I had my hair cut off and sold it because I couldn't have lived through Christmas without giving you a present. It'll grow out again—you won't mind, will you? I just had to do it. My hair grows awfully fast. Say 'Merry Christmas!', Jim, and let's be happy. You don't know what a nice— what a beautiful, nice gift I've got for you."

"You've cut off your hair?" asked Jim, laboriously, as if he had not arrived at that patent fact yet even after the hardest mental labor.

"Cut it off and sold it," said Della. "Don't you like me just as well, anyhow? I'm me without my hair, ain't I?"

Jim looked about the room curiously.

"You say your hair is gone?" he said, with an air almost of idiocy.

"You needn't look for it," said Della. "It's sold, I tell you—sold and gone, too. It's Christmas Eve, boy. Be good to me, for it went for you. Maybe the hairs of my head were numbered," she went on with a sudden, serious sweetness, "but nobody could ever count my love for you. Shall I put the chops on, Jim?"

Out of his trance Jim seemed quickly to wake. He enfolded his Della. For ten seconds let us regard with discreet scrutiny some inconsequential object in the other direction. Eight dollars a week or a million a year—what is the difference? A mathematician or a wit would give you the wrong answer. The magi brought valuable gifts, but that was not among them. This dark assertion will be illuminated later on.

Jim drew a package from his overcoat pocket and threw it upon the table.

"Don't make any mistake, Dell," he said, "about me. I don't think there's anything in the way of a haircut or a shave or a shampoo that could make me like my girl any less. But if you'll unwrap that package you may see why you had me going a while at first."

White fingers and nimble tore at the string and paper. And then an ecstatic scream of joy; and then, alas! a quick feminine change to hysterical tears and wails, necessitating the immediate employment of all the comforting powers of the lord of the flat.

For there lay The Combs—the set of combs, side and back, that Della had worshiped for long in a Broadway window. Beautiful combs, pure tortoise shell, with jeweled rims—just the shade to wear in the beautiful vanished hair. They were expensive combs, she knew, and her heart had simply craved and yearned over them without the least hope of possession. And now, they were hers, but the tresses that should have adorned the coveted adornments were gone.

But she hugged them to her bosom, and at length she was able to look up with dim eyes and a smile and say: "My hair grows so fast, Jim!"

And then Della leaped up like a little singed cat and cried, "Oh, oh!"

Jim had not yet seen his beautiful present. She held it out to him eagerly upon her open palm. The dull precious metal seemed to flash with a reflection of her bright and ardent spirit.

"Isn't it a dandy, Jim? I hunted all over town to find it. You'll have to look at the time a hundred times a day now. Give me your watch. I want to see how it looks on it."

Instead of obeying, Jim tumbled down on the couch and put his hands under the back of his head and smiled.

"Dell," said he, "let's put our Christmas presents away and keep 'em a while. They're too nice to use just at present. I sold the watch to get the money to buy your combs. And now suppose you put the chops on."

The magi, as you know, were wise men—wonderfully wise men—who brought gifts to the Babe in the manger. They invented the art of giving Christmas presents. Being wise, their gifts were no doubt wise ones, possibly bearing the privilege of exchange in case of duplication. And here I have lamely related to you the uneventful chronicle of two foolish children in a flat who most unwisely sacrificed for each other the greatest treasures of their house. But in a last word to the wise of these days let it be said that of all who give gifts these two were the wisest. Of all who give and receive gifts, such as they are wisest. Everywhere they are wisest. They are the magi.

*What was the real trouble when this
boy could not get along in school?*

Paul's Case

WILLA CATHER (1876–1947)

Willa Sibert Cather believed that the first two
years she spent as a child on the Western frontier,
where her parents moved from her birthplace at
Winchester, Virginia, when she was nine, were the
most important to her literary career. She felt that
the most vivid re-creation of experience depends
on recollection of the views seen with the fresh
eyes of childhood. Her family had English, Irish,
and Alsatian forebears, and when her father settled
on a ranch near Red Cloud, Nebraska, she took
quite naturally to the pioneer existence of the families of Scandinavians, Germans, Bohemians, and
French-Canadians that dwelt near them on this
harsh prairie.

She lived outdoors much, and studied at home
or with neighbors, since no school was near. She
first attended classes regularly when the family
moved to town and she entered high school. Her
favorite reading, the Latin and English classics, is
reflected in the chaste, classic balance and feeling

for the past that show in her novels and stories.

During her years at the University of Nebraska, from which she graduated in 1895, she wrote stories of immigrant life. Afterward she was telegraph editor and dramatic critic of the Pittsburgh Leader, then head of the Allegheny High School, and from 1904 to 1911 served on the staff of McClure's Magazine, most of the time as managing editor. The success of her stories enabled her to resign her post and indulge, as a free-lance writer, her taste for travel, music, and New York life. She never married.

Six universities gave her honorary degrees. One of her novels won the Pulitzer prize for 1922, and another in 1933 was awarded the French Prix Fémina Américaine. She was elected to the American Academy of Arts and Letters in 1938.

Her short stories are collected in The Troll Garden (1905), Youth and the Bright Medusa (1920), and Obscure Destinies (1932). Perhaps her best stories, like "Paul's Case" and "The Sculptor's Funeral," are those dealing, in the manner of her model Henry James, with the plight of the unappreciated and rejected artist by the "practical" pioneering temperament of America.

"Paul's Case" first appeared in McClure's Magazine in 1905, and was collected in The Troll Garden in the same year.

IT WAS PAUL'S AFTERNOON to appear before the faculty of the Pittsburgh High School to account for his various misdemeanors. He had been suspended a week ago, and his father had called at the Principal's office and confessed his perplexity about his son. Paul entered the faculty room suave and smiling. His clothes were a trifle outgrown, and the tan velvet on the collar of his open overcoat was frayed and worn; but for all that there was something of the dandy about him, and he wore an opal pin in his neatly knotted black four-in-hand, and a red carnation in his buttonhole. This latter adornment the faculty somehow felt was not properly significant of the contrite spirit befitting a boy under the ban of suspension.

Paul was tall for his age and very thin, with high, cramped shoulders and a narrow chest. His eyes were remarkable for a certain hysterical brilliancy, and he continually used them in a conscious, theatrical sort of way, peculiarly offensive in a boy. The pupils were abnormally large, as though he were addicted to belladonna, but there was a glassy glitter about them which that drug does not produce.

When questioned by the Principal as to why he was there, Paul stated, politely enough, that he wanted to come back to school. This was a lie, but Paul was quite accustomed to lying; found it, indeed, indispensable for overcoming friction. His teachers were asked to state their respective charges against him, which they did with such a rancor and aggrievedness as evinced that this was not a usual case. Disorder and impertinence were among the offenses named, yet each of his instructors felt that it was scarcely possible to put into words the real cause of the trouble, which lay in a sort of hysterically defiant manner of the boy's; in the contempt which they all knew he felt for them, and which he seemingly made not the least effort to conceal. Once, when he had been making a synopsis of a paragraph at the blackboard, his English teacher had stepped to his side and attempted to guide his hand. Paul had started back with a shudder and thrust his hands violently behind him. The astonished woman could scarcely have been more hurt and embarrassed had he struck at her. The insult was so involuntary and definitely personal as to be unforgettable. In one way and another, he had made all his teachers, men and women alike, conscious of the same feeling of physical aversion. In one class he habitually sat with his hand shading his eyes; in another he always looked out of the window during the recitation; in another he made a running commentary on the lecture, with humorous intent.

His teachers felt this afternoon that his whole attitude was symbolized by his shrug and his flippantly red carnation flower, and they fell upon him without mercy, his English teacher leading the pack. He stood through it smiling, his pale lips parted over his white teeth. (His lips were continually twitching, and he had a habit of raising his eyebrows that was contemptuous and irritating to the last degree.) Older boys than Paul had broken down and shed tears under that ordeal, but his set smile did not once desert him, and his only sign of discomfort was the nervous trembling of the fingers that toyed with the buttons of his overcoat, and an occasional jerking of the other hand which held his hat. Paul was always smiling, always glancing about him, seeming to feel that people might be watching him and trying to detect something. This conscious expression, since it was as far as possible from boyish mirthfulness, was usually attributed to insolence or "smartness."

As the inquisition proceeded, one of his instructors repeated an impertinent remark of the boy's, and the Principal asked him whether he thought that a courteous speech to make to a woman. Paul shrugged his shoulders slightly and his eyebrows twitched.

"I don't know," he replied. "I didn't mean to be polite or impolite, either. I guess it's a sort of way I have, of saying things regardless."

The Principal asked him whether he didn't think that a way it would be well to get rid of. Paul grinned and said he guessed so. When he was told that he could go, he bowed gracefully and went out. His bow was like a repetition of the scandalous red carnation.

His teachers were in despair, and his drawing master voiced the feeling of them all when he declared there was something about the boy which none of them understood. He added: "I don't really believe that smile of his comes altogether from insolence; there's something sort of haunted about it. The boy is not strong, for one thing. There is something wrong about the fellow."

The drawing master had come to realize that, in looking at Paul, one saw only his white teeth and the forced animation of his eyes. One warm afternoon the boy had gone to sleep at his drawing board, and his master had noted with amazement what a white, blue-veined face it was; drawn and wrinkled like an old man's about the eyes, the lips twitching even in his sleep.

His teachers left the building dissatisfied and unhappy; humiliated to have felt so vindictive toward a mere boy, to have uttered this feeling in cutting terms, and to have set each other on, as it were, in the gruesome game of intemperate reproach. One of them remembered having seen a miserable street cat set at bay by a ring of tormentors.

As for Paul, he ran down the hill whistling the Soldiers' Chorus from *Faust*, looking wildly behind him now and then to see whether some of his teachers were not there to witness his light-heartedness. As it was now late in the afternoon and Paul was on duty that evening as usher at Carnegie Hall, he decided that he would not go home to supper.

When he reached the concert hall the doors were not yet open. It was chilly outside, and he decided to go up into the picture gallery—always deserted at this hour—where there were some of Raffelli's gay studies of Paris streets and an airy blue Venetian scene or two that always exhilarated him. He was delighted to find no one in the gallery but the old guard, who sat in the corner, a newspaper on his knee, a black patch over one eye and the other closed. Paul possessed himself of the place and walked confidently up and down, whistling under his breath. After a while he sat down before a blue Rico and lost himself. When he bethought him to look at his watch, it was after seven o'clock, and he rose with a start and ran downstairs, making a face at Augustus Cæsar, peering out from the east-room, and an evil gesture at the Venus of Milo as he passed her on the stairway.

When Paul reached the ushers' dressing room half a dozen boys were there already, and he began excitedly to tumble into his uniform. It was one of the few that at all approached fitting, and Paul thought it very becoming—though he knew the tight, straight coat accentuated his narrow chest, about which he was exceedingly sensitive. He was always excited while he dressed, twanging all over to the tuning of the strings and the preliminary flourishes of the horns in the music-room; but tonight he seemed quite beside himself, and he teased and plagued the boys until, telling him that he was crazy, they put him down on the floor and sat on him.

Somewhat calmed by his suppression, Paul dashed out to the front of the house to seat the early comers. He was a model usher. Gracious and smiling he ran up and down the aisles. Nothing was too much trouble for him; he carried messages and brought programs as though it were his greatest pleasure in life, and all the people in his section thought him a charming boy, feeling that he remembered and admired them. As the house filled, he grew more and more vivacious and animated, and the color came to his cheeks and lips. It was very much as though this were a great reception and Paul were the host. Just as the musicians came out to take their places, his English teacher arrived with checks for the seats which a prominent manufacturer had taken for the season. She betrayed some embarrassment when she handed Paul the tickets, and a *hauteur* which subsequently made her feel very foolish. Paul was startled for a moment, and had the feeling of wanting to put her out; what business had she here among all these fine people and gay colors? He looked her over and decided that she was not appropriately dressed and must be a fool to sit downstairs in such togs. The tickets had probably been sent her out of kindness, he reflected, as he put down a seat for her, and she had about as much right to sit there as he had.

When the symphony began Paul sank into one of the rear seats with a long sigh of relief, and lost himself as he had done before the Rico. It was not that symphonies, as such, meant anything in particular to Paul, but the first sigh of the instruments seemed to free some hilarious spirit within him; something that struggled there like the Genius in the bottle found by the Arab fisherman. He felt a sudden zest of life; the lights danced before his eyes and the concert hall blazed into unimaginable splendor. When the soprano soloist came on, Paul forgot even the nastiness of his teacher's being there, and gave himself up to the peculiar intoxication such personages always had for him. The soloist chanced to be a German woman, by no means in her first youth, and the mother of many children; but she wore a satin gown and a tiara, and she had that indefinable air of achievement, that world-shine upon her, which always blinded Paul to any possible defects.

After a concert was over, Paul was often irritable and wretched until he got to sleep,—and tonight he was even more than usually restless. He had the feeling of not being able to let down; of its being impossible to give up this delicious excitement which was the only thing that could be called living at all. During the last number he withdrew and, after hastily changing his clothes in the dressing room, slipped out to the side door where the singer's carriage stood. Here he began pacing rapidly up and down the walk, waiting to see her come out.

Over yonder the Schenley, in its vacant stretch, loomed big and square through the fine rain, the windows of its twelve stories glowing like those of a lighted cardboard house under a Christmas tree. All the actors and singers of any importance stayed there when they were in the city, and a number of the big manufacturers of the place lived there in the winter. Paul had often hung about the hotel, watching the people go in and out, longing to enter and leave schoolmasters and dull care behind him forever.

At last the singer came out, accompanied by the conductor, who helped her into her carriage and closed the door with a cordial *auf wiedersehen*,—which set Paul to wondering whether she were not an old sweetheart of his. Paul followed the carriage over to the hotel, walking so rapidly as not to be far from the entrance when the singer alighted and disappeared behind the swinging glass doors which were opened by a Negro in a tall hat and a long coat. In the moment that the door was ajar, it seemed to Paul that he, too, entered. He seemed to feel himself go after her up the steps, into the warm, lighted building, into an exotic, a tropical world of shiny, glistening surfaces and basking ease. He reflected upon the mysterious dishes that were brought into the dining room, the green bottles in buckets of ice, as he had seen them in the supper party pictures of the Sunday supplement. A quick gust of wind brought the rain down with sudden vehemence, and Paul was startled to find that he was still outside in the slush of the gravel driveway; that his boots were letting in the water and his scanty overcoat was clinging wet about him; that the lights in front of the concert hall were out, and that the rain was driving in sheets between him and the orange glow of the windows above him. There it was, what he wanted—tangibly before him, like the fairy world of a Christmas pantomime; as the rain beat in his face, Paul wondered whether he were destined always to shiver in the black night outside, looking up at it.

He turned and walked reluctantly toward the car tracks. The end had to come some time; his father in his night clothes at the top of the stairs, explanations that did not explain, hastily improvised fictions that were forever tripping him up, his upstairs room and its horrible yellow wallpaper, the creaking bureau with the greasy plush collar-box, and over his painted wooden bed the pictures of George Washington and John Calvin, and the framed motto, "Feed my Lambs," which had been worked in red worsted by his mother, whom Paul could not remember.

Half an hour later, Paul alighted from the Negley Avenue car and went slowly down one of the side streets off the main thoroughfare. It was a highly respectable street, where all the houses were exactly alike, and where business men of moderate means begot and reared large families of children, all of whom went to Sabbath School and learned the shorter catechism, and were interested in arithmetic; all of whom were as exactly alike as their homes, and of a piece with the monotony in which they lived. Paul never went up Cordelia Street without a shudder of loathing. His home was next to the house of the Cumberland minister. He approached it tonight with the nerveless sense of defeat, the hopeless feeling of sinking back forever into ugliness and commonness that he had always had when he came home. The moment he turned into Cordelia Street he felt the waters close above his head. After each of these orgies of living, he experienced all the physical depression which follows a debauch; the loathing of respectable beds, of common food, of a house permeated by kitchen odors; a shuddering repulsion for the flavorless, colorless mass of everyday existence; a morbid desire for cool things and soft lights and fresh flowers.

The nearer he approached the house, the more absolutely unequal Paul felt to the sight of it all; his ugly sleeping chamber; the cold bathroom with the grimy zinc tub, the cracked mirror, the dripping spiggots; his father, at the top of the stairs, his hairy legs sticking out from his nightshirt, his feet thrust into carpet slippers. He was so much later than usual that there would certainly be inquiries and reproaches. Paul stopped short before the door. He felt that he could not be accosted by his father tonight; that he could not toss again on that miserable bed. He would not go in. He would tell his father that he had no carfare, and it was raining so hard he had gone home with one of the boys and stayed all night.

Meanwhile, he was wet and cold. He went around to the back of the house and tried one of the basement windows, found it open, raised it cautiously, and scrambled down the cellar wall to the floor. There he stood, holding his breath, terrified by the noise he had made; but the floor above him was silent, and there was no creak on the stairs. He found a soapbox, and carried it over to the soft ring of light that streamed from the furnace door, and sat down. He was horribly afraid of rats, so he did not try to sleep, but sat looking distrustfully at the dark, still terrified lest he might have awakened his father. In such reactions, after one of the experiences which made days and nights out of the dreary blanks of the calendar, when his senses were deadened, Paul's head was always singularly clear. Suppose his father had heard him getting in at the window and had come down and shot him for a burglar? Then, again, suppose his father had come down, pistol in hand, and he

had cried out in time to save himself, and his father had been hor-
rified to think how nearly he had killed him? Then, again, suppose
a day should come when his father would remember that night, and
wish there had been no warning cry to stay his hand? With this last
supposition Paul entertained himself until daybreak.

The following Sunday was fine; the sodden November chill was
broken by the last flash of autumnal summer. In the morning Paul
had to go to church and Sabbath School, as always. On seasonable
Sunday afternoons the burghers of Cordelia Street usually sat out
on their front "stoops," and talked to their neighbors on the next
stoop, or called to those across the street in neighborly fashion. The
men sat placidly on gay cushions placed upon the steps that led
down to the sidewalk, while the women, in their Sunday "waists,"
sat in rockers on the cramped porches, pretending to be greatly
at their ease. The children played in the streets; there were so
many of them that the place resembled the recreation grounds of a
kindergarten. The men on the steps—all in their shirt sleeves, their
vests unbuttoned—sat with the legs well apart, their stomachs
comfortably protruding, and talked of the prices of things, or told
anecdotes of the sagacity of their various chiefs and overlords. They
occasionally looked over the multitude of squabbling children,
listened affectionately to their high-pitched, nasal voices, smiling to
see their own proclivities reproduced in their offspring, and inter-
spersed their legends of the iron kings with remarks about their
sons' progress at school, their grades in arithmetic, and the amounts
they had saved in their toy banks. On this last Sunday of November,
Paul sat all the afternoon on the lowest step of his stoop, staring
into the street, while his sisters, in their rockers, were talking to the
minister's daughters next door about how many shirtwaists they
had made in the last week, and how many waffles someone had
eaten at the last church supper. When the weather was warm, and
his father was in a particularly jovial frame of mind, the girls made
lemonade, which was always brought out in a red-glass pitcher,
ornamented with forget-me-nots in blue enamel. This the girls
thought very fine, and the neighbors joked about the suspicious
color of the pitcher.

Today Paul's father, on the top step, was talking to a young man who shifted a restless baby from knee to knee. He happened to be the young man who was daily held up to Paul as a model, and after whom it was his father's dearest hope that he would pattern. This young man was of a ruddy complexion, with a compressed, red mouth, and faded, near-sighted eyes, over which he wore thick spectacles, with gold bows that curved about his ears. He was clerk to one of the magnates of a great steel corporation, and was looked upon in Cordelia Street as a young man with a future. There was a story that, some five years ago—he was now barely twenty-six—he had been a trifle "dissipated," but in order to curb his appetites and save the loss of time and strength that a sowing of wild oats might have entailed, he had taken his chief's advice, oft reiterated to his employees, and at twenty-one had married the first woman whom he could persuade to share his fortunes. She happened to be an angular schoolmistress, much older than he, who also wore thick glasses, and who had now borne him four children, all near-sighted, like herself.

The young man was relating how his chief, now cruising in the Mediterranean, kept in touch with all the details of the business, arranging his office hours on his yacht just as though he were at home, and "knocking off work enough to keep two stenographers busy." His father told, in turn, the plan his corporation was considering, of putting in an electric railway plant at Cairo. Paul snapped his teeth; he had an awful apprehension that they might spoil it all before he got there. Yet he rather liked to hear these legends of the iron kings, that were told and retold on Sundays and holidays; these stories of palaces in Venice, yachts on the Mediterranean, and high play at Monte Carlo appealed to his fancy, and he was interested in the triumphs of cash boys who had become famous, though he had no mind for the cash-boy stage.

After supper was over, and he had helped to dry the dishes, Paul nervously asked his father whether he could go to George's to get some help in his geometry, and still more nervously asked for carfare. This latter request he had to repeat, as his father, on principle, did not like to hear requests for money, whether much or little.

He asked Paul whether he could not go to some boy who lived nearer, and told him that he ought not to leave his school work until Sunday; but he gave him the dime. He was not a poor man, but he had a worthy ambition to come up in the world. His only reason for allowing Paul to usher was that he thought a boy ought to be earning a little.

Paul bounded upstairs, scrubbed the greasy odor of the dish-water from his hands with the ill-smelling soap he hated, and then shook over his fingers a few drops of violet water from the bottle he kept hidden in his drawer. He left the house with his geometry conspicuously under his arm, and the moment he got out of Cordelia Street and boarded a downtown car, he shook off the lethargy of two deadening days, and began to live again.

The leading juvenile of the permanent stock company which played at one of the downtown theaters was an acquaintance of Paul's, and the boy had been invited to drop in at the Sunday night rehearsals whenever he could. For more than a year Paul had spent every available moment loitering about Charley Edwards's dressing room. He had won a place among Edwards's following not only because the young actor, who could not afford to employ a dresser, often found him useful, but because he recognized in Paul something akin to what churchmen term "vocation."

It was at the theater and at Carnegie Hall that Paul really lived; the rest was but a sleep and a forgetting. This was Paul's fairy tale, and it had for him all the allurement of a secret love. The moment he inhaled the gassy, painty, dusty odor behind the scenes, he breathed like a prisoner set free, and felt within him the possibility of doing or saying splendid, brilliant things. The moment the cracked orchestra beat out the overture from *Martha*, or jerked at the serenade from *Rigoletto*, all stupid and ugly things slid from him, and his senses were deliciously, yet delicately fired.

Perhaps it was because, in Paul's world, the natural nearly always wore the guise of ugliness, that a certain element of artificiality seemed to him necessary in beauty. Perhaps it was because his experience of life elsewhere was so full of Sabbath School picnics, petty economies, wholesome advice as to how to succeed in life, and the unescapable odors of cooking that he found this existence so alluring, these smartly-clad men and women so attractive, that he was so moved by these starry apple orchards that bloomed perennially under the limelight.

It would be difficult to put it strongly enough how convincingly the stage entrance of that theater was for Paul the actual portal of Romance. Certainly none of the company ever suspected it, least of all Charley Edwards. It was very like the old stories that used to float about London of fabulously rich Jews, who had subterranean halls, with palms, and fountains, and soft lamps and richly apparelled women who never saw the disenchanting light of London day. So, in the midst of that smoke-palled city, enamored of figures and grimy toil, Paul had his secret temple, his wishing-carpet, his bit of blue-and-white Mediterranean shore bathed in perpetual sunshine.

Several of Paul's teachers had a theory that his imagination had been perverted by garish fiction; but the truth was, he scarcely ever read at all. The books at home were not such as would either tempt or corrupt a youthful mind, and as for reading the novels that some of his friends urged upon him—well, he got what he wanted much more quickly from music; any sort of music, from an orchestra to a barrel organ. He needed only the spark, the indescribable thrill that made his imagination master of his senses, and he could make plots and pictures enough of his own. It was equally true that he was not stage-struck—not, at any rate, in the usual acceptation of that expression. He had no desire to become an actor, any more than he had to become a musician. He felt no necessity to do any of these things; what he wanted was to see, to be in the atmosphere, float on the wave of it, to be carried out, blue league after blue league, away from everything.

After a night behind the scenes, Paul found the schoolroom more than ever repulsive; the bare floors and naked walls; the prosy men who never wore frock coats, or violets in their buttonholes; the women with their dull gowns, shrill voices, and pitiful seriousness about prepositions that govern the dative. He could not bear to have the other pupils think, for a moment, that he took these people seriously; he must convey to them that he considered it all trivial, and was there only by way of a joke, anyway. He had autograph pictures of all the members of the stock company which he showed his classmates, telling them the most incredible stories of his familiarity with these people, of his acquaintance with the soloists who came to Carnegie Hall, his suppers with them and the flowers he sent them. When these stories lost their effect, and his audience grew listless, he would bid all the boys good-by, announcing that he was going to travel for a while; going to Naples, to California, to Egypt. Then, next Monday, he would slip back, conscious and nervously smiling; his sister was ill, and he would have to defer his voyage until spring.

Matters went steadily worse with Paul at school. In the itch to let his instructors know how heartily he despised them, and how thoroughly he was appreciated elsewhere, he mentioned once or twice that he had no time to fool with theorems; adding—with a twitch of the eyebrows and a touch of that nervous bravado which so perplexed them—that he was helping the people down at the stock company; they were old friends of his.

The upshot of the matter was that the Principal went to Paul's father, and Paul was taken out of school and put to work. The manager at Carnegie Hall was told to get another usher in his stead; the doorkeeper at the theater was warned not to admit him to the house; and Charley Edwards remorsefully promised the boy's father not to see him again.

The members of the stock company were vastly amused when some of Paul's stories reached them—especially the women. They were hard-working women, most of them supporting indolent husbands or brothers, and they laughed rather bitterly at having stirred the boy to such fervid and florid inventions. They agreed with the faculty and with his father, that Paul's was a bad case.

The eastbound train was plowing through a January snowstorm; the dull dawn was beginning to show gray when the engine whistled a mile out of Newark. Paul started up from the seat where he had lain curled in uneasy slumber, rubbed the breath-misted window glass with his hand, and peered out. The snow was whirling in curling eddies above the white bottom lands, and the drifts lay already deep in the fields and along the fences, while here and there the long dead grass and dried weed stalks protruded black above it. Lights shone from the scattered houses, and a gang of laborers who stood beside the track waved their lanterns.

Paul had slept very little, and he felt grimy and uncomfortable. He had made the all-night journey in a day coach because he was afraid if he took a Pullman he might be seen by some Pittsburgh business man who had noticed him in Denny & Carson's office. When the whistle woke him, he clutched quickly at his breast pocket, glancing about him with an uncertain smile. But the little, clay-bespattered Italians were still sleeping, the slatternly women across the aisle were in open-mouthed oblivion, and even the crumby, crying babies were for the nonce stilled. Paul settled back to struggle with his impatience as best he could.

When he arrived at the Jersey City station, he hurried through his breakfast, manifestly ill at ease and keeping a sharp eye about him. After he reached the Twenty-third Street station, he consulted a cabman, and had himself driven to a men's furnishing establishment which was just opening for the day. He spent upward of two hours there, buying with endless reconsidering and great care. His new street suit he put on in the fitting-room; the frock coat and dress clothes he had bundled into the cab with his new shirts. Then he drove to a hatter's and a shoe house. His next errand was at Tiffany's, where he selected silver-mounted brushes and a scarf-pin. He would not wait to have his silver marked, he said. Lastly, he stopped at a trunk shop on Broadway, and had his purchases packed into various traveling bags.

It was a little after one o'clock when he drove up to the Waldorf, and, after settling with the cabman, went into the office. He registered from Washington; said his mother and father had been abroad, and that he had come down to await the arrival of their steamer. He told his story plausibly and had no trouble, since he offered to pay for them in advance, in engaging his rooms; a sleeping room, sitting room and bath.

Not once, but a hundred times Paul had planned this entry into New York. He had gone over every detail of it with Charley Edwards, and in his scrap book at home there were pages of description about New York hotels, cut from the Sunday papers.

When he was shown to his sitting room on the eighth floor, he saw at a glance that everything was as it should be; there was but one detail in his mental picture that the place did not realize, so he rang for the bell boy and sent him down for flowers. He moved about nervously until the boy returned, putting away his new linen and fingering it delightedly as he did so. When the flowers came, he put them hastily into water, and then tumbled into a hot bath. Presently he came out of his white bathroom, resplendent in his new silk underwear, and playing with the tassels of his red robe. The snow was whirling so fiercely outside his windows that he could scarcely see across the street; but within, the air was deliciously soft and fragrant. He put the violets and jonquils on the tabouret beside the couch, and threw himself down with a long sigh, covering himself with a Roman blanket. He was thoroughly tired; he had been in such haste, he had stood up to such a strain, covered so much ground in the last twenty-four hours, that he wanted to think how it had all come about. Lulled by the sound of the wind, the warm air, and the cool fragrance of the flowers, he sank into deep, drowsy retrospection.

It had been wonderfully simple; when they had shut him out of the theater and concert hall, when they had taken away his bone, the whole thing was virtually determined. The rest was a mere matter of opportunity. The only thing that at all surprised him was his own courage—for he realized well enough that he had always been tormented by fear, a sort of apprehensive dread that, of late years, as the meshes of the lies he had told closed about him, had been pulling the muscles of his body tighter and tighter. Until now, he could not remember a time when he had not been dreading something. Even when he was a little boy, it was always there—behind him, or before, or on either side. There had always been the shadowed corner, the dark place into which he dared not look, but from which something seemed always to be watching him—and Paul had done things that were not pretty to watch, he knew.

But now he had a curious sense of relief, as though he had at last thrown down the gauntlet to the thing in the corner.

Yet it was but a day since he had been sulking in the traces; but yesterday afternoon that he had been sent to the bank with Denny & Carson's deposit, as usual—but this time he was instructed to leave the book to be balanced. There was above two thousand dollars in checks, and nearly a thousand in the bank notes which he had taken from the book and quietly transferred to his pocket. At the bank he had made out a new deposit slip. His nerves had been steady enough to permit of his returning to the office, where he had finished his work and asked for a full day's holiday tomorrow, Saturday, giving a perfectly reasonable pretext. The bankbook, he knew, would not be returned before Monday or Tuesday, and his father would be out of town for the next week. From the time he slipped the bank notes into his pocket until he boarded the night train for New York, he had not known a moment's hesitation.

How astonishingly easy it had all been; here he was, the thing done; and this time there would be no awakening, no figure at the top of the stairs. He watched the snowflakes whirling by his window until he fell asleep.

When he awoke, it was four o'clock in the afternoon. He bounded up with a start; one of his precious days gone already! He spent nearly an hour in dressing, watching every stage of his toilet carefully in the mirror. Everything was quite perfect; he was exactly the kind of boy he had always wanted to be.

When he went downstairs, Paul took a carriage and drove up Fifth Avenue toward the Park. The snow had somewhat abated; carriages and tradesmen's wagons were hurrying soundlessly to and fro in the winter twilight; boys in woolen mufflers were shoveling off the doorsteps; the avenue stages made fine spots of color against the white street. Here and there on the corners whole flower gardens bloomed behind glass windows, against which the snowflakes stuck and melted; violets, roses, carnations, lilies of the valley —somehow vastly more lovely and alluring that they blossomed thus unnaturally in the snow. The Park itself was a wonderful stage winter-piece.

When he returned, the pause of the twilight had ceased, and the tune of the streets had changed. The snow was falling faster, lights streamed from the hotels that reared their many stories fearlessly up into the storm, defying the raging Atlantic winds. A long, black stream of carriages poured down the avenue, intersected here and there by other streams, tending horizontally. There were a score of cabs about the entrance of his hotel, and his driver had to wait. Boys in livery were running in and out of the awning stretched across the sidewalk, up and down the red velvet carpet laid from the door to the street. Above, about, within it all, was the rumble and roar, the hurry and toss of thousands of human beings as hot for pleasure as himself, and on every side of him towered the glaring affirmation of the omnipotence of wealth.

The boy set his teeth and drew his shoulders together in a spasm of realization; the plot of all dramas, the text of all romances, the nerve-stuff of all sensations was whirling about him like the snow-flakes. He burnt like a faggot in a tempest.

When Paul came down to dinner, the music of the orchestra floated up the elevator shaft to greet him. As he stepped into the thronged corridor, he sank back into one of the chairs against the wall to get his breath. The lights, the chatter, the perfumes, the bewildering medley of color—he had, for a moment, the feeling of not being able to stand it. But only for a moment; these were his own people, he told himself. He went slowly about the corridors, through the writing rooms, smoking rooms, reception rooms, as though he were exploring the chambers of an enchanted palace, built and peopled for him alone.

When he reached the dining room he sat down at a table near a window. The flowers, the white linen, the many-colored wine glasses, the gay toilettes of the women, the low popping of corks, the undulating repetitions of the *Blue Danube* from the orchestra, all flooded Paul's dream with bewildering radiance. When the roseate tinge of his champagne was added—that cold, precious, bubbling stuff that creamed and foamed in his glass—Paul wondered that there were honest men in the world at all. This was what all the world was fighting for, he reflected; this was what all the struggle was about. He doubted the reality of his past. Had he ever known a place called Cordelia Street, a place where fagged-looking business men boarded the early car? Mere rivets in a machine they seemed to Paul,—sickening men, with combings of children's hair always hanging to their coats, and the smell of cooking in their clothes. Cordelia Street—ah, that belonged to another time and country! Had he not always been thus, had he not sat here night after night, from as far back as he could remember, looking pensively over just such shimmering textures, and slowly twirling the stem of a glass like this one between his thumb and middle finger? He rather thought he had.

He was not in the least abashed or lonely. He had no especial desire to meet or to know any of these people; all he demanded was the right to look on and conjecture, to watch the pageant. The mere stage properties were all he contended for. Nor was he lonely later in the evening, in his loge at the Opera. He was entirely rid of his nervous misgivings, of his forced aggressiveness, of the imperative desire to show himself different from his surroundings. He felt now that his surroundings explained him. Nobody questioned the purple; he had only to wear it passively. He had only to glance down at his dress coat to reassure himself that here it would be impossible for anyone to humiliate him.

He found it hard to leave his beautiful sitting room to go to bed that night, and sat long watching the raging storm from his turret window. When he went to sleep, it was with the lights turned on in his bedroom; partly because of his old timidity, and partly so that, if he should wake in the night, there would be no wretched moment of doubt, no horrible suspicion of yellow wall paper, or of Washington and Calvin above his bed.

On Sunday morning the city was practically snow-bound. Paul breakfasted late, and in the afternoon he fell in with a wild San Francisco boy, a freshman at Yale, who said he had run down for a "little flyer" over Sunday. The young man offered to show Paul the night side of the town, and the two boys went off together after dinner, not returning to the hotel until seven o'clock the next morning. They had started out in the confiding warmth of a champagne friendship, but their parting in the elevator was singularly cool. The freshman pulled himself together to make his train, and Paul went to bed. He awoke at two o'clock in the afternoon, very thirsty and dizzy, and rang for ice water, coffee, and the Pittsburgh papers.

On the part of the hotel management, Paul excited no suspicion. There was this to be said for him, that he wore his spoils with dignity and in no way made himself conspicuous. His chief greediness lay in his ears and eyes, and his excesses were not offensive ones. His dearest pleasures were the gray winter twilights in his sitting room; his quiet enjoyment of his flowers, his clothes, his wide divan, his cigarette and his sense of power. He could not remember a time when he had felt so at peace with himself. The mere release from the necessity of petty lying, lying every day and every day, restored his self-respect. He had never lied for pleasure, even at school; but to make himself noticed and admired, to assert his difference from other Cordelia Street boys; and he felt a good deal more manly, more honest, even, now that he had no need for boastful pretensions, now that he could, as his actor friends used to say, "dress the part." It was characteristic that remorse did not occur to him. His golden days went by without a shadow, and he made each as perfect as he could.

On the eighth day after his arrival in New York, he found the whole affair exploited in the Pittsburgh papers, exploited with a wealth of detail which indicated that local news of a sensational nature was at a low ebb. The firm of Denny & Carson announced that the boy's father had refunded the full amount of his theft, and that they had no intention of prosecuting. The Cumberland minister had been interviewed, and expressed his hope of yet reclaiming the motherless lad, and Paul's Sabbath School teacher declared that she would spare no effort to that end. The rumor had reached Pittsburgh that the boy had been seen in a New York hotel, and his father had gone East to find him and bring him home.

Paul had just come in to dress for dinner; he sank into a chair, weak in the knees, and clasped his head in his hands. It was to be worse than jail, even; the tepid waters of Cordelia Street were to close over him finally and forever. The gray monotony stretched before him in hopeless, unrelieved years; Sabbath School, Young People's Meeting, the yellow-papered room, the damp dishtowels; it all rushed back upon him with sickening vividness. He had the old feeling that the orchestra had suddenly stopped, the sinking sensation that the play was over. The sweat broke out on his face, and he sprang to his feet, looked about him with his white, conscious smile, and winked at himself in the mirror. With something of the childish belief in miracles with which he had so often gone to class, all his lessons unlearned, Paul dressed and dashed whistling down the corridor to the elevator.

He had no sooner entered the dining room and caught the measure of the music, than his remembrance was lightened by his old elastic power of claiming the moment, mounting with it, and finding it all sufficient. The glare and glitter about him, the mere scenic accessories had again, and for the last time, their old potency. He would show himself that he was game, he would finish the thing splendidly. He doubted, more than ever, the existence of Cordelia Street, and for the first time he drank his wine recklessly. Was he not, after all, one of these fortunate beings? Was he not still himself, and in his own place? He drummed a nervous accompaniment to the music and looked about him, telling himself over and over that it had paid.

He reflected drowsily, to the swell of the violin and the chill sweetness of his wine, that he might have done it more wisely. He might have caught an outbound steamer and been well out of their clutches before now. But the other side of the world had seemed too far away and too uncertain then; he could not have waited for it; his need had been too sharp. If he had to choose over again, he would do the same thing tomorrow. He looked affectionately about the dining room, now gilded with a soft mist. Ah, it had paid indeed!

Paul was awakened next morning by a painful throbbing in his head and feet. He had thrown himself across the bed without undressing, and had slept with his shoes on. His limbs and hands were lead heavy, and his tongue and throat were parched. There came upon him one of those fateful attacks of clear-headedness that never occurred except when he was physically exhausted and his nerves hung loose. He lay still and closed his eyes and let the tide of realities wash over him.

His father was in New York; "stopping at some joint or other," he told himself. The memory of successive summers on the front stoop fell upon him like a weight of black water. He had not a hundred dollars left; and he knew now, more than ever, that money was everything, the wall that stood between all he loathed and all he wanted. The thing was winding itself up; he had thought of that on his first glorious day in New York, and had even provided a way to snap the thread. It lay on his dressing table now; he had got it out last night when he came blindly up from dinner,—but the shiny metal hurt his eyes, and he disliked the look of it, anyway.

He rose and moved about with a painful effort, succumbing now and again to attacks of nausea. It was the old depression exaggerated; all the world had become Cordelia Street. Yet somehow he was not afraid of anything, was absolutely calm; perhaps because he had looked into the dark corner at last, and knew. It was bad enough, what he saw there; but somehow not so bad as his long fear of it had been. He saw everything clearly now. He had a feeling that he had made the best of it, that he had lived the sort of life he was meant to live, and for half an hour he sat staring at the revolver. But he told himself that was not the way, so he went downstairs and took a cab to the ferry.

When Paul arrived at Newark, he got off the train and took another cab, directing the driver to follow the Pennsylvania tracks out of the town. The snow lay heavy on the roadways and had drifted deep in the open fields. Only here and there the dead grass or dried weed stalks projected, singularly black, above it. Once well into the country, Paul dismissed the carriage and walked, floundering along the tracks, his mind a medley of irrelevant things. He seemed to hold in his brain an actual picture of everything he had seen that morning. He remembered every feature of both his drivers, the toothless old woman from whom he had bought the red flowers in his coat, the agent from whom he had got his ticket, and all of his fellow-passengers on the ferry. His mind, unable to cope with vital matters near at hand, worked feverishly and deftly at sorting and grouping these images. They made for him a part of the ugliness of the world, of the ache in his head, and the bitter burning on his tongue. He stooped and put a handful of snow into his mouth as he walked, but that, too, seemed hot. When he reached a little hillside, where the tracks ran through a cut some twenty feet below him, he stopped and sat down.

The carnations in his coat were drooping with the cold, he noticed; all their red glory over. It occurred to him that all the flowers he had seen in the show windows that first night must have gone the same way, long before this. It was only one splendid breath they had, in spite of their brave mockery at the winter outside the glass. It was a losing game in the end, it seemed, this revolt against the homilies by which the world is run. Paul took one of the blossoms carefully from his coat and scooped a little hole in the snow, where he covered it up. Then he dozed a while, from his weak condition, seeming insensible to the cold.

The sound of an approaching train woke him, and he started to his feet, remembering only his resolution, and afraid lest he should be too late. He stood watching the approaching locomotive, his teeth chattering, his lips drawn away from them in a frightened smile; once or twice he glanced nervously sidewise, as though he were being watched. When the right moment came, he jumped. As he fell, the folly of his haste occurred to him with merciless clearness, the vastness of what he had left undone. There flashed through his brain, clearer than ever before, the blue of Adriatic water, the yellow of Algerian sands.

He felt something strike his chest,—his body was being thrown swiftly through the air, on and on, immeasurably far and fast, while his limbs gently relaxed. Then, because the picture-making mechanism was crushed, the disturbing visions flashed into black, and Paul dropped back into the immense design of things.

> "No, Henry, we ain't seen your wife
> around today." . . .

The Lost Phœbe

THEODORE DREISER (1871–1945)

The twelfth of thirteen children, Theodore Herman Albert Dreiser was born into an impoverished German immigrant family in Terre Haute, Indiana. He got most of his schooling in Warsaw, Indiana, and later, at the expense of a kindly teacher, spent a year at Indiana University.

His chief education came, however, from voluminous reading, attendance at the theater, and many years of newspaper work and magazine editing in Chicago, St. Louis, Pittsburgh, and New York, where he finally became editor in chief of the Butterick publications. An early piece of writing, untouched by the grim naturalism for which he was later remembered, was the chorus of the popular song, "On the Banks of the Wabash," for which his brother, Paul Dresser, wrote the music.

His first novel was published in 1900 on the recommendation of Frank Norris, but almost immediately was withdrawn by the publisher as likely to shock its readers. After 1911, success as a novelist

enabled Dreiser to live by his writings. He made a
trip to Russia in 1927.

Aside from fiction, he turned out plays, essays,
and several volumes of autobiography. Dreiser's
wide outlook and ponderous style made him more
at home in the novel than in the confines of the
short story, but he published several volumes of
human portraits in Free (1918), Twelve Men
(1919), Chains (1927), and A Gallery of Women
(1929).

"The Lost Phœbe" first appeared in 1916 in
Century Magazine.

THEY LIVED TOGETHER in a part of the country which
was not so prosperous as it had once been, about three miles from
one of those towns that, instead of increasing in population, is
steadily decreasing. The territory was not very thickly settled; perhaps a house every other mile or so, with large areas of corn- and
wheatland and fallow fields that at odd seasons had been sown
to timothy and clover. Their particular house was part log and part
frame, the log portion being the old original home of Henry's
grandfather. The new portion, of now rain-beaten, time-worn slabs,
through which the wind squeaked in the chinks at times, and which
several overshadowing elms and a butternut tree made picturesque
and reminiscently pathetic, but a little damp, was erected by Henry
when he was twenty-one and just married.

That was forty-eight years before. The furniture inside, like the
house outside, was old and mildewy and reminiscent of an earlier
day. You have seen the what-not of cherry wood, perhaps, with
spiral legs and fluted top. It was there. The old-fashioned four-
poster bed, with its ball-like protuberances and deep curving in-

cisions, was there also, a sadly alienated descendant of an early Jacobean ancestor. The bureau of cherry was also high and wide and solidly built, but faded-looking, and with a musty odor. The rag carpet that underlay all these sturdy examples of enduring furniture was a weak, faded, lead and pink colored affair woven by Phœbe Ann's own hands, when she was fifteen years younger than she was when she died. The creaky wooden loom on which it had been done now stood like a dusty, bony skeleton, along with a broken rocking chair, a worm-eaten clothes press—Heaven knows how old—a lime-stained bench that had once been used to keep flowers on outside the door, and other decrepit factors of household utility, in an east room that was a lean-to against this so-called main portion. All sorts of other broken-down furniture were about this place; an antiquated clotheshorse, cracked in two of its ribs; a broken mirror in an old cherry frame, which had fallen from a nail and cracked itself three days before their youngest son, Jerry, died; an extension hat-rack, which once had had porcelain knobs on the ends of its pegs; and a sewing machine, long since outdone in its clumsy mechanism by rivals of a newer generation.

The orchard to the east of the house was full of gnarled old apple trees, worm-eaten as to trunks and branches, and fully ornamented with green and white lichens, so that it had a sad, greenish-white, silvery effect in moonlight. The low outhouses, which had once housed chickens, a horse or two, a cow, and several pigs, were covered with patches of moss as to their roof, and the sides had been free of paint for so long that they were blackish-gray as to color, and a little spongy. The picket fence in front, with its gate squeaky and askew, and the side fences of the stake-and-rider type were in an equally run-down condition. As a matter of fact, they had aged synchronously with the persons who lived here, old Henry Reifsneider and his wife Phœbe Ann.

They had lived here, these two, ever since their marriage, forty-eight years before, and Henry had lived here before that from his childhood up. His father and mother, well along in years when he was a boy, had invited him to bring his wife here when he had first fallen in love and decided to marry; and he had done so. His father and mother were the companions of himself and his wife for ten years after they were married, when both died; and then Henry and Phœbe were left with their five children growing lustily apace. But all sorts of things had happened since then. Of the seven children, all told, that had been born to them, three had died; one girl had gone to Kansas; one boy had gone to Sioux Falls, never even to be heard of after; another boy had gone to Washington; and the last girl lived five counties away in the same State, but was so burdened with cares of her own that she rarely gave them a thought. Time and a commonplace home life that had never been attractive had weaned them thoroughly, so that, wherever they were, they gave little thought as to how it might be with their father and mother.

Old Henry Reifsneider and his wife Phœbe were a loving couple. You perhaps know how it is with simple natures that fasten themselves like lichens on the stones of circumstance and weather their days to a crumbling conclusion. The great world sounds widely, but it has no call for them. They have no soaring intellect. The orchard, the meadow, the cornfield, the pigpen, and the chicken-lot measure the range of their human activities. When the wheat is headed it is reaped and threshed; when the corn is browned and frosted it is cut and shocked; when the timothy is in full head it is cut, and the haycock erected. After that comes winter, with the hauling of grain to market, the sawing and splitting of wood, the simple chores of fire-building, meal-getting, occasional repairing, and visiting. Beyond these and the changes of weather—the snows, the rains, and the fair days—there are no immediate, significant things. All the rest of life is a far-off, clamorous phantasmagoria, flickering like northern lights in the night, and sounding as faintly as cowbells tinkling in the distance.

Old Henry and his wife Phœbe were as fond of each other as it is possible for two old people to be who have nothing else in this life to be fond of. He was a thin old man, seventy when she died, a queer, crotchety person with coarse gray-black hair and beard, quite straggly and unkempt. He looked at you out of dull, fishy, watery eyes that had deep-brown crow's-feet at the sides.

His clothes, like the clothes of many farmers, were aged and angular and baggy, standing out at the pockets, not fitting about the neck, protuberant and worn at elbow and knee. Phœbe Ann was thin and shapeless, a very umbrella of a woman, clad in shabby black, and with a black bonnet for her best wear. As time had passed, and they had only themselves to look after, their movements had become slower and slower, their activities fewer and fewer. The annual keep of pigs had been reduced from five to one grunting porker, and the single horse which Henry now retained was a sleepy animal, not overnourished and not very clean. The chickens, of which formerly there was a large flock, had almost disappeared, owing to ferrets, foxes, and the lack of proper care, which produces disease. The former healthy garden was now a straggling memory of itself, and the vines and flowerbeds that formerly ornamented the windows and dooryard had now become choking thickets. A will had been made which divided the small tax-eaten property equally among the remaining four, so that it was really of no interest to any of them. Yet these two lived together in peace and sympathy, only that now and then old Henry would become unduly cranky, complaining almost invariably that something had been neglected or mislaid which was of no importance at all.

"Phœbe, where's my corn knife? You ain't never minded to let my things alone no more."

"Now you hush, Henry," his wife would caution him in a cracked and squeaky voice. "If you don't, I'll leave yuh. I'll git up and walk out of here some day, and then where would y' be? Y' ain't got anybody but me to look after yuh, so yuh just behave yourself. Your corn knife's on the mantel where it's allus been unless you've gone an' put it summers else."

Old Henry, who knew his wife would never leave him under any circumstances, used to speculate at times as to what he would do if she were to die. That was the one leaving that he really feared. As he climbed on the chair at night to wind the old, long-pendulumed, double-weighted clock, or went finally to the front and the back door to see that they were safely shut in, it was a comfort to know that Phœbe was there, properly ensconced on her side of the bed, and that if he stirred restlessly in the night, she would be there to ask what he wanted.

"Now, Henry, do lie still! You're as restless as a chicken."

"Well, I can't sleep, Phœbe."

"Well, yuh needn't roll so, anyhow. Yuh kin let me sleep."

This usually reduced him to a state of somnolent ease. If she wanted a pail of water, it was a grumbling pleasure for him to get it; and if she did rise first to build the fires, he saw that the wood was cut and placed within easy reach. They divided this simple world nicely between them.

As the years had gone on, however, fewer and fewer people had called. They were well-known for a distance of as much as ten square miles as old Mr. and Mrs. Reifsneider, honest, moderately Christian, but too old to be really interesting any longer. The writing of letters had become an almost impossible burden too difficult to continue or even negotiate via others, although an occasional letter still did arrive from the daughter in Pemberton County. Now and then some old friend stopped with a pie or cake or a roasted chicken or duck, or merely to see that they were well; but even these kindly minded visits were no longer frequent.

One day in the early spring of her sixty-fourth year Mrs. Reifsneider took sick, and from a low fever passed into some indefinable ailment which, because of her age, was no longer curable. Old Henry drove to Swinnerton, the neighboring town, and procured a doctor. Some friends called, and the immediate care of her was taken off his hands. Then one chill spring night she died, and old Henry, in a fog of sorrow and uncertainty, followed her body to the nearest graveyard, an unattractive space with a few pines growing in it. Although he might have gone to the daughter in Pemberton or sent for her, it was really too much trouble and he was too weary and fixed. It was suggested to him at once by one friend and another that he come to stay with them awhile, but he did not see fit. He was so old and so fixed in his notions and so accustomed to the exact surroundings he had known all his days, that he could not think of leaving. He wanted to remain near where they had put his Phœbe; and the fact that he would have to live alone did not trouble him in the least. The living children were notified and the care of him offered if he would leave, but he would not.

"I kin make a shift for myself," he continually announced to old Dr. Morrow, who had attended his wife in this case. "I kin cook a little, and, besides, it don't take much more'n coffee an' bread in the mornin's to satisfy me. I'll get along now well enough. Yuh jest let me be." And after many pleadings and proffers of advice, with supplies of coffee and bacon and baked bread duly offered and accepted, he was left to himself. For a while he sat idly outside his door brooding in the spring sun. He tried to revive his interest in farming, and to keep himself busy and free from thought by looking after the fields, which of late had been much neglected. It was a gloomy thing to come in of an evening, however, or in the afternoon, and find no shadow of Phœbe where everything suggested her. By degrees he put a few of her things away. At night he sat beside his lamp and read in the papers that were left him occasionally or in a Bible that he had neglected for years, but he could get little solace from these things. Mostly he held his hand over his mouth and looked at the floor as he sat and thought of what had become of her, and how soon he himself would die. He made a great business of making his coffee in the morning and frying himself a little bacon at night; but his appetite was gone. The shell in which he had been housed so long seemed vacant, and its shadows were suggestive of immedicable griefs. So he lived quite dolefully for five long months, and then a change began.

It was one night, after he had looked after the front and the back door, wound the clock, blown out the light, and gone through all the selfsame motions that he had indulged in for years, that he went to bed not so much to sleep as to think. It was a moonlight night. The green-lichen-covered orchard just outside and to be seen from his bed where he now lay was a silvery affair, sweetly spectral. The moon shone through the east windows, throwing the pattern of the panes on the wooden floor, and making the old furniture, to which he was accustomed, stand out dimly in the room. As usual he had been thinking of Phœbe and the years when they had been young together, and of the children who had gone, and the poor shift he was making of his present days. The house was coming to be in a very bad state indeed. The bedclothes were in disorder and not clean, for he made a wretched shift of washing. It was a terror to him. The roof leaked, causing things, some of them, to remain damp for weeks at a time, but he was getting into that brooding state where he would accept anything rather than exert himself. He preferred to pace slowly to and fro or to sit and think.

By twelve o'clock of this particular night he was asleep, however, and by two had waked again. The moon by this time had shifted to a position on the western side of the house, and it now shone in through the windows of the living room and those of the kitchen beyond. A certain combination of furniture—a chair near a table with his coat on it, the half-open kitchen door casting a shadow, and the position of a lamp near a paper—gave him an exact representation of Phœbe leaning over the table as he had often seen her do in life. It gave him a great start. Could it be she—or her ghost? He had scarcely ever believed in spirits; and still— He looked at her fixedly in the feeble half-light, his old hair tingling oddly at the roots, and then sat up. The figure did not move. He put his thin legs out of the bed and sat looking at her, wondering if this could really be Phœbe. They had talked of ghosts often in their lifetime, of apparitions and omens; but they had never agreed that such things could be. It had never been a part of his wife's creed that she could have a spirit that could return to walk the earth. Her afterworld was quite a different affair, a vague heaven, no less, from which the righteous did not trouble to return. Yet here she was now, bending over the table in her black skirt and gray shawl, her pale profile outlined against the moonlight.

"Phœbe," he called, thrilling from head to toe, and putting out one bony hand, "have yuh come back?"

The figure did not stir, and he arose and walked uncertainly to the door, looking at it fixedly the while. As he drew near, however, the apparition resolved itself into its primal content—his old coat over the high-backed chair, the lamp by the paper, the half-open door.

"Well," he said to himself, his mouth open, "I thought shore I saw her." And he ran his hand strangely and vaguely through his hair, the while his nervous tension relaxed. Vanished as it had, it gave him the idea that she might return.

Another night, because of this first illusion, and because his mind was now constantly on her and he was old, he looked out of the window that was nearest his bed and commanded a hencoop and pigpen and a part of the wagon-shed, and there, a faint mist exuding from the damp of the ground, he thought he saw her again. It was one of those little wisps of mist, one of those faint exhalations of the earth that rise in a cool night after a warm day, and flicker like small white cypresses of fog before they disappear. In life it had been a custom of hers to cross this lot from her kitchen door to the pigpen to throw in any scrap that was left from her cooking, and here she was again. He sat up and watched it strangely, doubt-fully, because of his previous experience, but inclined, because of the nervous titillation that passed over his body, to believe that spirits really were, and that Phœbe, who would be concerned be-cause of his lonely state, must be thinking about him, and hence returning. What other way would she have? How otherwise could she express herself? It would be within the province of her charity so to do, and like her loving interest in him. He quivered and watched it eagerly; but, a faint breath of air stirring, it wound away toward the fence and disappeared.

A third night, as he was actually dreaming, some ten days later, she came to his bedside and put her hand on his head.

"Poor Henry!" she said. "It's too bad."

He roused out of his sleep, actually to see her, he thought, moving from his bedroom into the one living room, her figure a shadowy mass of black. The weak straining of his eyes caused little points of light to flicker about the outlines of her form. He arose, greatly astonished, walked the floor in the cool room, convinced that

Phœbe was coming back to him. If he only thought sufficiently, if he made it perfectly clear by his feeling that he needed her greatly, she would come back, this kindly wife, and tell him what to do. She would perhaps be with him much of the time, in the night, anyhow; and that would make him less lonely, this state more endurable.

In age and with the feeble it is not such a far cry from the subtleties of illusion to actual hallucination, and in due time this transition was made for Henry. Night after night he waited, expecting her return. Once in his weird mood he thought he saw a pale light moving about the room, and another time he thought he saw her walking in the orchard after dark. It was one morning when the details of his lonely state were virtually unendurable that he woke with the thought that she was not dead. How he had arrived at this conclusion it is hard to say. His mind had gone. In its place was a fixed illusion. He and Phœbe had had a senseless quarrel. He had reproached her for not leaving his pipe where he was accustomed to find it, and she had left. It was an aberrated fulfillment of her old jesting threat that if he did not behave himself she would leave him.

"I guess I could find yuh ag'in," he had always said. But her cackling threat had always been:

"Yuh'll not find me if I ever leave yuh. I guess I kin git some place where yuh can't find me."

This morning when he arose he did not think to build the fire in the customary way or to grind his coffee and cut his bread, as was his wont, but solely to meditate as to where he should search for her and how he should induce her to come back. Recently the one horse had been dispensed with because he found it cumbersome and beyond his needs. He took down his soft crush hat after he had dressed himself, a new glint of interest and determination in his eye, and taking his black crook cane from behind the door, where he had always placed it, started out briskly to look for her among the nearest neighbors. His old shoes clumped soundly in the dust as he walked, and his gray-black locks, now grown rather long, straggled out in a dramatic fringe or halo from under his hat. His short coat stirred busily as he walked, and his hands and face were peaked and pale.

"Why, hello, Henry! Where're yuh goin' this mornin'?" inquired Farmer Dodge, who, hauling a load of wheat to market, encountered him on the public road. He had not seen the aged farmer in months, not since his wife's death, and he wondered now, seeing him looking so spry.

"Yuh ain't seen Phœbe, have yuh?" inquired the old man, looking up quizzically.

"Phœbe who?" inquired Farmer Dodge, not for the moment connecting the name with Henry's dead wife.

"Why, my wife Phœbe, o' course. Who do yuh s'pose I mean?" He stared up with a pathetic sharpness of glance from under his shaggy, gray eyebrows.

"Wall, I'll swan, Henry, yuh ain't jokin', are yuh?" said the solid Dodge, a pursy man, with a smooth, hard, red face. "It can't be your wife yuh're talkin' about. She's dead."

"Dead! Shucks!" retorted the demented Reifsneider. "She left me early this mornin', while I was sleepin'. She allus got up to build the fire, but she's gone now. We had a little spat last night, and I guess that's the reason. But I guess I kin find her. She's gone over to Matilda Race's, that's where she's gone."

He started briskly up the road, leaving the amazed Dodge to stare in wonder after him.

"Well, I'll be switched!" he said aloud to himself. "He's clean out'n his head. That poor old feller's been livin' down there till he's gone outen his mind. I'll have to notify the authorities." And he flicked his whip with great enthusiasm. "Geddap!" he said, and was off.

Reifsneider met no one else in this poorly populated region until he reached the whitewashed fence of Matilda Race and her husband three miles away. He had passed several other houses en route, but these not being within the range of his illusion were not considered. His wife, who had known Matilda well, must be here. He opened the picket-gate which guarded the walk, and stamped briskly up to the door.

"Why, Mr. Reifsneider," exclaimed old Matilda herself, a stout woman, looking out of the door in answer to his knock, "what brings yuh here this mornin'?"

"Is Phœbe here?" he demanded eagerly.

"Phœbe who? What Phœbe?" replied Mrs. Race, curious as to this sudden development of energy on his part.

"Why, my Phœbe, o' course. My wife Phœbe. Who do yuh s'pose? Ain't she here now?"

"Lawsy me!" exclaimed Mrs. Race, opening her mouth. "Yuh pore man! So you're clean out'n your mind now. Yuh come right in and sit down. I'll git yuh a cup o' coffee. O' course your wife ain't here; but yuh come in an' sit down. I'll find her fer yuh after a while. I know where she is."

The old farmer's eyes softened, and he entered. He was so thin and pale a specimen, pantalooned and patriarchal, that he aroused Mrs. Race's extremest sympathy as he took off his hat and laid it on his knees quite softly and mildly.

"We had a quarrel last night, an' she left me," he volunteered.

"Laws! laws!" sighed Mrs. Race, there being no one present with whom to share her astonishment as she went to her kitchen. "The pore man! Now somebody's just got to look after him. He can't be allowed to run around the country this way lookin' for his dead wife. It's turrible."

She boiled him a pot of coffee and brought in some of her new-baked bread and fresh butter. She set out some of her best jam and put a couple of eggs to boil, lying whole-heartedly the while.

"Now yuh stay right there, Uncle Henry, till Jake comes in, an' I'll send him to look for Phœbe. I think it's more'n likely she's over to Swinnerton with some o' her friends. Anyhow, we'll find out. Now yuh just drink this coffee an' eat this bread. Yuh must be tired. Yuh've had a long walk this mornin'." Her idea was to take counsel with Jake, "her man," and perhaps have him notify the authorities.

She bustled about, meditating on the uncertainties of life, while old Reifsneider thrummed on the rim of his hat with his pale fingers and later ate abstractedly of what she offered. His mind was on his wife, however, and since she was not here, or did not appear, it wandered vaguely away to a family by the name of Murray, miles away in another direction. He decided after a time that he would not wait for Jake Race to hunt his wife but would seek her for himself. He must be on, and urge her to come back.

"Well, I'll be goin'," he said, getting up and looking strangely about him. "I guess she didn't come here after all. She went over to the Murrays, I guess. I'll not wait any longer, Mis' Race. There's a lot to do over to the house today." And out he marched in the face of her protests, taking to the dusty road again in the warm spring sun, his cane striking the earth as he went.

It was two hours later that this pale figure of a man appeared in the Murrays' doorway, dusty, perspiring, eager. He had tramped all of five miles, and it was noon. An amazed husband and wife of sixty heard his strange query, and realized also that he was mad. They begged him to stay to dinner, intending to notify the authorities later and see what could be done; but though he stayed to partake of a little something, he did not stay long, and was off again to another distant farmhouse, his idea of many things to do and his need of Phœbe impelling him. So it went for that day and the next and the next, the circle of his inquiry ever widening.

The process by which a character assumes the significance of being peculiar, his antics weird, yet harmless, in such a community is often involute and pathetic. This day, as has been said, saw Reifsneider at other doors, eagerly asking his unnatural question, and leaving a trail of amazement, sympathy, and pity in his wake. Although the authorities were informed—the county sheriff, no less —it was not deemed advisable to take him into custody; for when those who knew old Henry, and had for so long, reflected on the condition of the county insane asylum, a place which, because of the poverty of the district, was of staggering aberration and sickening environment, it was decided to let him remain at large; for, strange to relate, it was found on investigation that at night he returned peacefully enough to his lonesome domicile there to discover whether his wife had returned, and to brood in loneliness until the morning. Who would lock up a thin, eager, seeking old man with iron-gray hair and an attitude of kindly, innocent inquiry, particularly when he was well known for a past of only kindly servitude and reliability? Those who had known him best rather agreed that he should be allowed to roam at large. He could do no harm. There were many who were willing to help him as to food, old clothes, the odds and ends of his daily life—at least at first. His figure after a time became not so much a commonplace as an accepted curiosity, and the replies, "Why, no, Henry; I ain't see her," or "No, Henry; she ain't been here today," more customary.

For several years thereafter then he was an odd figure in the sun and rain, on dusty roads and muddy ones, encountered occasionally in strange and unexpected places, pursuing his endless search. Undernourishment, after a time, although the neighbors and those who knew his history gladly contributed from their store, affected his body; for he walked much and ate little. The longer he roamed the public highway in this manner, the deeper became his strange hallucination; and finding it harder and harder to return from his more and more distant pilgrimages, he finally began taking a few utensils with him from his home, making a small package of them, in order that he might not be compelled to return. In an old tin coffee-pot of large size he placed a small tin cup, a knife, fork, and spoon, some salt and pepper, and to the outside of it, by a string forced through a pierced hole, he fastened a plate, which could be released, and which was his woodland table. It was no trouble for him to secure the little food that he needed, and with a strange, almost religious dignity, he had no hesitation in asking for that much. By degrees his hair became longer and longer, his once black hat became an earthen brown, and his clothes threadbare and dusty.

For all of three years he walked, and none knew how wide were his perambulations, nor how he survived the storms and cold. They could not see him, with homely rural understanding and forethought, sheltering himself in haycocks, or by the sides of cattle, whose warm bodies protected him from the cold, and whose dull understandings were not opposed to his harmless presence. Overhanging rocks and trees kept him at times from the rain, and a

friendly hayloft or corncrib was not above his humble consideration.

The involute progression of hallucination is strange. From asking at doors and being constantly rebuffed or denied, he finally
came to the conclusion that although his Phœbe might not be
in any of the houses at the doors of which he inquired, she might
nevertheless be within the sound of his voice. And so, from patient
inquiry, he began to call sad, occasional cries, that ever and anon
waked the quiet landscapes and ragged hill regions, and set to
echoing his thin "O-o-o Phœbe! O-o-o Phœbe!" It had a pathetic,
albeit insane, ring, and many a farmer or plowboy came to know it
even from afar and say, "There goes old Reifsneider."

Another thing that puzzled him greatly after a time and after
many hundreds of inquiries was, when he no longer had any particular dooryard in view and no special inquiry to make, which
way to go. These crossroads, which occasionally led in four or
even six directions, came after a time to puzzle him. But to solve
this knotty problem, which became more and more of a puzzle,
there came to his aid another hallucination. Phœbe's spirit or some
power of the air or wind or nature would tell him. If he stood at the
center of the parting of the ways, closed his eyes, turned thrice
about, and called "O-o-o Phœbe!" twice, and then threw his cane
straight before him, that would surely indicate which way to go,
for Phœbe, or one of these mystic powers, would surely govern its
direction and fall! In whichever direction it went, even though,
as was not infrequently the case, it took him back along the path
he had already come, or across fields, he was not so far gone in
his mind but that he gave himself ample time to search before
he called again. Also the hallucination seemed to persist that at
some time he would surely find her. There were hours when his feet
were sore, and his limbs weary, when he would stop in the heat
to wipe his seamed brow, or in the cold to beat his arms. Sometimes, after throwing away his cane, and finding it indicating the
direction from which he had just come, he would shake his head
wearily and philosophically, as if contemplating the unbelievable

or an untoward fate, and then start briskly off. His strange figure
came finally to be known in the farthest reaches of three or four
counties. Old Reifsneider was a pathetic character. His fame was
wide.

Near a little town called Watersville, in Green County, perhaps
four miles from that minor center of human activity, there was a
place or precipice locally known as the Red Cliff, a sheer wall of
red sandstone, perhaps a hundred feet high, which raised its sharp
face for half a mile or more above the fruitful cornfields and
orchards that lay beneath, and which was surmounted by a thick
grove of trees. The slope that slowly led up to it from the opposite
side was covered by a rank growth of beech, hickory, and ash,
through which threaded a number of wagon-tracks crossing at
various angles. In fair weather it had become old Reifsneider's
habit, so inured was he by now to the open, to make his bed in
some such patch of trees as this, to fry his bacon or boil his eggs
at the foot of some tree, before laying himself down for the night.
Occasionally, so light and inconsequential was his sleep, he would
walk at night. More often, the moonlight or some sudden wind
stirring in the trees or a reconnoitering animal arousing him, he
would sit up and think, or pursue his quest in the moonlight or
the dark, a strange, unnatural, half wild, half savage-looking but
utterly harmless creature, calling at lonely road crossings, staring
at dark and shuttered houses, and wondering where, where Phœbe
could really be.

That particular lull that comes in the systole-diastole of this
earthly ball at two o'clock in the morning invariably aroused him,
and though he might not go any farther he would sit up and contemplate the darkness or the stars, wondering. Sometimes in the
strange processes of his mind he would fancy that he saw moving
among the trees the figure of his lost wife, and then he would get
up to follow, taking his utensils, always on a string, and his cane.
If she seemed to evade him too easily he would run, or plead, or,
suddenly losing track of the fancied figure, stand awed or disap-
pointed, grieving for the moment over the almost insurmountable
difficulties of his search.

It was in the seventh year of these hopeless peregrinations, in the dawn of a similar springtime to that in which his wife had died, that he came at last one night to the vicinity of this selfsame patch that crowned the rise to the Red Cliff. His far-flung cane, used as a divining rod at the last crossroads, had brought him hither. He had walked many, many miles. It was after ten o'clock at night, and he was very weary. Long wandering and little eating had left him but a shadow of his former self. It was a question now not so much of physical strength but of spiritual endurance which kept him up. He had scarcely eaten this day, and now, exhausted, he set himself down in the dark to rest and possibly to sleep.

Curiously on this occasion a strange suggestion of the presence of his wife surrounded him. It would not be long now, he counseled with himself, although the long months had brought him nothing, until he should see her, talk to her. He fell asleep after a time, his head on his knees. At midnight the moon began to rise, and at two in the morning, his wakeful hour, was a large silver disk shining through the trees to the east. He opened his eyes when the radiance became strong, making a silver pattern at his feet and lighting the woods with strange lusters and silvery, shadowy forms. As usual, his old notion that his wife must be near occurred to him on this occasion, and he looked about him with a speculative, anticipatory eye. What was it that moved in the distant shadows along the path by which he had entered—a pale, flickering will-o'-the-wisp that bobbed gracefully among the trees and riveted his expectant gaze? Moonlight and shadows combined to give it a strange form and a stranger reality, this fluttering of bog-fire or dancing of wandering fireflies. Was it truly his lost Phœbe? By a circuitous route it passed about him, and in his fevered state he fancied that he could see the very eyes of her, not as she was when he last saw her in the black dress and shawl, but now a strangely younger Phœbe, gayer, sweeter, the one whom he had known years before as a girl. Old Reifsneider got up. He had been expecting and dreaming of this hour all these years, and now as he saw the feeble light dancing lightly before him he peered at it questioningly, one thin hand in his gray hair.

Of a sudden there came to him now for the first time in many years the full charm of her girlish figure as he had known it in boyhood, the pleasing, sympathetic smile, the brown hair, the blue sash she had once worn about her waist at a picnic, her gay, graceful movements. He walked around the base of the tree, straining with his eyes, forgetting for once his cane and utensils, and following eagerly after. On she moved before him, a will-o'-the-wisp of the spring, a little flame above her head, and it seemed as though among the small saplings of ash and beech and the thick trunks of hickory and elm that she signaled with a young, a lightsome hand.

"Oh, Phœbe! Phœbe!" he called. "Have yuh really come? Have yuh really answered me?" And hurrying faster, he fell once, scrambling lamely to his feet, only to see the light in the distance dancing illusively on. On and on he hurried until he was fairly running, brushing his ragged arms against the trees, striking his hands and face against impeding twigs. His hat was gone, his lungs were breathless, his reason quite astray, when coming to the edge of the cliff he saw her below among a silvery bed of apple trees now blooming in the spring.

"Oh, Phœbe!" he called. "Oh, Phœbe! Oh, no, don't leave me!" And feeling the lure of a world where love was young and Phœbe, as this vision presented her, a delightful epitome of their quondam youth, he gave a gay cry of "Oh, wait, Phœbe!" and leaped.

Some farmer-boys, reconnoitering this region of bounty and prospect some few days afterward, found first the tin utensils tied together under the tree where he had left them, and then later at the foot of the cliff, pale, broken, but elate, a molded smile of peace and delight upon his lips, his body. His old hat was discovered lying under some low-growing saplings, the twigs of which had held it back. No one of all the simple population knew how eagerly and joyously he had found his lost mate.

He was barely human, but he knew—
and kept—the secret of survival. . . .

The Fourth Man

JOHN RUSSELL (1885-   )

Russell was born in Davenport, Iowa. After spending two years at Northwestern University, he became, in 1908, a special correspondent for the New York Herald in Panama and Peru. Later he was a staff writer for the magazine section of the New York Sun. During World War I, he was in charge of United States government propaganda for Great Britain and Ireland. He has explored widely in Asia, South America, and the Pacific region. His knowledge of strange parts of the world has led to his employment as consultant by a number of motion-picture companies.

Since Russell began contributing to magazines in 1912, he has written more than a thousand short stories—most of them dealing with adventures in far places of the globe.

His first collected volume, The Red Mark (1919) (English edition, Where the Pavement Ends, 1921), was hailed by critics as "almost pure Kipling," and its writer was said to show "considerable skill in depicting the sensuous charm of the tropics." This volume, together with In Dark Places (1922) and Far Wandering Men (1928), has been published under one cover with the title, Color of the East (1930).

"The Fourth Man" first appeared in book form in The Red Mark. Set in the waters off New Caledonia, the French possession in the South Pacific that formerly held a penal colony, it is an excellent example of the story with a surprise ending that can legitimately be expected if the reader does not allow himself to be deftly led astray by the art of the storyteller.

THE RAFT MIGHT have been taken for a swath of cut sedge or a drifting tangle of roots as it slid out of the shadowy river mouth at dawn and dipped into the first ground swell. But while the sky brightened and the breeze came fresh offshore it picked a way among shoals and swampy islets with purpose and direction, and when at last the sun leaped up and cleared his bright eye of the morning mist it had passed the wide entrance to the bay and stood to open sea.

It was a curious craft for such a venture, of a type that survives here and there in the obscure corners of the world. The coracle maker would have scorned it. The first navigating pithecanthrope built nearly as well with his log and bush. A mat of pandanus leaves served for its sail and a paddle of *niaouli* wood for its helm. But it had a point of real seaworthiness. Its twin floats, paired as a catamaran, were woven of reed bundles and bamboo sticks upon triple rows of bladders. It was light as a bladder itself, elastic, fit to ride any weather. One other quality this raft possessed which recommended it beyond all comfort and all safety to its present crew. It was very nearly invisible. They had only to unstep its mast and lie flat in the cup of its soggy platform and they could not be spied half a mile away.

Four men occupied the raft. Three of them were white. Their bodies had been scored with brambles and blackened with dried blood, and on wrist and ankle they bore the dark and wrinkled stain of the gyves. The hair upon them was long and matted. They wore only the rags of blue canvas uniforms. But they were whites, members of the superior race—members of a highly superior race according to those philosophers who rate the criminal aberration as a form of genius.

The fourth was the man who had built the raft and was now sailing it. There was nothing superior about him. His skin was a layer of soot. His prognathous jaw carried out the angle of a low forehead. No line of beauty redeemed his lean limbs and knobby joints. Nature had set upon him her plainest stamp of inferiority, and his only attempts to relieve it were the twist of bark about his middle and the prong of pig ivory through the cartilage of his nose. Altogether a very ordinary specimen of one of the lowest branches of the human family—the Canaques of New Caledonia.

The three whites sat together well forward, and so they had sat in silence for hours. But at sunrise, as if some spell had been raised by the clang of that great copper gong in the east, they stirred and breathed deep of the salt air and looked at one another with hope in their haggard faces, and then back toward the land which was now no more than a gray-green smudge behind them. . . . "Friends," said the eldest, whose temples were bound with a scrap of crimson scarf, "friends—the thing is done."

With a gesture like conjuring he produced from the breast of his tattered blouse three cigarettes, fresh and round, and offered them.

"Nippers!" cried the one at his right. "True nippers—name of a little good man! And here? Doctor, I always said you were a marvel. See if they be not new from the box!"

Dr. Dubosc smiled. Those who had known him in very different circumstances about the boulevards, the lobbies, the clubs, would have known him again and in spite of all disfigurement by that smile. And here, at the bottom of the earth, it had set him still apart in the prisons, the cobalt mines, the chain gangs of a community not much given to mirth. Many a crowded lecture hall at Montpellier had seen him touch off some intellectual firework with just such a twinkle behind his bristly gray brows, with just such a thin curl of lip.

"By way of celebration," he explained. "Consider. There are seventy-five evasions from Nouméa every six months, of which not more than one succeeds. I had the figures myself from Dr. Pierre at the infirmary. He is not much of a physician, but a very honest fellow. Could anybody win on that percentage without dissipating? I ask you."

"Therefore you prepared for this?"

"It is now three weeks since I bribed the night guard to get these same nippers."

The other regarded him with admiration. Sentiment came readily upon this beardless face, tender and languid, but overdrawn, with eyes too large and soft, and oval too long. It was one of those faces familiar enough to the police which might serve as model for an angel were it not associated with some revolting piece of devilry. Fenayrou himself had been condemned "to perpetuity" as an incorrigible.

"Is not our doctor a wonder?" he inquired as he handed a cigarette along to the third white man. "He thinks of everything. You should be ashamed to grumble. See—we are free, after all. Free!"

The third was a gross, pockmarked man with hairless lids, known sometimes as Niniche, Trois Huit, Le Tordeur, but chiefly among *copains* as Perroquet—a name derived perhaps from his beaked nose, or from some perception of his jailbird character. He was a garrotter by profession, accustomed to rely upon his fists only for the exchange of amenities. Dubosc might indulge a fancy and Fenayrou seek to carry it as a pose, but The Parrot remained a gentleman of strictly serious turn. There is perhaps a tribute to

the practical spirit of penal administration in the fact that while
Dubosc was the most dangerous of these three and Fenayrou the
most depraved, Perroquet was the one with the official reputation,
whose escape would be signaled first among the "Wanted." He
accepted the cigarette because he was glad to get it, but he said
nothing until Dubosc passed a tin box of matches and the first
gulp of picadura filled his lungs. . . .

"Wait till you've got your two feet on a *pavé*, my boy. That will
be the time to talk of freedom. What? Suppose there came a
storm."

"It is not the season of storms," observed Dubosc.

But The Parrot's word had given them a check. Such spirits
as these, to whom the land had been a horror, would be slow to
feel the terror of the sea. Back there they had left the festering
limbo of a convict colony, oblivion. Out here they had reached
the rosy threshold of the big round world again. They were men
raised from the dead, charged with all the furious appetites of
lost years, with the savor of life, strong and sweet on their lips.
And yet they paused and looked about in quickened perception,
with the clutch at the throat that takes the landsman on big
waters. The spaces were so wide and empty. The voices in their
ears were so strange and murmurous. There was a threat in each
wave that came from the depths, a sinister vibration. None of them
knew the sea. None knew its ways, what tricks it might play, what
traps it might spread—more deadly than those of the jungle.

The raft was running now before a brisk chop with alternate
spring and wallow, while the froth bubbled in over the prow and
ran down among them as they sat. "Where is that cursed ship
that was to meet us here?" demanded Fenayrou.

"It will meet us right enough." Dubosc spoke carelessly, though
behind the blown wisp of his cigarette he had been searching
the outer horizon with keen glance. "This is the day, as agreed.
We will be picked up off the mouth of the river."

"You say," growled Perroquet. "But where is any river now?
Or any mouth? Sacred name, this wind will blow us to China if
we keep on."

"We dare not lie in any closer. There is a government launch at Torrien. Also the traders go armed hereabouts, ready for chaps like us. And don't imagine that the native trackers have given us up. They are likely to be following still in their proas."

"So far!"

Fenayrou laughed, for The Parrot's dread of their savage enemies had a morbid tinge.

"Take care, Perroquet. They will eat you yet."

"Is it true?" demanded the other, appealing to Dubosc. "I have heard it is even permitted these devils to keep all runaways they can capture—Name of God!—to fatten on."

"An idle tale," smiled Dubosc. "They prefer the reward. But one hears of convicts being badly mauled. There was a forester who made a break from Baie du Sud and came back lacking an arm. Certainly these people have not lost the habit of cannibalism."

"Piecemeal," chuckled Fenayrou. "They will only sample you, Perroquet. Let them make a stew of your brains. You would miss nothing."

But The Parrot swore.

"Name of a name—what brutes!" he said, and by a gesture recalled the presence of that fourth man who was of their party and yet so completely separated from them that they had almost forgotten him.

The Canaque was steering the raft. He sat crouched at the stern, his body glistening like varnished ebony with spray. He held the steering paddle, immobile as an image, his eyes fixed upon the course ahead. There was no trace of expression on his face, no hint of what he thought or felt or whether he thought or felt anything. He seemed not even aware of their regard, and each one of them experienced somehow that twinge of uneasiness with which the white confronts his brother of color—this enigma brown or yellow or black he is fated never wholly to understand or to fathom. . . .

"It occurs to me," said Fenayrou, in a pause, "that our friend here who looks like a shiny boot is able to steer us God knows where. Perhaps to claim the reward."

"Reassure yourself," answered Dubosc. "He steers by my order. Besides, it is a simple creature—an infant, truly, incapable of any but the most primitive reasoning."

"Is he incapable of treachery?"

"Of any that would deceive us. Also, he is bound by his duty. I made my bargain with his chief, up the river, and this one is sent to deliver us on board our ship. It is the only interest he has in us."

"And he will do it?"

"He will do it. Such is the nature of the native."

"I am glad you feel so," returned Fenayrou, adjusting himself indolently among the drier reeds and nursing the last of his cigarette. "For my part I wouldn't trust a figurehead like that for two sous. *Mazette!* What a monkey face!"

"Brute!" repeated Perroquet, and this man, sprung from some vile river-front slum of Argenteuil, whose home had been the dock pilings, the grog shop, and the jail, even this man viewed the black Canaque from an immeasurable distance with the look of hatred and contempt. . . .

Under the heat of the day the two younger convicts lapsed presently into dozing. But Dubosc did not doze. His tormented soul peered out behind its mask as he stood to sweep the skyline again under shaded hand. His theory had been so precise, the fact was so different. He had counted absolutely on meeting the ship—some small schooner, one of those flitting, half-piratical traders of the copra islands that can be hired like cabs in a dark street for any questionable enterprise. Now there was no ship, and here was no crossroads where one might sit and wait. Such a craft as the catamaran could not be made to lie to.

The doctor foresaw ugly complications for which he had not prepared and whereof he must bear the burden. The escape had been his own conception, directed by him from the start. He had picked his companions deliberately from the whole forced labor squad, Perroquet for his great strength, Fenayrou as a ready echo. He had made it plain since their first dash from the mine, during their skirmish with the military guards, their subsequent wander-

ings in the brush with bloodhounds and trackers on the trail—
through every crisis—that he alone should be the leader.

For the others, they understood well enough which of their
number was the chief beneficiary. Those mysterious friends on
the outside that were reaching half around the world to further
their release had never heard of such individuals as Fenayrou and
The Parrot. Dubosc was the man who had pulled the wires: that
brilliant physician whose conviction for murder had followed so
sensationally, so scandalously, upon his sweep of academic and
social honors. There would be clacking tongues in many a Parisian
salon, and white faces in some, when news should come of his
escape. Ah, yes, for example, they knew the high-flyer of the band,
and they submitted—so long as he led them to victory. They submitted, while reserving a depth of jealousy, the inevitable remnant
of caste persisting still in this democracy of stripes and shame.

By the middle of the afternoon the doctor had taken necessary
measures.

"Ho!" said Fenayrou sleepily. "Behold our colors at the mast-
head. What is that for, comrade?"

The sail had been lowered and in its place streamed the scrap
of crimson scarf that had served Dubosc as a turban.

"To help them sight us when the ship comes."

"What wisdom!" cried Fenayrou. "Always he thinks of everything, our doctor: everything—"

He stopped with the phrase on his lips, and his hand outstretched
toward the center of the platform. Here, in a damp depression
among the reeds, had lain the wicker-covered bottle of green glass
in which they carried their water. It was gone.

"Where is that flask?" he demanded. "The sun has grilled me
like a bone."

"You will have to grill some more," said Dubosc grimly. "This
crew is put on rations."

Fenayrou stared at him wide-eyed, and from the shadow of a
folded mat The Parrot thrust his purpled face. "What do you sing
me there? Where is the water?"

"I have it," said Dubosc.

They saw, in fact, that he held the flask between his knees, along with their single packet of food in its wrapping of coconut husk.

"I want a drink," challenged Perroquet.

"Reflect a little. We must guard our supplies like reasonable men. One does not know how long we may be floating here. . . ."

Fell a silence among them, heavy and strained, in which they heard only the squeaking of frail basketwork as their raft labored in the wash. Slow as was their progress, they were being pushed steadily outward and onward, and the last cliffs of New Caledonia were no longer even a smudge in the west, but only a hazy line. And still they had seen no moving thing upon the great round breast of the sea that gleamed in its corselet of brass plates under a brazen sun. "So that is the way you talk now?" began The Parrot, half choking. "You do not know how long? But you were sure enough when we started."

"I am still sure," returned Dubosc. "The ship will come. Only she cannot stay for us in one spot. She will be cruising to and fro until she intercepts us. We must wait."

"Ah, good! We must wait. And in the meantime, what? Fry here in the sacred heat with our tongues hanging out while you deal us drop by drop—*hein?*"

"Perhaps."

"But no!" The garrotter clenched his hands. "Blood of God, there is no man big enough to feed me with a spoon!"

Fenayrou's chuckle came pat, as it had more than once, and Dubosc shrugged.

"You laugh!" cried Perroquet, turning in fury. "But how about this lascar of a captain that lets us put to sea unprovided? What? He thinks of everything, does he? He thinks of everything! . . . Sacred farceur—let me hear you laugh again!"

Somehow Fenayrou was not so minded.

"And now he bids us be reasonable," concluded The Parrot. "Tell that to the devils in hell. You and your cigarettes, too. Bah—comedian!"

"It is true," muttered Fenayrou, frowning. "A bad piece of work for a captain of runaways."

But the doctor faced mutiny with his thin smile.

"All this alters nothing. Unless we would die very speedily, we must guard our water."

"By whose fault?"

"Mine," acknowledged the doctor. "I admit it. What then? We can't turn back. Here we are. Here we must stay. We can only do our best with what we have."

"I want a drink," repeated The Parrot, whose throat was afire since he had been denied.

"You can claim your share, of course. But take warning of one thing. After it is gone do not think to sponge on us—on Fenayrou and me."

"He would be capable of it, the pig!" exclaimed Fenayrou, to whom this thrust had been directed. "I know him. See here, my old, the doctor is right. Fair for one, fair for all."

"I want a drink."

Dubosc removed the wooden plug from the flask.

"Very well," he said quietly.

With a delicacy that lent something of legerdemain to all his gestures, he took out a small canvas wallet, the crude equivalent of the professional black bag, from which he drew a thimble. Meticulously he poured a brimming measure, and Fenayrou gave a shout at the grumbler's fallen jaw as he accepted that tiny cup between his big fingers. Dubosc served Fenayrou and himself with the same amount before he recorked the bottle.

"In this manner we should have enough to last us three days— maybe more—with equal shares among the three of us. . . ."

Such was his summing of the demonstration, and it passed without comment, as a matter of course in the premises, that he should count as he did—ignoring that other who sat alone at the stern of the raft, the black Canaque, the fourth man.

Perroquet had been outmaneuvered, but he listened sullenly while for the hundredth time Dubosc recited his easy and definite plan for their rescue, as arranged with his secret correspondents.

"That sounds very well," observed The Parrot, at last. "But what if these jokers only mock themselves of you? What if they have counted it good riddance to let you rot here? And us? Sacred name, that would be a famous jest! To let us wait for a ship and they have no ship!"

"Perhaps the doctor knows better than we how sure a source he counts upon," suggested Fenayrou slyly.

"That is so," said Dubosc, with great good humor. "My faith, it would not be well for them to fail me. Figure to yourselves that there is a safety vault in Paris full of papers to be opened at my death. Certain friends of mine could hardly afford to have some little confessions published that would be found there. . . . Such a tale as this, for instance—"

And to amuse them he told an indecent anecdote of high life, true or fictitious; it mattered nothing, so he could make Fenayrou's eyes glitter and The Parrot growl in wonder. Therein lay his means of ascendancy over such men, the knack of eloquence and vision. Harried, worn, oppressed by fears that he could sense so much more sharply than they, he must expend himself now in vulgar marvels to distract these ruder minds. He succeeded so far that when the wind fell at sunset they were almost cheerful, ready to believe that the morning would bring relief. They dined on dry biscuit and another thimbleful of water apiece and took watch by amiable agreement. And through that long, clear night of stars, whenever the one of the three who kept awake between his comrades chanced to look aft, he could see the vague blot of another figure—the naked Canaque, who slumbered there apart. . . .

It was an evil dawning. Fenayrou, on the morning trick, was aroused by a foot as hard as a hoof, and started up at Perroquet's wrathful face, with the doctor's graver glance behind.

"Idler! Good-for-nothing! Will you wake at least before I smash your ribs? Name of God, here is a way to stand watch!"

"Keep off!" cried Fenayrou wildly. "Keep off. Don't touch me!"

"Eh, and why not, fool? Do you know that the ship could have missed us? A ship could have passed us a dozen times while you slept?"

"*Bourrique!*"

"*Vache!*"

They spat the insults of the prison while Perroquet knotted his great fist over the other, who crouched away catlike, his mobile mouth twisted to a snarl. Dubosc stood aside in watchful calculation until against the angry red sunrise in which they floated there flashed the naked red gleam of steel.

"Enough. Fenayrou, put up that knife."

"The dog kicked me!"

"You were at fault," said Dubosc sternly.

"Perroquet!"

"Are we all to die that he may sleep?" stormed The Parrot.

"The harm is done. Listen now, both of you. Things are bad enough already. We may need all our energies. Look about."

They looked and saw the far, round horizon and the empty desert of the sea and their own long shadows that slipped slowly before them over its smooth, slow heaving, and nothing else. The land had sunk away from them in the night—some one of the chance currents that sweep among the islands had drawn them none could say where or how far. The trap had been sprung. "Good God, how lonely it is!" breathed Fenayrou in a hush.

No more was said. They dropped their quarrel. Silently they shared their rations as before, made shift to eat something with their few drops of water, and sat down to pit themselves one against another in the vital struggle that each could feel was coming—a sort of tacit test of endurance.

A calm had fallen, as it does between trades in this flawed belt, an absolute calm. The air hung weighted. The sea showed no faintest crinkle, only the maddening, unresting heave and fall in polished undulations on which the lances of the sun broke and drove in under their eyelids as white, hot splinters; a savage sun that kindled upon them with the power of burning glass, that sucked the moisture from poor human bits of jelly and sent them crawling to the shelter of their mats and brought them out again, gasping, to shrivel anew. The water, the world of water, seemed sleek and thick as oil. They came to loathe it and the rotting smell of it, and when the doctor made them dip themselves overside they found little comfort. It was warm, sluggish, slimed. But a curious thing resulted. . . .

While they clung along the edge of the raft they all faced inboard, and there sat the black Canaque. He did not join them. He did not glance at them. He sat hunkered on his heels in the way of the native, with arms hugging his knees. He stayed in his place at the stern, motionless under that shattering sun, gazing out into vacancy. Whenever they raised their eyes they saw him. He was the only thing to see.

"Here is one who appears to enjoy himself quite well," remarked Dubosc.

"I was thinking so myself," said Fenayrou.

"The animal!" rumbled Perroquet.

They observed him, and for the first time with direct interest, with thought of him as a fellow being—with the beginning of envy.

"He does not seem to suffer."

"What is going on in his brain? What does he dream of there? One would say he despises us."

"The beast!"

"Perhaps he is waiting for us to die," suggested Fenayrou with a harsh chuckle. "Perhaps he is waiting for the reward. He would not starve on the way home, at least. And he could deliver us—piecemeal."

They studied him.

"How does he do it, doctor? Has he no feeling?"

"I have been wondering," said Dubosc. "It may be that his fibers are tougher—his nerves."

"Yet we have had water and he none."

"But look at his skin, fresh and moist."

"And his belly, fat as a football!"

The Parrot hauled himself aboard.

"Don't tell me this black beast knows thirst!" he cried with a strange excitement. "Is there any way he could steal our supplies?"

"Certainly not."

"Then, name of a dog, what if he has supplies of his own hidden about?"

The same monstrous notion struck them all, and the others swarmed to help. They knocked the black aside. They searched the platform where he had sat, burrowing among the rushes, seeking some secret cache, another bottle or gourd. They found nothing.

"We were mistaken," said Dubosc.

But Perroquet had a different expression for disappointment. He turned on the Canaque and caught him by the kinky mop of the hair and proceeded to give him what is known as gruel in the cobalt mines. This was a little specialty of The Parrot's. He paused only when he himself was breathless and exhausted and threw the limp, unresisting body from him.

"There, lump of dirt! That will teach you. Maybe you're not so chipper now, my boy—*hein?* Not quite so satisfied with your luck. Pig! That will make you feel. . . ."

It was a ludicrous, a wanton, a witless thing. But the others said nothing. The learned Dubosc made no protest. Fenayrou had none of his usual jests at the garrotter's stupidity. They looked on as at the satisfaction of a common grudge. The white trampled the black with or without cause, and that was natural. And the black crept away into his place with his hurts and his wrongs and made no signs and struck no blow. And that was natural too.

The sun declined into a blazing furnace whereof the gates stood wide, and they prayed to hasten it and cursed because it hung enchanted. But when it was gone their blistered bodies still held the heat like things incandescent. The night closed down over them like a purple bowl, glazed and impermeable. They would have divided the watches again, though none of them thought of sleep, but Fenayrou made a discovery.

"Idiots!" he rasped. "Why should we look and look? A whole navy of ships cannot help us now. If we are becalmed, why, so are they!"

The Parrot was singularly put out.

"Is this true?" he asked Dubosc.

"Yes, we must hope for a breeze first."

"Then, name of God, why didn't you tell us so? Why did you keep on playing out the farce?"

He pondered it for a time. "See here," he said. "You are wise, eh? You are very wise. You know things we do not and you keep them to yourself." He leaned forward to peer into the doctor's face. "Very good. But if you think you're going to use that cursed smartness to get the best of us in any way—see here, my zig, I pull your gullet out like the string of an orange. . . . Like that. What?"

Fenayrou gave a nervous giggle and Dubosc shrugged, but it was perhaps about this time that he began to regret his intervention in the knife play.

For there was no breeze and there was no ship.

By the third morning each had sunk within himself, away from the rest. The doctor was lost in a profound depression, Perroquet in dark suspicion, and Fenayrou in bodily suffering, which he supported ill. Only two effective ties still bound their confederacy. One was the flask which Dubosc had slung at his side by a strip of the wickerwork. Every move he made with it, every drop he poured, was followed by burning eyes. And he knew, and he had no advantage of them in knowing, that the will to live was working its relentless formula aboard that raft. Under his careful saving there still remained nearly half of their original store.

The other bond, as it had come to be by strange mutation, was the presence of the black Canaque.

There was no forgetting the fourth man now, no overlooking of him. He loomed upon their consciousness, more formidable, more mysterious, more exasperating with every hour. Their own powers were ebbing. The naked savage had yet to give the slightest sign of complaint or weakness.

During the night he had stretched himself out on the platform as before, and after a time he had slept. Through the hours of darkness and silence, while each of the whites wrestled with despair, this black man had slept as placidly as a child, with easy, regular breathing. Since then he had resumed his place aft. And so he remained, unchanged, a fixed fact and a growing wonder.

The brutal rage of Perroquet, in which he had vented his distorted hate of the native, had been followed by superstitious doubts.

"Doctor," he said at last, in awed huskiness, "is this a man or a fiend?"

"It is a man."

"A miracle," put in Fenayrou.

But the doctor lifted a finger in a way his pupils would have remembered.

"It is a man," he repeated, "and a very poor and wretched example of a man. You will find no lower type anywhere. Observe his cranial angle, the high ears, the heavy bones of his skull. He is scarcely above the ape. There are educated apes more intelligent."

"Ah! Then what?"

"He has a secret," said the doctor.

That was a word to transfix them.

"A secret! But we see him—every move he makes, every instant. What chance for a secret?"

The doctor rather forgot his audience, betrayed by chagrin and bitterness.

"How pitiful!" he mused. "Here are we three—children of the century, products of civilization—I fancy none would deny that, at least. And here is this man who belongs before the Stone Age. In a set trial of fitness, of wits, of resource, is he to win? Pitiful!"

"What kind of secret?" demanded Perroquet, fuming.

"I cannot say," admitted Dubosc, with a baffled gesture. "Possibly some method of breathing, some peculiar posture that operates to cheat the sensations of the body. Such things are known among primitive peoples—known and carefully guarded—like the properties of certain drugs, the uses of hypnotism and complex natural laws. Then, again, it may be psychologic—a mental attitude persistently held. Who knows? . . .

"To ask him? Useless. He will not tell. Why should he? We scorn him. We give him no share with us. We abuse him. He simply falls back on his own expedients. He simply remains inscrutable—as he has always been and will always be. He never tells those innermost secrets. They are the means by which he has survived from the depth of time, by which he may yet survive when all our wisdom is dust."

"I know several very excellent ways of learning secrets," said Fenayrou as he passed his dry tongue over his lips. "Shall I begin?"

Dubosc came back with a start and looked at him.

"It would be useless. He could stand any torture you could invent. No, that is not the way."

"Listen to mine," said Perroquet, with sudden violence. "Me, I am wearied of the gab. You say he is a man? Very well. If he is a man, he must have blood in his veins. That would be, anyway, good to drink."

"No," returned Dubosc. "It would be hot. Also it would be salt. For food—perhaps. But we do not need food."

"Kill the animal, then, and throw him over!"

"We gain nothing."

"Well, sacred name, what do you want?"

"To beat him!" cried the doctor, curiously agitated. "To beat him at the game—that's what I want! For our own sakes, for our racial pride, we must, we must. To outlast him, to prove ourselves his masters. By better brain, by better organization and control. Watch him, watch him, friends—that we may ensnare him, that we may detect and defeat him in the end!"

But the doctor was miles beyond them.

"Watch?" growled The Parrot. "I believe you, old windbag. It is all one watch. I sleep no more and leave any man alone with that bottle."

To this the issue finally sharpened. Such craving among such men could not be stayed much longer by driblets. They watched. They watched the Canaque. They watched each other. And they watched the falling level in their flask—until the tension gave.

Another dawn upon the same dead calm, rising like a conflagration through the puddled air, cloudless, hopeless. Another day of blinding, slow-drawn agony to meet. And Dubosc announced that their allowance must be cut to half a thimbleful.

There remained perhaps a quarter of a liter—a miserable reprieve of bare life among the three of them, but one good swallow for a yearning throat.

At sight of the bottle, at the tinkle of its limpid contents, so cool and silvery green inside the glass, Fenayrou's nerve snapped. . . .

"More!" he begged, with pleading hands. "I die. More!"

When the doctor refused him he grovelled among the reeds, then rose suddenly to his knees and tossed his arms abroad with a hoarse cry:

"A ship! A ship!"

The others spun about. They saw the thin unbroken ring of this greater and more terrible prison to which they had exchanged; and that was all they saw, though they stared and stared. They turned back to Fenayrou and found him in the act of tilting the bottle. A cunning slash of his knife had loosed it from its sling at the doctor's side. . . . Even now he was sucking at the mouth, spilling the precious liquid—

With one sweep Perroquet caught up their paddle and flattened him, crushed him.

Springing across the prostrate man, Dubosc snatched the flask upright and put the width of the raft between himself and the big garrotter who stood wide-legged, his bloodshot eyes alight, rumbling in his chest.

"There is no ship," said The Parrot. "There will be no ship. We are done. Because of you and your rotten promises that brought us here—doctor, liar, ass!"

Dubosc stood firm.

"Come a step nearer and I break bottle and all over your head."

They stood regarding each other, and Perroquet's brows gathered in a slow effort of thought.

"Consider," urged Dubosc with his quaint touch of pedantry. "Why should you and I fight? We are rational men. We can see this trouble through and win yet. Such weather cannot last for ever. Besides, here are only two of us to divide the water now."

"That is true," nodded The Parrot. "That is true, isn't it? Fenayrou kindly leaves us his share. An inheritance—what? A famous idea. I'll take mine now."

Dubosc probed him keenly.

"My share, at once, if you please," insisted Perroquet, with heavy docility. "Afterward, we shall see. Afterward."

The doctor smiled his grim and wan little smile.

"So be it."

Without relinquishing the flask he brought out his canvas wallet once more—that wallet which replaced the professional black bag—and rolled out the thimble by some swift sleight of his flexible fingers while he held Perroquet's glance with his own.

"I will measure it for you."

He poured the thimbleful and handed it over quickly, and when Perroquet had tossed it off he filled again and again.

"Four—five," he counted. "That is enough."

But The Parrot's big grip closed quietly around his wrist at the last offering and pinioned him and held him helpless.

"No, it is not enough. Now I will take the rest. Ha, wise man! Have I fooled you at last?"

There was no chance to struggle, and Dubosc did not try, only stayed smiling up at him, waiting.

Perroquet took the bottle.

"The best man wins," he remarked. "Eh, my zig? A bright notion—of yours. The—best—"

His lips moved, but no sound issued. A look of the most intense surprise spread upon his round face. He stood swaying a moment, and collapsed like a huge hinged toy when the string is cut.

Dubosc stooped and caught the bottle again, looking down at his big adversary, who sprawled in brief convulsion and lay still, a bluish scum oozing between his teeth. . . .

"Yes, the best man wins," repeated the doctor, and laughed as he in turn raised the flask for a draught.

"The best wins!" echoed a voice in his ear.

Fenayrou, writhing up and striking like a wounded snake, drove the knife home between his shoulders.

The bottle fell and rolled to the middle of the platform, and there, while each strove vainly to reach it, it poured out its treasure in a tiny stream that trickled away and was lost.

. . .

It may have been minutes or hours later—for time has no count in emptiness—when next a sound proceeded from that frail slip of a raft, hung like a mote between sea and sky. It was a phrase of song, a wandering strain in half tones and fluted accidentals, not unmelodious. The black Canaque was singing. He sang without emotion or effort, quite casually and softly to himself. So might he sing by his forest hut to ease some hour of idleness. Clasping his knees and gazing out into space, untroubled, unmoved, enigmatic to the end, he sang—he sang.

And after all, the ship came.

She came in a manner befitting the sauciest little tops'l schooner between Nukahiva and the Pelews—as her owner often averred and none but the envious denied—in a manner worthy, too, of that able Captain Jean Guibert, the merriest little scamp that ever cleaned a pearl bank or snapped a cargo of labor from a scowling coast. Before the first whiff out of the west came the *Petite Susanne*, curtsying and skipping along with a flash of white frill by her forefoot, and brought up startled and stood shaking her skirts and keeping herself quite daintily to windward.

"And 'ere they are sure enough, by dam'!" said the polyglot Captain Jean in the language of commerce and profanity. "Zose passengers for us, hey? They been here all the time, not ten mile off—I bet you, Marteau. Ain't it 'ell? What you zink, my gar?"

His second, a tall and excessively bony individual of gloomy outlook, handed back the glasses.

"More bad luck. I never approved of this job. And now—see? —we have had our voyage for nothing. What misfortune!"

"Marteau, if that good Saint Pierre gives you some day a gold 'arp still you would holler bad luck—bad job!" retorted Captain Jean. "Do I 'ire you to stand zere and cry about ze luck? Get a boat over, and quicker zan zat!"

M. Marteau aroused himself sufficiently to take command of the boat's crew that presently dropped away to investigate. . . .

"It is even as I thought," he called up from the quarter when he returned with his report. "I told vou how it would be, Captain Jean."

"Hey?" cried the captain, bouncing at the rail. "Have you got zose passengers yet, *enfant de salaud?*"

"I have not," said Marteau in the tone of lugubrious triumph. There was nothing in the world that could have pleased him quite so much as this chance to prove Captain Jean the loser on a venture. "We are too late. Bad luck, bad luck—that calm. What misfortune! They are all dead!"

"Will you mind your business?" shouted the skipper.

"But still, the gentlemen are dead—"

"What is zat to me? All ze better, they will cost nozing to feed."

"But how—"

"Hogsheads, my gar," said Captain Jean paternally. "Zose hogsheads in the afterhold. Fill them nicely with brine, and zere we are!" And, having drawn all possible satisfaction from the other's amazement, he sprang the hub of his joke with a grin. "Ze gentlemen's passage is all paid, Marteau. Before we left Sydney, Marteau. I contrac' to bring back three escape' convicts, and so by 'ell I do— in pickle! And now if you'll kindly get zose passengers aboard like I said an' bozzer less about ze goddam luck, I be much oblige'. Also, zere is no green on my eye, Marteau, and you can dam' well smoke it!"

Marteau recovered himself with difficulty in time to recall another trifling detail. "There is a fourth man on board that raft, Captain Jean. He is a Canaque—still alive. What shall we do with him?"

"A Canaque?" snapped Captain Jean. "A Canaque! I have no word in my contrac' about any Canaque. . . . Leave him zere. He is only a dam' black. He'll do well enough where he is."

And Captain Jean was right, perfectly right, for while the *Petite Susanne* was taking aboard her grisly cargo the wind freshened from the west, and just about the time she was shaping away for Australia the "dam' black" spread his own sail of pandanus leaves and twirled his own helm of *niaouli* wood and headed the catamaran eastward, back toward New Caledonia.

Feeling somewhat dry after his exertion, he plucked at random from the platform a hollow reed with a sharp end, and, stretching himself at full length in his accustomed place, at the stern, he thrust the reed down into one of the bladders underneath and drank his fill of sweet water. . . .

He had a dozen such storage bladders remaining, built into the floats at intervals above the waterline—quite enough to last him safely home again.

"Miss Lucy Wessen's eyes were shining,
and I went the whole hog." . . .

I'm a Fool

SHERWOOD ANDERSON (1876–1941)

The scenes of "I'm a Fool" are drawn from the
author's boyhood as an odd-job worker at race
tracks and around Middle Western streets. His
father was a drifter, each of whose seven children
was born in a different town. Young Jobby, as he
was called, was born in Camden, Ohio, and he always had the look of a typical midlander.

His rebellion against the worst aspects of industrial civilization was based on a knowledge of
its seamy side. At seventeen he was a factory hand
in Chicago. After enlisting and serving in Cuba
in the Spanish-American War, he returned to
Chicago, entered the advertising business, and later
became manager of a paint factory in Elyria, Ohio.
This job he forsook in favor of the literary life,
dramatically leaving the factory in the middle of
dictating a letter.

His writing in the Dial and the Little Review
made him known as a member of the growing
"Chicago group." His first novel appeared in 1916.

Winesburg, Ohio (1919), a powerful collection of
tales and sketches which is a landmark in modern
fiction, brought him success. After winning the
Dial prize in 1921, he spent a year abroad. In 1925
he settled in Marion, Virginia, and began running
both of the town's newspapers, one Democratic
and one Republican.

His best short stories are found in Winesburg,
Ohio; The Triumph of the Egg (1921); Horses
and Men (1923); and Death in the Woods (1933).
"I'm a Fool" was first published in 1922 in the
Dial.

IT WAS A HARD JOLT for me, one of the most bitterest I
ever had to face. And it all came about through my own foolishness
too. Even yet, sometimes, I want to cry or swear or kick myself.
Perhaps, even now, after all this time, there will be a kind of satisfaction in making myself look cheap by telling of it.

It began at three o'clock one October afternoon as I sat in
the grandstand at the fall trotting and pacing meet at Sandusky,
Ohio.

To tell the truth, I felt a little foolish that I should be sitting in
the grandstand at all. During the summer before I had left my
home town with Harry Whitehead and, with a Negro named Burt,
had taken a job as swipe with one of the two horses Harry was
campaigning through the fall race meets that year. Mother cried
and my sister Mildred, who wanted to get a job as schoolteacher
in our town that fall, stormed and scolded about the house all
during the week before I left. They both thought it something
disgraceful that one of our family should take a place as a swipe
with race horses. I've an idea Mildred thought my taking the place

would stand in the way of her getting the job she'd been working so long for.

But after all I had to work and there was no other work to be got. A big lumbering fellow of nineteen couldn't just hang around the house and I had got too big to mow people's lawns and sell newspapers. Little chaps who could get next to people's sympathies by their sizes were always getting jobs away from me. There was one fellow who kept saying to everyone who wanted a lawn mowed or a cistern cleaned that he was saving money to work his way through college, and I used to lie awake nights thinking up ways to injure him without being found out. I kept thinking of wagons running over him and bricks falling on his head as he walked along the street. But never mind him.

I got the place with Harry and I liked Burt fine. We got along splendid together. He was a big Negro with a lazy sprawling body and soft kind eyes, and when it came to a fight he could hit like Jack Johnson. He had Bucephalus, a big black pacing stallion that could do 2.09 or 2.10 if he had to, and I had a little gelding named Doctor Fritz that never lost a race all fall when Harry wanted him to win.

We set out from home late in July in a box car with the two horses, and after that, until late November, we kept moving along to the race meets and the fairs. It was a peachy time for me, I'll say that. Sometimes, now, I think that boys who are raised regular in houses, and never have a fine Negro like Burt for best friend, and go to high schools and college, and never steal anything or get drunk a little, or learn to swear from fellows who know how, or come walking up in front of a grandstand in their shirt sleeves and with dirty horsey pants on when the races are going on and the grandstand is full of people all dressed up— What's the use talking about it? Such fellows don't know nothing at all. They've never had no opportunity.

But I did. Burt taught me how to rub down a horse and put the bandages on after a race and steam a horse out and a lot of valuable things for any man to know. He could wrap a bandage on a horse's leg so smooth that if it had been the same color you would think it was his skin, and I guess he'd have been a big driver, too, and got to the top like Murphy and Walter Cox and the others if he hadn't been black.

Gee whizz, it was fun. You got to a county seat town maybe, say, on a Saturday or Sunday, and the fair began the next Tuesday and lasted until Friday afternoon. Doctor Fritz would be, say, in the 2.25 trot on Tuesday afternoon and on Thursday afternoon Bucephalus would knock 'em cold in the "free-for-all" pace. It left you a lot of time to hang around and listen to horse talk, and see Burt knock some yap cold that got too gay, and you'd find out about horses and men and pick up a lot of stuff you could use all the rest of your life if you had some sense and salted down what you heard and felt and saw.

And then at the end of the week when the race meet was over, and Harry had run home to tend up to his livery stable business, you and Burt hitched the two horses to carts and drove slow and steady across country to the place for the next meeting so as not to overheat the horses, etc., etc., you know.

Gee whizz, gosh amighty, the nice hickorynut and beechnut and oaks and other kinds of trees along the roads, all brown and red, and the good smells, and Burt singing a song that was called Deep River, and the country girls at the windows of houses and everything. You can stick your colleges up your nose for all me. I guess I know where I got my education.

Why, one of those little burgs of towns you come to on the way, say now, on a Saturday afternoon, and Burt says, "Let's lay up here." And you did.

And you took the horses to a livery stable and fed them and you got your good clothes out of a box and put them on.

And the town was full of farmers gaping, because they could see you were race horse people, and the kids maybe never see a Negro before and was afraid and run away when the two of us walked down their main street.

And that was before prohibition and all that foolishness, and so you went into a saloon, the two of you, and all the yaps come and stood around, and there was always someone pretended he was horsey and knew things and spoke up and began asking questions, and all you did was to lie and lie all you could about what horses you had, and I said I owned them, and then some fellow said, "Will you have a drink of whisky?" and Burt knocked his eye out the way he could say, offhand like, "Oh, well, all right, I'm agreeable to take a little nip. I'll split a quart with you." Gee whizz.

But that isn't what I want to tell my story about. We got home late in November and I promised mother I'd quit the race horses for good. There's a lot of things you've got to promise a mother because she don't know any better.

And so, there not being any work in our town any more than when I left there to go to the races, I went off to Sandusky and got a pretty good place taking care of the horses for a man who owned a teaming and delivery and storage business there. It was a pretty good place with good eats and a day off each week and sleeping on a cot in the big barn, and mostly just shoveling in hay and oats to a lot of big good-enough skates of horses that couldn't have trotted a race with a toad. I wasn't dissatisfied and I could send money home.

And then, as I started to tell you, the fall races come to Sandusky and I got the day off and I went. I left the job at noon and had on my good clothes and my new brown derby hat I'd just bought the Saturday before, and a stand-up collar.

First of all I went downtown and walked about with the dudes. I've always thought to myself, "put up a good front," and so I did it. I had forty dollars in my pocket and so I went into the West House, a big hotel, and walked up to the cigar stand. "Give me three twenty-five cent cigars," I said. There was a lot of horse men and strangers and dressed-up people from other towns standing around in the lobby and in the bar, and I mingled amongst them. In the bar there was a fellow with a cane and a Windsor tie on, that it made me sick to look at him. I like a man to be a man and dress up, but not to go put on that kind of airs. So I pushed him aside, kind of rough, and had me a drink of whisky. And then he looked at me as though he thought he'd get gay, but he changed his mind and didn't say anything. And then I had another drink of whisky, just to show him something, and went out and had a hack out to the races all to myself, and when I got there I bought myself the best seat I could get up in the grandstand, but didn't go in for any of these boxes. That's putting on too many airs.

And so there I was, sitting up in the grandstand as gay as you please and looking down on the swipes coming out with their horses and with their dirty horsey pants on and the horse blankets swung over their shoulders same as I had been doing all the year before. I liked one thing about the same as the other, sitting up there and feeling grand and being down there and looking up at the yaps and feeling grander and more important too. One thing's about as good as another if you take it just right. I've often said that.

Well, right in front of me, in the grandstand that day, there was a fellow with a couple of girls and they was about my age. The young fellow was a nice guy all right. He was the kind maybe that goes to college and then comes to be a lawyer or maybe a newspaper editor or something like that, but he wasn't stuck on himself. There are some of that kind are all right and he was one of the ones.

He had his sister with him and another girl and the sister looked around over his shoulder, accidental at first, not intending to start anything—she wasn't that kind—and her eyes and mine happened to meet.

You know how it is. Gee, she was a peach. She had on a soft dress, kind of a blue stuff, and it looked carelessly made, but was well sewed and made and everything. I knew that much. I blushed when she looked right at me and so did she. She was the nicest girl I've ever seen in my life. She wasn't stuck on herself and she could talk proper grammar without being like a schoolteacher or something like that. What I mean is, she was O.K. I think maybe her father was well-to-do, but not rich to make her chesty because she was his daughter, as some are. Maybe he owned a drug store or a dry goods store in their home town, or something like that. She never told me and I never asked.

My own people are all O.K. too, when you come to that. My

grandfather was Welsh and over in the old country, in Wales, he was—but never mind that.

The first heat of the first race come off and the young fellow setting there with the two girls left them and went down to make a bet. I knew what he was up to, but he didn't talk big and noisy and let everyone around know he was a sport, as some do. He wasn't that kind. Well, he come back and I heard him tell the two girls what horse he'd bet on, and when the heat was trotted they all half got to their feet and acted in the excited, sweaty way people do when they've got money down on a race, and the horse they bet on is up there pretty close at the end, and they think maybe he'll come on with a rush, but he never does because he hasn't got the old juice in him, come right down to it.

And, then, pretty soon, the horses came out for the 2.18 pace and there was a horse in it I knew. He was a horse Bob French had in his string, but Bob didn't own him. He was a horse owned by a Mr. Mathers down at Marietta, Ohio.

This Mr. Mathers had a lot of money and owned a coal mine or something, and he had a swell place out in the country, and he was stuck on race horses, but was a Presbyterian or something, and I think more than likely his wife was one, too, maybe a stiffer one than himself. So he never raced his horses hisself, and the story round the Ohio race tracks was that when one of his horses got ready to go to the races he turned him over to Bob French and pretended to his wife he was sold.

So Bob had the horses and he did pretty much as he pleased and you can't blame Bob; at least, I never did. Sometimes he was out to win and sometimes he wasn't. I never cared much about that when I was swiping a horse. What I did want to know was that my horse had the speed and could go out in front if you wanted him to.

And, as I'm telling you, there was Bob in this race with one of Mr. Mathers' horses, was named "About Ben Ahem" or something like that, and was fast as a streak. He was a gelding and had a mark of 2.21, but could step in .08 or .09.

Because when Burt and I were out, as I've told you, the year before, there was a Negro Burt knew, worked for Mr. Mathers, and we went out there one day when we didn't have no race on at the Marietta Fair and our boss Harry had gone home.

And so everyone was gone to the fair but just this one Negro, and he took us all through Mr. Mathers' swell house and he and Burt tapped a bottle of wine Mr. Mathers had hid in his bedroom, back in a closet, without his wife knowing, and he showed us this Ahem horse. Burt was always stuck on being a driver, but didn't have much chance to get to the top, being a Negro, and he and the other Negro gulped that whole bottle of wine and Burt got a little lit up.

So the Negro let Burt take this About Ben Ahem and step him a mile in a track Mr. Mathers had all to himself, right there on the farm. And Mr. Mathers had one child, a daughter, kinda sick and not very good-looking, and she came home and we had to hustle and get About Ben Ahem stuck back in the barn.

I'm only telling you to get everything straight. At Sandusky, that afternoon I was at the fair, this young fellow with the two girls was fussed, being with the girls and losing his bet. You know how a fellow is that way. One of them was his girl and the other his sister. I had figured that out.

"Gee whizz," I says to myself, "I'm going to give him the dope."

He was mighty nice when I touched him on the shoulder. He and the girls were nice to me right from the start and clear to the end. I'm not blaming them.

And so he leaned back and I gave him the dope on About Ben Ahem. "Don't bet a cent on this first heat because he'll go like an oxen hitched to a plough, but when the first heat is over go right down and lay on your pile." That's what I told him.

Well, I never saw a fellow treat any one sweller. There was a fat man sitting beside the little girl that had looked at me twice by this time, and I at her, and both blushing, and what did he do but have the nerve to turn and ask the fat man to get up and change places with me so I could set with his crowd.

Gee whizz, amighty. There I was. What a chump I was to go

and get gay up there in the West House bar, and just because that dude was standing there with a cane and that kind of a necktie on, to go and get all balled up and drink that whisky, just to show off.

Of course, she would know, me setting right beside her and letting her smell of my breath. I could have kicked myself right down out of that grandstand and all around that race track and made a faster record than most of the skates of horses they had there that year.

Because that girl wasn't any mutt of a girl. What wouldn't I have given right then for a stick of chewing gum to chew, or a lozenger, or some licorice, or most anything. I was glad I had those twenty-five cent cigars in my pocket, and right away I give that fellow one and lit one myself. Then that fat man got up and we changed places and there I was plunked down beside her.

They introduced themselves, and the fellow's best girl he had with him was named Miss Elinor Woodbury, and her father was a manufacturer of barrels from a place called Tiffin, Ohio. And the fellow himself was named Wilbur Wessen and his sister was Miss Lucy Wessen.

I suppose it was their having such swell names got me off my trolley. A fellow, just because he has been a swipe with a race horse, and works taking care of horses for a man in the teaming, delivery and storage business, isn't any better or worse than anyone else. I've often thought that, and said it, too.

But you know how a fellow is. There's something in that kind of nice clothes, and the kind of nice eyes she had, and the way she looked at me, awhile before, over her brother's shoulder, and me looking back at her, and both of us blushing.

I couldn't show her up for a boob, could I?

I made a fool of myself, that's what I did. I said my name was Walter Mathers from Marietta, Ohio, and then I told all three of them the smashingest lie you ever heard. What I said was that my father owned the horse About Ben Ahem, and that he had let him out to this Bob French for racing purposes, because our family was proud and had never gone into racing that way, in our own name, I mean. Then I had got started, and they were all leaning over and listening, and Miss Lucy Wessen's eyes were shining, and I went the whole hog.

I told about our place down at Marietta, and about the big stables and the grand brick house we had on a hill, up above the Ohio River, but I knew enough not to do it in no bragging way. What I did was to start things and then let them drag the rest out of me. I acted just as reluctant to tell as I could. Our family hasn't got any barrel factory, and, since I've known us, we've always been pretty poor, but not asking anything of anyone at that, and my grandfather, over in Wales—but never mind that.

We set there talking like we had known each other for years and years, and I went and told them that my father had been expecting maybe this Bob French wasn't on the square, and had sent me up to Sandusky on the sly to find out what I could.

And I bluffed it through I had found out all about the 2.18 pace in which About Ben Ahem was to start.

I said he would lose the first heat by pacing like a lame cow and then he would come back and skin 'em alive after that. And to back up what I said I took thirty dollars out of my pocket and handed it to Mr. Wilbur Wessen and asked him would he mind, after the first heat, to go down and place it on About Ben Ahem for whatever odds he could get. What I said was that I didn't want Bob French to see me and none of the swipes.

Sure enough the first heat came off and About Ben Ahem went off his stride, up the back stretch, and looked like a wooden horse or a sick one, and come in to be last. Then this Wilbur Wessen went down to the betting place under the grandstand and there I was with the two girls, and when that Miss Woodbury was looking the other way once, Lucy Wessen kinda, with her shoulder you know, kinda touched me. You know how a woman can do. They get close, but not getting gay either. You know what they do. Gee whizz.

And then they give me a jolt. What they had done when I didn't know was to get together, and they had decided Wilbur Wessen would bet fifty dollars, and the two girls had gone and put in ten dollars each of their own money, too. I was sick then, but I was sicker later.

About the gelding, About Ben Ahem, and their winning their money I wasn't worried a lot about that. It come out O.K. Ahem stepped the next three heats like a bushel of spoiled eggs going to market before they could be found out, and Wilbur Wessen had got nine to two for the money. There was something else eating at me.

Because Wilbur come back after he had bet the money, and after that he spent most of his time talking to that Miss Woodbury, and Lucy Wessen and I was left alone together like on a desert island. Gee, if I'd only been on the square or if there had been any way of getting myself on the square. There ain't any Walter Mathers, like I said to her and them, and there hasn't ever been one, but if there was, I bet I'd go to Marietta, Ohio, and shoot him tomorrow.

There I was, big boob that I am. Pretty soon the race was over, and Wilbur had gone down and collected our money, and we had a hack downtown, and he stood us a swell dinner at the West House, and a bottle of champagne beside.

And I was with that girl and she wasn't saying much, and I wasn't saying much either. One thing I know. She wasn't stuck on me because of the lie about my father being rich and all that. There's a way you know. . . . Craps amighty. There's a kind of girl you see just once in your life, and if you don't get busy and make hay then you're gone for good and all and might as well go jump off a bridge. They give you a look from inside of them somewhere, and it ain't no vamping, and what it means is—you want that girl to be your wife, and you want nice things around her like flowers and swell clothes, and you want her to have the kids you're going to have, and you want good music played and no ragtime. Gee whizz.

There's a place over near Sandusky, across a kind of bay, and it's called Cedar Point. And when we had had that dinner we went over to it in a launch, all by ourselves. Wilbur and Miss Lucy and that Miss Woodbury had to catch a ten o'clock train back to Tiffin,

Ohio, because when you're out with girls like that you can't get careless and miss any trains and stay out all night like you can with some kinds of Janes.

And Wilbur blowed himself to the launch and it cost him fifteen cold plunks, but I wouldn't ever have knew it if I hadn't listened. He wasn't no tinhorn kind of a sport.

Over at the Cedar Point place we didn't stay around where there was a gang of common kind of cattle at all.

There was big dance halls and dining places for yaps, and there was a beach you could walk along and get where it was dark, and we went there.

She didn't talk hardly at all and neither did I, and I was thinking how glad I was my mother was all right, and always made us kids learn to eat with a fork at table and not swill soup and not be noisy and rough like a gang you see around a race track that way.

Then Wilbur and his girl went away up the beach and Lucy and I set down in a dark place where there was some roots of old trees the water had washed up, and after that, the time, till we had to go back in the launch and they had to catch their trains, wasn't nothing at all. It went like winking your eye.

Here's how it was. The place we were setting in was dark, like I said, and there was roots from that old stump sticking up like arms, and there was a watery smell, and the night was like—as if you could put your hand out and feel it—so warm and soft and dark and sweet like an orange.

I most cried and I most swore and I most jumped up and danced, I was so mad and happy and sad.

When Wilbur came back from being alone with his girl, and she saw him coming, Lucy she says, "We got to go to the train now," and she was most crying, too, but she never knew nothing I knew, and she couldn't be so all busted up. And then, before Wilbur and Miss Woodbury got up to where she was, she put her face up and kissed me quick and put her head up against me and she was all quivering and— Gee whizz.

Sometimes I hope I have cancer and die. I guess you know what I mean. We went in the launch across the bay to the train like that, and it was dark too. She whispered and said it was like she and I could get out of the boat and walk on the water, and it sounded foolish, but I knew what she meant.

And then quick, we were right at the depot, and there was a big gang of yaps, the kind that goes to the fairs, and crowded and milling around like cattle, and how could I tell her? "It won't be long because you'll write and I'll write to you." That's all she said.

I got a chance like a hay barn afire. A swell chance I got.

And maybe she would write me, down at Marietta that way, and the letter would come back, and stamped on the front of it by the U.S.A. "there ain't any such guy," or something like that, whatever they stamp on a letter that way.

And me trying to pass myself off for a bigbug and a swell—to her, as decent a little body as God ever made. Craps amighty. A swell chance I got.

And then the train come in and she got on, and Wilbur Wessen come and shook hands with me, and that Miss Woodbury was nice too, and bowed to me and I at her and the train went and I busted out and cried like a kid.

Gee, I could have run after that train and made Dan Patch look like a freight train after a wreck, but socks amighty, what was the use? Did you ever see such a fool?

I'll bet you what—if I had an arm broke right now or a train had run over my foot—I wouldn't go to no doctor at all. I'd go set down and let her hurt and hurt—that's what I'd do.

I'll bet you what—if I hadn't a drunk that booze I'd a never been such a boob as to go tell such a lie—that couldn't never be made straight to a lady like her.

I wish I had that fellow right here that had on a Windsor tie and carried a cane. I'd smash him for fair. Gosh darn his eyes. He's a big fool—that's what he is.

And if I'm not another you just go find me one and I'll quit working and be a bum and give him my job. I don't care nothing for working and earning money and saving it for no such boob as myself.

*Jim Kendall never knew that the last
and best joke was on him. . . .*

Haircut

RING LARDNER (1885–1933)

The sports writer who became a master of the colloquial short story was born Ringgold Wilmer
Lardner in Niles, Michigan. After graduating from
high school in his native city, he studied engineer-
ing for a semester at Armour Institute. Then, after
a series of odd jobs, he became a reporter on the
South Bend Times. Later he covered sports for the
Hearst papers and for two years edited a baseball
weekly, Sporting News, in St. Louis.

A set of humorous stories in the Saturday Evening Post about baseball players became widely
known, and Lardner's later serious work is sometimes overshadowed by his reputation as a mere
funny man. At heart he was a biting satirist who
charged himself with debunking phonies and fakes
of all kinds, but his scorn of the brute and the
boor shown in "Haircut" is balanced by the keen
enjoyment of human foibles revealed in such a
story as "Golden Honeymoon."

His genius in recording the way real people really

talk has led to the quotation of his dialogue in many studies of the modern American language. He collaborated on two successful Broadway plays, Elmer the Great and June Moon.

"Haircut" was first published in Liberty magazine in 1925 and later appeared in The Love Nest and Other Stories (1926). All the Lardner stories are collected in one volume in Round Up (1929).

I GOT ANOTHER BARBER that comes from Carterville and helps me out Saturdays, but the rest of the time I can get along all right alone. You can see for yourself that this ain't no New York City and besides that, the most of the boys works all day and don't have no leisure to drop in here and get themselves prettied up.

You're a newcomer, ain't you? I thought I hadn't seen you round before. I hope you like it good enough to stay. As I say, we ain't no New York City or Chicago, but we have pretty good times. Not as good, though, since Jim Kendall got killed. When he was alive, him and Hod Meyers used to keep this town in an uproar. I bet they was more laughin' done here than any town its size in America.

Jim was comical, and Hod was pretty near a match for him. Since Jim's gone, Hod tries to hold his end up just the same as ever, but it's tough goin' when you ain't got nobody to kind of work with.

They used to be plenty fun in here Saturdays. This place is jam-packed Saturdays, from four o'clock on. Jim and Hod would show up right after their supper, round six o'clock. Jim would set himself down in that big chair, nearest the blue spittoon. Whoever had been settin' in that chair, why they'd get up when Jim come in and give it to him.

You'd of thought it was a reserved seat like they have sometimes in a theayter. Hod would generally always stand or walk up and down, or some Saturdays, of course, he'd be settin' in this chair part of the time, gettin' a haircut.

Well, Jim would set there a w'ile without openin' his mouth only to spit, and then finally he'd say to me, "Whitey,"—my right name, that is, my right first name, is Dick, but everybody round here calls me Whitey—Jim would say, "Whitey, your nose looks like a rosebud tonight. You must of been drinkin' some of your aw de cologne."

So I'd say, "No, Jim, but you look like you'd been drinkin' somethin' of that kind or somethin' worse."

Jim would have to laugh at that, but then he'd speak up and say, "No, I ain't had nothing to drink, but that ain't sayin' I wouldn't like somethin'. I wouldn't even mind if it was wood alcohol."

Then Hod Meyers would say, "Neither would your wife." That would set everybody to laughin' because Jim and his wife wasn't on very good terms. She'd of divorced him only they wasn't no chance to get alimony and she didn't have no way to take care of herself and the kids. She couldn't never understand Jim. He *was* kind of rough, but a good fella at heart.

Him and Hod had all kinds of sport with Milt Sheppard. I don't suppose you've seen Milt. Well, he's got an Adam's apple that looks more like a mushmelon. So I'd be shavin' Milt and when I'd start to shave down here on his neck, Hod would holler, "Hey, Whitey, wait a minute! Before you cut into it, let's make up a pool and see who can guess closest to the number of seeds."

And Jim would say, "If Milt hadn't of been so hoggish, he'd of ordered a half a cantaloupe instead of a whole one and it might not of stuck in his throat."

All the boys would roar at this and Milt himself would force a smile, though the joke was on him. Jim certainly was a card!

There's his shavin' mug, settin' on the shelf, right next to Charley Vail's. "Charles M. Vail." That's the druggist. He comes in regular for his shave, three times a week. And Jim's is the cup next to

Charley's. "James H. Kendall." Jim won't need no shavin' mug no more, but I'll leave it there just the same for old time's sake. Jim certainly was a character!

Years ago, Jim used to travel for a canned goods concern over in Carterville. They sold canned goods. Jim had the whole northern half of the State and was on the road five days out of every week. He'd drop in here Saturdays and tell his experiences for that week. It was rich.

I guess he paid more attention to playin' jokes than makin' sales. Finally the concern let him out and he come right home here and told everybody he'd been fired instead of sayin' he'd resigned like most fellas would of.

It was a Saturday and the shop was full and Jim got up out of that chair and says, "Gentlemen, I got an important announcement to make. I been fired from my job."

Well, they asked him if he was in earnest and he said he was and nobody could think of nothin' to say till Jim finally broke the ice himself. He says, "I been sellin' canned goods and now I'm canned goods myself."

You see, the concern he'd been workin' for was a factory that made canned goods. Over in Carterville. And now Jim said he was canned himself. He was certainly a card!

Jim had a great trick that he used to play w'ile he was travelin'. For instance, he'd be ridin' on a train and they'd come to some little town like, well, like, we'll say, like Benton. Jim would look out the train window and read the signs on the stores.

For instance, they'd be a sign, "Henry Smith, Dry Goods." Well, Jim would write down the name and the name of the town and when he got to wherever he was goin' he'd mail back a postal card to Henry Smith at Benton and not sign no name to it, but he'd write on the card, well, somethin' like "Ask your wife about that book agent that spent the afternoon last week," or "Ask your Missus who kept her from gettin' lonesome the last time you was in Carterville." And he'd sign the card, "A Friend."

Of course, he never knew what really come of none of these

jokes, but he could picture what *probably* happened and that was enough.

Jim didn't work very steady after he lost his position with the Carterville people. What he did earn, doin' odd jobs round town, why he spent pretty near all of it on gin and his family might of starved if the stores hadn't of carried them along. Jim's wife tried her hand at dressmakin', but they ain't nobody goin' to get rich makin' dresses in this town.

As I say, she'd of divorced Jim, only she seen that she couldn't support herself and the kids and she was always hopin' that some day Jim would cut out his habits and give her more than two or three dollars a week.

They was a time when she would go to whoever he was workin' for and ask them to give her his wages, but after she done this once or twice, he beat her to it by borrowin' most of his pay in advance. He told it all round town, how he had outfoxed his Missus. He certainly was a caution!

But he wasn't satisfied with just outwittin' her. He was sore the way she had acted, tryin' to grab off his pay. And he made up his mind he'd get even. Well, he waited till Evans's Circus was advertised to come to town. Then he told his wife and two kiddies that he was goin' to take them to the circus. The day of the circus, he told them he would get the tickets and meet them outside the entrance to the tent.

Well, he didn't have no intentions of bein' there or buyin' tickets or nothin'. He got full of gin and laid round Wright's poolroom all day. His wife and the kids waited and waited and of course he didn't show up. His wife didn't have a dime with her, or nowhere else, I guess. So she finally had to tell the kids it was all off and they cried like they wasn't never goin' to stop.

Well, it seems, w'ile they was cryin', Doc Stair came along and he asked what was the matter, but Mrs. Kendall was stubborn and wouldn't tell him, but the kids told him and he insisted on takin' them and their mother in the show. Jim found this out afterwards and it was one reason why he had it in for Doc Stair.

Doc Stair come here about a year and a half ago. He's a mighty handsome young fella and his clothes always look like he has them made to order. He goes to Detroit two or three times a year and w'ile he's there he must have a tailor take his measure and then make him a suit to order. They cost pretty near twice as much, but they fit a whole lot better than if you just bought them in a store.

For a w'ile everybody was wonderin' why a young doctor like Doc Stair should come to a town like this where we already got old Doc Gamble and Doc Foote that's both been here for years and all the practice in town was always divided between the two of them.

Then they was a story got round that Doc Stair's gal had throwed him over, a gal up in the Northern Peninsula somewheres, and the reason he come here was to hide himself away and forget it. He said himself that he thought they wasn't nothin' like general practice in a place like ours to fit a man to be a good all-round doctor. And that's why he'd came.

Anyways, it wasn't long before he was makin' enough to live on, though they tell me that he never dunned nobody for what they owed him, and the folks here certainly has got the owin' habit, even in my business. If I had all that was comin' to me for just shaves alone I could go to Carterville and put up at the Mercer for a week and see a different picture every night. For instance, they's old George Purdy—but I guess I shouldn't ought to be gossipin'.

Well, last year, our coroner died, died of the flu. Ken Beatty, that was his name. He was the coroner. So they had to choose another man to be coroner in his place and they picked Doc Stair. He laughed at first and said he didn't want it, but they made him take it. It ain't no job that anybody would fight for and what a man makes out of it in a year would just about buy seeds for their garden. Doc's the kind, though, that can't say no to nothin' if you keep at him long enough.

But I was goin' to tell you about a poor boy we got here in town—Paul Dickson. He fell out of a tree when he was about ten years old. Lit on his head and it done somethin' to him and he ain't never been right. No harm in him, but just silly. Jim Kendall used to call him cuckoo; that's a name Jim had for anybody that was off their head, only he called people's head their bean. That was another of his gags, callin' head bean and callin' crazy people cuckoo. Only poor Paul ain't crazy, but just silly.

You can imagine that Jim used to have all kinds of fun with Paul. He'd send him to the White Front Garage for a left-handed monkey wrench. Of course they ain't no such thing as a left-handed monkey wrench.

And once we had a kind of a fair here and they was a baseball game between the fats and the leans and before the game started Jim called Paul over and sent him way down to Schrader's hardware store to get a key for the pitcher's box.

They wasn't nothin' in the way of gags that Jim couldn't think up, when he put his mind to it.

Poor Paul was always kind of suspicious of people, maybe on account of how Jim had kept foolin' him. Paul wouldn't have much to do with anybody only his own mother and Doc Stair and a girl here in town named Julie Gregg. That is, she ain't a girl no more, but pretty near thirty or over.

When Doc first came to town, Paul seemed to feel like here was a real friend and he hung round Doc's office most of the w'ile; the only time he wasn't there was when he'd go home to eat or sleep or when he seen Julie Gregg doin' her shoppin'.

When he looked out Doc's window and seen her, he'd run downstairs and join her and tag along with her to the different stores. The poor boy was crazy about Julie and she always treated him mighty nice and made him feel like he was welcome, though of course it wasn't nothin' but pity on her side.

Doc done all he could to improve Paul's mind and he told me once that he really thought the boy was gettin' better, that they was times when he was as bright and sensible as anybody else.

But I was goin' to tell you about Julie Gregg. Old Man Gregg was in the lumber business, but got to drinkin' and lost the most of his money and when he died, he didn't leave nothin' but the house and just enough insurance for the girl to skimp along on.

Her mother was a kind of a half invalid and didn't hardly ever leave the house. Julie wanted to sell the place and move somewheres else after the old man died, but the mother said she was born here and would die here. It was tough on Julie, as the young people round this town—well, she's too good for them.

She's been away to school and Chicago and New York and different places and they ain't no subject she can't talk on, where you take the rest of the young folks here and you mention anything to them outside of Gloria Swanson or Tommy Meighan and they think you're delirious. Did you see Gloria in *Wages of Virtue?* You missed somethin'!

Well, Doc Stair hadn't been here more than a week when he come in one day to get shaved and I recognized who he was as he had been pointed out to me, so I told him about my old lady. She's been ailin' for a couple of years and neither Doc Gamble or Doc Foote, neither one, seemed to be helpin' her. So he said he would come out and see her, but if she was able to get out herself, it would be better to bring her to his office where he could make a completer examination.

So I took her to his office and w'ile I was waitin' for her in the reception room, in come Julie Gregg. When somebody comes in Doc Stair's office, they's a bell that rings in his inside office so as he can tell they's somebody to see him.

So he left my old lady inside and come out to the front office and that's the first time him and Julie met and I guess it was what they call love at first sight. But it wasn't fifty-fifty. This young fella was the slickest lookin' fella she'd ever seen in this town and she went wild over him. To him she was just a young lady that wanted to see the doctor.

She'd come on about the same business I had. Her mother had been doctorin' for years with Doc Gamble and Doc Foote and without no results. So she'd heard they was a new doc in town and decided to give him a try. He promised to call and see her mother that same day.

I said a minute ago that it was love at first sight on her part.

I'm not only judgin' by how she acted afterwards but how she looked at him that first day in his office. I ain't no mind reader, but it was wrote all over her face that she was gone.

Now Jim Kendall, besides bein' a jokesmith and a pretty good drinker, well, Jim was quite a lady-killer. I guess he run pretty wild durin' the time he was on the road for them Carterville people, and besides that, he'd had a couple little affairs of the heart right here in town. As I say, his wife could of divorced him, only she couldn't.

But Jim was like the majority of men, and women, too, I guess. He wanted what he couldn't get. He wanted Julie Gregg and worked his head off tryin' to land her. Only he'd of said bean instead of head.

Well, Jim's habits and his jokes didn't appeal to Julie and of course he was a married man, so he didn't have no more chance than, well, than a rabbit. That's an expression of Jim's himself. When somebody didn't have no chance to get elected or somethin', Jim would always say they didn't have no more chance than a rabbit.

He didn't make no bones about how he felt. Right in here, more than once, in front of the whole crowd, he said he was stuck on Julie and anybody that could get her for him was welcome to his house and his wife and kids included. But she wouldn't have nothin' to do with him; wouldn't even speak to him on the street. He finally seen he wasn't gettin' nowheres with his usual line so he decided to try the rough stuff. He went right up to her house one evenin' and when she opened the door he forced his way in and grabbed her. But she broke loose and before he could stop her, she run in the next room and locked the door and phoned to Joe Barnes. Joe's the marshal. Jim could hear who she was phonin' to and he beat it before Joe got there.

Joe was an old friend of Julie's pa. Joe went to Jim the next day and told him what would happen if he ever done it again.

I don't know how the news of this little affair leaked out. Chances is that Joe Barnes told his wife and she told somebody else's wife and they told their husband. Anyways, it did leak out and Hod

Meyers had the nerve to kid Jim about it, right here in this shop. Jim didn't deny nothin' and kind of laughed it off and said for us all to wait; that lots of people had tried to make a monkey out of him, but he always got even.

Meanw'ile everybody in town was wise to Julie's bein' wild mad over the Doc. I don't suppose she had any idear how her face changed when him and her was together; of course she couldn't of, or she'd of kept away from him. And she didn't know that we was all noticin' how many times she made excuses to go up to his office or pass it on the other side of the street and look up in his window to see if he was there. I felt sorry for her and so did most other people.

Hod Meyers kept rubbin' it into Jim about how the Doc had cut him out. Jim didn't pay no attention to the kiddin' and you could see he was plannin' one of his jokes.

One trick Jim had was the knack of changin' his voice. He could make you think he was a girl talkin' and he could mimic any man's voice. To show you how good he was along this line, I'll tell you the joke he played on me once.

You know, in most towns of any size, when a man is dead and needs a shave, why the barber that shaves him soaks him five dollars for the job; that is, he don't soak *him*, but whoever ordered the shave. I just charge three dollars because personally I don't mind much shavin' a dead person. They lay a whole lot stiller than live customers. The only thing is that you don't feel like talkin' to them and you get kind of lonesome.

Well, about the coldest day we ever had here, two years ago last winter, the phone rung at the house w'ile I was home to dinner and I answered the phone and it was a woman's voice and she said she was Mrs. John Scott and her husband was dead and would I come out and shave him.

Old John had always been a good customer of mine. But they live seven miles out in the country, on the Streeter road. Still I didn't see how I could say no.

So I said I would be there, but would have to come in a jitney and it might cost three or four dollars besides the price of the shave. So she, or the voice, it said that was all right, so I got Frank Abbott to drive me out to the place and when I got there, who should open the door but old John himself! He wasn't no more dead than, well, than a rabbit.

It didn't take no private detective to figure out who had played me this little joke. Nobody could of thought it up but Jim Kendall. He certainly was a card!

I tell you this incident just to show you how he could disguise his voice and make you believe it was somebody else talkin'. I'd of swore it was Mrs. Scott had called me. Anyways, some woman.

Well, Jim waited till he had Doc Stair's voice down pat; then he went after revenge.

He called Julie up on a night when he knew Doc was over in Carterville. She never questioned but what it was Doc's voice. Jim said he must see her that night; he couldn't wait no longer to tell her somethin'. She was all excited and told him to come to the house. But he said he was expectin' an important long-distance call and wouldn't she please forget her manners for once and come to his office. He said they couldn't nothin' hurt her and nobody would see her and he just *must* talk to her a little w'ile. Well, poor Julie fell for it.

Doc always keeps a night light in his office, so it looked to Julie like they was somebody there.

Meanw'ile Jim Kendall had went to Wright's poolroom, where they was a whole gang amusin' themselves. The most of them had drank plenty of gin, and they was a rough bunch even when sober. They was always strong for Jim's jokes and when he told them to come with him and see some fun they give up their card games and pool games and followed along.

Doc's office is on the second floor. Right outside his door they's a flight of stairs leadin' to the floor above. Jim and his gang hid in the dark behind these stairs.

Well, Julie comes up to Doc's door and rung the bell and they was nothin' doin'. She rung it again and she rung it seven or eight times. Then she tried the door and found it locked. Then Jim made some kind of a noise and she heard it and waited a minute, and then she says, "Is that you, Ralph?" Ralph is Doc's first name.

They was no answer and it must of came to her all of a sudden that she'd been bunked. She pretty near fell downstairs and the whole gang after her. They chased her all the way home, hollerin', "Is that you, Ralph?" and "Oh, Ralphie, dear, is that you?" Jim says he couldn't holler it himself, as he was laughin' too hard.

Poor Julie! She didn't show up here on Main Street for a long, long time afterward.

And of course Jim and his gang told everybody in town, everybody but Doc Stair. They was scared to tell him, and he might of never knowed only for Paul Dickson. The poor cuckoo, as Jim called him, he was here in the shop one night when Jim was still gloatin' yet over what he'd done to Julie. And Paul took in as much of it as he could understand and he run to Doc with the story.

It's a cinch Doc went up in the air and swore he'd make Jim suffer. But it was a kind of a delicate thing, because if it got out that he had beat Jim up, Julie was bound to hear of it and then she'd know that Doc knew and of course knowin' that he knew would make it worse for her than ever. He was goin' to do somethin', but it took a lot of figurin'.

Well, it was a couple days later when Jim was here in the shop again, and so was the cuckoo. Jim was goin' duck-shootin' the next day and had came in lookin' for Hod Meyers to go with him. I happened to know that Hod had went over to Carterville and wouldn't be home till the end of the week. So Jim said he hated to go alone and he guessed he would call it off. Then poor Paul spoke up and said if Jim would take him he would go along. Jim thought a w'ile and then he said, well, well, he guessed a half-wit was better than nothin'.

I suppose he was plottin' to get Paul out in the boat and play some joke on him, like pushin' him in the water. Anyways, he said Paul could go. He asked him had he ever shot a duck and Paul said no, he'd never even had a gun in his hands. So Jim said he could set in the boat and watch him and if he behaved himself, he might lend him his gun for a couple of shots. They made a date to meet in the mornin' and that's the last I seen of Jim alive.

Next mornin', I hadn't been open more than ten minutes when Doc Stair come in. He looked kind of nervous. He asked me had I seen Paul Dickson. I said no, but I knew where he was, out duck-shootin' with Jim Kendall. So Doc says that's what he had heard, and he couldn't understand it because Paul had told him he wouldn't never have no more to do with Jim as long as he lived.

He said Paul had told him about the joke Jim had played on Julie. He said Paul had asked him what he thought of the joke and the Doc had told him that anybody that would do a thing like that ought not to be let live.

I said it had been a kind of a raw thing, but Jim just couldn't resist no kind of a joke, no matter how raw. I said I thought he was all right at heart, but just bubblin' over with mischief. Doc turned and walked out.

At noon he got a phone call from old John Scott. The lake where Jim and Paul had went shootin' is on John's place. Paul had came runnin' up to the house a few minutes before and said they'd been an accident. Jim had shot a few ducks and then give the gun to Paul and told him to try his luck. Paul hadn't never handled a gun and he was nervous. He was shakin' so hard that he couldn't control the gun. He let fire and Jim sunk back in the boat, dead.

Doc Stair, bein' the coroner, jumped in Frank Abbott's flivver and rushed out to Scott's farm. Paul and old John was down on the shore of the lake. Paul had rowed the boat to shore, but they'd left the body in it, waitin' for Doc to come.

Doc examined the body and said they might as well fetch it back to town. They was no use leavin' it there or callin' a jury, as it was a plain case of accidental shootin'.

Personally I wouldn't never leave a person shoot a gun in the same boat I was in unless I was sure they knew somethin' about guns. Jim was a sucker to leave a new beginner have his gun, let alone a half-wit. It probably served Jim right, what he got. But still we miss him round here. He certainly was a card!

Comb it wet or dry?

*America's greatest orator would argue
a case with Satan himself. . . .*

The Devil and Daniel Webster

STEPHEN VINCENT BENÉT (1898–1943)

Benét's interest in American history, folklore, and
fantasy, which are delightfully combined in his best
short stories, awoke in him as a youth, while he
browsed in his father's library.

His ancestors originally came from Spain and
Florida. Both his grandfather, for whom he was
named, and his father were West Point graduates
and army officers. His sister and his brother became
well known as poets, and Stephen's fame rests not
only upon his fiction but upon his epic John
Brown's Body, which won him the Pulitzer poetry
prize for 1928.

Born in Bethlehem, Pennsylvania, and growing
up at various army posts, Stephen began writing
early, contributing to the St. Nicholas League and
publishing a volume of monologues in verse when
he was only seventeen. He won a B.A. at Yale University in 1919 and an M.A. in 1920, and edited the
Yale Literary Magazine. He studied at the Sor-
bonne in Paris, and later went to France again on a

Guggenheim Fellowship to write his celebrated Civil War poem. He won many other honors, including the Nation poetry prize, the Shelley Memorial Award, the Roosevelt Medal, and a vice-presidency of the American Academy of Arts and Letters.

One volume of his Selected Works (1942) is devoted to his fiction, which comprises novels and stories of contemporary life as well as the re-creation of history and the creation of American legends, such as his stories of the great orator and statesman Daniel Webster. Of the origin of the story here presented, Benét said, "We have our own folk-gods and giants and figures of earth in this country—I wanted to write something about them."

"The Devil and Daniel Webster," which appeared in the Saturday Evening Post in 1936, was made into a play in 1939 and became the libretto of an opera in the same year, with music by Douglas Moore; it has also appeared as a motion picture.

IT'S A STORY they tell in the border country, where Massachusetts joins Vermont and New Hampshire.

Yes, Dan'l Webster's dead—or, at least, they buried him. But every time there's a thunderstorm around Marshfield, they say you can hear his rolling voice in the hollows of the sky. And they say that if you go to his grave and speak loud and clear, "Dan'l Webster—Dan'l Webster!" the ground'll begin to shiver and the trees begin to shake. And after a while you'll hear a deep voice saying, "Neighbor, how stands the Union?" Then you better answer the Union stands as she stood, rock-bottomed and copper-sheathed, one and indivisible, or he's liable to rear right out of the ground. At least, that's what I was told when I was a youngster.

You see, for a while, he was the biggest man in the country. He never got to be President, but he was the biggest man. There were thousands that trusted in him right next to God Almighty, and they told stories about him and all the things that belonged to him that were the stories of patriarchs and such. They said, when he stood up to speak, stars and stripes came right out of the sky, and once he spoke against a river and made it sink into the ground. They said, when he walked the woods with his fishing rod, Killall, the trout would jump out of the streams right into his pockets, for they knew it was no use putting up a fight against him; and, when he argued a case, he could turn on the harps of the blessed and the shaking of the earth underground. That was the kind of man he was, and his big farm up at Marshfield was suitable to him. The chickens he raised were all white meat down through the drumsticks, the cows were tended like children, and the big ram he called Goliath had horns with a curl like a morning-glory vine and could butt through an iron door. But Dan'l wasn't one of your gentlemen farmers; he knew all the ways of the land, and he'd be up by candlelight to see that the chores got done. A man with a mouth like a mastiff, a brow like a mountain and eyes like burning anthracite—that was Dan'l Webster in his prime. And the biggest case he argued never got written down in the books, for he argued it against the devil, nip and tuck and no holds barred. And this is the way I used to hear it told.

There was a man named Jabez Stone, lived at Cross Corners, New Hampshire. He wasn't a bad man to start with, but he was an unlucky man. If he planted corn, he got borers; if he planted potatoes, he got blight. He had good-enough land, but it didn't prosper him; he had a decent wife and children, but the more children he had, the less there was to feed them. If stones cropped up in his neighbor's field, boulders boiled up in his; if he had a horse with the spavins, he'd trade it for one with the staggers and give something extra. There's some folks bound to be like that, apparently. But one day Jabez Stone got sick of the whole business.

He'd been plowing that morning and he'd just broke the plow-share on a rock that he could have sworn hadn't been there yesterday. And, as he stood looking at the plowshare, the off horse began to cough—that ropy kind of cough that means sickness and horse doctors. There were two children down with the measles, his wife was ailing, and he had a whitlow on his thumb. It was about the last straw for Jabez Stone. "I vow," he said, and he looked around him kind of desperate, "I vow it's enough to make a man want to sell his soul to the devil! And I would, too, for two cents!"

Then he felt a kind of queerness come over him at having said what he'd said; though, naturally, being a New Hampshireman, he wouldn't take it back. But, all the same, when it got to be evening and, as far as he could see, no notice had been taken, he felt relieved in his mind, for he was a religious man. But notice is always taken, sooner or later, just like the Good Book says. And, sure enough, next day, about suppertime, a soft-spoken, dark-dressed stranger drove up in a handsome buggy and asked for Jabez Stone.

Well, Jabez told his family it was a lawyer, come to see him about a legacy. But he knew who it was. He didn't like the looks of the stranger, nor the way he smiled with his teeth. They were white teeth, and plentiful—some say they were filed to a point, but I wouldn't vouch for that. And he didn't like it when the dog took one look at the stranger and ran away howling, with his tail between his legs. But having passed the word, more or less, he stuck to it, and they went out behind the barn and made their bargain. Jabez Stone had to prick his finger to sign, and the stranger lent him a silver pin. The wound healed clean, but it left a little white scar.

After that, all of a sudden, things began to pick up and prosper for Jabez Stone. His cows got fat and his horses sleek, his crops were the envy of the neighborhood, and lightning might strike all over the valley, but it wouldn't strike his barn. Pretty soon he was one of the prosperous people of the county; they asked him to stand for selectman, and he stood for it; there began to be talk of running him for state senate. All in all, you might say the Stone family was as happy and contented as cats in a dairy. And so they were, except for Jabez Stone.

He'd been contented enough the first few years. It's a great thing when bad luck turns; it drives most other things out of your head. True, every now and then, especially in rainy weather, the little white scar on his finger would give him a twinge. And once a year, punctual as clockwork, the stranger with the handsome buggy would come driving by. But the sixth year the stranger lighted, and, after that, his peace was over for Jabez Stone.

The stranger came up through the lower field, switching his boots with a cane—they were handsome black boots, but Jabez Stone never liked the look of them, particularly the toes. And, after he'd passed the time of day, he said, "Well, Mr. Stone, you're a hummer! It's a very pretty property you've got here, Mr. Stone."

"Well, some might favor it and others might not," said Jabez Stone, for he was a New Hampshireman.

"Oh, no need to decry your industry!" said the stranger, very easy, showing his teeth in a smile. "After all, we know what's been done, and it's been according to contract and specifications. So when—ahem—the mortgage falls due next year, you shouldn't have any regrets."

"Speaking of that mortgage, mister," said Jabez Stone, and he looked around for help to the earth and the sky, "I'm beginning to have one or two doubts about it."

"Doubts?" said the stranger not quite so pleasantly.

"Why, yes," said Jabez Stone. "This being the U.S.A. and me always having been a religious man." He cleared his throat and got bolder. "Yes, sir," he said, "I'm beginning to have considerable doubts as to that mortgage holding in court."

"There's courts and courts," said the stranger, clicking his teeth. "Still, we might as well have a look at the original document." And he hauled out a big black pocketbook, full of papers. "Sherwin, Slater, Stevens, Stone," he muttered. " 'I, Jabez Stone, for a term of seven years—' Oh, it's quite in order, I think."

But Jabez Stone wasn't listening, for he saw something else

flutter out of the black pocketbook. It was something that looked like a moth, but it wasn't a moth. And as Jabez Stone stared at it, it seemed to speak to him in a small sort of piping voice, terrible small and thin, but terrible human. "Neighbor Stone!" It squeaked. "Neighbor Stone! Help me! For God's sake, help me!"

But before Jabez Stone could stir hand or foot, the stranger whipped out a big bandanna handkerchief, caught the creature in it, just like a butterfly, and started tying up the ends of the bandanna.

"Sorry for the interruption," he said. "As I was saying—"

But Jabez Stone was shaking all over like a scared horse.

"That's Miser Stevens' voice!" he said in a croak. "And you've got him in your handkerchief!"

The stranger looked a little embarrassed.

"Yes, I really should have transferred him to the collecting box," he said with a simper, "but there were some rather unusual specimens there and I don't want them crowded. Well, well, these little contretemps will occur."

"I don't know what you mean by contertan," said Jabez Stone, "but that was Miser Stevens' voice! And he ain't dead! You can't tell me he is! He was just as spry and mean as a woodchuck Tuesday!"

"In the midst of life . . ." said the stranger, kind of pious. "Listen!" Then a bell began to toll in the valley and Jabez Stone listened, with the sweat running down his face. For he knew it was tolled for Miser Stevens and that he was dead.

"These long-standing accounts," said the stranger with a sigh; "one really hates to close them. But business is business."

He still had the bandanna in his hand, and Jabez Stone felt sick as he saw the cloth struggle and flutter.

"Are they all as small as that?" he asked hoarsely.

"Small?" said the stranger. "Oh, I see what you mean. Why, they vary." He measured Jabez Stone with his eyes, and his teeth showed. "Don't worry, Mr. Stone," he said. "You'll go with a very good grade. I wouldn't trust you outside the collecting box. Now, a man like Dan'l Webster, of course—well, we'd have to build a special box for him, and even at that, I imagine the wing spread would astonish you. He'd certainly be a prize. I wish we could see our way clear to him. But, in your case, as I was saying—"

"Put that handkerchief away!" said Jabez Stone, and he began to beg and to pray. But the best he could get at the end was a three years' extension, with conditions.

But till you make a bargain like that, you've got no idea of how fast four years can run. By the last months of those years Jabez Stone's known all over the state and there's talk of running him for governor—and it's dust and ashes in his mouth. For every day, when he gets up, he thinks, "There's one more night gone," and every night, when he lies down, he thinks of the black pocketbook and the soul of Miser Stevens, and it makes him sick at heart. Till, finally, he can't bear it any longer, and, in the last days of the last year, he hitches up his horse and drives off to seek Dan'l Webster. For Dan'l was born in New Hampshire, only a few miles from Cross Corners, and it's well known that he has a particular soft spot for old neighbors.

It was early in the morning when he got to Marshfield, but Dan'l was up already, talking Latin to the farm hands and wrestling with the ram, Goliath, and trying out a new trotter and working up speeches to make against John C. Calhoun. But when he heard a New Hampshireman had come to see him, he dropped everything else he was doing, for that was Dan'l's way. He gave Jabez Stone a breakfast that five men couldn't eat, went into the living history of every man and woman in Cross Corners, and finally asked him how he could serve him.

Jabez Stone allowed that it was a kind of mortgage case.

"Well, I haven't pleaded a mortgage case in a long time, and I don't generally plead now, except before the Supreme Court," said Dan'l, "but if I can, I'll help you."

"Then I've got hope for the first time in ten years," said Jabez Stone and told him the details.

Dan'l walked up and down as he listened, hands behind his back, now and then asking a question, now and then plunging his eyes at the floor, as if they'd bore through it like gimlets. When Jabez

Stone had finished, Dan'l puffed out his cheeks and blew. Then he turned to Jabez Stone and a smile broke over his face like the sunrise over Monadnock.

"You've certainly given yourself the devil's own row to hoe, Neighbor Stone," he said, "but I'll take your case."

"You'll take it?" said Jabez Stone, hardly daring to believe.

"Yes," said Dan'l Webster. "I've got about seventy-five other things to do and the Missouri Compromise to straighten out, but I'll take your case. For if two New Hampshiremen aren't a match for the devil, we might as well give the country back to the Indians."

Then he shook Jabez Stone by the hand and said, "Did you come down here in a hurry?"

"Well, I admit I made time," said Jabez Stone.

"You'll go back faster," said Dan'l Webster, and he told 'em to hitch up Constitution and Constellation to the carriage. They were matched grays with one white forefoot, and they stepped like greased lightning.

Well, I won't describe how excited and pleased the whole Stone family was to have the great Dan'l Webster for a guest, when they finally got there. Jabez Stone had lost his hat on the way, blown off when they overtook a wind, but he didn't take much account of that. But after supper he sent the family off to bed, for he had most particular business with Mr. Webster. Mrs. Stone wanted him to sit in the front parlor, but Dan'l Webster knew front parlors and said he preferred the kitchen. So it was there they sat, waiting for the stranger, with a jug on the table between them and a bright fire on the hearth—the stranger being scheduled to show up on the stroke of midnight, according to specification.

Well, most men wouldn't have asked for better company than Dan'l Webster and a jug. But with every tick of the clock Jabez Stone got sadder and sadder. His eyes roved round, and though he sampled the jug you could see he couldn't taste it. Finally, on the stroke of 11:30 he reached over and grabbed Dan'l Webster by the arm.

"Mr. Webster, Mr. Webster!" he said, and his voice was shaking with fear and a desperate courage. "For God's sake, Mr. Webster, harness your horses and get away from this place while you can!"

"You've brought me a long way, neighbor, to tell me you don't like my company," said Dan'l Webster, quite peaceable, pulling at the jug.

"Miserable wretch that I am!" groaned Jabez Stone. "I've brought you a devilish way, and now I see my folly. Let him take me if he wills. I don't hanker after it, I must say, but I can stand it. But you're the Union's stay and New Hampshire's pride! He mustn't get you, Mr. Webster! He mustn't get you!"

Dan'l Webster looked at the distracted man, all gray and shaking in the firelight, and laid a hand on his shoulder.

"I'm obliged to you, Neighbor Stone," he said gently. "It's kindly thought of. But there's a jug on the table and a case in hand. And I never left a jug or a case half finished in my life."

And just at that moment there was a sharp rap on the door.

"Ah," said Dan'l Webster very coolly, "I thought your clock was a trifle slow, Neighbor Stone." He stepped to the door and opened it. "Come in!" he said.

The stranger came in—very dark and tall he looked in the firelight. He was carrying a box under his arm—a black japanned box with little air holes in the lid. At the sight of the box Jabez Stone gave a low cry and shrank into a corner of the room.

"Mr. Webster, I presume," said the stranger, very polite, but with his eyes glowing like a fox's deep in the woods.

"Attorney of record for Jabez Stone," said Dan'l Webster, but his eyes were glowing too. "Might I ask your name?"

"I've gone by a good many," said the stranger carelessly. "Perhaps Scratch will do for the evening. I'm often called that in these regions."

Then he sat down at the table and poured himself a drink from the jug. The liquor was cold in the jug, but it came steaming into the glass.

"And now," said the stranger, smiling and showing his teeth, "I shall call upon you, as a law-abiding citizen, to assist me in taking possession of my property."

Well, with that the argument began—and it went hot and heavy.

At first Jabez Stone had a flicker of hope, but when he saw Dan'l Webster being forced back at point after point, he just sat scrunched in his corner, with his eyes on that japanned box. For there wasn't any doubt as to the deed or the signature—that was the worst of it. Dan'l Webster twisted and turned and thumped his fist on the table, but he couldn't get away from that. He offered to compromise the case; the stranger wouldn't hear of it. He pointed out the property had increased in value, and state senators ought to be worth more; the stranger stuck to the letter of the law. He was a great lawyer, Dan'l Webster, but we know who's the King of Lawyers, as the Good Book tells us, and it seemed as if, for the first time, Dan'l Webster had met his match.

Finally, the stranger yawned a little. "Your spirited efforts on behalf of your client do you credit, Mr. Webster," he said, "but if you have no more arguments to adduce, I'm rather pressed for time . . ." and Jabez Stone shuddered.

Dan'l Webster's brow looked dark as a thundercloud.

"Pressed or not, you shall not have this man!" he thundered. "Mr. Stone is an American citizen, and no American citizen may be forced into the service of a foreign prince. We fought England for that in '12 and we'll fight all hell for it again!"

"Foreign?" said the stranger. "And who calls me a foreigner?"

"Well, I never yet heard of the dev—of your claiming American citizenship," said Dan'l Webster with surprise.

"And who with better right?" said the stranger with one of his terrible smiles. "When the first wrong was done to the first Indian, I was there. When the first slaver put out for the Congo, I stood on her deck. Am I not in your books and stories and beliefs, from the first settlements on? Am I not spoken of still in every church in New England? 'Tis true the North claims me for a Southerner and the South for a Northerner, but I am neither. I am merely an honest American like yourself—and of the best descent—for, to tell the truth, Mr. Webster, though I don't like to boast of it, my name is older in this country than yours."

"Aha!" said Dan'l Webster with the veins standing out in his forehead. "Then I stand on the Constitution! I demand a trial for my client!"

"The case is hardly one for an ordinary court," said the stranger, his eyes flickering. "And, indeed, the lateness of the hour—"

"Let it be any court you choose, so it is an American judge and an American jury!" said Dan'l Webster in his pride. "Let it be the quick or the dead; I'll abide the issue!"

"You have said it," said the stranger, and pointed his finger at the door. And with that, and all of a sudden, there was a rushing of wind outside and a noise of footsteps. They came, clear and distinct, through the night. And yet they were not like the footsteps of living men.

"In God's name, who comes by so late?" cried Jabez Stone in an ague of fear.

"The jury Mr. Webster demands," said the stranger, sipping at his boiling glass. "You must pardon the rough appearance of one or two; they will have come a long way."

And with that the fire burned blue and the door blew open and twelve men entered, one by one.

If Jabez Stone had been sick with terror before, he was blind with terror now. For there was Walter Butler, the loyalist, who spread fire and horror through the Mohawk Valley in the times of the Revolution; and there was Simon Girty, the renegade, who saw white men burned at the stake and whooped with the Indians to see them burn. His eyes were green, like a catamount's, and the stains on his hunting shirt did not come from the blood of the deer. King Philip was there, wild and proud as he had been in life, with the great gash in his head that gave him his death wound, and cruel Governor Dale, who broke men on the wheel. There was Morton of Merry Mount, who so vexed the Plymouth Colony, with his flushed, loose, handsome face and his hate of the godly. There was Teach, the bloody pirate, with his black beard curling on his breast. The Reverend John Smeet, with his strangler's hands and his Geneva gown, walked as daintily as he had to the gallows. The red print of the rope was still around his neck, but he carried a perfumed handkerchief in one hand. One and all, they came into the room with the fires of hell still upon them, and the stranger named their names and their deeds as they came, till the tale of twelve was told. Yet the stranger had told the truth—they had all played a part in America.

"Are you satisfied with the jury, Mr. Webster?" said the stranger mockingly, when they had taken their places.

The sweat stood upon Dan'l Webster's brow, but his voice was clear.

"Quite satisfied," he said. "Though I miss General Arnold from the company."

"Benedict Arnold is engaged upon other business," said the stranger with a glower. "Ah, you asked for a justice, I believe."

He pointed his finger once more, and a tall man, soberly clad in Puritan garb, with the burning gaze of the fanatic, stalked into the room and took his judge's place.

"Justice Hathorne is a jurist of experience," said the stranger. "He presided at certain witch trials once held in Salem. There were others who repented of the business later, but not he."

"Repent of such notable wonders and undertakings?" said the stern old justice. "Nay, hang them—hang them all!" And he muttered to himself in a way that struck ice into the soul of Jabez Stone.

Then the trial began, and, as you might expect, it didn't look anyways good for the defense. And Jabez Stone didn't make much of a witness in his own behalf. He took one look at Simon Girty and screeched, and they had to put him back in his corner in a kind of swoon.

It didn't halt the trial though; the trial went on, as trials do. Dan'l Webster had faced some hard juries and hanging judges in his time, but this was the hardest he'd ever faced, and he knew it. They sat there with a kind of glitter in their eyes, and the stranger's smooth voice went on and on. Every time he'd raise an objection, it'd be "Objection sustained," but whenever Dan'l objected, it'd be "Objection denied." Well, you couldn't expect fair play from a fellow like this Mr. Scratch.

It got to Dan'l in the end, and he began to heat, like iron in the forge. When he got up to speak he was going to flay that stranger with every trick known to the law, and the judge and jury too. He didn't care if it was contempt of court or what would happen to him for it. He didn't care any more what happened to Jabez Stone. He just got madder and madder, thinking of what he'd say. And yet, curiously enough, the more he thought about it, the less he was able to arrange his speech in his mind.

Till, finally, it was time for him to get up on his feet, and he did so, all ready to bust out with lightnings and denunciations. But before he started he looked over the judge and jury for a moment, such being his custom. And he noticed the glitter in their eyes was twice as strong as before, and they all leaned forward. Like hounds just before they get the fox, they looked, and the blue mist of evil in the room thickened as he watched them. Then he saw what he'd been about to do, and he wiped his forehead, as a man might who's just escaped falling into a pit in the dark.

For it was him they'd come for, not only Jabez Stone. He read it in the glitter of their eyes and in the way the stranger hid his mouth with one hand. And if he fought them with their own weapons, he'd fall into their power; he knew that, though he couldn't have told you how. It was his own anger and horror that burned in their eyes; and he'd have to wipe that out or the case was lost. He stood there for a moment, his black eyes burning like anthracite. And then he began to speak.

He started off in a low voice, though you could hear every word. They say he could call on the harps of the blessed when he chose. And this was just as simple and easy as a man could talk. But he didn't start out by condemning or reviling. He was talking about the things that make a country a country and a man a man.

And he began with the simple things that everybody's known and felt—the freshness of a fine morning when you're young, and the taste of food when you're hungry, and the new day that's every day when you're a child. He took them up and he turned them in his hands. They were good things for any man. But without freedom they sickened. And when he talked of those enslaved, and the sorrows of slavery, his voice got like a big bell. He talked of the early days of America and the men who had made those days. It wasn't a spread-eagle speech, but he made you see it. He admitted all the wrong that had ever been done. But he showed how, out of the wrong and the right, the suffering and the starvations, something new had come. And everybody had played a part in it, even the traitors.

Then he turned to Jabez Stone and showed him as he was—an ordinary man who'd had hard luck and wanted to change it. And, because he'd wanted to change it, now he was going to be punished for all eternity. And yet there was good in Jabez Stone, and he showed that good. He was hard and mean, in some ways, but he was a man. There was sadness in being a man, but it was a proud thing too. And he showed what the pride of it was till you couldn't help feeling it. Yes, even in hell, if a man was a man, you'd know it. And he wasn't pleading for any one person any more, though his voice rang like an organ. He was telling the story and the failures and the endless journey of mankind. They got tricked and trapped and bamboozled, but it was a great journey. And no demon that was ever foaled could know the inwardness of it—it took a man to do that.

The fire began to die on the hearth and the wind before morning to blow. The light was getting gray in the room when Dan'l Webster finished. And his words came back at the end to New Hampshire ground, and the one spot of land that each man loves and clings to. He painted a picture of that, and to each one of that jury he spoke of things long forgotten. For his voice could search the heart, and that was his gift and his strength. And to one his voice was like the forest and its secrecy, and to another like the sea and the storms of the sea; and one heard the cry of his lost nation in it, and another saw a little harmless scene he hadn't remembered for years. But each saw something. And when Dan'l Webster finished he didn't know whether or not he'd saved Jabez Stone. But he knew he'd done a miracle. For the glitter was gone from the eyes of judge and jury, and, for the moment, they were men again, and knew they were men.

"The defense rests," said Dan'l Webster and stood there like a mountain. His ears were still ringing with his speech, and he didn't hear anything else till he heard Judge Hathorne say, "The jury will retire to consider its verdict."

Walter Butler rose in his place and his face had a dark, gay pride on it.

"The jury has considered its verdict," he said and looked the stranger full in the eye. "We find for the defendant, Jabez Stone."

With that, the smile left the stranger's face, but Walter Butler did not flinch.

"Perhaps 'tis not strictly in accordance with the evidence," he said, "but even the damned may salute the eloquence of Mr. Webster."

With that, the long crow of a rooster split the gray morning sky, and judge and jury were gone from the room like a puff of smoke and as if they had never been there. The stranger returned to Dan'l Webster, smiling wryly.

"Major Butler was always a bold man," he said. "I had not thought him quite so bold. Nevertheless, my congratulations, as between two gentlemen."

"I'll have that paper first, if you please," said Dan'l Webster, and he took it and tore it into four pieces. It was queerly warm to the touch. "And now," he said, "I'll have you!" and his hand came down like a bear trap on the stranger's arm. For he knew that once you bested anybody like Mr. Scratch in fair fight, his power on you was gone. And he could see that Mr. Scratch knew it too.

The stranger twisted and wriggled, but he couldn't get out of that grip. "Come, come, Mr. Webster," he said, smiling palely. "This sort of thing is ridic—ouch!—is ridiculous. If you're worried about the costs of the case, naturally, I'd be glad to pay—"

"And so you shall!" said Dan'l Webster, shaking him till his teeth rattled. "For you'll sit right down at that table and draw up a document, promising never to bother Jabez Stone nor his heirs or assigns nor any other New Hampshireman till doomsday! For any hades we want to raise in this state, we can raise ourselves, without assistance from strangers."

"Ouch!" said the stranger. "Ouch! Well, they never did run very big to the barrel, but—ouch!—I agree!"

So he sat down and drew up the document. But Dan'l Webster kept his hand on his coat collar all the time.

"And now may I go?" said the stranger, quite humble, when Dan'l'd seen the document's in proper and legal form.

"Go?" said Dan'l, giving him another shake. "I'm still trying to figure out what I'll do with you. For you've settled the costs of the case, but you haven't settled with me. I think I'll take you back to Marshfield," he said, kind of reflective. "I've got a ram there named Goliath that can butt through an iron door. I'd kind of like to turn you loose in his field and see what he'd do."

Well, with that the stranger began to beg and to plead. And he begged and he pled so humble that finally Dan'l, who was naturally kindhearted, agreed to let him go. The stranger seemed terrible grateful for that and said, just to show they were friends, he'd tell Dan'l's fortune before leaving. So Dan'l agreed to that, though he didn't take much stock in fortunetellers ordinarily. But, naturally, the stranger was a little different.

Well, he pried and he peered at the lines in Dan'l's hands. And he told him one thing and another that was quite remarkable. But they were all in the past.

"Yes, all that's true, and it happened," said Dan'l Webster. "But what's to come in the future?"

The stranger grinned, kind of happily, and shook his head.

"The future's not as you think it," he said. "It's dark. You have a great ambition, Mr. Webster."

"I have," said Dan'l firmly, for everybody knew he wanted to be President.

"It seems almost within your grasp," said the stranger, "but you will not attain it. Lesser men will be made President and you will be passed over."

"And, if I am, I'll still be Daniel Webster," said Dan'l. "Say on."

"You have two strong sons," said the stranger, shaking his head. "You look to found a line. But each will die in war and neither reach greatness."

"Live or die, they are still my sons," said Dan'l Webster. "Say on."

"You have made great speeches," said the stranger. "You will make more."

"Ah," said Dan'l Webster.

"But the last great speech you make will turn many of your own against you," said the stranger. "They will call you Ichabod; they will call you by other names. Even in New England some will say you have turned your coat and sold your country, and their voices will be loud against you till you die."

"So it is an honest speech, it does not matter what men say," said Dan'l Webster. Then he looked at the stranger and their glances locked.

"One question," he said. "I have fought for the Union all my life. Will I see that fight won against those who would tear it apart?"

"Not while you live," said the stranger grimly, "but it will be won. And after you are dead, there are thousands who will fight for your cause, because of words that you spoke."

"Why, then, you long-barreled, slab-sided, lantern-jawed, fortune-telling note shaver," said Dan'l Webster with a great roar of laughter, "be off with you to your own place before I put my mark on you! For, by the thirteen original colonies, I'd go to the Pit itself to save the Union!"

And with that he drew back his foot for a kick that would have stunned a horse. It was only the tip of his shoe that caught the stranger, but he went flying out of the door with his collecting box under his arm.

"And now," said Dan'l Webster, seeing Jabez Stone beginning to rouse from his swoon, "let's see what's left in the jug, for it's dry work talking all night. I hope there's pie for breakfast, Neighbor Stone."

But they say that whenever the devil comes near Marshfield, even now, he gives it a wide berth. And he hasn't been seen in the state of New Hampshire from that day to this.

I'm not talking about Massachusetts or Vermont.

> *Jody loved to hear Grandfather tell*
> *about Indians and pioneers. . . .*

The Leader of the People

JOHN STEINBECK (1902–   )

The great San Joaquin Valley of California and the Monterey Peninsula on the nearby Pacific Coast are the settings of John Ernst Steinbeck's best books and stories. He was born in Salinas, where his father, of German descent, was county treasurer; his mother's family came from Northern Ireland.

After graduating from the local high school, young Steinbeck entered Stanford University at Palo Alto and spent several years there, learning to write, although he never sought a degree. He worked at various jobs—as a hod carrier in Madison Square Garden, as a reporter on a New York daily, as winter caretaker at Lake Tahoe, and as surveyor, fisherman, and fruit picker. For many years he was close to poverty; not until 1935 did one of his books hit the popular taste so that he was able to live in comfort and travel as he wished. During World War II he was a newspaper correspondent, and he visited Russia after the war.

[283]

Steinbeck is amazingly versatile and has succeeded as journalist, playwright, student of biology (The Sea of Cortez, 1941), writer of film scripts and adaptations, and short-story artist of high craftsmanship and feeling. He was awarded a Pulitzer prize in 1940 for his famed novel of the Okie migration, The Grapes of Wrath (1939), and was also elected to the National Institute of Arts and Letters.

"The Leader of the People" first appeared in The Long Valley (1938). Other volumes of Steinbeck stories are The Pastures of Heaven (1932) and The Red Pony (1937).

ON SATURDAY AFTERNOON Billy Buck, the ranch-hand, raked together the last of the old year's haystack and pitched small forkfuls over the wire fence to a few mildly interested cattle. High in the air small clouds like puffs of cannon smoke were driven eastward by the March wind. The wind could be heard whishing in the brush on the ridge crests, but no breath of it penetrated down into the ranch cup.

The little boy, Jody, emerged from the house eating a thick piece of buttered bread. He saw Billy working on the last of the haystack. Jody tramped down scuffing his shoes in a way he had been told was destructive to good shoeleather. A flock of white pigeons flew out of the black cypress tree as Jody passed, and circled the tree and landed again. A half-grown tortoise-shell cat leaped from the bunkhouse porch, galloped on stiff legs across the road, whirled and galloped back again. Jody picked up a stone to help the game along, but he was too late, for the cat was under the porch before the stone could be discharged. He threw the stone into the cypress tree and started the white pigeons on another whirling flight.

Arriving at the used-up haystack, the boy leaned against the barbed wire fence. "Will that be all of it, do you think?" he asked.

The middle-aged ranch-hand stopped his careful raking and stuck his fork into the ground. He took off his black hat and smoothed down his hair. "Nothing left of it that isn't soggy from ground moisture," he said. He replaced his hat and rubbed his dry leathery hands together.

"Ought to be plenty mice," Jody suggested.

"Lousy with them," said Billy. "Just crawling with mice."

"Well, maybe, when you get all through, I could call the dogs and hunt the mice."

"Sure, I guess you could," said Billy Buck. He lifted a forkful of the damp ground-hay and threw it into the air. Instantly three mice leaped out and burrowed frantically under the hay again.

Jody sighed with satisfaction. Those plump, sleek, arrogant mice were doomed. For eight months they had lived and multiplied in the haystack. They had been immune from cats, from traps, from poison and from Jody. They had grown smug in their security, overbearing and fat. Now the time of disaster had come; they would not survive another day.

Billy looked up at the top of the hills that surrounded the ranch. "Maybe you better ask your father before you do it," he suggested.

"Well, where is he? I'll ask him now."

"He rode up to the ridge ranch after dinner. He'll be back pretty soon."

Jody slumped against the fence post. "I don't think he'd care."

As Billy went back to his work he said ominously, "You'd better ask him anyway. You know how he is."

Jody did know. His father, Carl Tiflin, insisted upon giving permission for anything that was done on the ranch, whether it was important or not. Jody sagged farther against the post until he was sitting on the ground. He looked up at the little puffs of wind-driven cloud. "Is it like to rain, Billy?"

"It might. The wind's good for it, but not strong enough."

"Well, I hope it don't rain until after I kill those damn mice." He looked over his shoulder to see whether Billy had noticed the mature profanity. Billy worked on without comment.

Jody turned back and looked at the side-hill where the road from the outside world came down. The hill was washed with lean March sunshine. Silver thistles, blue lupins and a few poppies bloomed among the sage bushes. Halfway up the hill Jody could see Double-tree Mutt, the black dog, digging in a squirrel hole. He paddled for a while and then paused to kick bursts of dirt out between his hind legs, and he dug with an earnestness which belied the knowledge he must have had that no dog had ever caught a squirrel by digging in a hole.

Suddenly, while Jody watched, the black dog stiffened, and backed out of the hole and looked up the hill toward the cleft in the ridge where the road came through. Jody looked up too. For a moment Carl Tiflin on horseback stood out against the pale sky and then he moved down the road toward the house. He carried something white in his hand.

The boy started to his feet. "He's got a letter," Jody cried. He trotted away toward the ranch house, for the letter would probably be read aloud and he wanted to be there. He reached the house before his father did, and ran in. He heard Carl dismount from his creaking saddle and slap the horse on the side to send it to the barn where Billy would unsaddle it and turn it out.

Jody ran into the kitchen. "We got a letter!" he cried.

His mother looked up from a pan of beans. "Who has?"

"Father has. I saw it in his hand."

Carl strode into the kitchen then, and Jody's mother asked, "Who's the letter from, Carl?"

He frowned quickly. "How did you know there was a letter?"

She nodded her head in the boy's direction. "Big-Britches Jody told me."

Jody was embarrassed.

His father looked down at him contemptuously. "He is getting to be a Big-Britches," Carl said. "He's minding everybody's business but his own. Got his big nose into everything."

Mrs. Tiflin relented a little. "Well, he hasn't enough to keep him busy. Who's the letter from?"

Carl still frowned on Jody. "I'll keep him busy if he isn't careful." He held out a sealed letter. "I guess it's from your father."

Mrs. Tiflin took a hairpin from her head and slit open the flap. Her lips pursed judiciously. Jody saw her eyes snap back and forth over the lines. "He says," she translated, "he says he's going to drive out Saturday to stay for a little while. Why, this is Saturday. The letter must have been delayed." She looked at the postmark. "This was mailed day before yesterday. It should have been here yesterday." She looked up questioningly at her husband, and then her face darkened angrily. "Now what have you got that look on for? He doesn't come often."

Carl turned his eyes away from her anger. He could be stern with her most of the time, but when occasionally her temper arose, he could not combat it.

"What's the matter with you?" she demanded again.

In his explanation there was a tone of apology Jody himself might have used. "It's just that he talks," Carl said lamely. "Just talks."

"Well, what of it? You talk yourself."

"Sure I do. But your father only talks about one thing."

"Indians!" Jody broke in excitedly. "Indians and crossing the plains!"

Carl turned fiercely on him. "You get out, Mr. Big-Britches! Go on, now! Get out!"

Jody went miserably out the back door and closed the screen with elaborate quietness. Under the kitchen window his shamed, downcast eyes fell upon a curiously shaped stone, a stone of such fascination that he squatted down and picked it up and turned it over in his hands.

The voices came clearly to him through the open kitchen window. "Jody's damn well right," he heard his father say. "Just Indians and crossing the plains. I've heard that story about how the horses got driven off about a thousand times. He just goes on and on, and he never changes a word in the things he tells."

When Mrs. Tiflin answered her tone was so changed that Jody, outside the window, looked up from his study of the stone. Her voice had become soft and explanatory. Jody knew how her face would have changed to match the tone. She said quietly, "Look at it this way, Carl. That was the big thing in my father's life. He led a wagon train clear across the plains to the coast, and when it was finished, his life was done. It was a big thing to do, but it didn't last long enough. Look!" she continued. "It's as though he was born to do that, and after he finished it, there wasn't anything more for him to do but think about it and talk about it. If there'd been any farther west to go, he'd have gone. He's told me so himself. But at last there was the ocean. He lives right by the ocean where he had to stop."

She had caught Carl, caught him and entangled him in her soft tone.

"I've seen him," he agreed quietly. "He goes down and stares off west over the ocean." His voice sharpened a little. "And then he goes up to the Horseshoe Club in Pacific Grove, and tells people how the Indians drove off the horses."

She tried to catch him again. "Well, it's everything to him. You might be patient with him and pretend to listen."

Carl turned impatiently away. "Well, if it gets too bad, I can always go down to the bunkhouse and sit with Billy," he said irritably. He walked through the house and slammed the front door after him.

Jody ran to his chores. He dumped the grain to the chickens without chasing any of them. He gathered the eggs from the nests. He trotted into the house with the wood and interlaced it so carefully in the woodbox that two armloads seemed to fill it to overflowing.

His mother had finished the beans by now. She stirred up the fire and brushed off the stove-top with a turkey wing. Jody peered cautiously at her to see whether any rancor toward him remained. "Is he coming today?" Jody asked.

"That's what his letter said."

"Maybe I better walk up the road to meet him."

Mrs. Tiflin clanged the stove-lid shut. "That would be nice," she said. "He'd probably like to be met."

"I guess I'll just do it then."

Outside, Jody whistled shrilly to the dogs. "Come on up the hill," he commanded. The two dogs waved their tails and ran ahead. Along the roadside the sage had tender new tips. Jody tore off some pieces and rubbed them on his hands until the air was filled with the sharp wild smell. With a rush the dogs leaped from the road and yapped into the brush after a rabbit. That was the last Jody saw of them, for when they failed to catch the rabbit, they went back home.

Jody plodded on up the hill toward the ridge top. When he reached the little cleft where the road came through, the afternoon wind struck him and blew up his hair and ruffled his shirt. He looked down on the little hills and ridges below and then out at the huge green Salinas Valley. He could see the white town of Salinas far out in the flat and the flash of its windows under the waning sun. Directly below him, in an oak tree, a crow congress had convened. The tree was black with crows all cawing at once.

Then Jody's eyes followed the wagon road down from the ridge where he stood, and lost it behind a hill, and picked it up again on the other side. On that distant stretch he saw a cart slowly pulled by a bay horse. It disappeared behind the hill. Jody sat down on the ground and watched the place where the cart would reappear again. The wind sang on the hilltops and the puff-ball clouds hurried eastward.

Then the cart came into sight and stopped. A man dressed in black dismounted from the seat and walked to the horse's head. Although it was so far away, Jody knew he had unhooked the check-rein, for the horse's head dropped forward. The horse moved on, and the man walked slowly up the hill beside it. Jody gave a glad cry and ran down the road toward them. The squirrels bumped along off the road, and a road runner flirted its tail and raced over the edge of the hill and sailed out like a glider.

Jody tried to leap into the middle of his shadow at every step.

A stone rolled under his foot and he went down. Around a little bend he raced, and there, a short distance ahead, were his grandfather and the cart. The boy dropped from his unseemly running and approached at a dignified walk.

The horse plodded stumble-footedly up the hill and the old man walked beside it. In the lowering sun their giant shadows flickered darkly behind them. The grandfather was dressed in a black broadcloth suit and he wore kid congress gaiters and a black tie on a short, hard collar. He carried his black slouch hat in his hand. His white beard was cropped close and his white eyebrows overhung his eyes like mustaches. The blue eyes were sternly merry. About the whole face and figure there was a granite dignity, so that every motion seemed an impossible thing. Once at rest, it seemed the old man would be stone, would never move again. His steps were slow and certain. Once made, no step could ever be retraced; once headed in a direction, the path would never bend nor the pace increase nor slow.

When Jody appeared around the bend, Grandfather waved his hat slowly in welcome, and he called, "Why, Jody! Come down to meet me, have you?"

Jody sidled near and turned and matched his step to the old man's step and stiffened his body and dragged his heels a little. "Yes, sir," he said. "We got your letter only today."

"Should have been here yesterday," said Grandfather. "It certainly should. How are all the folks?"

"They're fine, sir." He hesitated and then suggested slyly, "Would you like to come on a mouse hunt tomorrow, sir?"

"Mouse hunt, Jody?" Grandfather chuckled. "Have the people of this generation come down to hunting mice? They aren't very strong, the new people, but I hardly thought mice would be game for them."

"No, sir. It's just play. The haystack's gone. I'm going to drive out the mice to the dogs. And you can watch, or even beat the hay a little."

The stern, merry eyes turned down on him. "I see. You don't eat them, then. You haven't come to that yet."

Jody explained, "The dogs eat them, sir. It wouldn't be much like hunting Indians, I guess."

"No, not much—but then later, when the troops were hunting Indians and shooting children and burning teepees, it wasn't much different from your mouse hunt."

They topped the rise and started down into the ranch cup, and they lost the sun from their shoulders. "You've grown," Grandfather said. "Nearly an inch, I should say."

"More," Jody boasted. "Where they mark me on the door, I'm up more than an inch since Thanksgiving even."

Grandfather's rich throaty voice said, "Maybe you're getting too much water and turning to pith and stalk. Wait until you head out, and then we'll see."

Jody looked quickly into the old man's face to see whether his feelings should be hurt, but there was no will to injure, no punishing nor putting-in-your-place light in the keen blue eyes. "We might kill a pig," Jody suggested.

"Oh, no! I couldn't let you do that. You're just humoring me. It isn't the time and you know it."

"You know Riley, the big boar, sir?"

"Yes. I remember Riley well."

"Well, Riley ate a hole into that same haystack, and it fell down on him and smothered him."

"Pigs do that when they can," said Grandfather.

"Riley was a nice pig, for a boar, sir. I rode him sometimes, and he didn't mind."

A door slammed at the house below them, and they saw Jody's mother standing on the porch waving her apron in welcome. And they saw Carl Tiflin walking up from the barn to be at the house for the arrival.

The sun had disappeared from the hills by now. The blue smoke from the house chimney hung in flat layers in the purpling ranch cup. The puff-ball clouds, dropped by the falling wind, hung listlessly in the sky.

Billy Buck came out of the bunkhouse and flung a wash basin of soapy water on the ground. He had been shaving in midweek, for Billy held Grandfather in reverence, and Grandfather said that Billy was one of the few men of the new generation who had not gone soft. Although Billy was in middle age, Grandfather considered him a boy. Now Billy was hurrying toward the house too.

When Jody and Grandfather arrived, the three were waiting for them in front of the yard gate.

Carl said, "Hello, sir. We've been looking for you."

Mrs. Tiflin kissed Grandfather on the side of his beard, and stood still while his big hand patted her shoulder. Billy shook hands solemnly, grinning under his straw moustache. "I'll put up your horse," said Billy, and he led the rig away.

Grandfather watched him go, and then, turning back to the group, he said as he had said a hundred times before, "There's a good boy. I knew his father, old Mule-tail Buck. I never knew why they called him Mule-tail except he packed mules."

Mrs. Tiflin turned and led the way into the house. "How long are you going to stay, Father? Your letter didn't say."

"Well, I don't know. I thought I'd stay about two weeks. But I never stay as long as I think I'm going to."

In a short while they were sitting at the white oilcloth table eating their supper. The lamp with the tin reflector hung over the table. Outside the dining-room windows the big moths battered softly against the glass.

Grandfather cut his steak into tiny pieces and chewed slowly. "I'm hungry," he said. "Driving out here got my appetite up. It's like when we were crossing. We all got so hungry every night we could hardly wait to let the meat get done. I could eat about five pounds of buffalo meat every night."

"It's moving around does it," said Billy. "My father was a government packer. I helped him when I was a kid. Just the two of us could about clean up a deer's ham."

"I knew your father, Billy," said Grandfather. "A fine man he was. They called him Mule-tail Buck. I don't know why except he packed mules."

"That was it," Billy agreed. "He packed mules."

Grandfather put down his knife and fork and looked around the table. "I remember one time we ran out of meat—" His voice dropped to a curious low singsong, dropped into a tonal groove the story had worn for itself. "There was no buffalo, no antelope, not even rabbits. The hunters couldn't even shoot a coyote. That was the time for the leader to be on the watch. I was the leader, and I kept my eyes open. Know why? Well, just the minute the people began to get hungry they'd start slaughtering the team oxen. Do you believe that? I've heard of parties that just ate up their draft cattle. Started from the middle and worked toward the ends. Finally they'd eat the lead pair, and then the wheelers. The leader of a party had to keep them from doing that."

In some manner a big moth got into the room and circled the hanging kerosene lamp. Billy got up and tried to clap it between his hands. Carl struck with a cupped palm and caught the moth and broke it. He walked to the window and dropped it out.

"As I was saying," Grandfather began again, but Carl interrupted him. "You'd better eat some more meat. All the rest of us are ready for our pudding."

Jody saw a flash of anger in his mother's eyes. Grandfather picked up his knife and fork. "I'm pretty hungry, all right," he said. "I'll tell you about that later."

When supper was over, when the family and Billy Buck sat in front of the fireplace in the other room, Jody anxiously watched Grandfather. He saw the signs he knew. The bearded head leaned forward; the eyes lost their sternness and looked wonderingly into the fire; the big lean fingers laced themselves on the black knees. "I wonder," he began, "I just wonder whether I ever told you how those thieving Piutes drove off thirty-five of our horses."

"I think you did," Carl interrupted. "Wasn't it just before you went up into the Tahoe country?"

Grandfather turned quickly toward his son-in-law. "That's right. I guess I must have told you that story."

"Lots of times," Carl said cruelly, and he avoided his wife's eyes. But he felt the angry eyes on him, and he said, " 'Course I'd like to hear it again."

Grandfather looked back at the fire. His fingers unlaced and laced again. Jody knew how he felt, how his insides were collapsed and empty. Hadn't Jody been called a Big-Britches that very afternoon? He rose to heroism and opened himself to the term Big-Britches again. "Tell about Indians," he said softly.

Grandfather's eyes grew stern again. "Boys always want to hear about Indians. It was a job for men, but boys want to hear about it. Well, let's see. Did I ever tell you how I wanted each wagon to carry a long iron plate?"

Everyone but Jody remained silent. Jody said, "No. You didn't."

"Well, when the Indians attacked, we always put the wagons in a circle and fought from between the wheels. I thought that if every wagon carried a long plate with rifle holes, the men could stand the plates on the outside of the wheels when the wagons were in the circle and they would be protected. It would save lives and that would make up for the extra weight of the iron. But of course the party wouldn't do it. No party had done it before and they couldn't see why they should go to the expense. They lived to regret it, too."

Jody looked at his mother, and knew from her expression that she was not listening at all. Carl picked at a callus on his thumb and Billy Buck watched a spider crawling up the wall.

Grandfather's tone dropped into its narrative groove again. Jody knew in advance exactly what words would fall. The story droned on, speeded up for the attack, grew sad over the wounds, struck a dirge at the burials on the great plains. Jody sat quietly watching Grandfather. The stern blue eyes were detached. He looked as though he were not very interested in the story himself.

When it was finished, when the pause had been politely respected as the frontier of the story, Billy Buck stood up and stretched and hitched his trousers. "I guess I'll turn in," he said. Then he faced Grandfather. "I've got an old powder horn and a cap and ball pistol down to the bunkhouse. Did I ever show them to you?"

Grandfather nodded slowly. "Yes, I think you did, Billy. Reminds me of a pistol I had when I was leading the people across."

Billy stood politely until the little story was done, and then he said, "Good night," and went out of the house.

Carl Tiflin tried to turn the conversation then. "How's the country between here and Monterey? I've heard it's pretty dry."

"It is dry," said Grandfather. "There's not a drop of water in the Laguna Seca. But it's a long pull from '87. The whole country was powder then, and in '61 I believe all the coyotes starved to death. We had fifteen inches of rain this year."

"Yes, but it all came too early. We could do with some now." Carl's eye fell on Jody. "Hadn't you better be getting to bed?"

Jody stood up obediently. "Can I kill the mice in the old haystack, sir?"

"Mice? Oh! Sure, kill them all off. Billy said there isn't any good hay left."

Jody exchanged a secret and satisfying look with Grandfather. "I'll kill every one tomorrow," he promised.

Jody lay in his bed and thought of the impossible world of Indians and buffaloes, a world that had ceased to be forever. He wished he could have been living in the heroic time, but he knew he was not of heroic timber. No one living now, save possibly Billy Buck, was worthy to do the things that had been done. A race of giants had lived then, fearless men, men of staunchness unknown in this day. Jody thought of the wide plains and of the wagons moving across like centipedes. He thought of Grandfather on a huge white horse, marshaling the people. Across his mind marched the great phantoms, and they marched off the earth and they were gone.

He came back to the ranch for a moment, then. He heard the dull rushing sound that space and silence make. He heard one of the dogs, out in the doghouse, scratching a flea and bumping his elbow against the floor with every stroke. Then the wind arose again and the black cypress groaned and Jody went to sleep.

He was up half an hour before the triangle sounded for breakfast. His mother was rattling the stove to make the flames roar when Jody went through the kitchen. "You're up early," she said. "Where are you going?"

"Out to get a good stick. We're going to kill the mice today."

"Who is 'we'?"

"Why, Grandfather and I."

"So you've got him in it. You always like to have someone with you in case there's blame to share."

"I'll be right back," said Jody. "I just want to have a good stick ready for after breakfast."

He closed the screen door after him and went out into the cool blue morning. The birds were noisy in the dawn and the ranch cats came down from the hill like blunt snakes. They had been hunting gophers in the dark, and although the four cats were full of gopher meat, they sat in a semicircle at the back door and mewed pitiously for milk. Double-tree Mutt and Smasher moved sniffing along the edge of the brush, performing the duty with rigid ceremony, but when Jody whistled, their heads jerked up and their tails waved. They plunged down to him, wriggling their skins and yawning. Jody patted their heads seriously, and moved on to the weathered scrap pile. He selected an old broom handle and a short piece of inch-square scrap wood. From his pocket he took a shoelace and tied the ends of the sticks loosely together to make a flail. He whistled his new weapon through the air and struck the ground experimentally, while the dogs leaped aside and whined with apprehension.

Jody turned and started down past the house toward the old haystack ground to look over the field of slaughter, but Billy Buck, sitting patiently on the back steps, called to him, "You better come back. It's only a couple minutes till breakfast."

Jody changed his course and moved toward the house. He leaned his flail against the steps. "That's to drive the mice out," he said. "I'll bet they're fat. I'll bet they don't know what's going to happen to them today."

"No, nor you either," Billy remarked philosophically, "nor me, nor anyone."

Jody was staggered by this thought. He knew it was true. His imagination twitched away from the mouse hunt. Then his mother came out on the back porch and struck the triangle, and all thoughts fell in a heap.

Grandfather hadn't appeared at the table when they sat down. Billy nodded at his empty chair. "He's all right? He isn't sick?"

"He takes a long time to dress," said Mrs. Tiflin. "He combs his whiskers and rubs up his shoes and brushes his clothes."

Carl scattered sugar on his mush. "A man that's led a wagon train across the plains has got to be pretty careful how he dresses."

Mrs. Tiflin turned on him. "Don't do that, Carl! Please don't!" There was more of threat than of request in her tone. And the threat irritated Carl.

"Well, how many times do I have to listen to the story of the iron plates, and the thirty-five horses? That time's done. Why can't he forget it, now it's done?" He grew angrier while he talked, and his voice rose. "Why does he have to tell them over and over? He came across the plains. All right! Now it's finished. Nobody wants to hear about it over and over."

The door into the kitchen closed softly. The four at the table sat frozen. Carl laid his mush spoon on the table and touched his chin with his fingers.

Then the kitchen door opened and Grandfather walked in. His mouth smiled tightly and his eyes were squinted. "Good morning," he said, and he sat down and looked at his mush dish.

Carl could not leave it there. "Did—did you hear what I said?"

Grandfather jerked a little nod.

"I don't know what got into me, sir. I didn't mean it. I was just being funny."

Jody glanced in shame at his mother, and he saw that she was looking at Carl, and that she wasn't breathing. It was an awful thing that he was doing. He was tearing himself to pieces to talk like that. It was a terrible thing to him to retract a word, but to retract it in shame was infinitely worse.

Grandfather looked sidewise. "I'm trying to get right side up," he said gently. "I'm not being mad. I don't mind what you said, but it might be true, and I would mind that."

"It isn't true," said Carl. "I'm not feeling well this morning. I'm sorry I said it."

"Don't be sorry, Carl. An old man doesn't see things sometimes. Maybe you're right. The crossing is finished. Maybe it should be forgotten, now it's done."

Carl got up from the table. "I've had enough to eat. I'm going to work. Take your time, Billy!" He walked quickly out of the dining room. Billy gulped the rest of his food and followed soon after. But Jody could not leave his chair.

"Won't you tell any more stories?" Jody asked.

"Why, sure I'll tell them, but only when—I'm sure people want to hear them."

"I like to hear them, sir."

"Oh! Of course you do, but you're a little boy. It was a job for men, but only little boys like to hear about it."

Jody got up from his place. "I'll wait outside for you, sir. I've got a good stick for those mice."

He waited by the gate until the old man came out on the porch. "Let's go down and kill the mice now," Jody called.

"I think I'll just sit in the sun, Jody. You go kill the mice."

"You can use my stick if you like."

"No, I'll just sit here a while."

Jody turned disconsolately away, and walked down toward the old haystack. He tried to whip up his enthusiasm with thoughts of the fat juicy mice. He beat the ground with his flail. The dogs coaxed and whined about him, but he could not go. Back at the house he could see Grandfather sitting on the porch, looking small and thin and black.

Jody gave up and went to sit on the steps at the old man's feet. "Back already? Did you kill the mice?"

"No, sir. I'll kill them some other day."

The morning flies buzzed close to the ground and the ants dashed about in front of the steps. The heavy smell of sage slipped down the hill. The porch boards grew warm in the sunshine.

Jody hardly knew when Grandfather started to talk. "I shouldn't stay here, feeling the way I do." He examined his strong old hands. "I feel as though the crossing wasn't worth doing." His eyes moved up the side-hill and stopped on a motionless hawk perched on a dead limb. "I tell those old stories, but they're not what I want to tell. I only know how I want people to feel when I tell them.

"It wasn't Indians that were important, nor adventures, nor even getting out here. It was a whole bunch of people made into one big crawling beast. And I was the head. It was westering and westering. Every man wanted something for himself, but the big beast that was all of them wanted only westering. I was the leader, but if I hadn't been there, someone else would have been the head. The thing had to have a head.

"Under the little bushes the shadows were black at white noonday. When we saw the mountains at last, we cried—all of us. But it wasn't getting here that mattered, it was movement and westering.

"We carried life out here and set it down the way those ants carry eggs. And I was the leader. The westering was as big as God, and the slow steps that made the movement piled up and piled up until the continent was crossed.

"Then we came down to the sea, and it was done." He stopped and wiped his eyes until the rims were red. "That's what I should be telling instead of stories."

When Jody spoke, Grandfather started and looked down at him. "Maybe I could lead the people some day," Jody said.

The old man smiled. "There's no place to go. There's the ocean to stop you. There's a line of old men along the shore hating the ocean because it stopped them."

"In boats I might, sir."

"No place to go, Jody. Every place is taken. But that's not the worst—no, not the worst. Westering has died out of the people. Westering isn't a hunger any more. It's all done. Your father is right. It is finished." He laced his fingers on his knee and looked at them.

Jody felt very sad. "If you'd like a glass of lemonade I could make it for you."

Grandfather was about to refuse, and then he saw Jody's face. "That would be nice," he said. "Yes, it would be nice to drink a lemonade."

Jody ran into the kitchen where his mother was wiping the last of the breakfast dishes. "Can I have a lemon to make a lemonade for Grandfather?"

His mother mimicked—"And another lemon to make a lemonade for you."

"No, ma'am. I don't want one."

"Jody! You're sick!" Then she stopped suddenly. "Take a lemon out of the cooler," she said softly. "Here, I'll reach the squeezer down to you."

The intrepid hero flew grimly into the
raging hurricane. . . .

The Secret Life of Walter Mitty

JAMES THURBER (1894–   )

Our neurotic era found its portrayer in Thurber,
whose humorous writing and droopy cartoons have
been a feature of the New Yorker magazine for the
past quarter of a century.

Thurber grew up in his birthplace, Columbus,
Ohio, where a childhood accident with a bow and
arrow damaged his eyesight. Unable for this reason to serve in the army in World War I, he became a code clerk in the State Department in
Washington and later in the American Embassy
in Paris. He stayed in Paris as a newspaper correspondent until 1926, when he came to New York
and began an association with the New Yorker that
has lasted ever since. He lives most of the time in
Connecticut but travels frequently. His eyesight
has always troubled him, and he draws and writes
with great difficulty. In addition to his illustrations
and short humorous pieces, he has written several
books for children and collaborated with Elliot
Nugent on a popular play, The Male Animal.

[301]

"The Secret Life of Walter Mitty" first appeared in the New Yorker in 1939; it has been made into a motion picture. Most of Thurber's best fiction appears in The Thurber Carnival *(1945).*

WE'RE GOING THROUGH!" The Commander's voice was like thin ice breaking. He wore his full-dress uniform, with the heavily braided white cap pulled down rakishly over one cold gray eye. "We can't make it, sir. It's spoiling for a hurricane, if you ask me." "I'm not asking you, Lieutenant Berg," said the Commander. "Throw on the power lights! Rev her up to 8,500! We're going through!" The pounding of the cylinders increased: ta-pocketa-pocketa-pocketa-*pocketa-pocketa*. The Commander stared at the ice forming on the pilot window. He walked over and twisted a row of complicated dials. "Switch on No. 8 auxiliary!" he shouted. "Switch on No. 8 auxiliary!" repeated Lieutenant Berg. "Full strength in No. 3 turret!" shouted the Commander. "Full strength in No. 3 turret!" The crew, bending to their various tasks in the huge, hurtling eight-engined Navy hydroplane, looked at each other and grinned. "The Old Man'll get us through," they said to one another. "The Old Man ain't afraid of Hell!" . . .

"Not so fast! You're driving too fast!" said Mrs. Mitty. "What are you driving so fast for?"

"Hmm?" said Walter Mitty. He looked at his wife, in the seat beside him, with shocked astonishment. She seemed grossly unfamiliar, like a strange woman who had yelled at him in a crowd. "You were up to fifty-five," she said. "You know I don't like to go more than forty. You were up to fifty-five." Walter Mitty drove on toward Waterbury in silence, the roaring of the SN202 through the worst storm in twenty years of Navy flying fading in the remote, intimate airways of his mind. "You're tensed up again," said Mrs. Mitty.

"It's one of your days. I wish you'd let Dr. Renshaw look you over."

Walter Mitty stopped the car in front of the building where his wife went to have her hair done. "Remember to get those overshoes while I'm having my hair done," she said. "I don't need overshoes," said Mitty. She put her mirror back into her bag. "We've been through all that," she said, getting out of the car. "You're not a young man any longer." He raced the engine a little. "Why don't you wear your gloves? Have you lost your gloves?" Walter Mitty reached in a pocket and brought out the gloves. He put them on, but after she had turned and gone into the building and he had driven on to a red light, he took them off again. "Pick it up, brother!" snapped a cop as the light changed, and Mitty hastily pulled on his gloves and lurched ahead. He drove around the streets aimlessly for a time, and then he drove past the hospital on his way to the parking lot.

. . . "It's the millionaire banker, Wellington McMillan," said the pretty nurse. "Yes?" said Walter Mitty, removing his gloves slowly. "Who has the case?" "Dr. Renshaw and Dr. Benbow, but there are two specialists here, Dr. Remington from New York and Dr. Pritchard-Mitford from London. He flew over." A door opened down a long, cool corridor and Dr. Renshaw came out. He looked distraught and haggard. "Hello, Mitty," he said. "We're having the devil's own time with McMillan, the millionaire banker and close personal friend of Roosevelt. Obstreosis of the ductal tract. Tertiary. Wish you'd take a look at him." "Glad to," said Mitty.

In the operating room there were whispered introductions: "Dr. Remington, Dr. Mitty. Dr. Pritchard-Mitford, Dr. Mitty." "I've read your book on streptothricosis," said Pritchard-Mitford, shaking hands. "A brilliant performance, sir." "Thank you," said Walter Mitty. "Didn't know you were in the States, Mitty," grumbled Remington. "Coals to Newcastle, bringing Mitford and me up here for a tertiary." "You are very kind," said Mitty. A huge, complicated machine, connected to the operating table, with many tubes and wires, began at this moment to go pocketa-pocketa-pocketa. "The new anaesthetizer is giving way!" shouted an interne. "There is no one in the East who knows how to fix it!"

"Quiet, man!" said Mitty, in a low, cool voice. He sprang to the machine, which was now going pocketa-pocketa-queep-pocketa-queep. He began fingering delicately a row of glistening dials. "Give me a fountain pen!" he snapped. Someone handed him a fountain pen. He pulled a faulty piston out of the machine and inserted the pen in its place. "That will hold for ten minutes," he said. "Get on with the operation." A nurse hurried over and whispered to Renshaw, and Mitty saw the man turn pale. "Coreopsis has set in," said Renshaw nervously. "If you would take over, Mitty?" Mitty looked at him and at the craven figure of Benbow, who drank, and at the grave, uncertain faces of the two great specialists. "If you wish," he said. They slipped a white gown on him; he adjusted a mask and drew on thin gloves; nurses handed him shining . . .

"Back it up, Mac! Look out for that Buick!" Walter Mitty jammed on the brakes. "Wrong lane, Mac," said the parking-lot attendant, looking at Mitty closely. "Gee. Yeh," muttered Mitty. He began cautiously to back out of the lane marked "Exit Only." "Leave her sit there," said the attendant. "I'll put her away." Mitty got out of the car. "Hey, better leave the key." "Oh," said Mitty, handing the man the ignition key. The attendant vaulted into the car, backed it up with insolent skill, and put it where it belonged.

They're so damn cocky, thought Walter Mitty, walking along Main Street; they think they know everything. Once he had tried to take his chains off, outside New Milford, and he had got them wound around the axles. A man had had to come out in a wrecking car and unwind them, a young, grinning garageman. Since then Mrs. Mitty always made him drive to a garage to have the chains taken off. The next time, he thought, I'll wear my right arm in a sling; they won't grin at me then. I'll have my right arm in a sling and they'll see I couldn't possibly take the chains off myself. He kicked at the slush on the sidewalk. "Overshoes," he said to himself, and he began looking for a shoe store.

When he came out into the street again, with the overshoes in a box under his arm, Walter Mitty began to wonder what the other thing was his wife had told him to get. She had told him, twice, before they set out from their house for Waterbury. In a way he hated these weekly trips to town—he was always getting something wrong. Kleenex, he thought, Squibb's, razor blades? No. Toothpaste, toothbrush, bicarbonate, carborundum, initiative and referendum? He gave it up. But she would remember it. "Where's the what's-its-name?" she would ask. "Don't tell me you forgot the what's-its-name." A newsboy went by shouting something about the Waterbury trial.

. . . "Perhaps this will refresh your memory." The District Attorney suddenly thrust a heavy automatic at the quiet figure on the witness stand. "Have you ever seen this before?" Walter Mitty took the gun and examined it expertly. "This is my Webley-Vickers 50.80," he said calmly. An excited buzz ran around the courtroom. The Judge rapped for order. "You are a crack shot with any sort of firearms, I believe?" said the District Attorney, insinuatingly. "Objection!" shouted Mitty's attorney. "We have shown that the defendant could not have fired the shot. We have shown that he wore his right arm in a sling on the night of the fourteenth of July." Walter Mitty raised his hand briefly and the bickering attorneys were stilled. "With any known make of gun," he said evenly, "I could have killed Gregory Fitzhurst at three hundred feet *with my left hand*." Pandemonium broke loose in the courtroom. A woman's scream rose above the bedlam and suddenly a lovely, dark-haired girl was in Walter Mitty's arms. The District Attorney struck at her savagely. Without rising from his chair, Mitty let the man have it on the point of the chin. "You miserable cur!" . . .

"Puppy biscuit," said Walter Mitty. He stopped walking and the buildings of Waterbury rose up out of the misty courtroom and surrounded him again. A woman who was passing laughed. "He said 'Puppy biscuit,' " she said to her companion. "That man said 'Puppy biscuit' to himself." Walter Mitty hurried on. He went into an A. & P., not the first one he came to but a smaller one farther up the street. "I want some biscuit for small, young dogs," he said to the clerk. "Any special brand, sir?" The greatest pistol shot in the world thought a moment. "It says 'Puppies Bark for It' on the box," said Walter Mitty.

His wife would be through at the hairdresser's in fifteen minutes, Mitty saw in looking at his watch, unless they had trouble drying it; sometimes they had trouble drying it. She didn't like to get to the hotel first; she would want him to be there waiting for her as usual. He found a big leather chair in the lobby, facing a window, and he put the overshoes and the puppy biscuit on the floor beside it. He picked up an old copy of *Liberty* and sank down into the chair. "Can Germany Conquer the World Through the Air?" Walter Mitty looked at the pictures of bombing planes and of ruined streets.

. . . "The cannonading has got the wind up in young Raleigh, sir," said the sergeant. Captain Mitty looked up at him through tousled hair. "Get him to bed," he said wearily, "with the others. I'll fly alone." "But you can't, sir," said the sergeant anxiously. "It takes two men to handle that bomber and the Archies are pounding hell out of the air. Von Richtman's circus is between here and Saulier." "Somebody's got to get that ammunition dump," said Mitty. "I'm going over. Spot of brandy?" He poured a drink for the sergeant and one for himself. War thundered and whined around the dugout and battered at the door. There was a rending of wood and splinters flew through the room. "A bit of a near thing," said Captain Mitty carelessly. "The box barrage is closing in," said the sergeant. "We only live once, Sergeant," said Mitty, with his faint, fleeting smile. "Or do we?" He poured another brandy and tossed it off. "I never see a man could hold his brandy like you, sir," said the sergeant. "Begging your pardon, sir." Captain Mitty stood up and strapped on his huge Webley-Vickers automatic. "It's forty kilometers through hell, sir," said the sergeant. Mitty finished one last brandy. "After all," he said softly, "what isn't?" The pounding of the cannon increased; there was the rat-tat-tatting of machine guns, and from somewhere came the menacing pocketa-pocketa-pocketa of the new flame throwers. Walter Mitty walked to the door of the dugout humming "Auprès de Ma Blonde." He turned and waved to the sergeant. "Cheerio!" he said. . . .

Something struck his shoulder. "I've been looking all over this hotel for you," said Mrs. Mitty. "Why do you have to hide in this old chair? How did you expect me to find you?" "Things close in," said Walter Mitty vaguely. "What?" Mrs. Mitty said. "Did you get the what's-its-name? The puppy biscuit? What's in that box?" "Overshoes," said Mitty. "Couldn't you have put them on in the store?" "I was thinking," said Walter Mitty. "Does it ever occur to you that I am sometimes thinking?" She looked at him. "I'm going to take your temperature when I get you home," she said.

They went out through the revolving doors that made a faintly derisive whistling sound when you pushed them. It was two blocks to the parking lot. At the drug store on the corner she said, "Wait here for me. I forgot something. I won't be a minute." She was more than a minute. Walter Mitty lighted a cigarette. It began to rain, rain with sleet in it. He stood up against the wall of the drug store, smoking. . . . He put his shoulders back and his heels together. "To hell with the handkerchief," said Walter Mitty scornfully. He took one last drag on his cigarette and snapped it away. Then, with that faint, fleeting smile playing about his lips, he faced the firing squad; erect and motionless, proud and disdainful, Walter Mitty the Undefeated, inscrutable to the last.

*To find the animal he feared, the boy ranged the
wilderness, unarmed and alone. . . .*

The Bear

WILLIAM FAULKNER (1897–   )

Born of an aristocratic Southern family in New
Albany, Mississippi, Faulkner has spent most of his
life at Oxford, site of the University of Mississippi.
He became a flyer in World War I, but not
choosing to ally himself with the "Yankees," he enlisted in the Canadian Air Force. At the end of the
war he was a lieutenant in the RAF, having served
in France as an observer and been wounded when
a plane was shot down under him. He returned to
Oxford and took a number of courses at the University, supporting himself as a house painter. He
drifted to New Orleans where, by the help of Sherwood Anderson, he had his first poem published
and began writing novels. After wandering in New
York and Europe, he returned to take a job at Oxford, shoveling coal on the night shift at a power
plant. Here he rewrote his best known novels, and
after 1931 he was able to support himself by his
writing, which later included some scripts for

Hollywood films. Most of his novels and tales deal
with the same families, and together form a macabre chronicle of the decline of the proud Southern
aristocracy, told with morbid ingenuity and some
grotesque humor. His time away from his desk is
spent at hunting, fishing, and farming. He won
first prize in the O. Henry Memorial Award in
1939, and was elected to the National Institute of
Arts and Letters. The award of the Nobel prize in
literature for 1949 "for his powerful and artistically
independent contribution to the new American
novel" focused international attention upon his
work.

"The Bear" first appeared in the Saturday Evening Post, May 9, 1942; a greatly expanded version
appears in Go Down, Moses (1942). Faulkner's
other books of short stories include These 13
(1931) and Dr. Martino (1934). His Collected
Stories appeared in 1950.

HE WAS TEN. But it had already begun, long before that day
when at last he wrote his age in two figures and he saw for the
first time the camp where his father and Major de Spain and old
General Compson and the others spent two weeks each November
and two weeks again each June. He had already inherited then,
without ever having seen it, the tremendous bear with one trap-
ruined foot which, in an area almost a hundred miles deep, had
earned itself a name, a definite designation like a living man.

He had listened to it for years; the long legend of corncribs
rifled, of shoats and grown pigs and even calves carried bodily

into the woods and devoured, of traps and deadfalls overthrown
and dogs mangled and slain, and shotgun and even rifle charges
delivered at point-blank range and with no more effect than so
many peas blown through a tube by a boy—a corridor of wreckage
and destruction beginning back before he was born, through which
sped, not fast but rather with the ruthless and irresistible deliberation of a locomotive, the shaggy tremendous shape.

It ran in his knowledge before ever he saw it. It looked and
towered in his dreams before he even saw the unaxed woods where
it left its crooked print, shaggy, huge, red-eyed, not malevolent
but just big—too big for the dogs which tried to bay it, for the
horses which tried to ride it down, for the men and the bullets
they fired into it, too big for the very country which was its con-
stricting scope. He seemed to see it entire with a child's complete
divination before he ever laid eyes on either—the doomed wilderness whose edges were being constantly and punily gnawed at by
men with axes and plows who feared it because it was wilderness,
men myriad and nameless even to one another in the land where
the old bear had earned a name, through which ran not even a
mortal animal but an anachronism, indomitable and invincible, out
of an old dead time, a phantom, epitome and apotheosis of the old
wild life at which the puny humans swarmed and hacked in a fury
of abhorrence and fear, like pygmies about the ankles of a drowsing
elephant: the old bear solitary, indomitable and alone, widowered,
childless, and absolved of mortality—old Priam reft of his old wife
and having outlived all his sons.

Until he was ten, each November he would watch the wagon
containing the dogs and the bedding and food and guns and his
father and Tennie's Jim, the Negro, and Sam Fathers, the Indian,
son of a slave woman and a Chickasaw chief, depart on the road
to town, to Jefferson, where Major de Spain and the others would
join them. To the boy, at seven, eight, and nine, they were not
going into the Big Bottom to hunt bear and deer, but to keep
yearly rendezvous with a bear which they did not even intend to
kill. Two weeks later they would return, with no trophy, no head
and skin. He had not expected it. He had not even been afraid

it would be in the wagon. He believed that even after he was ten and his father would let him go too, for those two weeks in November, he would merely make another one, along with his father and Major de Spain and General Compson and the others, the dogs which feared to bay at it and the rifles and shotguns which failed even to bleed it, in the yearly pageant of the old bear's furious immortality.

Then he heard the dogs. It was in the second week of his first time in the camp. He stood with Sam Fathers against a big oak beside the faint crossing where they had stood each dawn for nine days now, hearing the dogs. He had heard them once before, one morning last week—a murmur, sourceless, echoing through the wet woods, swelling presently into separate voices which he could recognize and call by name. He had raised and cocked the gun as Sam told him and stood motionless again while the uproar, the invisible course, swept up and past and faded; it seemed to him that he could actually see the deer, the buck, blond, smoke-colored, elongated with speed, fleeing, vanishing, the woods, the gray solitude, still ringing even when the cries of the dogs had died away.

"Now let the hammers down," Sam said.

"You knew they were not coming here too," he said.

"Yes," Sam said. "I want you to learn how to do it when you didn't shoot. It's after the chance for the bear or the deer has done already come and gone that men and dogs get killed."

"Anyway," he said, "it was just a deer."

Then on the tenth morning he heard the dogs again. And he readied the too-long, too-heavy gun as Sam had taught him, before Sam even spoke. But this time it was no deer, no ringing chorus of dogs running strong on a free scent, but a moiling yapping an octave too high, with something more than indecision and even abjectness in it, not even moving very fast, taking a long time to pass completely out of hearing, leaving even then somewhere in the air that echo, thin, slightly hysterical, abject, almost grieving, with no sense of a fleeing, unseen, smoke-colored, grass-eating shape ahead of it, and Sam, who had taught him first of all to cock the gun and take position where he could see everywhere and then never move again, had himself moved up beside him; he could hear Sam breathing at his shoulder and he could see the arched curve of the old man's inhaling nostrils.

"Hah," Sam said. "Not even running. Walking."

"Old Ben!" the boy said. "But up here!" he cried. "Way up here!"

"He do it every year," Sam said. "Once. Maybe to see who in camp this time, if he can shoot or not. Whether we got the dog yet that can bay and hold him. He'll take them to the river, then he'll send them back home. We may as well go back, too; see how they look when they come back to camp."

When they reached the camp the hounds were already there, ten of them crouching back under the kitchen, the boy and Sam squatting to peer back into the obscurity where they huddled, quiet, the eyes luminous, glowing at them and vanishing, and no sound, only that effluvium of something more than dog, stronger than dog and not just animal, just beast, because still there had been nothing in front of that abject and almost painful yapping save the solitude, the wilderness, so that when the eleventh hound came in at noon and with all the others watching—even old Uncle Ash, who called himself first a cook—Sam daubed the tattered ear and the raked shoulder with turpentine and axle grease, to the boy it was still no living creature, but the wilderness which, leaning for the moment down, had patted lightly once the hound's temerity.

"Just like a man," Sam said. "Just like folks. Put off as long as she could having to be brave, knowing all the time that sooner or later she would have to be brave to keep on living with herself, and knowing all the time beforehand what was going to happen to her when she done it."

That afternoon, himself on the one-eyed wagon mule which did not mind the smell of blood nor, as they told him, of bear, and with Sam on the other one, they rode for more than three hours through the rapid, shortening winter day. They followed no path, no trail even that he could see; almost at once they were in a country which he had never seen before. Then he knew why

Sam had made him ride the mule which would not spook. The sound one stopped short and tried to whirl and bolt even as Sam got down, blowing its breath, jerking and wrenching at the rein, while Sam held it, coaxing it forward with his voice, since he could not risk tying it, drawing it forward while the boy got down from the marred one.

Then, standing beside Sam in the gloom of the dying afternoon, he looked down at the rotted overturned log, gutted and scored with claw marks and, in the wet earth beside it, the print of the enormous warped two-toed foot. He knew now what he had smelled when he peered under the kitchen where the dogs huddled. He realized for the first time that the bear which had run in his listening and loomed in his dreams since before he could remember to the contrary, and which, therefore, must have existed in the listening and dreams of his father and Major de Spain and even old General Compson, too, before they began to remember in their turn, was a mortal animal, and that if they had departed for the camp each November without any actual hope of bringing its trophy back, it was not because it could not be slain, but because so far they had had no actual hope to.

"Tomorrow," he said.

"We'll try tomorrow," Sam said. "We ain't got the dog yet."

"We've got eleven. They ran him this morning."

"It won't need but one," Sam said. "He ain't here. Maybe he ain't nowhere. The only other way will be for him to run by accident over somebody that has a gun."

"That wouldn't be me," the boy said. "It will be Walter or Major or—"

"It might," Sam said. "You watch close in the morning. Because he's smart. That's how come he has lived this long. If he gets hemmed up and has to pick out somebody to run over, he will pick out you."

"How?" the boy said. "How will he know—" He ceased. "You mean he already knows me, that I ain't never been here before, ain't had time to find out yet whether I—" He ceased again, looking at Sam, the old man whose face revealed nothing until it smiled. He said humbly, not even amazed, "It was me he was watching. I don't reckon he did need to come but once."

The next morning they left the camp three hours before day-light. They rode this time because it was too far to walk, even the dogs in the wagon; again the first gray light found him in a place which he had never seen before, where Sam had placed him and told him to stay and then departed. With the gun which was too big for him, which did not even belong to him, but to Major de Spain, and which he had fired only once—at a stump on the first day, to learn the recoil and how to reload it—he stood against a gum tree beside a little bayou whose black still water crept without movement out of a canebrake and crossed a small clearing and into cane again, where, invisible, a bird—the big woodpecker called Lord-to-God by Negroes—clattered at a dead limb.

It was a stand like any other, dissimilar only in incidentals to the one where he had stood each morning for ten days; a territory new to him, yet no less familiar than that other one which, after almost two weeks, he had come to believe he knew a little—the same solitude, the same loneliness through which human beings had merely passed without altering it, leaving no mark, no scar, which looked exactly as it must have looked when the first ancestor of Sam Fathers' Chickasaw predecessors crept into it and looked about, club or stone ax or bone arrow drawn and poised; different only because, squatting at the edge of the kitchen, he smelled the hounds huddled and cringing beneath it and saw the raked ear and shoulder of the one who, Sam said, had had to be brave once in order to live with herself, and saw yesterday in the earth beside the gutted log the print of the living foot.

He heard no dogs at all. He never did hear them. He only heard the drumming of the woodpecker stop short and knew that the bear was looking at him. He never saw it. He did not know whether it was in front of him or behind him. He did not move, holding the useless gun, which he had not even had warning to cock and which even now he did not cock, tasting in his saliva that taint as of brass which he knew now because he had smelled it when he peered under the kitchen at the huddled dogs.

Then it was gone. As abruptly as it had ceased, the woodpecker's dry, monotonous clatter set up again, and after a while he even believed he could hear the dogs—a murmur, scarce a sound even, which he had probably been hearing for some time before he even remarked it, drifting into hearing and then out again, dying away. They came nowhere near him. If it was a bear they ran, it was another bear. It was Sam himself who came out of the cane and crossed the bayou, followed by the injured bitch of yesterday. She was almost at heel, like a bird dog, making no sound. She came and crouched against his leg, trembling, staring off into the cane.

"I didn't see him," he said. "I didn't, Sam!"

"I know it," Sam said. "He done the looking. You didn't hear him, neither, did you?"

"No," the boy said. "I—"

"He's smart," Sam said. "Too smart." He looked down at the hound, trembling faintly and steadily against the boy's knee. From the raked shoulder a few drops of fresh blood oozed and clung. "Too big. We ain't got the dog yet. But maybe someday. Maybe not next time. But someday."

So I must see him, he thought. I must look at him. Otherwise, it seemed to him that it would go on like this forever, as it had gone on with his father and Major de Spain, who was older than his father, and even with old General Compson, who had been old enough to be a brigade commander in 1865. Otherwise, it would go on so forever, next time and next time, after and after and after. It seemed to him that he could see the two of them, himself and the bear, shadowy in the limbo from which time emerged, becoming time; the old bear absolved of mortality and himself partaking, sharing a little of it, enough of it. And he knew now what he had smelled in the huddled dogs and tasted in his saliva. He recognized fear. So I will have to see him, he thought, without dread or even hope. I will have to look at him.

It was in June of the next year. He was eleven. They were in camp again, celebrating Major de Spain's and General Compson's birthdays. Although the one had been born in September and the other in the depth of winter and in another decade, they had met for two weeks to fish and shoot squirrels and turkey and run coons and wildcats with the dogs at night. That is, he and Boon Hoggenbeck and the Negroes fished and shot squirrels and ran the coons and cats, because the proved hunters, not only Major de Spain and old General Compson, who spent those two weeks sitting in a rocking chair before a tremendous iron pot of Brunswick stew, stirring and tasting, with old Ash to quarrel with about how he was making it and Tennie's Jim to pour from the demijohn into the tin dipper from which he drank, but even the boy's father and Walter Ewell, who were still young enough, scorned such, other than shooting the wild gobblers with pistols for wagers on their marksmanship.

Or, that is, his father and the others believed he was hunting squirrels. Until the third day, he thought that Sam Fathers believed that too. Each morning he would leave the camp right after breakfast. He had his own gun now, a Christmas present. He went back to the tree beside the bayou where he had stood that morning. Using the compass which old General Compson had given him, he ranged from that point; he was teaching himself to be a better-than-fair woodsman without knowing he was doing it. On the second day he even found the gutted log where he had first seen the crooked print. It was almost completely crumbled now, healing with unbelievable speed, a passionate and almost visible relinquishment, back into the earth from which the tree had grown.

He ranged the summer woods now, green with gloom; if anything, actually dimmer than in November's gray dissolution, where, even at noon, the sun fell only in intermittent dappling upon the earth, which never completely dried out and which crawled with snakes—moccasins and water snakes and rattlers, themselves the color of the dappled gloom, so that he would not always see them until they moved, returning later and later, first day, second day, passing in the twilight of the third evening the little log pen enclosing the log stable where Sam was putting up the horses for the night.

"You ain't looked right yet," Sam said.

He stopped. For a moment he didn't answer. Then he said peacefully, in a peaceful rushing burst as when a boy's miniature dam in a little brook gives way, "All right. But how? I went to the bayou. I even found that log again. I—"

"I reckon that was all right. Likely he's been watching you. You never saw his foot?"

"I," the boy said, "I didn't—I never thought—"

"It's the gun," Sam said. He stood beside the fence, motionless —the old man, the Indian, in the battered faded overalls and the frayed five-cent straw hat which in the Negro's race had been the badge of his enslavement and was now the regalia of his freedom. The camp—the clearing, the house, the barn and its tiny lot with which Major de Spain in his turn had scratched punily and evanescently at the wilderness—faded in the dusk, back into the immemorial darkness of the woods. *The gun*, the boy thought. *The gun.*

"Be scared," Sam said. "You can't help that. But don't be afraid. Ain't nothing in the woods going to hurt you unless you corner it, or it smells that you are afraid. A bear or a deer, too, has got to be scared of a coward the same as a brave man has got to be."

The gun, the boy thought.

"You will have to choose," Sam said.

He left the camp before daylight, long before Uncle Ash would wake in his quilts on the kitchen floor and start the fire for breakfast. He had only the compass and a stick for snakes. He could go almost a mile before he would begin to need the compass. He sat on a log, the invisible compass in his invisible hand, while the secret night sounds, fallen still at his movements, scurried again and then ceased for good, and the owls ceased and gave over to the waking of day birds, and he could see the compass. Then he went fast yet still quietly; he was becoming better and better as a woodsman, still without having yet realized it.

He jumped a doe and a fawn at sunrise, walked them out of the bed, close enough to see them—the crash of undergrowth, the white scut, the fawn scudding behind her faster than he had believed it could run. He was hunting right, upwind, as Sam had taught him; not that it mattered now. He had left the gun; of his own will and relinquishment he had accepted not a gambit, not a choice, but a condition in which not only the bear's heretofore inviolable anonymity but all the old rules and balances of hunter and hunted had been abrogated. He would not even be afraid, not even in the moment when the fear would take him completely —blood, skin, bowels, bones, memory from the long time before it became his memory—all save that thin, clear, immortal lucidity which alone differed him from this bear and from all the other bear and deer he would ever kill in the humility and pride of his skill and endurance, to which Sam had spoken when he leaned in the twilight on the lot fence yesterday.

By noon he was far beyond the little bayou, farther into the new and alien country than he had ever been. He was traveling now not only by the compass but by the old, heavy, biscuit-thick silver watch which had belonged to his grandfather. When he stopped at last, it was for the first time since he had risen from the log at dawn when he could see the compass. It was far enough. He had left the camp nine hours ago; nine hours from now, dark would have already been an hour old. But he didn't think of that. He thought, *All right. Yes. But what?* and stood for a moment, alien and small in the green and topless solitude, answering his own question before it had formed and ceased. It was the watch, the compass, the stick—the three lifeless mechanicals with which for nine hours he had fended the wilderness off; he hung the watch and compass carefully on a bush and leaned the stick beside them and relinquished completely to it.

He had not been going very fast for the last two or three hours. He went no faster now, since distance would not matter even if he could have gone fast. And he was trying to keep a bearing on the tree where he had left the compass, trying to complete a circle which would bring him back to it or at least intersect itself, since direction would not matter now either. But the tree was not there, and he did as Sam had schooled him—made the next circle in the opposite direction, so that the two patterns would bisect somewhere, but crossing no print of his own feet, finding the tree **at** last, but in the wrong place—no bush, no compass, no watch—and the tree not even the tree, because there was a down log beside it and he did what Sam Fathers had told him was the next thing and the last.

As he sat down on the log he saw the crooked print—the warped, tremendous, two-toed indentation which, even as he watched it, filled with water. As he looked up, the wilderness coalesced, solidified—the glade, the tree he sought, the bush, the watch and the compass glinting where a ray of sunlight touched them. Then he saw the bear. It did not emerge, appear; it was just there, immobile, solid, fixed in the hot dappling of the green and windless noon, not as big as he had dreamed it, but as big as he had expected it, bigger, dimensionless against the dappled obscurity, looking at him where he sat quietly on the log and looked back at it.

Then it moved. It made no sound. It did not hurry. It crossed the glade, walking for an instant into the full glare of the sun; when it reached the other side it stopped again and looked back at him across one shoulder while his quiet breathing inhaled and exhaled three times.

Then it was gone. It didn't walk into the woods, the undergrowth. It faded, sank back into the wilderness as he had watched a fish, a huge old bass, sink and vanish into the dark depths of its pool without even any movement of its fins.

He thought, *It will be next fall.* But it was not next fall, nor the next nor the next. He was fourteen then. He had killed his buck, and Sam Fathers had marked his face with the hot blood, and in the next year he killed a bear. But even before that accolade he had become as competent in the woods as many grown men with the same experience; by his fourteenth year he was a better woodsman than most grown men with more. There was no territory within thirty miles of the camp that he did not know—bayou, ridge, brake, landmark, tree and path. He could have led anyone to any point in it without deviation, and brought them out again. He knew the game trails that even Sam Fathers did not know; in his thirteenth year he found a buck's bedding place, and unbeknown to his father he borrowed Walter Ewell's rifle and lay in wait at dawn and killed the buck when it walked back to the bed, as Sam had told him how the old Chickasaw fathers did.

But not the old bear, although by now he knew its footprints better than he did his own, and not only the crooked one. He could see any one of the three sound ones and distinguish it from any other, and not only by its size. There were other bears within these thirty miles which left tracks almost as large, but this was more than that. If Sam Fathers had been his mentor and the back-yard rabbits and squirrels at home his kindergarten, then the wilderness the old bear ran was his college, the old male bear itself, so long unwifed and childless as to have become its own ungendered progenitor, was his alma mater. But he never saw it.

He could find the crooked print now almost whenever he liked, fifteen or ten or five miles, or sometimes nearer the camp than that. Twice while on stand during the three years he heard the dogs strike its trail by accident; on the second time they jumped it seemingly, the voices high, abject, almost human in hysteria, as on that first morning two years ago. But not the bear itself. He would remember that noon three years ago, the glade, himself and the bear fixed during that moment in the windless and dappled blaze, and it would seem to him that it had never happened, that he had dreamed that too. But it had happened. They had looked at each other, they had emerged from the wilderness old as earth, synchronized to that instant by something more than the blood that moved the flesh and bones which bore them, and touched, pledged something, affirmed something more lasting than the frail web of bones and flesh which any accident could obliterate.

Then he saw it again. Because of the very fact that he thought of nothing else, he had forgotten to look for it. He was still-hunting with Walter Ewell's rifle. He saw it cross the end of a long blowdown, a corridor where a tornado had swept, rushing through rather than over the tangle of trunks and branches as a locomotive would have, faster than he had ever believed it could move, almost as fast as a deer even, because a deer would have spent most of that time in the air, faster than he could bring the rifle sights up to it, so that he believed the reason he never let off the shot was that he was still behind it, had never caught up with it. And now he knew what had been wrong during all the three years. He sat on a log, shaking and trembling as if he had never seen the woods before nor anything that ran them, wondering with incredulous amazement how he could have forgotten the very thing which Sam Fathers had told him and which the bear itself had proved the next day and had now returned after three years to affirm.

And now he knew what Sam Fathers had meant about the right dog, a dog in which size would mean less than nothing. So when he returned alone in April—school was out then, so that the sons of farmers could help with the land's planting, and at last his father had granted him permission, on his promise to be back in four days—he had the dog. It was his own, a mongrel of the sort called by Negroes a fyce, a ratter, itself not much bigger than a rat and possessing that bravery which had long since stopped being courage and had become foolhardiness.

It did not take four days. Alone again, he found the trail on the first morning. It was not a stalk; it was an ambush. He timed the meeting almost as if it were an appointment with a human being. Himself holding the fyce muffled in a feed sack and Sam Fathers with two of the hounds on a piece of a plowline rope, they lay down-wind of the trail at dawn of the second morning. They were so close that the bear turned without even running, as if in surprised amazement at the shrill and frantic uproar of the released fyce, turning at bay against the trunk of a tree, on its hind feet; it seemed to the boy that it would never stop rising, taller and taller, and even the two hounds seemed to take a desperate and despairing courage from the fyce, following it as it went in.

Then he realized that the fyce was actually not going to stop. He flung, threw the gun away, and ran; when he overtook and grasped the frantically pinwheeling little dog, it seemed to him that he was directly under the bear.

He could smell it, strong and hot and rank. Sprawling, he looked up to where it loomed and towered over him like a cloudburst and colored like a thunderclap, quite familiar, peacefully and even

lucidly familiar, until he remembered: This was the way he had
used to dream about it. Then it was gone. He didn't see it go.
He knelt, holding the frantic fyce with both hands, hearing the
abashed wailing of the hounds drawing farther and farther away,
until Sam came up. He carried the gun. He laid it down quietly
beside the boy and stood looking down at him.

"You've done seed him twice now with a gun in your hands,"
he said. "This time you couldn't have missed him."

The boy rose. He still held the fyce. Even in his arms and clear
of the ground, it yapped frantically, straining and surging after the
fading uproar of the two hounds like a tangle of wire springs. He
was panting a little, but he was neither shaking nor trembling now.

"Neither could you!" he said. "You had the gun! Neither did
you!"

"And you didn't shoot," his father said. "How close were you?"

"I don't know, sir," he said. "There was a big wood tick inside
his right hind leg. I saw that. But I didn't have the gun then."

"But you didn't shoot when you had the gun," his father said.
"Why?"

But he didn't answer, and his father didn't wait for him to,
rising and crossing the room, across the pelt of the bear which
the boy had killed two years ago and the larger one which his
father had killed before he was born, to the bookcase beneath
the mounted head of the boy's first buck. It was the room which
his father called the office, from which all the plantation business
was transacted; in it for the fourteen years of his life he had heard
the best of all talking. Major de Spain would be there and sometimes old General Compson, and Walter Ewell and Boon Hoggenbeck and Sam Fathers and Tennie's Jim, too, were hunters, knew
the woods and what ran them.

He would hear it, not talking himself but listening—the wilderness, the big woods, bigger and older than any recorded document
of white man fatuous enough to believe he had bought any fragment of it or Indian ruthless enough to pretend that any fragment
of it had been his to convey. It was of the men, not white nor

black nor red, but men, hunters with the will and hardihood to endure and the humility and skill to survive, and the dogs and the bear and deer juxtaposed and reliefed against it, ordered and compelled by and within the wilderness in the ancient and unremitting contest by the ancient and immitigable rules which voided all regrets and brooked no quarter, the voices quiet and weighty and deliberate for retrospection and recollection and exact remembering, while he squatted in the blazing firelight.

His father returned with the book and sat down again and opened it. "Listen," he said. He read the five stanzas aloud, his voice quiet and deliberate in the room where there was no fire now because it was already spring. Then he looked up. The boy watched him. "All right," his father said. "Listen." He read again, but only the second stanza this time, to the end of it, the last two lines, and closed the book and put it on the table beside him. "She cannot fade, though thou hast not thy bliss, for ever wilt thou love, and she be fair," he said.

"He's talking about a girl," the boy said.

"He had to talk about something," his father said. Then he said, "He was talking about truth. Truth doesn't change. Truth is one thing. It covers all things which touch the heart—honor and pride and pity and justice and courage and love. Do you see now?"

He didn't know. Somehow it was simpler than that. There was an old bear, fierce and ruthless, not merely just to stay alive, but with the fierce pride of liberty and freedom, proud enough of that liberty and freedom to see it threatened without fear or even alarm; nay, who at times even seemed deliberately to put that freedom and liberty in jeopardy in order to savor them, to remind his old strong bones and flesh to keep supple and quick to defend and preserve them. There was an old man, son of a Negro slave and an Indian king, inheritor on the one side of the long chronicle of a people who had learned humility through suffering, and pride through the endurance which survived the suffering and injustice, and on the other side, the chronicle of a people even longer in the land than the first, yet who no longer existed in the land at all save in the solitary brotherhood of an old Negro's alien blood and the wild and invincible spirit of an old bear. There was a boy who wished to learn humility and pride in order to become skillful and worthy in the woods, who suddenly found himself becoming so skillful so rapidly that he feared he would never become worthy because he had not learned humility and pride, although he had tried to, until one day and as suddenly he discovered that an old man who could not have defined either had led him, as though by the hand, to that point where an old bear and a little mongrel dog showed him that, by possessing one thing other, he would possess them both.

And a little dog, nameless and mongrel and many-fathered, grown, yet weighing less than six pounds, saying as if to itself, "I can't be dangerous, because there's nothing much smaller than I am; I can't be fierce, because they would call it just noise; I can't be humble, because I'm already too close to the ground to genuflect; I can't be proud, because I wouldn't be near enough to it for anyone to know who was casting that shadow; and I don't even know that I'm not going to heaven, because they have already decided that I don't possess an immortal soul. So all I can be is brave. But it's all right. I can be that, even if they still call it just noise."

That was all. It was simple, much simpler than somebody talking in a book about a youth and a girl he would never need to grieve over, because he could never approach any nearer her and would never have to get any farther away. He had heard about a bear, and finally got big enough to trail it, and he trailed it four years and at last met it with a gun in his hands and he didn't shoot. Because a little dog— But he could have shot long before the little dog covered the twenty yards to where the bear waited, and Sam Fathers could have shot at any time during that interminable minute while Old Ben stood on his hind feet over them. He stopped. His father was watching him gravely across the spring-rife twilight of the room; when he spoke, his words were as quiet as the twilight, too, not loud, because they did not need to be because they would last. "Courage, and honor, and pride," his father said, "and pity, and love of justice and of liberty. They all touch the heart, and what the heart holds to becomes truth, as far as we know the truth. Do you see now?"

Sam, and Old Ben, and Nip, he thought. And himself too. He had been all right too. His father had said so. "Yes, sir," he said.

APPENDIXES

OTHER AMERICAN SHORT-STORY
CLASSICS FOR FURTHER READING

Aiken, Conrad: *Mr. Arcularis; Silent Snow, Secret Snow*
Aldrich, Thomas Bailey: *Margery Daw*
Anderson, Sherwood: *I Want to Know Why*
Austin, William: *Peter Rugg, the Missing Man*
Benét, Stephen Vincent: *Daniel Webster and the Sea Serpent; Johnny Pye and the Fool-Killer*
Bierce, Ambrose: *The Damned Thing; A Horseman in the Sky*
Bradford, Roark: *How Come Christmas?*
Brush, Katharine: *Night Club*
Bunner, H. C.: *The Love-Letters of Smith*
Butler, Ellis Parker: *Pigs Is Pigs*
Cable, George Washington: *Posson Jone'*
Caldwell, Erskine: *Kneel to the Rising Sun*
Cather, Willa: *The Sculptor's Funeral*
Cobb, Irvin S.: *The Belled Buzzard; The Escape of Mr. Trimm*
Connell, Richard: *The Most Dangerous Game*
Crane, Stephen: *The Blue Hotel*
Crawford, F. Marion: *The Upper Berth*
Davis, Richard Harding: *Gallegher; The Bar Sinister*
Dobie, Charles Caldwell: *The Open Window*
Edmonds, Walter D.: *The Death of Red Peril*
Faulkner, William: *That Evening Sun; Turnabout; A Rose for Emily*

Ferber, Edna: *Roast Beef, Medium*

Fisher, Dorothy Canfield: *Flint and Fire*

Fitzgerald, F. Scott: *Babylon Revisited; The Diamond as Big as the Ritz*

Freeman, Mary E. Wilkins: *A New England Nun; The Revolt of Mother*

Garland, Hamlin: *The Return of a Private; Up the Coolly*

Gilman, Charlotte P.: *The Yellow Wall-Paper*

Gordon, Caroline: *Old Red*

Granberry, Edwin: *A Trip to Czardis*

Hale, Edward Everett: *The Man Without a Country*

Harte, Bret: *The Luck of Roaring Camp; Tennessee's Partner; How Santa Claus Came to Simpson's Bar*

Hawthorne, Nathaniel: *The Minister's Black Veil; The Great Stone Face; Ethan Brand; Rappaccini's Daughter; Young Goodman Brown; The Birthmark; Dr. Heidigger's Experiment*

Hemingway, Ernest: *The Snows of Kilmanjaro; The Undefeated; My Old Man; The Gambler, the Nun and the Radio; The Killers*

Henry, O.: *The Furnished Room; The Ransom of Red Chief; The Cop and the Anthem; Roads of Destiny; A Municipal Report; The Whirligig of Life*

Hergesheimer, Joseph: *Tol'able David*

Hull, Helen R.: *Clay Shuttered Doors*

Hurst, Fannie: *Humoresque*

Irving, Washington: *The Legend of Sleepy Hollow; The Devil and Tom Walker*

James, Henry: *The Lesson of the Master; The Turn of the Screw; The Madonna of the Future; The Beast in the Jungle*

Jewett, Sarah Orne: *A White Heron*

Kantor, MacKinlay: *The Romance of Rosy Ridge*

Kyne, Peter B.: *The Go-Getter*

Lardner, Ring: *Champion; The Golden Honeymoon*

Lewis, Sinclair: *Young Man Axelbrod*

London, Jack: *To Build a Fire; The Seed of McCoy*

Melville, Herman: *Benito Cereno; The* Town-Ho's *Story*

Norris, Frank: *A Deal in Wheat*
O'Brien, Fitz-James: *The Diamond Lens; What Was It?*
Page, Thomas Nelson: *Marse Chan*
Parker, Dorothy: *Big Blonde; A Telephone Call*
Poe, Edgar Allan: *William Wilson; The Black Cat; The Tell-Tale Heart; The Pit and the Pendulum; The Fall of the House of Usher; The Gold Bug; The Murders in the Rue Morgue; Ligeia*
Porter, Katherine Anne: *Flowering Judas; Pale Horse, Pale Rider*
Post, Melville Davisson: *The Doomdorf Mystery*
Ross, Leonard Q.: *The Education of Hyman Kaplan*
Russell, John: *The Price of the Head*
Saroyan, William: *The Daring Young Man on the Flying Trapeze*
Steele, Wilbur Daniel: *The Shame Dance; Blue Murder; The Yellow Cat; The Woman at Seven Brothers*
Steinbeck, John: *The Chrysanthemums; Breakfast*
Suckow, Ruth: *Golden Wedding*
Thurber, James: *The Catbird Seat*
Twain, Mark: *The Man That Corrupted Hadleyburg*
Van Dyke, Henry: *The Other Wise Man*
Welty, Eudora: *Death of a Traveling Salesman; The Petrified Man; A Piece of News*
Wharton, Edith: *Xingu*
Wister, Owen: *Philosophy 4*
Zangwill, Israel: *A Rose of the Ghetto*

LETTER TO THE READER

Can You Read?

This question is not intended to insult you. Naturally, everyone who has spent some years in school believes he knows how to read—to run his eyes over the printed lines and pick out various statements and recall the usual meanings of most of the words.

To read for full understanding, however, requires much more than this easygoing process. The kind of reading here recommended is *intensive* reading, which enables one to get all the meanings and implications on the page and to avoid getting false interpretations that cannot be supported by good judgment on the basis of what the author has written.

This kind of reading power is not common. Many people never learn to read in this active way. Teachers have discovered that even many college students have never learned how to understand the printed page properly. Former Chancellor Robert M. Hutchins of the University of Chicago has said that he was never taught to read in college, and that not until he graduated and went into law school—where exactness in interpretation of meanings is of prime importance—did he master this art of careful reading. Yet you will find many situations in life wherein getting all the meaning from written words will be of the utmost concern to you.

Anyone can greatly improve his skill in intensive reading if he sets out to do so with the same enthusiasm he needs in tackling any other branch of study. Reading fiction is an especially good

way to practice this skill, because almost everyone enjoys reading
stories and because good fiction offers the reader many chances
to exercise his ability to get the impressions the author wished
him to get.

Why Read Fiction?

We read for many reasons. Reading to enjoy a piece of literature
differs from reading to obtain facts alone. Some people overlook
this difference, and read a story or a poem in the same way that
they would read an encyclopedia, a road sign, a mathematical formula, or a science textbook. Fiction reading gives a great many
satisfactions, as will be suggested in a moment, but the main demand it makes upon the reader is not merely factual and mental
but pleasurable and emotional. The easiest introduction to reading
fiction may be found in reading the short story.

What Is the Short Story?

The short story we are talking about here is not just any story that
is short. It is a special kind of prose fiction that has developed in
little more than the past hundred years, whereas some other kinds,
equally enjoyable, have existed for centuries, going back perhaps
to the campfire yarns of the cave man. At first it may be easier
to say what the short story is *not*. It is not an anecdote or a mere
episode. It is not a myth, legend, folk tale, or fairy tale. It is not
a parable, fable, fabliau, or animal tale (such as the Reynard the
Fox stories or the Hindu Jataka tales). It is not an essay, a sermon,
or a mere sketch in which no conclusive action happens. It is not
a character portrait or a piece of history or biography. It is not a
"tale" such as the Arabian Nights adventures or the German tales
of Hoffman. All these kinds of literature have narrative elements,
and a few closely resemble the short story, but each lacks one or
more qualities of this definition:

> *The short story is a piece of prose fiction which can be read
> at a single sitting; it presents an artistic and unified impression*

of life through many devices, especially (a) theme, (b) characters, (c) action involving conflict and crisis, (d) setting, and (e) style.

The story, like any other piece of literature, is a work of art. Both art and science attempt to describe the universe in which we live. Science tries to do so by setting up general laws of behavior, whereas art—as in a story, poem, painting, or piece of music—tries to give us a specific impression of this universe.

The short story differs from the longer forms of prose fiction, the novel and the novelette, not merely in length. Its particular quality is unity of impression. It aims, in the words of Clayton Hamilton, "to produce a single narrative effect with the greatest economy of means that is consistent with the utmost emphasis." There is room in the longer kinds of fiction, such as the novel, for many more incidents, for a variety of lines of action, for a much larger cast of characters, for development of character over a longer period, and for a much fuller reporting of events. In the short story, the need to make every word contribute toward the final impression demands that the author make the strongest kind of effect with the fewest number of words, incidents, and characters. Even the best stories can do little more than show one important person making one important struggle to gain one important result.

Why Read Short Stories?

Within these rather rigid limits, however, the best writers of the short story can give the careful reader a marvelous variety of values. Any study of the short story should insist on bringing out these manifold values, which the careless reader does not get because he has never been shown that they are there in the story for him to enjoy.

Enjoyment is the purpose of all art—pleasure for the reader, the observer, or the listener. But a particular work may not be pleasurable on first acquaintance; first impressions are often changed later, and the road to appreciation consists in learning as much as we can about the work and opening our minds to the possibility of wider and deeper kinds of enjoyment. Again, a work may be pleasurable at first on a childish level, of which the mind soon tires; as we grow up, we are not satisfied merely with the nursery-rhyme kind of literature. Finally, since there are many values that a good short story can bring, we should ask ourselves, "Which, of the many kinds of pleasure that reading fiction can bring us, does this story offer?"

The rewards of fiction are many, and may vary for different readers or for the same reader at different times. Anyone who has studied literature should be able to list at least twenty rewards that reading can bring him. One that is frequently mentioned is the fact that understanding fiction can help the reader to understand life; we can quickly get acquainted with people and situations in literature that enable us to appreciate better the real world in which we must exist and act—and act often upon the slightest cues to human nature and social customs. This motive for reading literature might be better than some others. For instance, some people read to escape from life rather than to understand life. Sometimes, of course, it is good to brighten our humdrum existence by adventuring into the world of stories. However, if all fiction were at all times to be considered only as a drug, to stimulate or relax the reader, and stories were never anything more than a "shot in the arm," the reader would judge every story solely on this single quality and would miss many other possible rewards that would bring a variety of satisfactions.

How Do You Read a Short Story?

Now, to get down to the business of seeing how we may discover the manifold values of fiction, let us ask, "How should you study a short story?" We know, unfortunately, how most people respond when they are asked what they think about a story they have read. They say simply, "I liked it," or "I didn't like it." If pressed for details, they will embark on a tiresome recital of the plot or an attempt to describe the main character.

Stating a judgment on liking or not liking a story is perhaps the last thing that a reader should do after finishing it, rather than the first thing. Appreciation of the many qualities of the story cannot be compressed into such a simple utterance. We are more inclined to like some parts of a thing than others; criticism, to be useful, should be specific. Even the great stories collected in this book are not perfect in all respects; some are better than others in characterization, emotional range, or exciting incident.

Taste, then, is selective. If everybody liked everything about everything, this would be a dull world and criticism would not exist. Appreciation is not a simple matter of liking or not liking, on first acquaintance, a complex work of art. It requires some consideration of the various qualities in view—in other words, it calls for analysis.

A scheme for analyzing a short story to increase the appreciation of the reader is here presented for your use. It consists of a list of thirty questions. Questions 1–20 can be applied to any story for study and comment; questions 21–30 will be more useful with some stories than with others. This question list will furnish a working plan for the systematic approach to judgment on all the stories that you will read in future. Refer to it whenever you have read or re-read a story upon which you wish to make a criticism. If you are tempted to feel that "I've read this story but I don't know what to say about it," these questions should suggest plenty of things that you might talk about. If any terms used are not familiar to you, look them up in a good dictionary. If you cannot answer all the questions, look again at the story. That is the first and last court of appeal, for the author's text is the only common ground on which the author and the reader can meet. A sample analysis, to show how all these questions might be answered for the first story in this collection, will be found in Appendix C; but do not look at these answers until you have studied the story first and tried to answer them yourself.

Some of the questions on the list are matters of *technique*. Do not let this word frighten you. Technique, or craftsmanship, is merely a name for the means by which the writer achieves the impression he set out to achieve. We can obtain enjoyment from seeing an expert craftsman at work. At a piano recital, for instance, the person who knows something about the instrument and about music can enjoy not only *what* the pianist plays, but also *how* he plays it. In the same way, we can enjoy the technique of a literary craftsman.

Remember that each question in the list is raised not for its own sake but for the value that the answer will contribute toward the total appreciation of the whole story. In literature, the whole is always greater than the sum of its parts.

Main Questions for the Study of a Short Story

1. THEME. What is the theme? In other words, what important comment on life does the author make in the story? Can you state it in a single sentence, beginning with: "This story shows that . . ."? Do you think that this theme is true or false? The theme might be called the *main idea* of the story; it is *not* a conclusion of fact or a moral message. A great story should be rich in its comment on life. It may be hard to find a brief paraphrase of its complex and organic meaning, but unless we try to say "what the story is about," we may go far astray on judging all the other qualities. Since almost any idea might be the theme of a story, it is impossible to classify even the greatest themes of fiction. Usually, a theme that has universality is likely to produce a better story than a narrow and too specific theme. Sometimes a theme is so rich that it embodies an entire philosophy.

2. UNITY OF THEME. Does the story have unity of theme? The one main idea should emerge in all its implications as the story goes on, until finally the author's answer in this specific situation is clear and gives a single effect. There is no room in a short story for the presentation of a variety of complicated themes.

3. CHARACTERIZATION. What does characterization contribute to the total effect? Fiction is essentially people doing things. In the short story there is not enough space to show much *development* of character, but the short story can give *revelation* of character. Now, who are the chief characters? What is each character like? What does each want (motivation)? Why does each do what he

does? Do the characters succeed or fail in attaining their desires? Are their desires presented as admirable or unadmirable? What do their actions (including what they say or think) reveal about them? Are traits presented by mere description or statement, or do we assume them from actions? Who are the minor characters, and what are they like? Do the characters seem to be individuals or individualized types, or are they mere straw men or personifications of abstract terms? Do they seem to act because they must or because they are puppets moved about by the author to fit the plot? Is the hero a superman and the villain a fiend, or are the characters presented with some virtues and some human failings? Does the story violate usual experience by having all the good people in one group and all the bad ones in the opposition group?

4. UNITY OF CHARACTERIZATION. Does the story have unity of characterization? In the short story there is usually one, and only one, main character, the one to whom the events of the story mean the most. Who is the main character to whom this story belongs? What does he want? What is the main conflict of the main character? Does he fail or succeed in attaining his purpose? This character is presented as having certain prominent traits and desires which carry him through the story; at the end, would you say that what happens to him is *inevitable* under these conditions? Are there any unnecessary characters in the cast? If the main character is a *type*, can he or she be classed, for example, as one of the following: prodigal son, Cinderella, romantic dreamer, lovable rogue or Robin Hood, lucky simpleton, mastermind, clever weakling, patient wife, Frankenstein?

5. ACTION. What does the action of the story contribute to the total effect? The action is the series of happenings in the story; these may be physical, mental, or emotional events. Action, or plot, in a well-planned story makes the *main character* face a *problem* by going through *conflicts* or struggles which increase in importance and which result in some *crisis* and a final *significant event* which ends that line of conflict one way or another. Plots may vary from a single incident to a highly complicated series of interlocking events; if characterization or setting is of high im-

portance, the events need not be complex, whereas in a mystery story or one of dramatic action, the plot may be extremely complicated. Now, does the action of this story develop the theme and follow logically from the natures of the characters? Are there major and minor conflicts among the characters? Is this story about:

   a. A trivial incident?
   b. A representative incident?
   c. An apparently trivial incident which is actually important?
   d. An intrinsically important event in the lives of the main characters?

Is the action well motivated through characterization, or is there much action merely for the sake of action, resulting in farce or melodrama?

Conflicts are clashes of persons, forces, ideas, or emotions. The conflicts which arise during the action of a short story may be of the following kinds, and one or more of these kinds may appear in the same story: animal vs. animal; man vs. animal; man and animal vs. animal; man and animal vs. man and animal; man vs. the forces of nature; man vs. man in physical struggle, mental struggle or struggle of wits, and psychological struggle or struggle of wills; man vs. society; man vs. himself (dual personality, rival forces within the same man); man vs. supernatural forces (ghosts, magic); and man vs. fate. Which of these kinds of conflict do you find in the story?

6. UNITY OF ACTION. Does the story have unity of action? What is the most important conflict in the story, which exemplifies the theme and reveals the main trait or traits of the main character? Does this main action carry through from a beginning to a logical conclusion? Is there too little action, or too much? Is there any incident that could be omitted without damaging the total effect?

7. SETTING. What does the setting contribute to the total effect? The setting is the area in time and space in which the action goes on. The author's theme may hold good for various times and places, and then the setting need not be important. On the other hand, theme, characterization, and action may be made more sig-

nificant by the choice of a proper time and place. Setting is important if it is unusual or if its details are a main part of the action or if it works upon the emotions of the characters. Within the brief limits of the short story, elaborate setting for its own sake is seldom justified. But if the setting is an active part of the story—so much so that it might be considered as a motivating force upon the characters—then a story of atmosphere or local color results. Is this, then, an atmosphere or local-color story? Does the author avoid static description and weave the setting into the action? Does he avoid describing beyond the needs of the story? Are details chosen which are emotionally significant and which have suggestion value? Are the various senses appealed to, other than sight?

8. UNITY OF SETTING. Does the story have unity of setting (time and place)? Or does it shift the reader all over the map without need? Incidents and setting should work together to give an effect of consistency; certain happenings could occur more suitably in one place and time than in another. Is there any indication when the story takes place—century, day, season, hour? One story may cover only a few minutes of life; another may cover a much longer period. A good story should have no unnecessary shifts in place and time.

9. STYLE. Does the style of the story (including diction and dialogue) contribute consistently to the final effect? The style of a writer reveals his power of artistic composition—the best choice of words and sounds to fit his material. The style of good narrative need not be flowery or pedantic. It has many of the qualities of good poetic style—such as figures of speech, euphony, exact choice of words, skillful repetition, and use of selected, revealing details which have power to suggest—but these are used for storytelling purposes rather than for poetic purposes. *Diction* is the choice of words. *Dialogue* is the words the characters speak (in a first-person narrative, the entire story might be considered as a monologue in which the diction should be suited to the speaker). Do you think the story could be told better by using a higher or lower level of speech or style? If dialect appears, is it convincing and lively, and not too confusing? Does the diction avoid being commonplace,

trite, discursive, or offensive through use of vulgar, brutal, or repulsive details?

10. UNITY OF STYLE. Does the story have unity of style? In other words, is the style consistent with the desired effect, or does the writer seem to be jumping from one style to another? The style should be suitable throughout and fit the main tone of humor, tragedy, somberness, satire, seriousness, gaiety, or the like. This does not mean that the style should lack variety, but merely that the author should not damage his main effect by incongruous shifts in style and tone.

11. NARRATOR. Who is the narrator, and what does the choice of this narrator add to the total effect? A story may be told by one or more of the following narrators:

a. Main character in the story (in first person).
b. Minor character who tells the story (in first person) as an observer.
c. Author who tells the story as an omniscient observer (in first person or, better, in third person), using the convention of knowing all about the actions and thoughts of:
   1) The main character.
   2) A minor character.
   3) Several characters.
d. Writers of diaries, letters or other documents.

First-person stories lend an air of reality and human testimony, but it is hard for a "hero" to tell his own story without seeming boastful or conceited. A minor character or the author as a human observer may use the first person, but such a narrator must then be placed where he can witness all the important events of the story—"How does he know this?" we ask ourselves—and this may again strain plausibility (see 17 below). The interpretation of events told by such a narrator will be colored by personal bias; this can be harmful or useful to the story. Using the convention of the omniscient observer—the author who is presumed to know everything and see everywhere—gives an air of unbiased and objective truth. This method, particularly when it sticks close to the viewpoint of one character in the story, lends immediacy and enables us to share closely in the feelings and thoughts of the character, who then becomes a central means of perception for us. Establishing and keeping such a means of perception throughout the story avoids baffling shifts from one character to another—shifts which strain the reader's attention and which require too much space for the short story. Letters and other documents may sometimes be a good means of telling all or part of a story. A *frame* story is one which starts out (in either first- or third-person narrative) with a scene that sets the stage, and then has a character in that scene tell the main story. A poor choice of the means of narrating may spoil an otherwise good story. Where surprise is important, as in a detective story, a human narrator who does not properly interpret all the events would be a good choice for the author.

12. STRUCTURE. What is the structure of the story? Structure is the arrangement of the various elements in the story in order of presentation, so as to give artistic continuity to the whole. Aristotle's division of a work into beginning, middle, and end is still useful. One story may have a structure like that of a simple chain of events; another may be more like a play, with several scenes and rising dramatic interest; another may go in a circle and return to the starting place; another may have its incidents arranged in a steadily increasing intensity to the final line; another may end with a complete reversal of the situation, as in the common sort of surprise ending. The skillful author arranges the pace of presentation—summary, straight narrative, description, exposition, dramatic scene, dialogue, flashbacks, thoughts of a character, and so on—in order to lend variety and rising intensity to the structure. Some of these kinds of narrative require more space than others; is each worth the space it takes? For instance, a full scene treatment, with all dialogue and actions given, takes up much space, but may be worth it, particularly at the climax of the story. Summary is the most economical kind of narrative, but mere statement of what happened may be flat, unconvincing, and lacking in emotional value.

13. BEGINNING. Does the beginning of the story skillfully set the action going, suggest the theme, sketch in the background,

introduce the main characters and their problems, handle the exposition of previous events, arouse suspense, and hint at the probable outcome? Is the beginning too exciting, so that there must be a letdown after the opening and hence a drop in interest? Is the exposition of earlier events—what we must know in order to understand the situation the characters are facing—given in a lump of bare statement, or is it woven into the story and shown quickly through speech and action?

14. CLIMAXES. What is the climax of the story—the point of highest interest, at which the conflict is resolved and the outcome is clear? The climax should come at the "end of the middle" of the story and should be followed quickly by the end of the story. A climax may be merely a physical event, or it may be mental or emotional. Some readers are expert enough to pick out three kinds of climax rather than only one. The *climax of theme* is the point in the story at which full illumination comes to the reader concerning the main meaning of the story. The *climax of action* is the event which shows conclusively the final outcome of the main conflict. The *climax of character* is the point at which the fate of the main character becomes definitely clear. These three climaxes may or may not come at exactly the same point in the story.

15. ENDING. Does the ending of the story come too quickly, or too slowly, to make the needed final effect? If the story does not end soon after the point of climax, it will suffer anticlimax. What are the satisfactions that the particular ending brings? (For instance, would you enjoy a story in which a thoroughly vicious person is generously rewarded for his villainy and escapes all punishment?) Looking back, do you feel that the story ending was inevitable in this situation or that it came by pure chance or coincidence? Do you believe that a valid answer has been given to the main problem raised, or do you feel that the author has either dodged the question or invented a fake answer which does not agree with common sense? If the ending is a surprise, is it one that might have been fairly foreseen by an astute reader?

16. SUSPENSE. Is there suspense in the story which makes you continue to read with interest? Suspense may merely appeal to

curiosity about answering a riddle that the author has propounded, or it may awaken deep concern regarding what the author has to say about life. Does the author arouse curiosity about any point without satisfying it later? Is all the suspense concentrated on the outcome of the main action, or does the author arouse and satisfy suspense concerning minor incidents of the story?

17. PLAUSIBILITY. Is the story plausible? Does the author avoid the use of improbable events or strained coincidences? Do you feel, as you read, that the events of the story could really happen in this way? A good story need not be true to life in the sense that it supplies easily recognized or familiar characters, incidents, or settings. In the first place, only a person wholly familiar with the scene or character depicted would qualify as a judge of whether or not it is factually exact. More important for judgment of the artistry of the story is this question: Does the story have a logic of its own and state some truth about human existence? Truth is stranger than fiction, and sometimes harder to believe. What is wanted in fiction is verisimilitude—the appearance of truth. A good story is not, then, a relation of something that actually happened; rather it relates events that might be true or ought to be true. The story need not be true to life so long as it is true to fiction, for fiction is the world in which we look for the order that we seldom find in real life. Stories of fantasy and imagination, such as *Alice's Adventures in Wonderland*, might in this sense be true. The skillful writer prepares the way for our belief by foreshadowing coming events, until we are ready to accept them as following logically.

18. EMOTIONS. Which of the main human emotions or feelings are presented by the author in this story? Does he rely upon two or three obvious emotions (revenge, courage, fear) or does he deal with a wider range of emotions? On the other hand, does he concentrate on emotions which are too special to arouse universality of response? Does his presentation of emotion ring true to your experience? Is the story marred by sentimentality (the presentation of emotion that is much more intense than the situation warrants)? Do the emotions appeal to us through our own feelings—that is, does the author make us feel, or just tell us how we ought to feel?

Note that there may be a difference between the emotions the character undergoes in the story and the emotion the reader feels while reading about the character (for instance, the character may feel despair, the reader then feels pity).

19. BLENDING. Are the ingredients blended successfully in the right proportions, so that the reader gets the total effect? For example, do the characters, action, and setting best exemplify the theme? Does the action of the story spring logically from the characters? Does the setting help to make effective the theme, characterization, and action? Does the style suit the theme, characterization, action, and setting? Is the final story a well-unified whole?

20. JUDGMENT. Finally, do you like the story? Do you see and appreciate the manifold values in it which may bring satisfaction? Do you think you would find other values if you read the story a second or third time? If you do not like the story, can you say exactly why you do not?

Special Questions

21. TITLE. Does the title of the story give any clue to its theme or tone, or awaken interest in reading it? Many titles are only labels; others arouse suspense or suggest important meanings.

22. TYPE. One or more of the four main qualities of a story may be predominant, and thus we may classify a story as primarily one of theme, character, action, or setting. These may be subdivided according to type of theme, type of character, type of action (adventure, mystery, detection), type of setting (Western, historical, sports, sea), or chief emotions (love, terror, humor). Recognizing the type of story is useful if it helps us to understand the main features and enables us to compare it with other types or other stories of the same type. Two stories of the same type may be quite different in other respects, however, so that we have only begun to study a story when we have labeled it as belonging to one or another type.

23. LITERARY BACKGROUND. Would your appreciation of this story be heightened by knowing its literary background (the au-

thor's life and times, other works by this author, works by other authors of this period or this type)? Such background knowledge may be very useful, so long as one remembers that biography is not criticism, although it may improve the soundness of criticism.

24. SPECIAL CONTRIBUTIONS. Does the story offer you any special contributions? These might be humor; lively dialogue; allusions; historical fact; geographical information; scientific information; facts on social customs or manners; quotable passages; confirmation of your own ideas; thoughts on current economic, political, or social problems; or moral opinions.

25. SCALE. What is the scale of the story? Is it too long or too short to achieve its best effect, or is it about the right length?

26. INTENSITY. What is the intensity of the story? Is it relatively of high-voltage interest throughout, or is there a restful change of intensity now and then?

27. PATTERNS. Are there any patterns in the story? Pattern is made by repetition of elements, usually repetition with variation. Its effect may be merely cumulative, or it may be climactic. Patterns may be found in theme statement, characterization, incidents of action, settings, diction, structure, or the like.

28. DIGRESSIONS. Does the author refrain from inserting his own opinions on various subjects, or preaching at the reader? Or are apparent digressions in the story actually a skillful means of obtaining the desired final effect?

29. IRONY OF SITUATION. Is there irony of situation in the story? An ironic outcome is one which is the reverse of what was expected or hoped—an outcome that is almost mockingly the opposite, contrasting promise and fulfillment, for example, or appearance and reality. Use of this contrast, which may be heavy or subtle, often reveals much about the real beliefs of the author, and may give the effect that "life is like that."

30. SYMBOLISM. Has the author attained his effect by skillful use of symbolic actions or objects? A symbol is a person, object, or act which stands for something else or suggests something greater than itself. Recognition that a symbol is present at once establishes at least two levels of meaning in the story.

SAMPLE ANALYSIS OF "RIP VAN WINKLE"

To try out the list of questions given in Appendix B, let us see if we can answer all of them on one story, "Rip Van Winkle," in the hope that insights will emerge to give us greater appreciation of this story. If you do not agree with these answers, there is just one thing you can do—take another look at the story and study these qualities further, so that you can finally make up your mind about them.

1. THEME. The story shows that an idler, like a man under a magic spell, may dream away many years and arouse to find the old order gone forever (see also 22 and 23 below). This theme is not a message such as "never take a drink with strangers." The one-sentence statement of theme above omits the many implications and qualifications given during the entire story, but most careful readers would agree that the main idea is close to this statement. The theme seems true and universal.

2. UNITY OF THEME. The author sticks quite well to his main theme throughout, so that his conclusions regarding this idea give a single narrative effect at the end. No confusing subthemes appear.

3. CHARACTERIZATION. Characterization contributes much to the total effect of this story. It certainly has more deep and clear characterization than most of the supernatural stories that preceded it, whose main appeal was made to the sense of wonder. The chief characters are Rip (see 4 below) and his wife. His main trait is desire to escape being henpecked; hers is shrewishness, and hence

she is in direct opposition to his desire. He succeeds dramatically in attaining his wish. His aim is presented as being natural and admirable. The wife is not sympathetic to us, and we are on Rip's side. Traits are presented both through the narrator's bare statement (for instance, in paragraph 5) and through deductions by the reader on the basis of given actions (as in paragraph 9 we deduce the dog's state of mind from his acts). Minor characters are Wolf, the dog; Vedder, the innkeeper; Van Bummel, the schoolmaster; young Rip; Judith Gardinier, old Rip's daughter; members of the crowd, led by the "self-important old gentleman"; Peter Vanderdonk; and the ghosts of Hendrick Hudson and his crew. The dog serves as Rip's friend and ally; the men of the village are his friends but take no active part in supporting his attempt to solve his problem; the crowd and Rip's children help in the revelation; and the ghosts are a part of the machinery of the magic spell that causes the complication. Dame Van Winkle is a mere type; Rip is much more individualized; the rest are properly given only as much individuality as is needed to enact Rip's story. All the minor characters are needed, but mainly as supporting figures; the only one individualized beyond the needs of the story is Vedder, whose portrayal in paragraph 11 is amusing in itself, but unconnected with Rip's adventures. The hero, Rip, is far from heroic beyond belief, and his wife is humanly motivated—she has some good qualities, such as neatness in housekeeping, nor is her scolding completely without cause, for after all Rip is not a model husband.

4. UNITY OF CHARACTERIZATION. This story certainly belongs to Rip and no one else. Our comments would be far astray, for instance, if we made them on the assumption that this is a tragedy about the sorrows of Dame Van Winkle. Rip is quite properly the most strongly individualized person in the cast. His traits are given as easygoing good nature, neighborliness, kindness to children, shiftlessness at home but industriousness at hunting and helping friends, and fondness for tavern society (these are all quite likable human qualities). His main trait, of course, is dislike of being a henpecked husband, and only when he is "reduced almost to despair" by his wife's nagging does he seek to escape by wandering in the hills. He

succeeds—overwhelmingly and ironically—when he escapes into oblivion while a whole generation passes him by. A modern critic might say that Rip does not act much himself, but is acted upon; surely his tippling of the strangers' liquor brings a much more violent reaction than it might well be expected to bring. The picture of Rip given in this story was so strongly done that it has captured the imagination of readers ever since, and his name has entered our language as a symbol of his type. To call a person a Rip Van Winkle brings up an image in the minds even of people who have never read the story or seen the play based on it.

5. ACTION. Synopsis: A likable, henpecked husband seeks to escape his wife's scolding. He drinks with some mysterious strangers and unsuspectingly falls asleep for twenty years. When he awakens he comes to realize that while he has slept the world has passed him by. This *character* thus meets a *problem* (escaping wife); the *complication* is that he escapes for twenty years; the *crisis* is that he realizes this fact; the *solution* is that he continues to live on, unchanged except that he has been delivered from his wife and now has a wondrous tale to tell. Since character and setting are highly important in this story, the plot does not need to be as complicated as that in a strong action story. The action does, however, develop the theme and fit the character. The main conflict is not very great; Rip does not battle for his freedom, but merely falls into an enchanted sleep. Nor is the opposition to his action very strong. The main conflicts are Rip vs. wife; Rip vs. supernatural forces; Rip vs. society, until he is convinced of what has happened to him. There are some minor conflicts among characters (for example, in paragraph 12 Rip's wife is opposed to his friends, such as Vedder), but there is no scene in which Rip and his allies are pitted against his wife and her allies, if any. The story is about an intrinsically important event in the life of the main character. The actions of the characters are on the whole well motivated; the story is neither farce nor melodrama.

6. UNITY OF ACTION. The most important conflict is Rip's attempt to escape from his wife's nagging (see 5 above), and this conflict carries through from the beginning up to the point where

he learns that she is dead. The story has, perhaps, too little action for the modern taste and does not begin fast enough to arouse suspense. No incident in the story could easily be omitted.

7. SETTING. That setting was important to the author is shown by the fact that the story opens with a detailed description of the place where the remarkable events occur. Probably one intention of the author was to show that even his young nation might hold some spots hallowed by legends like those written about in the Old World. The setting takes an active part in the story—which would be entirely different if Rip lived, say, in a Los Angeles apartment house. This is, then, a local-color story that could best happen in this way in this particular sort of place. The details are fairly well selected, and not many of them seem to be given for their own sake. Many details are, however, stated directly by the author, and the opening suggests an empty stage after the scene painters have left and before the actors have appeared. Most details appeal to our sight (Irving once wanted to become a painter), but some details appeal to other senses.

8. UNITY OF SETTING. All events occur in the village or the nearby mountains and seem to occur naturally in these places. The span of the action is twenty years (a long period for a short story), but events are highly selected and the time passes for us rapidly—as it does in Rip's dreamless sleep. The action really begins "on a fine autumnal day" in colonial times, the 1760's. Rip awakens and returns on a morning after the Revolution is over and the United States is a nation, twenty years later. The mountain glen where Rip's enchantment begins is an appropriately spooky place.

9. STYLE. The style is an enjoyable part of this story, which would well repay reading aloud. Irving was favorably influenced by the best writers read in his day, including Addison, Steele, Goldsmith, and Defoe. The leisurely life of the village and the adventures of the easygoing hero are suggested by the slow-moving rhythm of Irving's long words and lengthy sentences. The story opens with a genre piece of description, a kind less popular now than in Irving's own time. He uses some similes but not too many: paragraph 5, "a rod as long and heavy as a Tartar's lance"; paragraph

7, "trooping like a colt at his mother's heels," "as a fine lady does her train in bad weather." Another quality of the style is the occasional use of proverbial sayings: paragraph 8, "rather starve on a penny than work for a pound"; paragraph 10, "a sharp tongue is the only edged tool that grows keener with constant use." The author's choice of rather general adjectives (as in paragraph 15, "rich woodland," "silent but majestic course," "purple cloud," "glassy bosom," "blue highlands") was common in his time but is considered vague today. On the other hand, some details are sharp and realistic, as when Rip awakens and fears that he may suffer an attack of rheumatism. Diction is well used to give a suggestion of the supernatural when Rip's enchantment is narrated. The diction of the story as a whole is fitting and satisfying. Dialogue does not appear, except when Rip talks to himself, until paragraph 32; there are spots earlier where indirect discourse could have been replaced by some dialogue to add interest. The level of speech is suitable for the story. A few localisms or archaic words are used, but only enough to suggest time and place. Even though this is a local-color story, Irving was wise not to include a large number of dialect words; it is remarkable that, although he gives the effect that this is a region where the Dutch settlers predominated, there is not a single Dutch word used, except names of people. The story would not still be enjoyed as much today had Irving told it in a heavy Dutch dialect. The diction as a whole avoids being commonplace, trite, or offensive, although it is sometimes rather discursive.

10. UNITY OF STYLE. The style is consistent and all of a piece; there are no distasteful shifts in style. The main tones are whimsical, mock-historical, and satirical; one is reminded that Irving's first book was a burlesque history of New York that contained the same sort of satire of social conditions that he gives in "Rip Van Winkle." The touch of the supernatural does not conflict with the main tone.

11. NARRATOR. In a foreword to his story, Irving explained that it was found among the papers of old Diedrich Knickerbocker, a historian, who is presumably the "I" in such phrases as "I have observed" (paragraph 3). This narrator says in the final paragraph

of the story that Rip told his adventure again and again until "it at last settled down precisely to the tale I have related." The narrator is thus the writer of a historical document based on Rip's personal narrative, with added comments by the historian. This old device attempts to give some authority to the tale and allows a more objective presentation than could be given by Rip's first-person narrative. Yet the focus is on Rip, for the most part; we share his thoughts but not those of any other actor in the story. The choice of narrator here is thus not a bad one.

12. STRUCTURE. The beginning comprises the first thirteen paragraphs; the middle takes up all but the last four paragraphs, which constitute the ending. The pace is rather leisurely, and all events are given in straight chronological order. The beginning is pure description. The end is straight narrative. The middle is narrative aided by description and some thoughts of the main character; at the crisis (paragraphs 30 through 56) there is a single long scene, with all action given, which increases the intensity and dramatic power. A scene of this kind may have its own structure corresponding to that of an entire story. Setting: At the door of the inn when Rip has returned to the village. Characters: Rip and the crowd, led by the "self-important old gentleman"; later, young Rip, Judith Gardinier, the old neighbor woman, and Peter Vanderdonk. Problem: Can Rip discover what has happened to him? Action: Rip gradually is convinced that he has slept for twenty years. Conflict: Rip is in danger of attack by the crowd until the facts slowly emerge. Crisis: Rip does not know who he is (paragraph 44). Conclusion: Rip and the others are convinced of the truth, and the problem is definitely answered. This scene is worth the space it takes, since this crisis is the high point of interest in the story. Intensity would certainly be lost if Irving had replaced this scene with a summary, such as: "Rip was baffled for a while, but finally convinced himself that his sleep had lasted for twenty years."

13. BEGINNING. The opening is slow; there is little action or suspense, and the main character is not introduced until the second page. The reader is not gripped at once; he must take it on faith that something worth reading about will eventually happen. The

theme is suggested by the amount of description given to the plight of the henpecked hero. The tone suggests that this will be a whimsical story of setting, and this background is given in great detail. The exposition of previous events is given in straight form rather than being woven into the action.

14. CLIMAXES. Climax of theme: The idea is not complete until the last sentence of the story; the slow ending is useful mainly to say the last word on the theme of the henpecked husband. Climax of action: This comes not later than paragraph 52, when Rip learns that his wife is dead and the conflict is definitely ended. Climax of character: This comes not later than paragraph 58, where we are told that "Rip now resumed his old walks and habits," and we know that he is not going to change his ways in the future. These climaxes do not come so early in the story that we feel the ending drags.

15. ENDING. Something would be lost if we omitted the last four paragraphs of the story. The main action is over, but points on theme and on Rip's adjustment to later life need to be made. There is no bad anticlimax. The ending is suitable and satisfying; it would be spoiled, for instance, if Rip became a reformed man and a leader in the community, if he were murdered as a Tory spy, or if he discovered a chest full of pirate gold. The ending seems a logical one for Rip's adventures. There is no shock of surprise, but we might be rudely surprised if an ending were tacked on that showed Rip to have been acting a part all along, and never really to have been henpecked at all. Irving's ending is implicit in the beginning of the story; in this sleepy village, nothing is going to be changed greatly, even by a revolution.

16. SUSPENSE. No problem is raised early in the story, except for the rather weak one: "What is Rip Van Winkle like?" Not until paragraph 23 can we state the main problem: "What has happened to Rip?" However, the author does withhold until late in the story the answer to the suspenseful minor question: "Who are the mysterious strangers on the mountain?" At the end, Irving answers rather fully the question of what happened to all the main characters in after years. By modern standards, "Rip Van

Winkle" is low in suspense value; we keep on reading the early pages for other reasons.

17. PLAUSIBILITY. The incident of the ghosts and the twenty-year sleep would be completely improbable in real life, and coincidence is used to arrange for Rip to meet the ghosts at just this critical period in his career. Irving uses several devices—such as many realistic details—to make it seem that the long sleep is just as factual as the dress of the Dutchman with the keg or the rust on the worm-eaten firelock Rip finds when he wakes; but the main event of the tale is still what Huckleberry Finn would call a "stretcher." Yet if, for the sake of the story, the reader suspends his disbelief and accepts this one improbability, he finds few other places where the story violates its own inner logic. From what we know of this old-fashioned community, all these events could happen in just this way. Note also that in the final paragraph it is said that some people insisted that Rip had been out of his head, an idea that allows a natural explanation of his strange story. The author uses foreshadowing; for example, since we know that Rip likes to go to the tavern, we are not surprised that he enjoys a drink from the keg of the strangers on the mountain.

18. EMOTIONS. The author presents a wide range of emotions. For instance, Rip feels successively—during a few pages of the action—despair, desire to escape his wife, sympathy for his dog, weariness, enjoyment of scenery, fear of returning home, apprehension at the cry of the stranger, surprise at his appearance, shyness and distrust, wonderment, awe, curiosity about the strange men, fear, desire to taste liquor, intoxication, mental confusion on awakening, physical discomfort, astonishment at the change in the stream bed, perplexity at losing his dog, hunger, dread, anxiety, surprise at sight of villagers, amazement at the growth of his beard, fear that he has been bewitched, awe at sight of his home, sadness that the dog seems to have forgotten him, and surprise at changes at the inn. All these emotions are mentioned by the author as being felt by the main character—a fairly generous and varied range for a story which is not primarily emotional or psychological. The main emotions of the story are properly despair, desire to escape,

wonderment during the adventure in the mountains, growing fear at recognition of his plight, and joy at discovery of his daughter. In general, the author tells us what the characters feel rather than makes us share the emotions by being given the stimuli that would arouse them in us. The story does not indulge in unmotivated sentimentality.

19. BLENDING. The qualities of theme, characterization, action, setting, and style work together quite well; each reinforces the others. The story as a whole is unified.

20. JUDGMENT. This is a great piece of fiction, especially when we remember that it is historically the earliest American short story. It would repay being read several times; its value does not lie in a single trick or surprise. It has many satisfying qualities (see other answers in this appendix). Perhaps its best points are a true theme of wide appeal; creation of a great symbolic figure; graphic presentation of an unusual setting and quaint characters; and a rich and amusing style.

21. TITLE. The title is a label, but the Dutch name suggests the setting, and the comic sound of it suggests that the style will be light in tone.

22. TYPE. Setting and characterization are somewhat more important than theme or action. The idea of an enchanted sleep that extends over years is found in the folklore of many lands. In a note to his story, Irving mentioned the German superstition about the sleep of Emperor Frederick Barbarossa as a possible source. Actually, he borrowed his story very greatly from a tale, "Peter Klaus," by the German writer Otmar. "Rip Van Winkle" is historically closer in form to the tale than it is to the present-day short story.

23. LITERARY BACKGROUND. This story was one of the first to be written by Washington Irving, the man with whom the history of the American short story begins. He had been living in Europe, reading old German tales of wonderful events and visiting Sir Walter Scott, from whom he heard the old legend of Thomas the Rhymer and his enchanted sleep. The writing of "Rip Van Winkle" was begun in a lonely room in Birmingham, England, in 1818, during the years when Irving was living far away from America. The

author's frame of mind is beautifully suggested by Dr. Stanley T. Williams in *The Life of Washington Irving*: "He, too, to escape a way of life as irksome as Dame Van Winkle herself, might dream away the years; he, too, an idler imprisoned in another realm, might return after decades only to find strange faces and the old order changed forever. He, too, by the tale's gossamer fancy, too fragile to be explained by allegory, might also satisfy, though he did not guess how well, his longing to make his native mountains, like Scott's hills, blossom with legend, a longing born when he was writing Knickerbocker's history, and renewed during his tour in Wales in 1815—the longing to give America 'a colour of romance and tradition.'"

24. SPECIAL CONTRIBUTIONS. Readily found are humor (including some satire on early American social conditions), a dash of history and geography, and some sage opinions of the narrator. There are few or no allusions or quotations from other authors. The epigraph by Cartright at the head of the story suggests that this is a highly veracious tale that the author swears is true, and this quotation before a story of the incredible is a mild joke.

25. SCALE. The story runs to about six thousand words—rather long by modern standards. The tale of "Peter Klaus" that Irving adapted was only about a fourth as long, but lacked Irving's special contributions and intensity. The craftsman of today would probably have to tell Rip's story in less than five thousand words. However, if we were to condense Irving's story very much it would lose its particular leisurely flavor.

26. INTENSITY. A reader accustomed only to the rapid-fire action of a modern adventure story may find Irving's writing a bit too deliberate. But we should realize that Irving gives us a rich profusion of sensuous detail that the usual plot story must omit. The beginning is not so intense that it causes a letdown later. Peaks of interest for most readers are the appearance of the strange old Dutchman and the mysterious bowling game, Rip's awakening, Rip's growing wonder at what has happened to him, and the dramatic scene in front of the inn. The ending is not abrupt, but is not so drawn out as to give anticlimax to the story.

27. PATTERNS. Few patterns are found. There are no personifying habits of speech to distinguish the various characters, but the occasional sententious remarks and proverbs of the narrator do form a pattern in diction. In characterization, Rip's son (paragraphs 7 and 43) is a repetition of his father in appearance. A pattern in setting, showing repetition with some contrast, is given in the descriptions of the village inn before and after the Revolution—the George III sign has become a picture of Washington, and so on. The shifts in setting have a simple pattern—the village, the mountains, and once more the village.

28. DIGRESSIONS. The narrator, old Knickerbocker, indulges in some opinions, proverbs, and moralizing that the modern writer might omit. There are no large chunks of digression, however, that could easily be cut out of the story to improve it.

29. IRONY OF SITUATION. The main outcome is ironic—Rip seeks to escape his wife, and escapes her for the disproportionate term of twenty years. There is also irony in the fact that the reader catches on to his plight more quickly than Rip does himself and waits with ironic expectation for his realization of it. There is also irony in the contrast between the life of the village before and after the Revolution—there is really no great change, but rather an ironic appearance of change.

30. SYMBOLISM. Rip's twenty-year sleep is presented as an actual event, but we can interpret it also as symbolic of the theme. There are few other symbols in the story. We should note that, historically, Rip himself—as we might see him mentioned today in a newspaper editorial—has become the symbol of a certain type of dreamer.